THE
LIGHTHOUSE
WITCHES

C.J. Cooke is an acclaimed, award-winning poet, novelist and academic with numerous other publications as Carolyn Jess-Cooke. Her work has been published in twenty-three languages to date. Born in Belfast, C.J. has a PhD in Literature from Queen's University, Belfast, and is currently Reader in Creative Writing at the University of Glasgow, where she researches creative writing interventions for mental health. C.J. Cooke lives in Glasgow with her husband and four children.

Keep in touch with C.J.:

www.cjcookeauthor.com
@cjcooke_author
@CJessCooke
/CJCookeBooks

Also by C.J. Cooke

The Guardian Angel's Journal
The Boy Who Could See Demons
I Know My Name
The Blame Game
The Nesting

LIGHTHOUSE WITCHES

'Right from the start, I was hooked on this eerie, cryptic novel. I don't know how C.J. Cooke does it, but every time I pick up one of her books, I can't stop reading until the last page'   Samantha Downing

'A gripping modern gothic thriller . . . wonderfully atmospheric and compelling'   Rosamund Lupton

'Beautiful prose and potent, pacy chapters . . . Like a lighthouse roving atmospheric waters, its secrets are revealed glimpse by tantalizing glimpse'   Cari Thomas

'A gripping meditation on terror and superstition'
                                                        Sara Sheridan

'This is C.J. Cooke's best yet! A fascinating and enthralling read'   Nina Pottell, *Prima*

'A compelling story and very satisfying'   Kate Sawyer

'Seething with gothic menace, *The Lighthouse Witches* interweaves myth, superstition and history in a way which feels strikingly relevant and gripping'   Caroline Lea

'A flawless read . . . the themes remain starkly relevant today'   Elizabeth Lee

'Surprising and inventive'   Sarah Burton

'A complex and haunting story, beautifully told . . . Tense, unsettling and ultimately incredibly moving'
                                                            Amanda Mason

'Utterly enthralling, original and atmospheric. C.J. Cooke writes with such haunting beauty'   N.J. Simmonds

'Clever, emotional and brilliantly written. An atmospheric beauty of a book, with a feminist voice that rang clear from every page'   Anna Day

'Wonderful writing with a beautifully haunting tone. Gothic at its best'   Rhiannon Ward

'A seductive page-turner, it's a perfect blend of historical fiction and thriller!'   Constance Sayers

'A perfect mix of propulsive plot and shivers-up-the-spine spookiness'   *Good Housekeeping*

THE
LIGHTHOUSE
WITCHES

C.J. COOKE

HarperCollins*Publishers*

HarperCollins*Publishers* Ltd
1 London Bridge Street
London SE1 9GF

www.harpercollins.co.uk

HarperCollins*Publishers*
1st Floor, Watermarque Building, Ringsend Road
Dublin 4, Ireland

First published by HarperCollins*Publishers* 2021
This paperback edition 2022
1

A catalogue record for this book is available from the British Library

ISBN: 978-0-00-845544-6

Set in Sabon by Palimpsest Book Production Ltd, Falkirk, Stirlingshire

Printed and bound in the UK using 100% renewable electricity
at CPI Group (UK) Ltd

This book is produced from independently certified FSC™ paper to ensure
responsible forest management.

For more information visit: www.harpercollins.co.uk/green

for Amy Hyndman (d. 1662)
and all witches
past
present
and future

'A sad tale's best for winter: I have one of sprites and goblins.'

William Shakespeare, *The Winter's Tale*

'Those who can make you believe absurdities can make you commit atrocities.'

Voltaire

They bind our feet and ankles, tear off our clothes and douse us with alcohol. Amy's crying and shaking like a new lamb, and I want to reach out to her but Stevens' knife is held to my throat, his face so close I can smell his disgusting breath. He uncurls his fingers to show me the stones before shoving them into my mouth, breaking my teeth. I gag on blood and broken molars.

They start to cut Amy's hair, hacking off her silky black locks so close to the skin that blood oozes darkly from her pale scalp. With a terrific lunge Stevens plunges his knife deep into my chest, scraping my collarbone, the shock of it causing my knees to buckle. I cannot breathe, nor speak. Amy lets out a long cry, like a wounded animal.

Already I can smell the fire. I do not fear it.

Wait for me, Amy. Wait.

LIV, 1998

Lòn Haven
The Black Isle, Scotland

I

The lighthouse was called The Longing. Pitched amidst tessellations of rock black as coke, thrashed for over a hundred years by disconsolate squalls, it needled upwards, spine-straight, a white bolt locking earth, sky, and ocean together. It was lovely in its decrepitude, feathery paint gnawed off by north winds and rust-blazed window frames signatures of use and purpose. I always thought lighthouses were beautiful symbols, but this one was more than that – it was hauntingly familiar.

Night was drawing in and we hadn't yet met the owner. We'd driven hundreds of miles over mountains, through sleepy villages and along winding roads, usually behind herds of cattle. We had taken a ferry, and got lost four times, on account of using an outdated, coffee-stained A–Z road map with several pages missing.

I parked up behind an old Range Rover. 'We're here,' I

told the girls, who had fallen asleep against each other in the back. I wrapped my raincoat around Clover – she was wearing only a swimsuit over a pair of jeans – and lifted her up to walk a little way along the rocky beach daubed with spiky patches of marram and tough white flowers.

The four of us scanned the bay. It was a raw scene: a full moon hiding behind purple cloud, ocean thrashing against black cliffs. Gulls wheeling and shrieking above us. Trees stood like pitchforks, flayed by the wind. They hemmed the island, watching.

II

The lighthouse keeper's bothy was a squat stone dwelling built close to the lighthouse. Smoke plumed from the chimney, pressing the earthy smell of peat into our noses. A woman stepped out to greet us. 'Olivia?' she said.

'Hi,' I said. 'Sorry I'm earlier than expected . . .'

'No trouble at all. Come on in out of the cold.'

We found ourselves in a cramped hallway, where someone had pinned a shark's jawbone to the inner wall. Luna reached out to touch one of the teeth and I tugged her back.

Saffy nodded at it. 'Is that from a great white?'

'Porbeagle shark,' the woman – Isla – said with a tilt of her chin. 'We don't get great whites. Porbeagles are just as big, mind, and every bit as dangerous.'

'I don't like sharks, Mummy,' Clover whispered.

'We have a basking shark that tends to hang around the bay,' Isla said. She glanced down at Luna, who threw me a panicked look. 'You'll be fine with a basking shark. No teeth, you see. Basil, he's called.'

'Is this where we'll be staying?' Saffy asked warily, eyeing the shark jaw.

'It is indeed,' Isla said. She turned to the girls. 'I'm Isla Kissick, and it's absolutely thrilling to meet all of you. But I'm afraid I only know your mummy's name. Why don't you tell me your names?'

'I'm Luna,' Luna said. 'I'm nine.'

'Luna,' Isla said. 'What a lovely name.'

'It means "moon",' Luna said, a little shy.

'Mine's Clover,' Clover said, elbowing Luna out of the way. 'I'm seven and a half and my name means clover, like the plant.'

'Also a lovely name,' Isla said. 'And I bet you already know that clovers are meant to bring good luck?'

Clover nodded. 'Mm-hmmm. But my mummy said you make your own luck.'

'Very wise,' Isla said, glancing at me approvingly. She turned to Saffy, who flushed red.

'And who might this lovely one be?' Isla said.

'Sapphire,' Saffy mumbled to the floor. 'I'm fifteen.'

'Well now, that's lovely,' Isla said. 'My daughter, Rowan, is fifteen. I'm sure you'll meet soon enough. Now, come and sit down. I've made you all some supper.'

I nodded at the girls to leave their bin bags in the hall before following Isla to a kitchen at the back, where the smell of freshly baked bread and tomato soup made my mouth water.

I'd supposed that Isla was Mr Roberts' partner, but she turned out to be his housekeeper. She was short and lithe with long copper hair neatly pinned up, and her quick, round eyes searched all of us up and down. She had a beautiful Scottish brogue and spoke fast, as though the words were too hot to hold in her mouth for long. She was smartly turned out – a crisp white shirt, grey check trousers, polished ankle boots. The bothy was incongruously old-fashioned. I would learn that Lòn Haven, its inhabitants included, was full of skewed time spheres. The absence of modern retail chains and its breathtakingly rugged land-scapes made the place feel like you'd stepped back in time, perhaps to the very beginnings of the earth. The lighthouse itself was built upon an ancient Scottish broch that was built upon a Neolithic fort which in turn was built upon late Jurassic rock, like an architectural babushka doll.

III

'There you go,' Isla said, placing bowls of steaming hot soup before each of us. I apologized again for the mix-up about our arrival. I'd planned to begin the commission a few weeks from now but decided to head north on the spur of the moment. Or the middle of the night, to be exact. We'd driven the whole way from York to Cromarty, only to find that the ferry was cancelled for the day on account of high winds. The girls and I had to endure a very cold and uncomfortable night at a rest stop, sleeping in the car.

'It's no trouble,' Isla said. 'Mr Roberts is away, of course, but I'm to take care of everything until he returns.'

'Are we sleeping in the car again?' Clover said, wiping her mouth on the back of her sleeve.

'In the car?' Isla repeated, looking to me for explanation.

'I'm sure there are plenty of beds for all of us,' I said quickly, and this time I was the one to look to Isla for confirmation. I didn't want to mention that we'd had to sleep rough.

8

'Of course there are,' she said. 'Shall I give you the grand tour?'

The bothy was small but efficiently organized. A door at the rear of the kitchen led to a scullery with a washing machine and loo. Three bedrooms provided ample sleeping space with freshly made-up beds, and a bathroom with a shower cubicle.

We followed Isla to the living room at the front of the house, overlooking the garden.

'Now, you'll have noticed it's a bit chilly on the island. So you're not to worry if you need to turn the heater on.' She nodded at the wood burning stove. 'You'll find a shed at the side of the bothy stocked with wood. And I've put plenty of blankets in the cupboards for you to coorie down in the evenings. Which reminds me. Sometimes the electricity goes off. Nothing to worry about. You know how to manage an oil lantern?'

I followed her gaze to an old-fashioned oil lamp in the windowsill, which I'd assumed was for decoration. I caught Isla rolling her eyes as it became clear that no, I didn't know how to manage an oil lantern.

'I'll be sure to leave instructions,' she said with a tight smile.

'Does Mr Roberts live here?' Saffy asked.

'This is *one* of his properties,' Isla said. 'But no, he doesnae live here. His main residence is north of here, twenty minutes or so by car.'

'Will you tell him I've arrived?' I asked.

'Well, I'd love to,' Isla said brusquely, 'but he's at sea just now.'

'At sea?'

'Aye, for all he has a half-dozen houses dotted about the place he prefers to be out on his boat.'

'I have a boat,' Clover offered.

Isla lifted an eyebrow. 'Do ye, now?'

'It's green with a purple chimney and I play with it in the bath.'

'Well, Mr Roberts' boat is a wee bit bigger than that, I'd wager,' Isla said, chuckling. 'He tends to sail to Shetland at this time of year.'

'He's a pirate, then?' Clover said, astonished.

Isla bent down to Clover's eye level. 'No. But I reckon he'd be a good 'un.'

'Do you come from Shetland?' Clover asked, running her fingertips along the stubbly woodchip wallpaper. Woodchip was her favourite texture.

'No,' Isla said. 'I come from Lòn Haven. Where d'*you* come from?'

'My mummy's vagina,' Clover said.

I watched Isla's face drop. 'Girls, go have a look at your bedrooms,' I said, ushering Clover quickly away. 'Do you know when I'm to discuss the commission with Mr Roberts?'

'He said to give you this.' Isla reached into her trouser pocket and pulled out a piece of folded paper. I opened it up to find an elaborate and highly abstract sketch, a diagram of sorts. Lots of lines and arrows and circles, like a zodiac.

'What is it?' I said, turning the page to the side. There was no indication which way the sketch was meant to be viewed.

'It's the mural,' Isla said flatly. 'The thing you're painting inside the Longing.'

I stared at her, wondering if I'd misheard. 'This? This is the mural?'

She cocked her head. 'Is something the matter?'

10

'No, no . . .' I said, though I didn't sound convincing, even to my own ears. 'I suppose I thought there might be more to it than this. Written instructions, perhaps.'

'That's all Mr Roberts has given me. He said I'm to fetch whatever equipment you need to do the job. So perhaps you can write me a list of whatever you'll require and I'll get on to it in the morning.'

Still dumbfounded by the sketch, I said I would, but that I'd need to see inside the Longing first.

'Ah, now that would be an idea,' she said, straightening a lampshade. 'How about I show you just now?'

Outside, harsh winds buffeted us on the rocks, and I saw movement on the far reaches of the island. Seals, Isla told us. I was astonished at how close they were to the bothy, but she told me they were shy creatures, despite their size. They'd not bother us. I watched them slip off the stones into the black water, their shape in the dark almost human.

The lighthouse stood twenty feet away from the bothy towards the far end of the cliff. We all pushed against the wind towards the heavy metal door at the base. I could make out an object wrapped around the handle. A tree branch. I made to pull it off, thinking it had been blown on there by the wind and become stuck. Isla stopped me.

'Rowan wood,' she said. 'It's for protection.'

I had no idea what she meant, but I stepped back as she tried to leverage the door open. Finally, it shifted. I lifted Clover on to my hip and held Luna's hand tight as we followed Isla inside.

'Bloody hell,' Saffy said, looking around. 'This place is rank.' I shushed her, but couldn't help agreeing internally.

I'd never been inside a lighthouse before. I'd expected

floor-levels, an enclosed staircase. The Longing, however, was a grim, granite cone. A rickety staircase was pinned loosely against the wall, spiralling Hitchcock-style to the lantern room at the very top. The place reeked of damp and rotting fish. I wondered why we were standing in an inch of black liquid, until Isla explained that one of the lower windows was broken, and seawater had poured inside and pooled on the floor.

'I gather you'll need something to pump it out before you start,' she said.

'Mr Roberts is turning it into a writing studio, is that right?' I asked, and Isla nodded.

'He's not published,' she added. 'Just a hobby. I wouldn't be expecting him to produce *The Iliad* or anything like that. He bought it last year and didn't seem to know what to do with it. Next thing I know, he's asking me about getting a painter in to prettify it, make it into a writing studio.' She gave a shrill laugh. 'Whoever heard of such a thing? Surely all you need to write is a pen and paper.'

'Maybe the views will inspire him,' I offered.

'Aye. Inspire him to go off sailing, more like.'

We were shrouded in darkness. Clover was clutching on to her toy giraffe, whimpering to go home. Bats flitted overhead. Moonlight dribbled from the small upper windows, revealing the height of the place.

'It's a hundred and forty-nine feet tall,' Isla said, swinging her torchlight to the very top. 'A hundred and thirty-eight steps to the lantern room. Braw views up there. I can show you when it's light.' Her torchlight rested on patches of paint that had crumbled off, revealing raw stone. About halfway up someone had graffitied a section of the wall in garish shades of lime-green and black.

'There was a break-in,' Isla said darkly. 'Outsiders, you see. We get them here a lot more now, since the rental properties on the east side opened up. And the Neolithic museum, that's new. You should take your girls.'

Isla reassured us that break-ins like this were rare, that tourists – or 'outsiders' – didn't frequent the place often. Lòn Haven's population was predominantly grassroots, with sixty or so archaeologists from 'the University' working at the Neolithic sites. Some of the younger population had inherited crofts that they didn't want to live in, so they'd started renting them out. The older population objected strongly both to the younger islanders moving away ('all of them want to live in Edinburgh or London,' she told us with a sneer) and, as a result, drawing 'outsiders' to the island to rent out the crofts.

Break-in aside, I was intrigued by the Longing. As an artist, two of my favourite things were shadows and curved angles, and this place had both in spades. The shadows seemed alive, like the wings of a giant bird stirred by our presence. It was creepy, yes, but also elegant – I loved how the staircase whirled upwards in increasingly narrower circles within the cylinder of the structure, how the lack of right angles gave every small edge extra significance, how the architecture drew my gaze upwards.

'Has the lighthouse ever been submerged?' I asked. I could hear wind pummelling the stone walls, the loud suck and slap of the waves close by.

'We get our fair share of storms,' Isla said, and I could tell she was choosing her words carefully so as not to put me off. 'But the Longing has been standing for a hundred years amidst all that Mother Nature and the sea gods have to throw at her, and I daresay she'll stand a hundred more.'

A pause. 'So long as you keep rowan on the door, you'll be fine.'

It was as she said this that I felt a wave of déjà vu pass over me. Saffy, Luna, and Isla were beginning to head towards the door to leave, but the feeling of familiarity was so strong that I paused, as though someone had spoken and I was trying to understand what they'd said.

'Liv?' Saffy said from behind. I turned all the way around, moved by absolute certainty that something was in the corner by the stairs, just underneath it, as though I'd left it there.

'Everything all right?' Isla said as I sloshed through the oily water to the staircase. Her torchlight fell upon something floating on the black water ahead of me. The slender white limb of a baby's corpse.

Luna gave a scream that bounced off the surfaces of the lighthouse.

'What is it?' Isla said, rushing forward.

Luna was still shrieking, clawing at me and crying, 'No! No!' She turned to rush out, and I grabbed her, reaching down with my free hand to scoop the little body out of the filthy water.

It wasn't a baby. It was only a doll, one of those naked newborn dolls that Clover liked to play with.

As I looked down into the grotesque face of that doll, its eyes blacked out with felt tip, adrenaline flashed brightly through my body. I had known it was a doll. I had known it was there before I saw it, and that we'd mistake it for a dead child. Like a memory.

But that was ridiculous. I had never been there before.

IV

The next morning, I woke at sunrise, disoriented and stiff. I gave a start at the scene squared off by the musty bedroom window, a grey wave reaching above rock like a ghostly hand. Wind whistled through the cracked windowpane, and an albatross sat on the windowsill, eyeing me boldly. When it stretched its wings and lifted into the sky, a lighthouse appeared on the outcrop. I reminded myself: I was in Scotland, on a tiny island on the eastern shore of the Highlands. I was here to paint a mural inside that lighthouse.

I got up, made coffee, and tried to work out how to turn on the TV. There was no aerial attached so we couldn't get a single channel. In the TV cabinet was a VCR player but no videotapes. We'd left York in such haste that I'd only packed the bare essentials – a few outfits, a handful of toys for the girls, and definitely no videotapes. I gave up and sat down with the page Isla had given me spread across the kitchen table. The mural for the lighthouse.

What was it? A crop circle? Some kind of zodiac?

It would have made a pretty tattoo for someone, but as a mural for the inside of a building as big as the Longing it was . . . unusual. I had expected a scene, something that told a story – a nautical scene, perhaps. A galleon with white sails full of winds, a sky transitioning from day to starry night, and heaving seas with whales and cephalopods lurking in the dark depths – something of that nature would look fabulous in the lighthouse, logistics notwithstanding. But this . . . it was like a physics equation, dry and strange.

I traced the symbols with my index finger to tease out a pattern. Two triangles, one upside down, overlapping at the narrowest point, and a smaller triangle overlapping the two larger ones, with a rectangular frame. That was the base of the diagram, and from that central design, lines, arrows and other shapes fanned outwards in all directions over the rectangle. Some of them were like the lines of a family tree, others like the right-angled spokes of a spider diagram. Some of the lines were crossed with three shorter lines, others were Cs and backwards Cs, and others looked like swastikas.

Swastikas?

Bloody hell. Was I working for a Nazi?

Some of the symbols floated within the rectangle frame alongside the triangles. They looked older in style, and I wondered if they might be Egyptian hieroglyphs. How the hell was I going to paint something like this on the inside of a *lighthouse*? I tried to imagine how this would even be physically possible. The walls of the Longing were sectioned by the staircase, so the mural would be carved up by the stairs and I'd have to take enormous care to ensure it matched up. Also, there was the small matter of the curved walls. The sketch had been drawn by hand, but evidently rulers and protractors had been used, given how straight the lines were. To achieve such straightness in a curved building was going to be a logistical nightmare.

I went to check on Saffy in the small loft bedroom to ask her opinion about the symbols at the fringes of the diagram. She'd taken an interest in mythological symbols for a school project and the last time we'd had an actual conversation she was showing me a painting she'd done of the Eye of Horus, explaining excitedly about how it was meant to protect against evil.

But the bed was empty, her boots and coat gone from the hallway. My heart thumped in my throat. Where was she?

'Morning, Mummy,' Luna said from the stairwell, her brown hair askew and limp with grease.

'Have you seen your sister?' I asked her.

'She's still asleep in your bed.'

'No, not Clover. Have you seen Saffy?'

Luna yawned and shook her head.

I kissed the top of her head. 'Stay inside, please.'

'Where are you going?'

'To find Saffy.'

I walked quickly outside to the Longing. A wave slapped against the rocks and sprayed me as I tugged the heavy door open and stepped inside. The smell of the place hit me, and I covered my mouth and nostrils with a hand as I looked around.

'Saffy?' I called.

At the very top of the staircase, I spotted someone in

17

the lantern room. A child, with long white-blonde hair. A girl, I thought. A flash of a pale shoulder told me she had no top on, and she was small – about five years old. It was dangerous for her to be up there.

'Saffy!' I shouted. 'Are you up there?'

No answer. I took to the stairs, running as quickly as I could and cursing myself for being so unfit. By the time I reached the top my heart was beating so hard in my throat I thought I might be sick. I forced myself to look down all the way to the bottom. I don't have a problem with heights, but all that stood between me and breaking my neck on concrete was a rusty banister. I took the next flight to the lantern room, determined to order Saffy downstairs.

Light poured into the lantern room through dozens of honeycomb windowpanes. It offered views of the west side of the island, as far as the towering white hills that marked the boundary between the desolate west and the more populated east, jagged as a spine. But it was empty.

'Hello?' I said. 'Anyone here?'

I looked around in case another flight of stairs might appear, or a doorway to another room in which a child might be hiding. In the centre of the room was an old metal frame upon which I imagined a Fresnel lens had once thrown a bright beam of light across the North Sea. The plaster was crumbling, and those patches that did remain were covered in graffiti.

I spotted a handle on one of the windows, and a chill ran up my spine. A flash of a frightened child reaching for that handle darted through my mind. I wrapped my hand tentatively around it and pushed. The window swung easily open, the hiss of the sea and the groaning wind rushing in. Below, the roof of the bothy and the mossy rocks of the island rested in the sunlight. On the left side of the island, a blonde-haired figure sat on the rocks, her feet dangling in the water.

Saffy.

I made my way back down the stairs as fast as I could and ran out to where she sat. She'd drawn a fresh Celtic squiggle on the back of her neck in biro – a preparatory tattoo, she liked to say. In her hand was an old book that I guessed she'd taken from the bothy. Clutched in her other hand, an old skeleton key. The bothy was full of clutter – books, ornaments, dried sea urchins, shark jaws pinned to the wall, for God's sake – and Saffy was a scavenger, always had been. Even when she was a toddler I'd discover odd things sequestered beneath her bed – bottle tops, cutlery, weeds she'd plucked from the front garden. I'd learn that she gathered such things with no plan to play with them, no purpose at all, other than the act of taking and hiding, of holding a secret.

She had her headphones on, a heavy beat bleeding out the sides. Even when I managed to get her to make eye contact she didn't take them off. Frustrated, I reached down and yanked them off her head.

'What are you *doing*?' she screamed. 'Give those back!'

Immediately I regretted it. She snatched them back.

'Did you see a little girl?' I said. 'In the lighthouse?'

She screwed her face up. 'What?'

'I saw a girl in the lantern room. Did you see her?'

'I have literally no idea what you're talking about . . .'

'Fine. Look, I need your help with something.'

'I'm busy,' she said, putting her headphones back on and opening up her book. 'Isn't that what *you* always say?' she added. '"Sorry, kids. Mum's *busy*."'

I ignored the dig. 'It's about a symbol. I could do with your help, Saffy.'

19

For about a minute, she did nothing, and I waited. Eventually she said, 'What symbol?'

I told her it was back in the bothy as I started to walk away. She slowly rose to her feet, tucked the book under her arm and followed behind, the hems of her jeans trailing in the rock pools.

V

By the time she arrived in the kitchen I'd put a kettle on and poured us both a cup of tea. She was holding a small book and sat at the table, absorbed by its pages.

'What are you reading?'

'It's a grimoire.'

'A what?'

I handed her a cup, careful to avoid the book she'd placed on the table in front of her. It looked old, the paper yellowed and delicate.

'Where'd you get that?' I asked.

'On the bookshelf in the living room. It's a book of spells. Some of the writing looks like it's Icelandic. And there's some stuff about witches.'

'Witches?'

'Yeah. There were witch hunts in Scotland as well as England. Worst witch hunts in Europe, apparently. Did you know that?'

I shook my head. Right then I was more concerned about

how she was handling Mr Roberts' book. 'Be careful with that, Saff,' I said. 'It might be valuable.'

'Hardly,' she scoffed. 'Why would anyone leave it lying around in this place if it was valuable?'

'Look, it's not yours, OK?'

I handed her a cup and spread the mural in front of her. 'That *is* a swastika, isn't it?' I said, pointing at one of the symbols.

She stared at it and sat down. I relished the closeness of her. It had been weeks since she'd sat with me like this, and although she was sullen and reluctant, she was still here.

'What is this?' she said, turning to me. 'Is this what they want you to paint inside the Longing?'

I nodded, and she laughed.

'They're taking the piss a bit.'

'A bit, yeah.'

She looked again at the symbol. 'Yes. That is indeed a swastika.'

I felt my heart sink. 'I can't paint bloody Nazi symbols,' I muttered, though I had no choice. I needed the money.

'Well, the swastika *is* a Nazi symbol,' Saffy said. 'It's also a Hindu symbol. And a Buddhist symbol. And Roman, and ancient Greek.' She laced her fingers and lifted her blue eyes to mine. 'You want me to go on?'

I was puzzled. 'So . . . he's not a Nazi, then.'

'Who's not a Nazi?'

'Mr Roberts. The man who wants me to paint the Longing.'

She shrugged. 'Maybe he is. All I'm saying is that the swastika's been around since three thousand BCE. So has this symbol.' She pointed at the overlapping triangles.

'It has?'

'It's a variation on the Borromean rings, or the Holy Trinity. You can't remove one without removing the other. It's a sign of infinity.'

'What about this one?' I asked, pointing at the one that looked like an Egyptian hieroglyph.

'Ah,' she said. 'I *could* tell you what that one means, but it'll cost you.'

I stared at her. 'How much?'

'Twenty quid.'

Twenty quid could buy a week's worth of groceries for the four of us. She held out her hand, expectant.

'No thanks,' I said. 'I'll go to a library.'

'Maybe you should think before you judge everyone to be a Nazi, Liv.'

The 'Liv' stung, just as she'd intended. 'Maybe I should.'

At that, she tucked her book under her armpit and got up sharply to leave, knocking her tea across the table and all over the mural.

'Saffy!' I yelled. 'Look what you've done!' I lunged forward to snatch the mural away, but the tea had covered the page. All I could do was hold it up, allowing the tea to slide off so that it wouldn't soak through.

'It's just a fucking piece of paper!' she shouted.

'Just a piece of paper?' I said, desperately flapping the sheet to get the liquid off. 'This is the only copy of the mural I've got!'

'Well, just ask for another one,' she said, hurling her cup into the sink with a clatter. 'Last I checked a piece of paper was pretty easy to come by. Or are we really *that* poor?'

I reeled at her comment, at how unapologetic she was. 'What the hell is wrong with you?'

'I think you should ask yourself the same question,' she

said, turning and squaring up to me. She was already four inches taller than me. 'Dragging all of us in the middle of the night to the back of beyond. You think that's good parenting?'

I knew what was buried inside that horrible question, the torrent of accusations folded within it. 'Maybe it isn't good parenting,' I said, trying not to show how much her words stung. 'But when *you* have kids, you can show us all how much of a better mother you are than me . . .'

Her eyes narrowed. 'You've certainly kept the bar low.'

Before I knew what I was doing I lifted a hand and slapped her hard across the face, a loud crack ringing through the air. She clasped a hand to her cheek, staring at me with wild horror.

'I'm sorry,' I said, reeling from what I'd done. 'Saffy. I'm so, so sorry.'

Her face crumpled, her eyes filling with tears and a sob escaping her mouth. For a moment the perfected mask of teenage haughtiness fell, and her hurt was laid nakedly before me – just for a second, she was my little girl again, reeling from the fact that I had struck her. That I had crossed a line I had promised never, ever to cross.

I took her arm to help her up, but she pulled away from me, her hands reaching for the back of her head. She was injured.

I turned and ran into the kitchen, searching the tiny icebox of the fridge for ice. Nothing. I grabbed a rag and held it under the cold tap, then returned to the living room.

But Saffy had gone.

The front door gaped open like a wound.

SAPPHIRE, 1998

I

Sapphire stumbles blindly across the road away from the Longing.

It's early, the sky like polished silver, the ocean sinewy and muscular, crackling as it reaches the stones at the edge of the causeway. She turns, out of breath from anger and wading, and looks back at the bothy. *What a shithole. No KFC or McDonald's on the whole bloody island.* And the lighthouse – she's always loved the idea of lighthouses, the romance of a building designed to throw light out across the ocean to keep ships safe and draw them home. But this one is creepy. It's tall and white with big sections of flaked paint, and the windows are smashed. It doesn't even work as a lighthouse. It's just a big phallic eyesore.

The cool, salty air has taken the sting away from her cheek. She narrows her eyes and watches the bothy, wishing she could set it alight with her mind. *What kind of mother hits their kid like that?* And after dragging them all up here too, to the arse-end of nowhere, right in the middle of Saffy's GCSEs. Saffy loves her school back in York. She loves her friends, and her boyfriend, Jack, who she's been seeing for six months.

She *hates* her mum. She wishes she would just die and let Saffy be adopted by someone normal. Maybe her biological dad will come back and he'll have a nice wife and some other kids and Saffy will have an actual normal life. Not one that involves living on boats and sometimes even in tents, and now a bothy on an island. A life with boundaries and bedtimes, clothes that don't come from charity shops.

Lately, she's been thinking about her stepdad, Sean. How much she misses him. Things were *normal* when he was alive, and they were happy. Even her mum was different. She wasn't as thin as she is now, but more importantly she was kind of calm. Now, she has this weird, nervous energy. Skittish as a river bird. And dazed, as if she's half asleep or permanently daydreaming. Sean was the one who made everything wonderful. He was like sunshine, bringing out the colours in everyone he met.

When Liv had told her that Sean had been injured in a car accident, Saffy had asked, 'Is he going to die?', because this was her worst fear. And when Liv said yes, it was likely that he would, Saffy had promised herself that she would be there when he did. It was what she'd held on to, the promise that she'd hold his hand, that the last thing he'd see was her there with him. She couldn't change the fact that he wasn't her *real* dad, but she could be there for him when he died.

But Liv insisted that Saffy go home with her uncle Liam, and nothing Saffy said or did persuaded her otherwise. Saffy wailed and pleaded, but still Liam took her firmly by the hand and drove her home. Not even an hour had passed before the phone rang with the news that Sean had passed.

If Sean had been her *real* dad, her mum would have let her stay. She's sure of it. But because he wasn't, she was told to leave, and therefore the precious chance to hold his hand as he slipped into the next world was ripped from her forever. He died without knowing how much she cared. She will never, *ever* forgive her mother for that.

A sob forms in her throat as stumbles on blindly towards the clutch of trees across the road, hugging the grimoire to her chest.

II

She slips inside the cool of the forest, noticing the mineral smell that has replaced the saltiness of the bay. *Things grow in the forest,* she thinks, *but die on the beach*. The ground feels soft underfoot, quilted by pine needles and leaf litter, the view above a watercolour of greens and blues. Within a minute she's feeling better, now that she's hidden away from everyone.

She weaves her way through the barcode of trunks, her anger lessening as she spies squirrels zipping into the branches. She finds a river, and beside it is an animal, crouched down. The copper fur and long white tail tells her it's a fox. She's never seen a fox, not in real life. She approaches carefully, not wanting it to dart off. Only when she's within touching distance does she realize that the fox is dead. Someone or something has cut it open.

She backs away, rubbing her hands on her jeans as though the very air around the dead animal might be infected. She turns in the opposite direction and finds an old wooden hut, hidden in a far corner of the wood. It's like it's been waiting for her. Inside it's dry and small, maybe an old hut used by a forest ranger or something. There are cobwebs and dried leaves in corners, an old mug stain on a wooden bench. She sets the grimoire down and arranges herself in a reading position, the small of her back pressed against the wall, knees to her chest.

Outside, it begins to rain, a heavy shower that bends the branches on the tree closest to the hut. The roof drums and the ground outside crackles and hisses, but no water comes inside her hut. A feeling of panic arises – what if the door has jammed? What if she's trapped? She gets up, checks that she can open the door. On finding that she can, she closes it with relief behind her.

Then, she returns to her book.

The GRIMOIRE of Patrick Roberts

I ought to start at the beginning, right at that first meeting.

My father moved us all to the north when we were very young – I was just turned eleven, my brother was nine and my mother was pregnant with our sister – and I remember how suspicious people were of us, as though our forlorn and scabby arrival into the town marked some kind of siege. It took a while for people to be friendly, but I remember one family, the Hyndmans, going out of their way to make us feel welcome and help us find our feet. They'd moved there the year before and conveyed how they'd experienced a similar reception. 'They're strange around here,' the wife said. Finwell, she was called, and the husband was called Hamish. Hamish and my father formed a strong bond, he helped my father find work, and when my mother gave birth to my sister – a stillborn – Finwell spent a lot of time at our house, bringing meals and consoling my mother. She named the little girl Elizabeth, after my grandmother. There was no visible reason at all why my sister should have died a day before she was due to be born, but of course such things happened and still happen. I don't believe my mother was ever the same after that.

Finwell's daughters helped out, too. Jenny and Amy. Jenny was thirteen, a long dark plait like a muscle down her back, a face like stone and a hard way about her. Amy was a few months older than me and preferred playing with me than helping her mother with preparing food and cleaning our house. She was a feral-looking child, like something raised by wolves – she was small and scrawny with a mane of crow-black hair that never seemed to be brushed and stuck out in all directions, usually snagged with berries and leaves as though she'd been dragged through a bush. She had these piercing moss-green eyes that shone out of her face like a mystic. Her skin was pale as fresh milk and her front teeth had grown in at weird angles. She was usually laughing at something or other, baring all her angled teeth. When I think of her as a child I see her mid-cackle, her head thrown all the way back, her two scrawny legs like twigs. Somehow she always had muddy knees – her mother made a point of complaining about it every time she set eyes on her – and her clothes were perpetually ripped and stained.

We lived our lives by magic. I was prone to nosebleeds,

and my mother would often gather her friends to hold a ceremony to stop them. The stream where we gathered our water was a fairy stream, and if you drank it and told a lie, you risked your tongue swelling until it filled your mouth. A sheep's skull smeared with blood and tar could show you the way to treasure if you threw it on the ground without fear of the demons that stood near, wanting to hide the treasure from your grasp. Few of us could do this – to not fear the beings that existed beyond the veil was difficult.

Most of us used the methods of magic as tools, but some were gifted, and used their gifts to help others. Amy's mother Finwell was gifted. A midwife renowned for preventing death in childbirth, she also had a reputation for being able to transfer the pains of childbirth from the labouring woman to her spouse, if so desired, and although this was never proven, I was aware of her being paid more than any other midwife in the village for her services, with mothers not only surviving childbirth whilst in Finwell's care, but in raptures about it.

We lived in dangerous times. The events at North Berwick were now legendary, the story of how hundreds of witches had raised a storm against King James VI as he and his wife sailed across the sea from Norway to Leith known by all of us. It was witches we were threatened with as children by our parents if we didn't go to bed. Witches would enchant us, boil our innards or shoot us with a fairy dart, and hand us over to the Devil.

The punishments meted out to the witches of North Berwick were recounted from generation to generation. Agnes Sampson, an elderly woman and a healer from Haddington, was the ringleader. She'd been kept in a scold's bridle, a fearful instrument wrought of iron that enclosed the head. Four sharp blades penetrated the mouth of the witch to keep her quiet, and doubtless to ruin her tongue for a long time thereafter. In Agnes' case, the bridle was chained to the wall of her cell, and therefore she was forced to endure countless days unable to speak, eat, or sleep, enduring the humiliation of opening her bowels or bladder without being able to attend to herself, and doubtless in a terrible amount of pain without a moment's relief.

After spending days thus, she confessed to raising the storm in partnership with the Devil, though I always thought that if I'd had to suffer days on end in a cell wearing such a monstrous instrument I'd have confessed to being Satan himself. No mercy was bestowed for Agnes' confession, however – she was swiftly garrotted and burnt at the stake.

At first, the people were glad of King James VI and his mission to rid the world of witches. Thank God for his witch finders, to protect us all from such wickedness! They well knew the unseen world was all around them, hidden behind a veil but every bit as potent as the summer sun. They knew that magic came in two forms – the good kind, which was used by healers, and the wicked kind, which belonged to Satan.

It turned out that Amy had inherited her mother's gifts of healing, aided by stones with symbols on them that she said came from the distant north. I recognized the symbols. Finwell had put them all over their house – on door handles, on whetstones, shoes, the bottoms of barrels. I'd asked Amy why anyone would go to the trouble of drawing on the bottom of a barrel. 'How's anyone supposed to see it?' I said. She gave me a withering look.

'It is not for decoration, Patrick.' And that was all she said.

The stones bore those same symbols, like constellations, arrows, and sometimes like pitchforks, carefully and impressively etched into them by hand. The stones were runes from Iceland, passed down by Amy's great-great-grandmother. The pictures were magical staves, or symbols. They conveyed messages to some kind of spirit realm and, if used by the right person, had the power to make things happen, good and bad.

I had not put much faith in them. Until I'd seen how they worked.

Amy and I had gathered some fish to keep as pets. Amy had poured them into a bucket and named them.

'They shall have babies,' she said.

'And then we will sell them?' I asked. She looked at me as though I'd gone mad.

'No. Then I will name their babies. We'll be the king and queen of the fish colony.'

But the next morning all the fish were floating at the top of the bucket. Amy was upset. She started slapping herself. I told her to stop.

'They're just fish, Amy,' I said. 'We can fetch more.'

'But I killed them,' she cried. 'I didn't mean to.'

Later that day, she asked me to go to the woods with her. I watched as she hefted the bucket full of dead fish all the way into the forest, then lit a small fire in a clearing. She was agitated, her face still red *and puffy from crying. She reached into a pocket and pulled out a large white stone with a red picture on it. A rune.*

'This one is rebirth,' she said, and I looked over the series of crosses and arrows grooved in the stone. The stone was quartz, she said, and was as old as the earth.

'What's the red from?' I asked, pointing at the stave carved deep into the stone.

'Birth blood,' she said, sniffing. 'For hundreds of years, each woman in my family has given of her blood each time she's birthed a child.'

I wiped my hands on my shirt.

Then she set the stone in the middle of the flames.

She made me hold hands with her over the fire, and we had to sit awkwardly so we wouldn't get burned. She closed her eyes and said some words in a language I didn't recognize. I remember the wind picked up, and I felt dizzy, but nothing happened. Except, of course, all the fish came alive.

'Look! Look!' Amy shrieked, bouncing up and down and pointing at the bucket. 'It worked!'

I tell no lie – those fish had been floating before, and now they were all swimming in the water. I made her pour one out into her palm to show me, and it flopped around, its tiny mouth gasping until she plopped it back in.

I was stunned, but above all I was happy for her.

I wasn't yet wise enough to be terrified.

LUNA, 2021

I

Luna swims to the surface of sleep and lurches upright with a gasp.

She had the dream again. The one about her mother killing her.

This time her mother made her sit in the lantern room of the Longing, the sky outside dark and sequinned with stars. On the ground, a silky, plum-dark liquid swirled around her feet.

'Hold still,' her mother said, and she squeezed her knees together as she had a hundred times before, when her mother braided her hair and ordered her to sit still. Only this time, her mother wasn't braiding her hair. She was smashing Luna's head with a hammer. The liquid on the ground was her blood.

The tapping sound of the hammer continues, seeping into her conscious thoughts. She realizes she didn't dream that part at all – it's coming from the front door.

She gets up awkwardly, cradling her stomach with a hand as she moves one leg at a time over the side of the bed, the round of it fitting neatly into her palm. Up until twenty weeks she had no bump at all, no proof of her cargo. She fretted about it, mostly because her pregnancy app depicted a cartoon of a woman with a neat round melon and all she'd developed was a kind of spare tyre around her waistline that sagged over her jeans. Somewhere around week twenty-four her belly seemed to erupt. Now she can't go an hour without peeing, could eat beef tomatoes until the cows come home. She eats them like apples, letting the sweet red juice run down the sides of her mouth, seeds corralling in her cleavage.

The knocking continues. She pulls the door open to find Margaret standing there, their neighbour from the flat upstairs. Margaret's in her seventies and generally aggrieved about something or other. Today is no exception.

'I *really* do think I'm a very patient neighbour, but this really takes both the cake and the biscuit!'

'I'm sorry, what?' Luna's eyes fall on the object that Margaret is holding in front of her like evidence of some sort. It's a limpet shell.

'I have no objection to you running a business from home,' Margaret says, 'and when Ethan said he wanted to clean his tools in the front garden, did I quibble? Not a word did you hear from me. But when you decide to fill your bin until it explodes all over the street, I *really* must speak out. I could have twisted my ankle!'

'I don't know what you're . . .' Luna steps forward, following the sweep of Margaret's hand to the wheelie bin left out on the kerb. Someone has dumped another two bags of rubbish inside, leaving the lid flipped open. The top bag has ripped, revealing hundreds of shells that spew over the garden path: cockles, whelks, periwinkles, barnacles, and even what she used to call smacked lugs, the purple and black ear-shape of mussel shells. Someone's shell collection, perhaps, or a home school project.

Margaret follows her to the bin, where she stoops down, trying to pick up one of the burst bags to stuff it back into the bin.

'I can't for the life of me work out why you'd gather so many shells,' Margaret says, aggrieved. 'Nor why you'd put them in the general waste.'

'I didn't.' Luna says it with a sigh. Her head throbs and it's suddenly difficult to breathe.

'Ethan must have done it,' Margaret decides, folding her arms.

'Ethan's not here.'

'Not here? Well, where is he?'

Luna turns and places her hands on the old woman's shoulders. 'I'll clean it up,' she says with a forced smile.

'But . . . but . . .'

Before Margaret can think of another stream of questions Luna has headed back inside, locking the door behind her.

II

Light from the window washes the surfaces of Luna's flat: a Pilates reformer, her sewing table, the life-sized orthopaedic skeleton she bought Ethan as a gift when he started his physiology course, her handmade necklaces of leather and driftwood hanging from an ironing board. The plan was to sell the necklaces on Etsy and buy baby things with the extra cash, but the orders haven't exactly been flooding in. Ethan has taken on extra Pilates classes to cover their rent, but he failed his last physiology exams. On the coffee table – an upturned crate they plucked out of a skip – there's a stack of textbooks borrowed from the library for Monday's re-sit.

She sinks down on the sofa, anger crackling in her ears, fizzing in her wrists. The dream of her mother dances around her head like shards of glass. Every time she thinks or dreams of her mother, it happens. Ethan calls the day after such dreams a rage-hangover – the massive comedown from some intense build-up of fury – and as usual she's drained and weepy. Her memories of Lòn Haven are still so fragmented, little more than shattered slivers of a mirror.

The psychiatrist said trauma can cause memory loss. Whatever happened was so terrible it caused her to dissociate, effectively checking out of the horror. But the memories will be in there somewhere, buried deep in the earth of her mind. It makes her angry, the forgetting. What she *does* know – or what her social services file states – is that her mother, Liv, abandoned her there when she was nine. No explanation. No apparent motivation. Just dumped her in the woods and vanished into thin air.

She's never been back to Lòn Haven, never so much as googled it. The very thought of that place triggers a panic attack.

She cradles the small grey triangle of a limpet shell in her hand. A limpet will wear away a patch of rock to fit its shell exactly. A home scar, it's called, sealing it to the rock. Creating a tight fit to its home. Limpets move around at night to feed, but they always return to the home scar.

Where did she learn that? A few images begin to coalesce in her mind: her mother at a garden gate, bending down to pick up a limpet shell. There's a raging sea behind her. And a lighthouse.

It's Lòn Haven.

Luna gives a shudder and sets the shell down, as though it's white-hot. She doesn't dare touch it. Ethan is coming to pick her up shortly for the hospital scan. She'll ask him to sweep up the shells when he arrives.

III

'Done,' Ethan says, washing his hands in the sink.

'You moved them? Both bags?'

He nods. 'I put them in number ten's bin. It was half-empty.'

'And you swept up the shells?'

'Yep.'

She's relieved. Today, of all days, she wants to feel free of Lòn Haven.

They travel to the hospital in Luna's car. Technically, they both own the car, and the flat is mortgaged in joint names, but Luna has both for now. A permanent separation isn't yet on the cards.

'Mum says hi,' Ethan says after a long silence. 'She's wondering if you'd like her to knit blue baby blankets or gender neutral.'

'I don't mind,' she says. 'Grey? Or maybe she'd rather wait until . . .'

She falls silent, thinking of the last time Ethan's mother started knitting for their baby. They'd got all the way to fourteen weeks with that one, had proudly told everyone they knew right after the twelve-week scan revealed a squirming foetus, apparently as healthy as could be. The night before the miscarriage she'd been sitting in Alison's house, where Ethan is living just now, admiring the blanket she'd begun knitting.

'It's going to be fine,' Ethan says now, resting his hand on top of hers. She pulls it away. He sighs and slides his hands between his knees.

'I found a flat a few streets away from ours,' he says, looking out the window. 'I was thinking it might be smart to grab it before someone else does.'

It takes her a moment to work out that he's asking if they're to continue to live separately.

'It's up to you,' she says, stung. 'It was your decision to move out in the first place.'

'We're going over this again, are we?'

The sign for the hospital appears at the side of the road, and she indicates to turn. 'I said I wasn't ready to marry you, Ethan. I didn't say I wanted us to split up.'

She parks, and he fixes his dark, sad eyes on her. They have had this conversation so many times, over and over, never resolving it.

'I need you to be honest with me,' he says in a measured voice. She senses that he's prepared a speech. She's still attracted to him, still in love with him. He has honest eyes, beautifully straight teeth, thick black dreads to his shoulders, a smooth, radio-presenter voice. He was born and raised in Coventry, with Trinidadian heritage. He is striking to look at: six foot four, square-jawed, muscular as a gladiator. She used to feel short and unattractive beside him, barely scraping five foot four, boring brown bob, nothing at all striking about her looks, but he's always acted as though he's the luckiest man alive to be with her. When she has her period he buys her ice cream and rubs her feet, and after each miscarriage he cried without embarrassment. Marriage is important to Ethan, especially since they've been trying for a baby.

'Look,' he says, and she notices that he's nervous. Is he seeing someone else? The thought of it pierces her.

But he's talking, and she has zoned out, mentally sifting through possibilities. Jenn from the Pilates club has always been flirty with him, even in front of Luna. She knows that Uche from the flat across the road is always a little more friendly when Luna's not around. Or maybe it's his ex, Maeve, who still comments on his Facebook posts.

'I don't care about the piece of paper, either,' he says. 'But I want to know what's changed your mind. I mean, if you don't want to marry me after six years together, when we're finally having a baby, do you really want to be with me?' His voice catches, and he looks down. 'For the record, I don't want us to split up either. I just wanted to give you space.'

So, he isn't seeing someone. Relief washes across her like a warm bath. What was it he asked? Oh yes; does she want to be with him. *Yes*, she thinks. *I really do.* But the stubborn resistance to marriage is still there, and she doesn't know why. Marriage was always on the cards. They said it would happen when they had enough money, when they could get time off work, when the time was *right*. And now it's the perfect time to get married.

But when Ethan got down on one knee on New Year's Eve, when she knew marriage was finally feasible, something inside her bolted.

And she said no.

IV

The sonographer shows them their baby boy on the screen, the occasional ribbon of blue or red showing where he's drinking amniotic fluid or sucking his thumb. Luna has seen him on this screen so many times now – the single benefit of being high risk – but today she's especially relieved to see that he is wriggling around like an eel. The appearance of the shells had made her fear that something might be wrong, that they were an omen, somehow, of their baby's imminent departure.

'Is everything OK?' she asks the sonographer when she seems to be frowning at something.

There's a fraught silence. She and Ethan share a terrified look. *This is it*, she thinks, and she feels her heart plummet.

'Ah, there we go,' the sonographer says. 'The screen had frozen. Baby's absolutely fine.'

She breathes out with relief and laughs. Ethan takes her hand and she squeezes it tight.

Later, as they're waiting in the reception area for her pregnancy notes to be returned, she picks up her phone and scrolls quickly to her Facebook pages, 'Have you seen Clover Stay?' and 'Help Find Sapphire Stay!' Clover's page features a handful of photographs and a home video of Clover doing handstands in a field. She's wearing a cotton dress over jeans. Her brown wavy hair is teased by the wind and she talks to the camera, which is held by their mother. 'Is it on?' she asks several times. A voice off-camera – Liv – says 'yeah'. Luna must have watched the clip a thousand times over and yet the sound of her mother's voice still feels like a horse kick. On camera, Clover raises both arms in the air, lifts her right knee, and lowers her hands to the grass, swinging her legs high above her until she is perfectly straight. Then she counts quickly to one hundred, wobbling as she holds her balance. She finishes with a flourish, walking two steps forward on her hands and throwing her legs over her head into a crab's bend. Then she leaps up and runs towards the camera with a laugh, her whole face filling the frame.

She doesn't have a Facebook page for her mother. She has a single photograph of Liv, sent by her uncle, that she keeps in her bedside drawer. Her mother is kneeling by a canvas propped on an easel on the stern of the houseboat where they lived for a while. She's wearing old dungarees covered in paint, and her brown hair is worn in two girlish ponytails. She's slim, with tattoos on both arms, and her face is turned to the camera in a wide smile, as though she's laughing with the photographer about the painting she's doing. In the corner of the frame, Luna can make out a child of around eighteen months old, wearing just a nappy. She's never been able to work out if the child in the photograph is her or Clover.

The photos and video were donated by old school friends

from Bristol and York. Sapphire's page has only two pictures that she managed to source from the school, a good quality school photo from Year Seven in which Saffy is smiling so broadly that she doesn't resemble the sullen, angry girl that Luna knew. The other is a scan of a blurry photo Saffy's ex-boyfriend Jack sent – he'd found it in the back of a school notebook. It shows Saffy's rakish frame as she stands in front of the Longing. She's wearing jeans and a black ribbed polo neck, her blonde hair scraped up off her face in a topknot, revealing her long, pale neck – this is exactly how Luna remembers her. From the scowl Saffy is wearing, it's likely Luna is the one who took the photo, using her mother's Polaroid camera.

No bodies were ever found, despite extensive searches. The disappearance of an entire family may well have attracted substantial media attention, especially given Lòn Haven's history. But barely a week after Liv disappeared, an explosion at the nuclear power station near Glasgow drew the eyes of the national press and the government for months afterwards, and the mystery of her family was all but forgotten.

The phone buzzes in her hand. She lifts it hastily, hoping to see her foster mother Grace's name on the screen, but instead finds NO CALLER ID. She lifts her thumb to cancel it, let the caller go to voicemail, but changes her mind and answers quietly instead.

'Hello?'

'Is that Luna Stay?'

'Yes?'

'Hello there, this is Police Constable Cullen. I'm calling you from the station here in Dingwall.'

The line is bad. She rises, heading out of the reception area. 'Where?'

'Dingwall? In Scotland? We have you down as a named contact in the case of finding a missing person.'

She walks quickly towards the window at the end of the corridor, where, at last, three bars of signal appear on her phone.

'Hi, are you there?'

'I'm here.'

'You said a missing person . . .'

'Yes. Clover Stay. Your sister, is that correct?'

Luna holds the phone away from her face and catches her breath. Is this actually happening? Did the police officer on the other end of the line just say that Clover has been found?

'Yes, yes,' she says, her voice thin. 'You said Clover, right? Is she there with you now?'

'Can I take a few details from you first, please?'

He asks for her full name, date of birth, current address. She is shaking from head to toe, her palms clammy and her breaths quick and light. She can't believe this is actually happening. Once he's satisfied she is Luna Stay, he gives full disclosure. 'She was brought to us last night. An ambulance has just taken her to the hospital in Inverness.'

Luna stops pacing. 'What happened? Is she all right?'

'I'll let the social worker talk you through that.' Then, quickly: 'She's OK, by the looks of things. Dehydrated, and they've sedated her to get some rest, but otherwise sturdy enough. Nothing life-threatening. I'll need consent to pass your number to social services for them to get in touch.'

Her throat is dry, and the link between her brain and her mouth seems to have been severed. 'Of course, yes. Yes, please. Which hospital?'

He tells her. She gets him to spell out the postcode and makes sure to write it down as she's certain she'll forget. 'I'll be there as soon as I can.'

She's pressing a hand to her mouth, as though she might be sick, when Ethan approaches.

'What's wrong?' he asks.

'They've found my sister.' She whispers it. She has had false alarms before. The last one was four years ago and she cried for weeks afterwards.

Ethan stares at her. 'They've found . . .?'

'Clover. Clover, Ethan.'

'Are you sure it's her?'

She's weeping and laughing at once. 'That's what they said. Oh, God.'

'Did you see her? I mean, didn't they FaceTime you, let you speak with her?'

'They just said she's in a hospital in Inverness. She has to stay in for another day, maybe two.'

'I'll drive you there . . .'

She shakes her head. 'You've got work.'

He's insistent. 'This is more important, Luna.'

At their flat, she packs as much food as the cool box will hold and fills an empty milk bottle with water. Luckily their old car has just been serviced, though it still has a kayak attached to the roof and there won't be time to take it off. Ethan empties the gin bottle filled with loose change to fill up with petrol. Luna taps the postcode into Google Maps, a long wavy line snaking from their home to the Scottish Highlands. They should reach the hospital by 6pm.

She kneels by their bed, reaches under it for the small box she has kept all this time. Inside is Clover's toy giraffe,

Gianni. There are some photographs, too, the ones she has scanned with her phone and added to the Facebook pages. She tucks them into her bag, noticing that her hands are shaking.

V

'So how old will she be?' Ethan asks once they hit the road. 'She was seven when she went missing, right?'

'She's twenty-nine now,' Luna says.

So many people told her to accept that Clover was dead. Accept that both she and Saffy were swept away by the sea, drowned. Or murdered, their bodies dumped in a shallow grave in a forest. The theory that Saffy had run away had merit, but it was unlikely that a child as young as Clover could have survived the wilds on her own. Most likely, she had fallen off the cliffs and drowned, or she'd been kidnapped.

That's what they'd said.

The social worker calls from the hospital. Eilidh, she's called. *Ay-lee*. The line is frustratingly bad, and when she tries to tell Luna what ward Clover's in Luna can't make her out.

'I'm wearing a teal-blue jumper and a black skirt,' Eilidh says. 'I'll meet you outside the main entrance.'

Just before she ends the call, Eilidh refers to Clover as

'a wee girl'. *She must be very thin*, Luna thinks. What has happened to her? She can barely bring herself to think.

They stop off at a town with a name she can't pronounce, buy coffee that tastes like dishwater. A Highland cow snorts at her from a field nearby, its jaw working a mouthful of grass. Emerald mountains disappear into wispy clouds, the valley cradles a turquoise lake. She feels sick with nerves and excitement, she can't decide which.

It's just after 6pm when Ethan pulls into the hospital car park. They put on their masks. At the entrance she sees a woman, similarly masked, wearing a teal-blue jumper, searching the car park as though she's waiting for someone.

She must be Eilidh.

'Lovely to meet you, Luna,' she says when they approach her. 'Now, are you ready to see your sister?'

VI

'This way,' Eilidh says, leading Luna and Ethan through the hospital doors and along the corridor.

Luna is aware that Eilidh is talking but can't make out what she says. Her mind is turned to the carbolic smell of the corridor, the photographs of puffins on the hospital walls, an elderly man in a wheelchair with bloodied dressings across both eyes. She clutches the toy giraffe to her chest, her mouth running dry.

'It says on the form that you're next of kin,' Eilidh says, flipping through a paper file.

'Yes,' Luna says. 'She's my sister.'

'Clover mentioned that she was living with your mother when she went missing, is that right?'

'Our mother?' Luna says. 'My . . . she went missing many years ago.' It's clear to everyone that the words are difficult to say, even all these years later. Ethan squeezes her hand. This could be the moment, she thinks. The riddle of her childhood solved.

She follows Eilidh into a ward with walls covered in cartoon figures. A sign reads 'Children's Ward'.

'Are you sure it's this way?' she hears Ethan ask.

In a moment she's in a side room, and she sees the figure on the bed, the chestnut shades in her hair lit up by a side lamp, hands folded in her lap, the lines of her face strikingly familiar. The delicate mouth, those denim-blue, deep-set eyes, that wide, wise brow. Luna raises a hand to her mouth. She must sway a little in shock, for Ethan is quickly beside her, his arm around her waist.

'Hello, Clover,' Eilidh says brightly. 'Your sister Luna is here.'

The figure in the bed is a child of around seven years. Her hair is scraped back from her face, the ends matted with dirt. She is pale, and her lips are dry and chapped. There are dressings on her knees and arms from where she's been wounded. She is hooked up to an IV and a handful of teddy bears have been tucked into the bed beside her for company. On the chart above her bed, someone has written 'CLOVER' in black marker.

'Here we are,' Eilidh says, smiling. But Luna frowns at her, searching her face for explanation. Where is her sister? Who is this child?

'She's to stay at least one more night for observation,' Eilidh is saying, mistaking Luna's look for a query regarding the child's care. 'She has a concussion and is a bit dehydrated. And there's an injury on her hip that the doctors would like to speak with you about.'

'Is she taking me to Mummy?' the girl asks Eilidh in a weak voice.

'I'm sure that's on the cards,' Eilidh tells her with a smile. 'You'll be home soon enough, sweetheart.'

Ethan gives a heavy sigh and rests his hand on Luna's shoulder. 'I'm sorry,' he says under his breath. He begins to pull out his car keys, because clearly they've driven all this way for nothing. They've come to collect a grown woman, but there's been a terrible mix-up and here they are, presented with someone else's missing child.

He turns to walk out, gesturing for Luna to follow – but she can't. She turns back towards the girl, staring.

The child looks up, shyly taking in the sight of the woman in front of her. Luna lowers her mask to her chin, looking to Eilidh for approval.

'How come you have my giraffe?' the child asks, sitting straighter.

'You recognize it, Clover?' Eilidh says, encouraged by this exchange.

'It's Gianni,' she says, itching to get him. 'Can I have him, please?' Luna finds herself handing over the toy, dumbfounded as the child squeezes it to her cheek. Exactly as Clover used to do. 'I missed you, Gianni.'

'I've had him a long time,' Luna finds herself saying, but Clover is already talking again, explaining that she set him down just the other day and when she went to cuddle him in bed he was gone.

'I put him right on the bedside table. Didn't I, Gianni? And then I got dressed and he was gone.'

Eilidh leans over to Clover and glances up at Luna. 'Do you recognize your sister, Luna? It's OK if you need a wee while.'

'You're called Luna?' the girl asks, narrowing her eyes. Luna nods.

'Well, isn't that lovely?' Eilidh says. 'Two sisters, reunited. As soon as you're well you'll be returning home with Luna.'

Luna opens her mouth to say something, but she is overwhelmed with a dozen emotions at once. The girl looks so like Clover, it's uncanny. Same pale, freckled face, same brown hair that curls at the bottom and those round, denim-blue eyes fixed in the same intelligent, challenging stare – just like Luna's. She has the same nose as Luna, too, a little too wide, and her ears stick out. She's missing two front teeth, and her left cheek dimples slightly when she talks. Just like Saffy's.

But she can't be Clover. She's more than twenty years too young.

A nurse comes in then, keen to check Clover's drip. Luna can feel Ethan's eyes on her, expectant, the air between them filled with questions. She knows he wants her to leave, now that it's evident that this is all a mistake. But her heart is racing, her instinct shouting every bit as loud as her fear.

Who is she, if not Clover?

LIV, 1998

I

I sat at the kitchen table holding the hand that had slapped Saffy, as though it belonged to someone else.

What have I done?

I was strongly against corporal punishment, had never lifted so much as a finger against my children. Saffy's words had riled me, yes, and I remembered feeling shaken by the sight of the little girl in the lighthouse, a little girl I had doubtless imagined . . . but clearly I was losing my grip.

After I struck her, Saffy ran out of the bothy. I'd taken Luna and Clover with me and driven up and down the main road, trying to find her, but there was no sign.

I'd returned to the bothy, hoping that Saffy might have blown off steam and returned. Shaken by the empty rooms, I'd called Isla and asked her to keep an eye out for Saffy on the main island of Lòn Haven. I tried to keep the details vague, but she didn't hesitate in prying.

'Strange for Sapphire to be out walking alone, isn't it?' she'd said. 'Given that she knows no one here.'

'There was a bit of a disagreement this morning,' I'd said awkwardly. 'She's just upset.'

'I see. Perhaps it's a hard adjustment for her, this place.'

'Perhaps.'

'She couldn't have stayed back in England with her father? Or grandparents?'

I'd bristled. Isla didn't know me well enough to be asking such things.

'If you see Saffy,' I'd said, biting back stronger words, 'could you tell her to stay put, please, and call me to let me know where she is?'

'I'll do you one better,' Isla had said, suddenly obsequious. 'How about Row and I take a drive around the island just now, see if we can find her, and when we do I'll take the girls out for a coffee. Give them a chance to become pals. How does that sound?'

I had hesitated. 'Sounds . . . great. Thank you.'

Until Saffy was found, I was helpless.

'Did you and Saffy have an argument?' Luna asked as I was making breakfast. She was always the most perceptive of the three, highly in tune with the emotions of others.

No,' I said, smiling. 'She's just out exploring, that's all.'

Mothers are the best actors.

Once Clover and Luna were set up at the dining table with bowls of breakfast cereal, I went outside, taking in the sight of the grey ocean swaying beyond the cliffs, a mackerel sky troubled by seabirds swooping and screaming beneath the clap of the waves. Saffy had never been an easy child. Defiant and headstrong, she was born with a will already forged in iron. Nonetheless, I'd always expected that having a teenager would be a turning point, the part of parenthood where everything got better. Throughout those early years of nappies, teething, tantrums and night terrors I'd consoled myself by imagining a time when my girls were old enough to be self-sufficient. Maybe then I wouldn't be pulled in three different directions, always spinning plates. But Saffy's defiance had grown into disrespect and contempt. I felt as though I needed an emotional suit of armour to protect myself from her spiteful comments. She resented every thought, cell, breath, and ounce of me.

I turned and glanced inside the bothy, noticing at once that Luna and Clover were now playing on the floor of the living room with their dinosaur toys. I left them to it, picking up my Polaroid camera and heading to the lighthouse for another look.

II

The Longing was still intimidating in the light of day. The sheer height of it made my mouth run dry. I waded quickly through the filthy sludge on the floor towards the staircase. I took my time, focusing on every detail – the curl of the iron banister, the sound of the seabirds outside, the spots on the wall where the light rested. It was the most beautiful building I'd ever laid eyes on, and the saddest. Both cathedral and asylum. A monument to hope, and to loneliness.

The elements and island wildlife had all but claimed the place. I wasn't an expert on pest control but I had worked on a number of projects that brought me into close contact with vermin; here, the upper floors were inhabited by a sizeable community of bats, while the presence of seabirds – black with white heads, a kind I'd never seen before – on the windowsills told me there were nests.

I headed up to the lantern room at the very top. The stairs narrowed at the last flight, and the climb into the little room itself was a bit of a squeeze. I'd only spent a moment or two in this room the day before, but now I was able to appreciate the space and the views it afforded across the island. The sun was beginning to burn off the haar, flinging out the beauty of Lòn Haven – the vast emerald ocean, muscular, shining cliffs, hills dotted with cairns and lush forests. Dusty floorboards creaked beneath my feet, but they seemed in good enough order, and the room had been cleaned and tidied recently. Perhaps this was where Mr Roberts was going to install his writing studio.

I took several pictures of the walls, then the views, with the Polaroid camera. The views would serve as my inspiration for the mural. Yes, I had the symbols that Mr Roberts wanted, but a mural requires depth – layers of images, if you like. So, I needed to think about the base layer. A palette of oceanic colours, even. I took more photos, careful not to overthink it too much – whatever drew my eye. The seals on the rocks below. The lavender tufts of heather in the fields, the white-tipped waves, the way they charged up the bay like white horses. The strange, black-headed seabirds hovering in the wind outside.

And I thought about how I arrived here. Here, in this lighthouse, with these girls and this *life*. I'd felt so proud accepting my place at the Glasgow School of Art. I was set to conquer the world, one brush stroke at a time. Later, in my gown and cap and in the toilet of a Costa, I'd discovered I was pregnant. I'd had a blink-and-you'll-miss-it fling with a textiles postgrad. He was an exchange student from the Netherlands and I'd admired his crochet sculptures. He was already long gone, backpacking around Europe.

A termination wasn't on the cards; a school friend had had one and relayed the procedure to a group of us in tears. Excruciating, she said, and humiliating. I preferred denial, right up until I went into labour and the midwives left me alone with a tiny blonde cherub that was apparently mine. I moved the cherub and myself into a bedsit in Bristol. Over time, I got used to the routine of staggering through the days, drunk with sleep deprivation.

I fell in love. Sean was an artist I met while teaching at Bristol College. We were happy. Sean taught ceramics and encouraged me to exhibit my work. We both had a collection at the Lime Tree Gallery at one point, and they sold so well that we were able to go on our first family holiday. We went to Nice. We had Luna, then Clover. They looked like twins, despite being two and a half years apart, both with Sean's big blue Irish eyes.

Clover had just turned two when Sean went out for a drink with a friend. Peter was three times over the limit when he took a bend at a hundred and eight miles an hour. The car spun out and hit a wall. Peter was killed instantly; Sean clung on for three days. They told us to say our goodbyes and switched off the machine.

It's a blur, that soul-shredding chapter of my life. We were homeless a lot, drifting from place to place and relying on the mercy of friends. I was a single mother to three girls, trying to juggle painting commissions and zero-hour teaching contracts with school runs and homework.

I thought of the sleeping bodies of my daughters tangled beside me when I woke that morning, and most mornings, legs and arms akimbo.

Did I love them?

More than my own life.

Would I have done it all again, knowing what I know now?

No, I don't think I would.

I'd had such high hopes for motherhood. And I wanted everything for my children. But every single day I had to confront the glaring reality that I simply wasn't able to provide the kind of life they deserved. And it crushed me.

III

I took the stairs back down, holding tightly to the banister that was only partially secured to the wall of the lighthouse. I tried not to look down into the abyss of that tall stone tower. I was used to heights – murals usually involved cherry pickers, or the cranes people associate with fire-fighters rescuing cats from tall trees. But the drop here was nerve-jangling. I had good balance, decent core strength – yet even so, I took those stairs as carefully as I could, keeping my eyes away from the vortex of the centre of the lighthouse. One slip, one distraction from each step would land me on solid concrete and break my back. Or kill me.

At the bottom of the staircase, I recalled the episode from the night before.

The doll in the dirty water.

It was still there, and much less eerie in the cool light of day. But I remembered how I'd felt a pull towards the section of the floor beneath the stairs. I moved towards it, sloshing through the water, feeling a bit stupid. My foot hit against something. A piece of wood.

I reached down and felt the hard edge of a slab of wood, about two-foot square. It wasn't heavy, and as soon as I lifted it the water started to gurgle and pour down into whatever the wood had been covering. A good thing, as far as I was concerned, as the dark water started to go down.

I assumed the wood had been covering a drain, but as I looked closer, I saw the grille wasn't a standard drain covering. The bars were old and rusty, fixed in place by a heavy lock. The water continued to pour down through the bars, a long echo indicating that there was quite a deep drop there. I couldn't see the bottom.

Luna and Clover were already outside when I emerged from the lighthouse, playing tag and laughing. I started to tell them off for leaving the bothy when they'd been instructed to stay indoors, but they were laughing so hard my words died in the wind.

At lunchtime, the old Range Rover that I recognized as Isla's pulled up outside. Through the window I saw a cloud of blonde hair emerge from the passenger side. Saffy, followed by another girl.

I ran outside, unable to stop myself from bursting into tears and throwing my arms around her. Luna, Clover, and I had scoured the area around the lighthouse, searching the caves dotting the cliffs further along the bay. We'd gone into the forest, then drove into the little town, Strallaig, in case she'd made it that far, but there had been no sign of her. I'd told myself that if she didn't turn up by two o'clock I'd call the police. It was half past one.

Saffy tolerated my hug – I guessed because we had an audience – and I thanked Isla for finding her. There was a man in the driving seat. An older man, mid-sixties, with a stone-cold stare.

'This is my husband, Bram,' Isla said.

'Hello,' I said. He didn't smile or say hello back, but I wasn't bothered. I was just grateful to have Saffy home.

'Where was she?' I asked.

'We spotted her walking along Salters Road, about a mile that way,' she said, turning to point left. 'We've just stopped by the café for a cuppa, haven't we, girls?'

The other girl, Rowan, introduced herself as Isla's daughter. At fifteen, she was the same age as Saffy, and just as shy and awkward, but she was friendly with it, too. She had long hair dyed raven black – an inch of copper roots betrayed her true colour – and heavy black eye make-up. An oversized Marilyn Manson T-shirt and studded Doc Martens indicated that she was somewhat of a goth. I invited her and Isla in for a coffee.

'Oh, we've just been to Mum's café,' Rowan said. She laughed nervously when she spoke, a light tinkle of bells.

'Wheesht,' Isla said, which I remembered meant 'be quiet'. Then, to me: 'We'd love to, but I've to open the café for a crafts workshop.'

She explained that 'the café' was her café in the town of Strallaig. She ran it while looking after properties, like the Longing, on the side.

'Another time, then,' I said.

She nodded. 'Oh, before I forget – I've ordered all the things you asked for. The paints, the harnesses, brushes, extension poles, a thirty-meter cherry picker. They'll take another week or so to arrive, but they're on their way.'

I was astonished. 'You found a cherry picker?'

'The thingamajig that looks like a fireman's lift?'

'Yes.'

'Aye. Took a bit of finding, that, but I got it. And I've

got a plasterer coming out to sort out all the bits of the interior wall that need fixing.'

I told her I owed her. 'Not at all,' she said brightly. Then, turning to get back into her car, she added, 'Why don't you come over one night? Bring the girls.' She winked. 'We can have that coffee with a dram of whisky.'

IV

I registered the girls at the local school, a small joined-up primary-through-secondary school with a hundred kids. It was very relaxed, with a lot of focus on the outdoors, and I tried not to think about where I would register them once I finished the mural.

I decided to keep the girls at home for a week longer so we could spend some time together before I started work, and specifically to try to get myself back into Saffy's good graces. The weather played nice for us, those grim scenes of lashing waves and witchy trees we'd been met with on our first night ripening to lush vistas of emerald fields, golden beaches, and rich blue ocean. The wildlife, too, was something else – we came to recognize the seals that seemed to reside on the rocks behind the Longing, the big grey one who shuffled and grunted in response when Clover called hello to him each morning, and the two slim black ones who often played together in the water, slick and quick as missiles.

'Sharks!' Luna shouted one morning. I raced outside to

find her pointing at a dorsal fin moving slowly through the water, only twenty feet or so from where we stood. A fishing boat was nearby, and I saw a man leaning over the side, sliding a pole into the water. The dorsal fin turned and began heading towards him. Clover clapped a hand to her mouth.

'The sharks are going to eat him!' she squealed.

The man was shouting something.

'What did he say?' Luna said.

'It's Basil,' he said, waving his arm at us. 'Basil!'

'Basil?' I called back.

'Oh, the basking shark,' Luna said. 'Remember? Isla told us about him when we arrived.'

We watched, speechless, as the shark lifted its snout out of the water to the fisherman's pole. And instead of feeding it, the fisherman used the pole to rub up and down the shark's body.

'He likes a good scratch,' the man shouted.

And every morning after that, a similar scene – the fisherman, whose name we learned was Angus McPherson, stopped off at the bay on his way back from his morning catch to say hello to Basil, our friendly neighbourhood basking shark.

We visited Camhanaich, the ancient standing stones set in a circle, which, according to Saffy, was likely used by Neolithic settlers for ritualistic slaughter. We drove through a sea fret, which was like driving through milk, and watched coal-black storm clouds roll in like travelling mountains. From an outcrop on the south shore, we saw a pod of killer whales through a pair of old binoculars, their dorsal fins cutting high through the waves. We explored the island's numerous forests, spotted otters and kingfishers the rivers, and the clock-round face of an owl in flight. We picked wildflower bouquets and took them back to the bothy, identifying each plant using an old encyclopaedia of Scottish flowers: fair-grass, fool's parsley, bog myrtle, hop-clover. We dried and hung them from the windows of the bothy.

We took old tin trays that I'd found in a cupboard at the bothy and went sledding down the grassy slopes of Braemeith, the tall hill in the middle of the island, until we got told off – Braemeith was a fairy hill, a farmer told us crossly, and it was bad luck for any human to step on it. The girls thought this was fascinating.

And at the Neolithic museum, we learned that the Longing was built on an old broch, a fortified dry-stone tower from around 500 BC. The guide at the museum gave the girls a leaflet each and flinched when I said we were staying in the bothy.

'You're staying at the Longing?' he said, raising an eyebrow. 'Quite a history, that place.'

'I can see that,' I said, flicking through the leaflet, my eyes falling on an artist's rendition of people being burned at the stake.

'Why's it called the Longing?' Luna asked him.

'It's named for the people who lost loved ones,' he said. 'Sometimes they'd visit the site where the Longing was built and . . . pay their respects.'

'That's tragic,' I said, and he nodded, but said nothing more.

LUNA, 2021

I

'Luna? Do you want to tell me what's going on?' Ethan says as they get into the car.

Her jaw is tight. 'Just drive.'

It's almost 8pm. They follow the directions on Google Maps to the B&B that Eilidh recommended, the air between them loud with a thousand unasked questions. She can't be Clover, she thinks. *Except*, a voice in her head says, *she is.*

They check into the B&B, a four-storey terrace with rooms that haven't been updated since the seventies. Luna feels a sense of relief as Ethan closes the bedroom door, the four walls of the room giving her space to begin to lay out all the tangled thoughts in her mind.

Ethan sits down in the wicker chair by the window.

'Who *was* that?' he says after a while.

She is studying a picture hanging on the opposite wall, a sun-faded oil painting of a vase of lilies. 'Who was what?'

'The girl in the hospital.'

'She's my sister.'

He coughs out a laugh. 'I don't understand. You said . . . I mean, she can't be more than, what, six or seven? You said Clover was twenty-nine.'

'There has to be a reason for how young she is,' she hears herself say. 'It has to be genetic, or hormonal. Some kind of condition that prevents ageing. Benjamin Button disease, or something. Toddlers with wrinkles and brittle bones. Clover obviously has something similar in reverse.'

'Luna . . .'

'Age regression, or suspension.' She looks up. 'We'll get her checked out. We'll find a specialist.'

His expression is so full of pity that she glances down to see if she's spilled coffee down her dress. It wouldn't be the first time. But no, it's not that. Her dress is fine.

'I *know* how hard this is,' he says earnestly.

'She looks exactly like Clover,' she says. 'Sounds like her, smells like her. She even knew the name of the giraffe. That was Clover's special toy that she'd had from birth.'

He's reaching out for her, nodding, as though she's lost her mind. 'I absolutely understand what you've been through . . .'

'No,' she says firmly. 'No, you don't. You haven't spent the last twenty-two years trying to figure out why your mother dumped you in a forest. You haven't spent the last twenty-two years tormented by what happened to your baby sister when you were supposed to be looking after her.'

'Luna . . .'

She stands, unable to sit any longer, her hands reaching for her cheeks. Her throat is burning with that same fierce knot that settled there the day Clover went missing all those years ago. Her emotions are the only thing that ring true – her memories about what happened before and after

Clover going missing are like pieces of a shattered mirror. She remembers going into foster care, and her first night spent in a stranger's house. She has random memories of those years – a neighbour in St Ives who used to smoke a purple pipe, a cat that had nine snow-white kittens in a cardboard box, long afternoons bouncing alone on a trampoline. She can remember a meal she had at a school friend's house, a steaming pot of mussels. Her friend told her the mussels were mermaid's lips, only to laugh hysterically when Luna believed her and bolted from the table in fright. And she recalls a Girl Guides' camp where they were instructed on knot-making, and the girls started tying one another to a tree, and Luna grew so distressed while being tied up that she vomited over one of the leaders.

The story of her past is not like other people's, she thinks. Most people's pasts can be viewed like cleaved water left in the wake of a boat. Hers? It's a tangled weave of spider webs and nightmares, never to make sense.

II

From the window, Luna locates the flat square of the hospital roof amidst the cityscape. She thinks of what the doctor said before they left. About the injury on Clover's hip. He wanted to know if it had happened before she went missing, or during.

'What injury?' she asked. He'd turned to Clover. She was asleep, curled around the teddies donated by the nurses. Very gently, he'd lifted up Clover's hospital gown and peeled back a white dressing on her hip to reveal a small red blotch. Perhaps a rash. Measles? No. Luna was sure they'd all been vaccinated. She'd lowered herself to look at it. The mark was singular, a handful of red-raw scratches within a raised circle of skin, angry and inflamed. Like a burn.

'Is it an insect bite?'

'We think it's a wound inflicted by a human.'

She'd straightened, searching his face. 'Who?'

'Well, I was hoping you might be able to shed a bit of light on it,' the doctor said. 'Can you make out the numbers?'

'*Numbers?*'

She bent quickly once more to see the mark, closer this time, but Clover had moaned and squirmed to change position.

'I can't make it out,' she said. 'What numbers?'

'It's very small, as you can see, but on closer inspection we found four digits. The numbers two zero two one.'

Luna leaned forward and stared hard. There they were: four numbers etched lightly into the skin in a vertical row.

2
0
2
1

Someone had carved numbers into Clover's skin.

'The police are looking into it,' she tells Ethan. 'Apparently it could be anything. A gang sign. A code.'

They both fall silent. How can this have happened? And why? Ethan rises from his chair and wraps his arms around her, holding her tight.

'I'm sorry,' he says. 'But . . .'

'She *is* Clover,' she snaps, pulling away. 'I don't care what you think.'

'OK.' For a while neither of them speaks. 'So . . . you think she's still a child because of what she's been through?'

She covers her face with her hands. 'It's my fault. It's my fault she went missing.'

'You can't say that.'

She snaps her head up, fixing him with a glare. 'It. Was. My. Fault.'

'You were *ten*, Luna.'

'You weren't there, Ethan. You don't know . . .'

'How were you to blame, exactly?'

She falters. 'I just know I was. I can't remember the details.'

But suddenly it's there, the memory of Sapphire coming into her room and talking to her. She knows instantly this was it, *this* was how it happened. Where has this been, this slice of her past? Where has it been lingering?

'I think it started with Saffy,' she says, closing her eyes. 'She went missing. But on purpose.'

He tilts his head. 'What do you mean, "on purpose"?'

'I think that Saffy and my mother had had a falling-out.'

'What about?'

'I'm not sure. Saffy stopped speaking to her and was sulking for ages. I think . . . she came to me and asked for a favour.'

As she speaks, a memory crystallizes in her mind, her senses relaying micro-images and smells that cohere into something that makes sense. She remembers Saffy coming into her room after school.

'I need a favour,' she'd asked.

Saffy hadn't done anything to deserve a favour but Luna had been curious. For a moment, she had glimpsed what other girls with an older sister experienced: a kind of friendship instead of constant humiliation and venom. Favours earned and requested, conversation that took place with words instead of silences.

'OK,' she'd replied finally.

'Can I come in?' Saffy had asked, which was odd as she was already in Luna's bedroom, and she never asked to come in. Luna had nodded, and Saffy had closed the door and sat down on her bed. She'd studied her nails.

'I'm going into hiding,' she'd said flatly. 'And I need you to pretend you don't know.'

'What do you mean, you're going into hiding?'

Saffy had heaved an irritated sigh. 'I'm running away? From home? I'm telling you because I want you to keep it a secret.' She'd lowered her eyes. 'And I want you to tell me how Mum reacts. Like, if she's upset or if she doesn't care. She'll probably throw a party. Balloons and everything.'

Luna had felt a rush of relief at the thought of her sister no longer living with her. 'Where will you go?'

Saffy had turned her face to the window. 'I was thinking of that hut we found in the woods. Just for a few days, you know? Maybe a month or so.'

'What about food? Won't you be hungry?'

'Maybe you could bring me food?'

Luna had wanted to say no, why should she, but she found herself nodding. If she didn't bring Saffy food she might die. So Luna had agreed.

'I want you to write down how Mum reacts and tell me,' Saffy had said. 'Write down what she says, what she does.'

Luna had cocked her head. 'Why?'

Saffy had given her a hard stare. 'Just do it.'

'And what happened?' Ethan asks.

'She packed some stuff into her backpack and left that night,' Luna tells him, surprised at the sudden ease with which this information surfaces in her mind. 'She went to the woods.'

She remembers going to the hut where Saffy had said she'd be. She'd been afraid of the woods, after a boy at school had told her they were haunted.

Saffy had been sitting on the floor of the horrible, ivy-choked hut, her headphones on, smoking and reading an old book.

'Well?' Saffy had said when Luna entered. 'Has she organized the celebration party yet?'

'It's only been a day,' Luna said. 'She hasn't noticed.'

The words were out before she could stop them. Saffy's face had twisted.

'Well, you can hardly blame her,' Luna had said. 'You're always off somewhere with your friends, or sulking in your room.'

'She hates me.'

'Once she finds out she'll go mental. You know she will.'

'No, Luna. She won't.'

Luna had wanted to throttle her sister then, not least because of how terrified she was going to make their mum but also because it was Luna's birthday soon, and she could see now that the timing was deliberate. She'd thought Saffy was starting to become a proper big sister, at long last. But she'd been hoodwinked. This was all a scheme to ruin her birthday *and* freak out their mum in one fell swoop.

'I hope she gets fucking arrested,' Saffy had said, taking a long drag from her tab. 'Maybe the police will think she's murdered me. Wouldn't that be fun?'

'You *have* to come home,' Luna had said. She wanted to stamp her foot or kick her stupid sister for being so bloody selfish. 'If you don't come home I'm going to tell everyone that you're here, and Mum will ground you for*ever*.'

Saffy had rolled her cigarette on the ashtray she'd made out of stones, then looked up at Luna, thoughtfully.

'You promised you wouldn't tell anyone. You know you can't go back on a promise.'

'I *can*. You tricked me! I made a promise because I thought you were being nice, and you're not. You're just doing this so you can spoil my birthday!'

'And then what happened?' Ethan asks.

Luna presses a hand to her forehead. 'I think . . . I stormed out. I was going to go straight home and tell Mum where she was. But I didn't. Even though Mum was freaking out by then, I kept quiet. I don't know why.' She begins to cry. Why didn't she say something? Why didn't she tell *someone*?

'The next morning I took a loaf of bread and some milk to Saffy in the hut. But she was gone.'

'Gone?'

She nods, wiping away tears. 'The hut was empty. No note, no clothing. No sign of a fight. And we never saw her again. That's all I remember.'

He takes this in. 'You were just a kid, Luna . . .'

He says it gently, but he doesn't get it. How could he? She hasn't kept anything from him that she hasn't been keeping from herself. He doesn't get that truth and memory can be too complex, too tentacled, to boil down to a linear narrative. That sometimes, silence is a form of survival.

'I can only recall little fragments, like dreams. And it's all scrambled. None of it makes sense.'

'OK. But talking through it . . . maybe something will come back to you.'

She feels flustered, overwhelmed. She folds her arms and pinches the skin on her forearms as she recounts the facts. She and her mother and two sisters had only been on Lòn Haven a month or so when everything turned to shit.

'What happened before you stayed at the lighthouse?' Ethan prompts.

Before?

Before Lòn Haven, she was just a normal nine-year-old going to school every day, living with her mum and two sisters on a houseboat in Bristol. Well, almost a normal nine-year-old. Her and Clover's dad died when she was four. She barely remembers anything about him. She remembers moving around a lot. Their mother worked as an artist, and sometimes as a cleaner, and often she'd rise before dawn to work at a corner shop – anything that would pay the bills. She remembers her mum's dungarees covered in dried paint, and she remembers canvases stacked against the walls of the house and the ducks that would sit on the windowsill, looking for scraps.

III

They have dinner in a family-run diner in the centre of the town. She tries again to phone Grace to tell her about Clover, but finds she can't bring herself to make the call. Grace is the only foster mother she's stayed in touch with, more an aunt to her now than a foster mother. What if Grace doesn't believe her? What if, like Ethan, Grace tries to tell her that the girl can't possibly be Clover? What if she is forced into conflict with the other person she loves, if the discovery of her baby sister becomes a wedge in her most important relationships?

Back at the B&B, Ethan strips to his boxer shorts and falls asleep on top of the bedclothes, snoring loudly. She lies beside him, still reeling from the events of the day. The shells, the scan, then the phone call . . . She tries to force memories to the surface of her mind, picturing them as stones on the bottom of a lake that she has to push upwards.

But it doesn't work like that. Memories, like stones, have their own gravity.

She thinks instead of St Ives, of her years there with her

foster mother, Grace. She should be grateful for that life, and she is, but it should be *enough,* she thinks. She attended an excellent high school, developed a strong network of good friends. Yes, she fell into drugs. Yes, she had an almost insurmountable compulsion to steal, a compulsion that still nags at her. Even now, she's eyeing that painting of the lilies on the wall and wondering if it would fit in her bag. She shakes it off. The painting is gross, and she knows all too well the sinking shame that follows the thrill of slipping away undetected. Grace never gave up on her, no matter how many times Luna stole money from her. She was a devoted foster mother – dedicated, patient, capable of showering her with unlimited attention. Her other life was the one before that, with her birth mother, Liv, and her sisters, Saffy and Clover, a life that ended abruptly with her being dumped in a forest by her mother. Why?

The 'why' of her abandonment has all but pulled her apart over the years. She remembers vividly waiting for her mother, believing wholeheartedly that she'd come back for her. Weeks passed, months. She'd run up to strangers in the street, in the mall, shouting out 'Mum! Mum!' Christmases spent in foster homes. She'd sit by the living room window, watching the cars pass. She always believed her mother would come back.

But she didn't.

LIV, 1998

I

The day the girls started at school, the equipment and paint for the mural arrived. I'd planned to start setting up as soon as it came, but I had been feeling ill all day, laid up on the sofa with a hot water bottle on my stomach. By evening I felt better, and when the girls went to bed I headed out to check the delivery.

It was a wild, windy night, autumn descending on the island in a fury with all her gales and rain. I hurried quickly across the wet rocks, pulling the heavy door of the Longing open and shutting it tightly behind me.

The black sludge on the floor was gone, drained away to a film of slime. I made sure the piece of wood was put back carefully across the grille on the hole in the floor. Then, I pulled back the tarp that was covering the cherry picker and the rest of the equipment. It looked good. Enough paint to cover several lighthouses, and in the exact colours I'd requested. Brand-new paintbrushes, a wallpaper table, work lamps, and extenders for the hard-to-reach parts. Protective clothing, a harness, goggles. It was top-notch equipment, and I felt relieved.

I decided to store the paintbrushes and protective clothing in the lantern room, just in case the ground floor flooded again. It was dark, but my torchlight fell on something that definitely hadn't been there the day before.

On the floor, visible in a beam of moonlight, was a white triangle, made up of three objects.

I bent down carefully to take a look at it, retracing my steps in my mind. No, the lantern room had definitely been empty. I'd have spotted such a thing if it had been there.

Bones. The triangle was made out of three delicate animal bones, perhaps the leg bones of a fox, criss-crossed in the shape of a triangle.

Someone had been here. And they'd left me a message. Or a warning.

Just then, there was a noise from somewhere below. A loud creak, then a slam. Footsteps.

Someone was inside the Longing.

I felt sick. I listened, my heart roaring in my ears, for the sound of the footsteps. They were heavy and slow. So, definitely not one of my children.

There was no way out of the lantern room, and nowhere to hide. I was trapped. I would have to pray that whoever it was would leave. Or I'd have to confront them.

I'd like to say that I screwed my courage to the sticking place and went out to confront the intruder, but I was terrified. What kind of person would come out on a stormy night to a derelict lighthouse? The sort who would also kill an animal to make some horrible symbol like the one lying in front of me. I squeezed my eyes shut. I wanted it all just to go away.

And then, a sound. A tune. Whoever was downstairs was humming.

It was a familiar song. I opened my eyes, utterly confused. Was that . . . *Abba*?

I raced out to the top of the stairs and shone my torchlight downstairs.

'Who's there?'

A loud clatter followed, and several loud expletives. My torchlight fell on a man. He'd fallen flat on his arse and was holding his hand up against my torchlight. I moved quickly down the stairs, much faster than I should have.

'You scared the shit out of me,' I said, when I reached the bottom. I took pleasure in shining my torchlight directly in his eyes. Built like a tank, he looked like a Viking – a thick copper beard, a round belly stretching the fabric of an Iron Maiden T-shirt, long amber hair pulled back into a ponytail, tattoos covering his hands. Just then, a horrible thought occurred to me.

'Are you . . . Patrick Roberts?' I said, lowering my torch.

'Finn McAllen. Isla said you'd need of a plasterer.' He had a deep, booming voice that bounced off the walls. 'I can come back later if that's easier . . .'

'No, no,' I said. 'The dead of night is absolutely the right time for checking out a lighthouse . . .'

'It's only eight o'clock,' he said. 'I came as soon as I finished my other job.'

'You've not been in earlier?' I said, thinking back to the bones. 'There was something left in the lantern room . . .'

'Nope,' he said, dusting himself off. 'I had a big job on today. I told Isla I'd have come sooner but it's been manic . . .'

So he hadn't left the bones upstairs. That is, if he was

telling the truth. I watched him carefully in the cold glare of the torchlight.

'You're here to see what plastering needs doing, correct?'

'Correct. Isla mentioned the place is getting a mural or something painted inside. You're the painter, I take it?'

'Yes.'

'OK,' he said, in a way that suggested he was expecting a different answer. 'Show me what needs doing.'

Everything, I thought, but instead I pointed the torch at the sections of stonework that I couldn't paint over, not without the mural looking disjointed and uneven. We took to the stairs and climbed to the first turn.

'Place is a mess,' he said, wobbling the banister.

'Please don't do that,' I said. 'You're likely to pull it off.'

'Sorry. I thought Roberts would have sorted the place out before getting it decorated.'

'I think it would take quite a while to sort this place out.'

'Not at all,' he said with a sniff. 'Dynamite would sort it in seconds.'

'Oh, before I forget,' I said, shining the torch up at the bats flitting in the high corners beneath the lantern room. 'I need to get someone out to take care of the bats.'

'You mean, take care of the bats or *take care* of the bats?' he said, drawing a line across his throat at the second repeat.

'I don't want them harmed. But I've no idea if the paint will bother them.' As I said this, a large bat flitted closely overhead, making us both duck.

'I think they'll bother you more than you'll bother them,' he said, chuckling. 'I'll take care of them. I do a bit of pest control, on the side.'

'Didn't you say you do plastering on the side?'

He cocked an eyebrow. 'There's a lot of "on the side" when you live on an island.'

'You've dealt with bats before?'

He shrugged. 'Not much I haven't dealt with. Bats, seals, the occasional whale . . .'

'A whale isn't a pest, surely.'

'It was a joke.'

He had a dry sense of humour, which I appreciated more than I let on. 'How soon can you start?'

He produced a notepad and pen from his pocket and jotted something down. 'Tomorrow, if I move some things around. However, I can't do much about the time it takes plaster to dry.'

'I can start painting over here if you want to plaster that section first.'

He didn't answer, but spent a long while checking the walls with his fingertips, pulling at loose bits of stone. 'Been a while since I've been inside,' he said.

'You know the Longing well?'

He placed a hand thoughtfully on the newel post. 'He said it took him a year to make this.'

'Who?'

He turned to me. 'My great-grandfather. He made this banister. The whole thing. A hundred yards of iron. Beaten and welded by hand. There might even be a picture of him here.' He strode over to the wall behind the staircase, and I followed. My torchlight fell on a small gallery of picture frames. It was the first time I'd noticed them. 'There he is.' He wiped the glass with his fingertips. 'Angus McAllen.'

'He was a lighthouse keeper,' I said, noticing the photographs of men posed in their uniforms.

'Aye.'

'Your family ran the Longing?'

'Not for a long time, now. They cut the shipping routes. The Longing was decommissioned after that.'

'I'm sorry.'

'Hardly your fault, is it?' he said. 'My family owns – *owned* – the Longing and ten acres around the bay. Even the wee bothy you're staying in. It got passed down to me.'

He went to say more, but stopped short, busying himself with his inspection of the walls. I figured it was difficult for him, being here.

As a hired plasterer instead of the owner.

II

I barely slept that night. I couldn't help but mentally play out the scene of someone creeping past the bothy and into the Longing, clutching a pile of bones, wanting to scare me off. Wanting to threaten me.

The next morning, after the school run, I resolved to call Isla and get her take on the matter. But exhaustion rendered me barely coherent – I babbled down the line at her about bones and triangles and naked children. 'I was wondering if you'd heard anything,' I said. 'From the locals, about me being here. I know a single mother with three kids moving into the area doesn't always go down well . . .'

'Why don't you come over?' she said. 'We'll have a cuppa and a chat.'

Isla lived on the other side of the island. I found the south side more charming than the north, with a coastline scooped out by white beaches and turquoise sea. Sailing boats swayed in the port, and a row of pretty terraced houses painted in different colours – pink, blue, yellow, lilac, and orange – lined the street overlooking the North

Sea. Isla's house was at the end of a long driveway, a large barn conversion with immaculate gardens. Isla greeted me at the door and led me to the sitting room, where I found her daughter, Rowan, curled up in a white armchair with a tub of ice cream and a blanket. She was watching *Friends*.

'Row's off school today, as you can see,' Isla told me. Rowan turned and gave us both a beaming, contented smile, which only served to make Isla cock an eyebrow disapprovingly. 'Period pains never called for a day off when I was young. But here we are.'

'Olivia,' Rowan said as I sat on the sofa opposite. 'I hope you don't mind me saying, but your aura is dark. Is something wrong?'

I looked to Isla, not quite sure how to respond. It seemed like this was her usual kind of query posed to household guests.

'I . . . found a few odd things in the Longing,' I said carefully. 'I suppose I'm unnerved by it.'

Rowan nodded sympathetically, her gazed fixed above my head. 'Yes. When I heard you were coming I put a rowan branch on the door.'

'That was you?' I said, surprised. 'What a kind gesture.'

'The Longing is super grim,' Rowan said. 'I could come and cleanse it for you, if you like?'

'Cleanse?' I said. I heard Isla sigh behind me.

'It probably has a lot of negative energy. You should really cleanse it before you start work. I'm a witch, you see. Didn't Sapphire tell you?'

'As in, Wiccan?'

Row shook her head, her large blue eyes wide. 'No, not Wiccan. I'm a green witch. It's very different.'

'Off you go, Rowan,' Isla said, irritated.

Rowan threw me a shy smile and gathered up her blanket. 'I'll come and do a cleanse any time, just let me know.' And she floated off.

'Righty-ho,' Isla said, closing the door and handing me a cup of tea. She sat down and cocked her head. 'You sounded very panicked on the phone, my dear. Walk me through what happened.'

I told her about the bones in the lantern room. They definitely weren't there the day after we arrived, so sometime between then and yesterday someone had put them there.

She pursed her lips at this. 'Very strange. I can imagine why you're so rattled.'

I exhaled deeply at this. I worried that I'd overreacted.

'You know, any other time I'd have said Mr Roberts left them, but he's at sea just now.'

'Why would Mr Roberts leave bones in the lantern room?'

She pulled a face. 'He's a bit of an odd one, that Roberts. Folk aren't keen on him, keep their distance.'

Now I was even more puzzled. 'But . . . you work for him?'

'Doesn't mean I'm bosom buddies with the man,' she said. Then, leaning close: 'If anything, I work for him to keep a close eye, see what he's up to. You've never met him, have you?'

'No. I heard about the commission through a friend . . .'

She nodded. 'I see. Nobody knows anything about him. Keeps his cards close to his chest, you see. The island's mystery millionaire. And right now, I can tell you he's out at sea.'

I nodded, a little uneasy at what she'd said about Mr Roberts. 'You said the Longing had been vandalized before. Do you think it might be the same people?'

'I can't be sure. Like I said, I'm sure it was outsiders that graffitied the place. Tourists, you ken.'

'Why couldn't it have been someone local?'

She sighed. 'To be completely honest with you, most folk around here are too afraid to go near the Longing.'

'Why?'

'It has a wee bit of a history, that place.'

I thought back to my visit to the Neolithic museum. 'I've heard it was named for people who were grieving?'

Isla folded her arms and pursed her lips, visibly weighing up how to shortcut to the parts of history that mattered. 'A long time ago, the people that lived here burned a number of women who were accused of witchcraft. The accused were held until their trials at the site where the Longing is now.'

I thought about the hole I'd found, covered by the metal grille. The thought of people being held down there made me shiver. 'Were they held underground?'

A nod. 'I believe so.'

'But that was hundreds of years ago,' I said. 'Surely people aren't afraid for that reason?'

Isla gave a little laugh. 'Ah, well . . . when one of the witches was being burned at the stake, she cursed the island. Soon after that, things started happening that were . . . frightening. And folk have been wary ever since.'

I frowned. 'What things?'

'Look, I don't think the bones are anything to worry about. I tend to know most of the goings-on in this place and I'm fairly sure there's no one who poses a threat to you. It's probably animals. Maybe some kids having a lark.'

'What about a young child?' I said, thinking back to what I'd seen in the lantern room the day that I pushed

Saffy. 'Would a young child from the island be deterred from going inside?'

'No wains live near the bay,' she said, puzzled. 'Are you sure you saw one?'

I faltered. I couldn't say I was sure.

'You mention that people here are still wary,' I said. 'That the island was cursed. You don't believe that, do you?'

She flicked her hair. Isla could be direct all day long, but wasn't keen on receiving it. 'I can appreciate that a "curse" sounds very dramatic from the outside, but when you start to see the evidence . . .'

'What evidence?'

She lowered her eyes. 'About thirty years ago a child went missing on the island. My wee brother, Jamie.'

'Oh, Isla,' I said, horrified. 'That's terrible.'

A small sigh, and I could see she was growing upset. 'I was sixteen. We all adored him. He was only two. We were playing in the rock pools on the bay all afternoon. One minute he was there and the next . . .' She pressed her fingers to her mouth. 'We searched everywhere. Every inch of the island was covered. My parents never got over it.'

'I can imagine,' I said. 'What a terrible thing to happen.'

'Sadly, it wasn't the first time a child went missing. And it wasn't the last. About a year after we lost Jamie, another child went missing. A German family. The husband was here doing research at the Neolithic site. Little girl.' She moved her eyes to a corner of the room, lost in a memory. 'And then, another child. Wee Cam Maguire. Bonniest lad you've ever seen. Seven years old. Mother went out of her mind looking for him. But they never did find him.'

I took this in. 'Can I ask a personal question?'

'Of course.'

'If these things keep happening, why do you still live here?'

I asked it gently, hoping not to offend her. She raised her eyebrows. 'Well, you can see for yourself how beautiful Lòn Haven is. And I think I inherited some of my mother's stubbornness. My family has lived here for centuries. If you think I'm going to let something as small as a witch's curse send me packing, you've another think coming.' She rallied, clapping her hands together. 'Now then, how about that dram?'

III

I avoided the lantern room after that, with the exception of a quick dash inside to retrieve the paintbrushes I'd left there. I spotted the bones, still on the floor, and darted out again, as though I might be able to erase the whole incident by simply closing my eyes to it.

Finn was already at the Longing when I arrived. He was dressed in overalls, prepping plaster in a bucket. A small radio played heavy metal music. He turned it down as I entered.

'Morning,' he said, lifting a white cardboard box and holding it out to me. I saw it contained something.

'What's this?' I said.

'Seeing as you're a visitor to Scotland, my daughter Cassie and I made some shortbread last night.'

'How kind,' I said. 'Thank you.'

A quick bow. 'You're most welcome.'

The shortbread broke the ice, and it felt better to work alongside someone here, especially since Isla's history lesson had made me feel creeped out by the thought of women in a dungeon underneath us. On the wallpaper table, I spread the pencil outline I'd done of the mural on a sheet of paper. 'What is that?' Finn asked.

'Oh, it's the mural.'

He screwed his face up. 'The mural? Bit small, isn't it?'

'It's an outline,' I said dryly, and he chuckled.

He stepped closer, looking at it curiously. 'What is it? Prince's new name?'

'I'm just the artist. Mr Roberts wants it painted, and that's what he'll get.'

'Hope he's paying well enough.'

'Enough to keep my girls in pony comics.'

'Your girls? How many?'

'Three. My youngest's seven. Clover. Luna's nine, and Saffy's fifteen.'

'Fifteen,' he said with a whistle. 'What's that like?'

'You've watched Harry Enfield's *Kevin and Perry* sketch?'

'Yeah?'

'I'm realizing more and more that it isn't a sketch at all. It's a documentary.'

'Shit, don't tell me *that*. Cassie's ten and I'm already feeling like I'm in that scene in *Jaws*. You know, "We're gonna need a bigger boat"?'

'She's ten? She must be in Luna's class at school, then.'

'Not at school. She's still recovering.'

'Recovering?'

He stepped back from the plasterwork, wiped his brow. 'She had leukaemia last year. That's, uh, the reason I sold this place. The doctors here said they couldn't do anything more for her. But I found a doctor in America who had this fancy new treatment. So I took her out there, paid for the treatment. And, uh, she's still here.'

I could tell he felt awkward telling me this. He was sharing with me, and not just the news of his daughter's illness, either – he had given up his inheritance for her.

I asked how Cassie's mother felt about it and he told me she wasn't around, and hadn't been for a long time. It was rare for me to meet another single parent. I met a lot of people who co-parented, managing the difficult task of ferrying their kids from one home to another, dividing holidays and finances. It was a hard job, to be sure – but a single parent, an honest-to-God buck-stops-with-me single parent was a rare species. And yet, here was Finn, another of my small tribe. He knew the language. He knew the grind of it.

A song came on the radio: 'Waterloo'. Finn bent down and fiddled with the dial, finding another channel.

I smiled. 'I thought you liked Abba.'

He looked up, catching my meaning. 'Ah. You mean, the other night. You heard that, did you?'

'I did.'

'It was on the car radio and I got it stuck in my head. I'm not a fan. Promise.'

'OK.'

He flicked his hair back in a camp flourish. 'I might do a wee bit of karaoke in my living room every now and then, with my feather boa and my sequinned leg warmers, maybes my silver knee boots. Other than that, I'm against them.'

I laughed. 'My lips are sealed.'

He wiggled his hips, and I laughed louder.

'So, since we're sharing,' he said as I was testing out the cherry picker, 'can I ask you something?'

'Sure.'

'What really brought you to Lòn Haven?'

'The job, of course.'

'You can't tell me you came all this way to paint this god-forsaken lighthouse. Especially during a school term.'

I was taken aback. 'Well, I did . . .'

'OK.'

'Did you think I had an ulterior motive?'

'No, no,' he said, bending to clean his trowel. He cleared his throat. 'I just figured you were running from something, that's all.'

I tried to tell myself that he was joking, but his words had somehow peeled back the layer I'd worked so hard to create, digging at the truth beneath it. Out here, I'd almost succeeded in pushing away the reasons I'd dragged my daughters from their beds in the middle of the night and driven non-stop to the Highlands of Scotland.

'Excuse me,' I said, 'I need to . . .'

'Something wrong?'

I didn't finish my sentence. I pushed open the door of the lighthouse and ran out into the rain.

LUNA, 2021

I

'Morning,' a voice says from the doorway of their room in the B&B. Ethan, followed by the smell of coffee. He peeks around the door of the bathroom. 'Brought you breakfast.'

'Thanks.'

Luna washes her hands and gives a long yawn as she heads back into the bedroom. Ethan sets his haul on the bedside table: a croissant, a decaf coffee, and a tub of porridge with a small pot of honey and a plastic spoon.

'How'd you sleep?' he asks.

She shrugs, her mouth full of hot porridge. She rarely sleeps well when she's pregnant.

He sits down next to her. She can tell he's been churning the Clover situation over in his mind. 'She does look like your sister,' he says with resignation. 'The girl in the hospital.'

In her mind's eye she sees him awake at dawn, scrolling through the Facebook page she set up for Clover. A page he's seen a hundred times, but which he needs to check now to figure out what the deal is with this kid that Luna claims to be her sister.

'Look, I don't want this to come between us,' he says anxiously, moving closer. He rests his hand carefully, slowly, on hers. 'If you say she's Clover, then . . . fine, I believe you. OK?'

She can tell he's lying, but it's out of kindness, or maybe an effort to worm his way back into her good graces. This is his compromise – a willingness to go along with her, even though he doesn't understand. There is a long silence between them, and she knows he's waiting for a response. When she looks at his hand on hers she feels her heart stirring. His warm, broad hands have always made her feel safe, comforted. And seen.

So why did she say no? Why does she still shudder at the thought of marrying him, being *bound* to him, despite knowing she still loves him?

They head to the hospital to see Clover. It feels like a dream, winding through the hospital corridors to find her sister. And then the moment Luna sees her again, sitting upright in the bed. Gianni the giraffe tucked in beside her and colour returned to her cheeks. Still a child.

Luna feels a rush of emotion at the sight of her. Stunning familiarity, and yet disappointment. She had hoped, stupidly, to find a woman there instead of a little girl.

'Hi, Luna,' Clover says brightly.

'Hello,' Luna replies, glancing self-consciously at Ethan.

'Did you and your giraffe sleep well?' he asks.

Clover looks up warily. Someone has washed her hair, and a tray of cleared bowls and plates nearby shows she's just finished breakfast.

'She perked up a fair bit after you left,' a nurse says, pouring her a cup of water from a jug. 'Didn't you?'

Clover takes the cup of water, her eyes darting cautiously

to Luna. Luna sits on the bed next to her, absorbing the sight of her again. Physically, the girl's likeness to Clover is uncanny. But Luna is aware, painfully aware, of how desperate she is for this to be Clover. For the search to be over, for the two halves of her life to lace together into a perfect whole once and for all.

'Morning,' another voice says, and Luna turns to see Eilidh approaching with a wide smile. Beside her is another woman, who isn't smiling. She's tall with short black hair and a hard face, a document folder tucked under one arm and her hands tightly clasped. She fixes Luna in an unyielding stare, until Luna looks away.

'How are you today, sweetheart?' Eilidh asks Clover brightly. 'You're looking better already, now that your sister's here.'

Clover plucks Gianni from beneath the blanket and holds him tight. Eilidh turns to the woman beside her and says, 'that's the toy she remembered.' She nods at Luna. 'The one you brought for her.'

Luna nods, understanding now the point Eilidh is making – that the toy is proof.

She turns to the woman with the hard face and introduces her to Luna. 'This is my colleague, Shannon Young. She wants to have a wee chat, if that's OK. Just to sort things out before Clover's discharged.'

Luna follows Eilidh and Shannon as they look for 'somewhere quiet to chat', and her stomach is in knots. The presence of the other social worker doesn't bode well.

They find a small office in a side room and arrange three chairs in a tight triangle.

'Nothing to worry about,' Eilidh says, as they sit down. She glances at Shannon, then at Luna. 'We just have to fill in some paperwork before we let Clover go. Obviously we're glad you've been reunited, but we need to take some information from you.'

Luna swallows. 'Of course.'

'Wonderful,' Eilidh says, beaming. 'Now, if you have something with your name and address on it, I'll get it photocopied.'

Luna pulls out her wallet and finds her driving license. She hands it to Eilidh, who holds it towards Shannon. They both inspect it closely.

'Coventry?' Shannon says. 'You lived there long?'

There's a tone in Shannon's voice that strikes Luna as suspicious. 'I've lived there for nine years now.'

'And what is it you do there?'

'I work for a children's mental health organization,' she says. 'I specialize in arts therapies for Adverse Childhood Experiences. I use art to help children from abusive homes develop coping strategies.'

'And you live in Coventry with your partner?' Shannon says.

'Yes.' Luna doesn't think it worthwhile delving into the complexities of her relationship with Ethan.

'Your partner's full name?'

'Ethan Singh.'

'Can I ask about your mother?' Eilidh says gently. 'When I first spoke with Clover, I asked her who usually takes care of her. So we could contact her family, you see. She told her mummy looked after her, and her big sister, Luna. I couldn't find your mum, Olivia, but luckily I was able to find you.'

Luna draws a breath. 'Our mother passed away.'

Eilidh tuts in sympathy. 'Poor thing.'

'You were staying on Lòn Haven when Clover went missing?' Shannon asks, and Luna nods. 'So who was last taking care of Clover?'

Luna feels her cheeks flush and her throat tighten. How can she possibly tell them that twenty-two years have passed? They'll decide Clover isn't her sister and put her into care.

'Actually, I have some questions of my own, if that's all right,' Luna says. 'Where was Clover all this time?'

'You mean, where was she since Tuesday?' Shannon says. 'Clover said she'd only just left the cottage the night before. She said she went looking for *you*. And then she was found wandering on the side of the road.'

Eilidh clears her throat. 'Clover's memory is still very hazy. The toxicology report shows no sign of any drugs in her system, though she had a mild head injury.'

'Head injury?' Luna asks. 'Did someone hit her?'

'We don't know,' Eilidh sighs. 'A trauma can do funny things to a person. Especially to their memories. What we do know is that she had walked for miles through thick woodland in just her sandals and dress before being picked up by a farmer.'

Miles from where? Luna thinks. Who has been looking after Clover? She had to have been fed and sheltered. Twenty-two years. She must be deeply traumatized.

'What about the injury on her hip?' Luna asks. 'The doctor thought a human did it.'

Eilidh nods, frowning as she thinks of it. 'The psychiatrist asked Clover about that but she has no memory of receiving it. She insists she was with your mother one minute and the next she was walking along the roadside. Everything in between is still a blank. Poor wee thing.'

'What I'm still having trouble with,' Shannon says, referring to a sheet from the document folder, 'is Clover's date of birth. It says here that she was born on the twenty-second of August, 1991. I've checked with the officer at Dingwall and he says that's what he has in his report.' She glances up at Luna for explanation.

'It must be a mistake,' Luna says. Even to her own ears her tone is unconvincing.

'Yes, it must be,' Eilidh says. 'Otherwise it would make Clover a grown woman!'

Shannon purses her lips, turning the pages. 'So you're saying Clover's date of birth is the twenty-second of August . . . ?'

Luna does a quick sum in her head. '2014.'

She pulls a pen and notebook out of an inside pocket and scribbles down the date on a fresh page.

'Clover said she was with you *and* her mother when she went missing,' Shannon says. 'But you said your mother's been dead a while.'

Luna's heart is racing. She's certain neither of them believe a word she's saying. But just then, an answer comes rushing to the front of her mind. She turns to Eilidh. 'Didn't you say Clover had a concussion?'

Eilidh nods. 'Yes. That's right.' She turns to Shannon. 'I had a concussion once. Made me say all kinds of things. Thought my dad was the king of Spain!'

Shannon purses her lips, but says nothing more.

Eilidh makes a photocopy of Luna's driver's license and takes down her mobile number and email. As they head silently back to the ward she can sense Shannon's eyes on her, full of mistrust. Eilidh seems keen to send Clover home with Luna, but Shannon . . . Luna senses she's Eilidh's boss.

She hasn't answered all Shannon's questions, and she's not sure how much she can lie without some element of the truth tripping her up and unravelling everything. There's a strong chance, she thinks, that they won't allow Clover to go home with her.

Not until the story adds up.

II

Back on the ward, Clover is playing with Gianni and her other teddy bears in the bed. Ethan is pacing the corridor, checking his phone. His face lights up when he sees her.

'You OK?' he says, reaching for her hand. She gives him it and nods.

He flicks his eyes at Clover. 'She's been asking all sorts of questions about you. She wanted to know where you'd gone. I think she was worried you'd left.'

Luna turns and catches Clover's gaze. Quickly Clover looks away before glancing back, shyly.

'I'm still here,' she tells Clover softly as she takes the chair next to her. 'Did you think I'd gone away?'

Clover gives a small nod. 'Thank you for finding Gianni,' she says.

'You're welcome.'

Just then, Gianni topples to the floor. Luna stoops to pick it up and hand it back to Clover. As she does so, one of her fingers brushes against Clover's. It's just a momentary touch, and yet Luna feels a small spark, like static. A few seconds later, a pain in her head makes her gasp, and she gives a loud 'Oh!' that draws the nurse's attention.

'Are you all right?' a nurse asks.

'Yes,' Luna says, breathless, but when she opens her eyes, she finds she can't see properly. There's a ray of white lights around her vision, and everything looks as though it's seen through the prism of a smashed mirror. Her fingers tingle, and a sharp tug in her groin makes her shout out.

Someone brings a chair and insists she sits down. 'At least you're in the right place if you go into labour,' a nurse jokes. Luna tries to smile but finds she can't. Another tug makes her groan, and she tries to breathe it away. It can't be a contraction. She's only twenty-six weeks.

Far too early for the baby to come.

SAPPHIRE, 1998

I

Saffy can't sleep. She sits cross-legged in the small, rock-hard bed that some idiot thought to build into the tight loft, forcing its occupants to sleep with their heads jammed against the cobwebby window. Right now the sound of the waves outside would wake the dead. It's like they're roaring out there, howling with anger at the rocks that prevent them from climbing up on to the island to wreak havoc. She squints at the sky and the lighthouse standing darkly to the right of the island, silhouetted against the moon. A lighthouse without a light is unbearably creepy, she decides. And then there are the shapes of the rocks, slick with rain, some of them like hooded figures . . . until one of them moves.

She sits up, pressing her face against the window. The rain is lashing across the glass, and the wind picks up, lightning flashing across the sky. She's not sure what she's more afraid of – the weather, or the *thing* she's sure she saw outside.

Her heart is thrumming. She watches for a few minutes more in case something – or someone – emerges from the Longing. But they don't. A flicker in the glass of the lantern room catches her eye and then it's gone.

She sits back, wondering what to do. She won't risk telling Liv and being made to feel like a scared child for seeing shapes in the dark. Instead, she pulls out a notebook and starts to write a letter to Jack. By the time he reads it, the axe-murderer currently surveying the midnight landscape from the lantern room of the Longing will probably have slit her and her family's throats, and she mentions that, if this is indeed the case, he can have her CD collection. He's been hankering after her Björk album for forever – because it's signed – and she knows he'll be thrilled with this offering. Enough, perhaps, to contemplate slitting her throat himself.

She tells him all about how her mother dragged her and her sisters from their home in the middle of the night and drove like a madwoman to the Scottish Highlands, and now they're marooned on an island for a month or something. She finishes the letter by telling him not to go off with Stephanie Bennett, hahaha, then worries that she comes across as too needy. But on the other hand, the thought of Jack preferring someone else over her is genuinely terrifying. Maybe she should chuck the letter in the bin and start again.

She glances at her mother's Polaroid that she's 'borrowed' from the Longing and has left carelessly on the floor. Then she takes off her top. Leaning close to the small lamp, she pulls a contemplative pose and points the lens of the camera at her face, making sure her bare shoulders are in the shot.

In a moment the white rectangle slides out beneath the lens. She writes on the back.

Thinking of you. Are you thinking of me? Xxx

II

The GRIMOIRE of Patrick Roberts

Despite our initial failure to integrate with the community of Lòn Haven, my father's skills gained us favour with many of the townsfolk. Most of the year he worked at sea on a whaling ship, and when he was home he worked as a handyman, endowed with a knack for sniffing out both the problem and a solution to virtually any constructional issue by merely setting eyes on it. He had no formal training but hailed from a long line of similarly gifted and self-schooled labourers. Before coming to Lòn Haven we'd lived in the house that my great-grandfather had built with his own hands until it burned to the ground, leaving us homeless and riddled with fleas and rickets. My father couldn't solve the problem of a house turned to ash by a blazing furnace, but he could repair rooftops and chimneys, resize doors and fashion new ones, render walls and right stonework. He often called to neighbouring villages to solve their problems, too. At night, he set about building our house as we were renting and my father didn't believe in borrowing from anyone.

In hindsight, I believe this is where the trouble started. Ironically, my father's newfound success meant that he was away from home more often, and the vines that might have otherwise remained small buds snaked through our house, and the next, and the next, until they strangled us all.

The man's name was Duncan. He was a church elder and owned a lot of land. I probably played with his younger sons Gordon and Alasdair a couple of times on the fen, where all the kids tended to congregate after the summer solstice nights for games. He had brought milk, eggs, and occasionally meat from his farm to my mother when she was in mourning after losing my sister, but suddenly he was at our door every day, bringing her food or assisting her in her prayers. I believe she had told him that she didn't need his help to pray – he said she needed to pray for repentance. Even a child as young as I knew my mother had no need to repent for losing my sister – the Angel of Death had simply decided her time was up. But Duncan was persistent. My mother began to hide in the kitchen and send my brother and me to answer the door when he called.

One day, he called in the morning and again in the evening. As a child I didn't fully understand why he should be so anxious to get to my mother. She was pregnant again, and I knew that she was afraid of him, and afraid of telling my father that she was afraid of him, and within this curious quandary I was a cog turning a wheel for her escape.

'She's not in,' I told him for the second time, and I felt my cheeks flame all the way to my collarbone.

He smiled down at me, then rested his hands on his knees and brought his nose close to mine.

'We both know that's a lie,' he said. 'Do you know what happens to little boys who tell lies?'

I shook my head. I had a horrible feeling in my stomach, and suddenly I was aware that it was late, our neighbours all gone indoors for the night. There was just my mother and my brother in the house. With my father gone, I was the man of the house.

'I'll tell you what happens,' he continued, so close to me now I could only see that hooked nose and the pores in his skin, like strawberry seeds. 'They get their bellies cut.' He drew a long finger across my stomach. 'So how about I ask you the question again, and you tell me the truth. Is your mother home or not?'

I gulped and nodded. He straightened, looked past me into the house. I knew he knew my father was away for the night, in another town, fixing someone's roof.

'Knock, knock,' he said, rapping his knuckles on the door. He stepped past me, one foot at a time, across the threshold, then called out in a big booming voice that seemed to shake the walls. 'Anyone home?'

Finally, my mother emerged, and although she looked surprised to see him, as though he'd just caught her in the middle of something, I knew her well enough to understand that it was all an act, that she was scared.

111

She gave Duncan a tight smile. 'What brings you here so late?'

He closed the door behind him. 'Oh, you know. I reckoned I'd check up on you, see what's been ailing you of late. You've not been around. I've been dropping off supplies to your boys. We've never discussed payment so I thought, now's as good a time as any.'

Her smile widened, grew more false, and there was fear in her eyes. 'Oh, how very thoughtful. I'm fine, thank you. Just fine.'

'Are you sure?' he said, stepping closer.

She pressed a hand to her pregnant belly, protective. 'And my husband should be back soon. He's always tired, and he'll be expecting supper. So perhaps you could arrange to return in the morning when he's refreshed, and happy to discuss any payment you desire.'

He lowered his eyes, gave a heavy sigh. 'Send the boy to bed.'

She turned her head stiffly towards me. 'Patrick. Bed.'

I nodded and scarpered, fast as my legs could carry me. In my room I slammed the door, then slid beneath my bed and stuffed my fist in my mouth.

I don't know what happened that night. I can guess, but I don't know.

When I woke, it was light again and I still under the bed. I raced to the kitchen and found my mother preparing breakfast. I studied her carefully. I was relieved to see her there, and I could tell that Duncan was gone. She seemed unharmed, but there was a cloud in the air and something on the wind that only I could read. She was different. Whatever had happened had changed her, and in a different way to how my sister's death had changed her. The look in her eyes was different.

I said nothing, and she said nothing. I held her gaze as I walked across the kitchen floor, then wrapped my arms around her waist and bawled into her belly. The baby moved against my cheek, and I was so glad that it was still alive because I'd feared Duncan had harmed it, and if the baby died my mother would collapse into sadness again. I felt her hand cup my head, her arm around my shoulders. We held each other like that for a very long time.

She went to see Finwell, Amy's mother. I played with Amy in the barn while she visited Finwell, and when she emerged she seemed better. Finwell had done a fine job of healing her, she said.

About a week thereafter Duncan fell ill with some kind of pox that no healer could cure. It was the talk of the village; I heard old Mrs Dunbar telling a neighbour about it, describing boils the size of sparrows' eggs filled with smelly green pus, and how his body was absolutely covered in them. Not an inch of flesh to be seen. The boils were inside his body, too, and he vomited hot black fluid day and night. His wife and sons kept vigil by his bed, and he whispered to them that he'd been cursed by witches.

My mother hadn't told a soul what had happened that night. But it turned out that someone had heard, or seen, because within a few weeks it was whispered throughout the village.

Amy told me. I went to her house and she was plucking pheasants, ripping the feathers out and laying them in a bowl for her mum to make pillows.

'Are you all right?' she asked me when I sat down.

'I'm well,' I said. She glanced around to check her brothers and sisters were out of earshot before signalling me to come closer. I didn't want to. I had always been squeamish, and the bloodless creature on the table turned my stomach. It made me think of my mother, and what Duncan had done to her.

'Look,' Amy said finally. 'I'm not sorry what I did to Duncan. But I'm sorry about what they're saying about your mum. I'm working on making it stop, all right?'

I screwed up my eyes and tried to process what she'd just said. There seemed to be whole chapters in those three sentences that I'd missed, somehow.

'What are you talking about?' I said. 'What you did to Duncan?'

I saw her cheeks turn red. This only happened when her mother shouted at her. Amy's mother was keen on the Wooden Spoon School of Discipline and she was the only person alive who commanded Amy's full respect.

She wiped her hands on her dress before sitting down opposite me.

'I cursed Duncan,' she said. 'I put a hex on him to make him sick. As payment for what he did. You know this.'

I shook my head. 'No, I didn't.'

She studied me with her huge, feline eyes. 'Yes, you do, Patrick. You know what I can do. No one else does. Not even my parents.' She chewed her lip. I wiped my nose on the back of my hand. It had started to bleed. 'Morag started a rumour about your *mum. She said she heard some commotion from your house. She said she saw him go in and have his way with your mum.'*

I felt like she'd slapped me. 'She saw?'

Amy nodded. I leaped to my feet, tears burning my eyes, and screamed in her face. 'If she saw, why didn't she do anything?'

'Sit down,' Amy said, unaffected by my outburst. I collapsed into my seat and buried my face in my hands. Amy let me sit there for a long time, not saying anything until I'd managed to calm down.

'Lots of people are saying that your ma caused Duncan's illness.' Her voice was soft now, and I knew she was worried.

I looked up. I had no idea what this meant but her voice was lined with worry.

'Why are they saying that?'

She looked away. 'I don't know.' She reached out and took my hand. I didn't even bother to pull away, despite how sticky it was.

When I went home, Mum was sewing by the lantern. She only had to look up for me to know something had happened.

'Where's Dad?' I asked.

'Gone,' she said, keeping her eyes on her sewing.

'Gone-gone?' I asked.

She nodded.

'Should I dig up his treasure box?' I asked. My father had told me that he had buried his inheritance in the hill near the large oak, and that if anything were to happen to him we were to dig it up. Now that he was gone, I couldn't see how we would survive.

Mother shook her head. I walked over to her and, very slowly, wrapped my arms around her. I buried my face in her shoulder and cried, and she let me. Then I let go and went to bed without saying a word.

It didn't happen the next day, or the day after. Dad had taken his axe, so he definitely was gone-gone. I came back from the fields to find church elders at the door, and Mum being taken away. Her wrists were bound and her head bowed. I ran up to her but one of the men pushed me back.

'Mum!' I shouted, as they threw her in the carriage. 'Mum! Stop! Where are you taking her?'

Some of the neighbours had come out, and I thought they were here to help. But they just stood there and watched.

'Witch,' one of them said in a low voice. Then someone else said it, then another. In a moment it was a deafening chant, and it didn't relent, not even when I cried out for them to stop, when I shouted that she was innocent, that he'd hurt her.

Not even then.

III

It's late morning. Saffy's at school, though once again the teacher is forcing them all to have class outdoors in the freezing cold and rain. Saffy has no idea why the woman insists on this, beyond punishment for the sake of it. It's almost October, and it's raining again. It always bloody rains here. Saffy has never seen rain like it, nor so many varieties. Rain that's like a mist, making her blonde hair all frizzy and fat. Rain that bounces up from the ground, rain that blisters the windows and drums the roof of the bothy. Rain that seeps inside your bones and chills you from the inside out. It was blue skies and sunshine when they left England. She didn't even bring a coat, and now she's had to borrow some old wax coat that smells of dead fish.

Today, the small group of teenage pupils are in the valley on the other side of the island writing poems about nature. Their teacher, Mrs McGrath, is clearly a poetry freak as that's all they seem to do. Saffy can't help but wind her up. 'Poetry makes me want to gouge my eyes out,' she says repeatedly, and finally Mrs McGrath snaps.

'Sapphire, I'm going to have to ask you to keep your opinions to yourself,' she says, pushing her glasses further up her nose with a wiry finger. 'There'll be plenty of time for other subjects, but this morning, we're doing poetry.' She throws a hard stare across the class, who are sat on tree stumps. 'Anyone else got a problem with that?'

They all shake their heads, resignedly. Saffy pouts, annoyed that nobody else has taken the cue to rib their teacher. Cowards.

An older boy leans into her. Brodie. 'Impressive,' he says. 'I've been waiting for ages for someone to stand up to that mean old bitch.'

Her chest fills with a warm glow, the kind that follows approval. She smiles broadly at him, and he winks. He's handsome. She noticed him the first day she started school, but up close his beauty is striking. He's Rowan's boyfriend, and so she hasn't paid him any mind. But Rowan's sitting with another girl on the other side of the group. Maybe they've broken up.

She doesn't hear what Mrs McGrath says next, and she doesn't quite see the page so clearly either – suddenly Brodie's proximity to her has made the world swampy, underwater somehow.

'I'm writing about butterflies,' she hears Rowan announce. 'About how the caterpillar changing into a butterfly is a metaphor for me becoming who I want to be.'

'Very good, Rowan,' Mrs McGrath says. 'Though please do write in silence? You use up your creative energy by explaining your project.'

My project, Saffy thinks. *Creative energy*. She scribbles on the page, keeping Brodie firmly in her field of vision. He looks up at her every now and then. He's seventeen, she remembers. He has stubble on his jaw and curly brown hair.

'I'm going to divide you all into small groups,' Mrs McGrath says. 'I'll assign you a part of the forest to explore so you don't waste time chatting.' Saffy finds herself in a group with Brodie and the weird twins, Fia and Fen, who don't talk to anyone else but each other. They're assigned to a vague part of the forest that looks spray-painted with neon-green moss. She remembers that sphagnum moss is an antiseptic, that the Celts used it to pack their wounds after battle. Soldiers in World War One did the same. She likes to cling on to bits of information like that, the type that links the ancient past to the near-present. It makes the strangeness of the present less strange.

Mrs McGrath tells them to do pencil rubbings of five different kinds of leaves and name the tree from which they came, then write a poem from the perspective of each tree that identifies how it grows, its fruit or leaves, and what happens to it during each season. To the others, this appears an easy task, but Saffy has no clue. Birds, she knows about, but trees? She can just about name five – oak, birch, fir, cherry, pine – but identify them? Not a chance.

'You OK?'

She looks up to find Brodie standing over her. The twins have slunk off, leaving her and Brodie alone in a clutch of towering conifers. Immediately blood rushes to her face, her heart catapulting in her chest. For a moment, Jack's face sweeps across her mind, and she feels a pang of guilt.

'Yeah,' she murmurs weakly. 'Just . . . trying to remember the name of this one.'

'That's a maple,' he says.

She rises to her full height. Saffy's tall, five foot eight, but Brodie looks down at her, making her feel tiny.

'You lived in the city, didn't you?' Brodie says.

She nods.

'I was born in Glasgow. West End.'

'West End,' she repeats.

He grins. 'I couldn't tell an elm from a monkey puzzle when I came here.'

'Monkey puzzle?'

He raises his dark eyes to the trees around them, his face lit in pearlescent afternoon light that leaks through the canopy. It's a scene that reminds her of one of those Dutch paintings, as though the gods in Mount Olympus have spotted one of their own.

'No monkey puzzles in this wood. That there's an elm, though.' He bends to retrieve a leaf. 'See? Looks like nettle leaves. It's a hermaphrodite, that tree.'

She swallows. Is he mocking her or being serious? 'Shut up.'

He looks at her, wounded, and she wants to collapse to the ground and beg forgiveness.

'I mean, a hermaphrodite?' she says, backpedalling. 'I didn't know trees had genitals.'

He laughs, and she laughs, too, but it's a desperate, kill-me-now laugh. 'It means that the flowers of the tree have both female and male reproductive parts. No genitals.'

'That's a relief. Can you imagine how awkward that would be? A forest full of penises and vaginas?'

Shut up, Saffy, she tells herself, wanting to die. *Shut. Up.*

'Imagine,' he says, and he holds her gaze a moment too long. He is dissolving her into a kind of vapour, one cell at a time. Never in her whole life has she seen such lips.

She looks away, embarrassed. 'I, uh, read that this place has some kind of history. Involving witches?'

'Yeah. That's what they say.'

She takes a breath, willing herself to stop overthinking her every movement. 'I read that they burned about four thousand witches here in Scotland. Or, you know, women.'

'I think some of them were men.'

'Yeah, like *two*.'

'Well, yeah. Not all of them were burned on Lòn Haven.'

'Obviously,' she says, then flushes red.

'You're staying at the Longing, aren't you?' Brodie says, and she nods. 'Do you know what the Longing's built on?'

She's puzzled. 'Rock?'

He laughs, and her cheeks burn. His stare peels layers off her, one at a time. She understands now the saying 'weak at the knees', because he has removed all of her bones just by existing. She feels wobbly and melty and stupid.

'It's built on an old broch from the Iron Age,' he says.

'Oh yeah, I heard about that.'

'Yeah. It's like a kind of round tower made of stone, though a lot shorter than the Longing. A Scottish chieftain would have lived there.'

She remembers this from the Neolithic museum but can tell Brodie's enjoying sharing this. 'Yeah?'

'A lot of people say it's cursed. They built a lighthouse on top of it and everyone who worked there died young.'

'You don't believe that, do you?' she says. 'The curse thing.'

He shrugs. 'Do you believe in witches?'

She's not sure how to answer. 'Well, yeah. Rowan's a witch, isn't she?'

He looks away. She's pleased to see what looks like irritation on his face at the mention of her. 'So she says. She meditates and collects crystals. That's about it.'

'So, the broch is cursed?' she says, circling him back to the topic.

'Oh yeah. They chucked witches into the hole. Tortured them for a few months, then set them on fire. People say the witches cursed the island for it.'

'The witches cursed Lòn Haven?' Saffy says, intrigued. 'Like – how?'

'Legend has it that they made a pact with the fae, to give them human form so they could take revenge on humankind.'

'The fae?'

'Fairies.'

She's never heard this term but commits it to memory. *Fae.* 'Why did they want revenge?'

'For taking over their lands. Destroying the forests, killing the animals. You follow?'

She nods.

'So the witches were all burned, wiped out. But now the fae could now take on human form. People called them "wildlings". They just have to touch a human to transform into them. Usually children.'

A shiver rolls up Saffy's spine. 'And why would they do that?'

'To kill everyone in the family. It happened. That's what they say. Whole bloodlines wiped out in a few weeks. The only way to stop them coming back to life is to kill them.'

'That's creepy shit,' Saffy says, relishing how dark the tale is. The only stories she ever heard about fairies involved tea parties inside tulips. 'But . . . you don't believe it, do you?'

His gaze moves past her, into the distance. She turns and searches behind her. 'What?'

'People have been killing wildlings in these woods for hundreds of years.' He moves his eyes back to her face. 'Want me to show you?'

She follows him through the trees, her curiosity quickened. They cross a small river, then pass a waterfall feathering down a bank of rock.

'What if we get lost?' she says.

'We won't,' he says. 'I've spent a lot of time in these woods, trust me.'

, He stops at a thick grove of trees. Five have burn marks on their trunks, a black mouth of shiny charcoaled bark on the trunks. The upper branches are untouched, but she can make out signs of regrowth on the lower branches where they've previously been destroyed. The lower trunk on one old tree has been gnawed away by flame. Perhaps a lightning strike, she thinks, or – more thrillingly – an act of arson. She walks up to one and holds out a hand to touch it.

'Don't,' Brodie says. There's a warning in his voice, and she turns, intrigued. 'They're sycamores.' He bends to pick up something from the ground. She starts, mistaking the teardrop pericarps of a sycamore seed for a moth. He tosses it into the air, where it twirls like helicopter blades. 'Helicopter seeds. That's how you can remember them.'

'So . . . what burned them? Lightning?'

He gives her a dark look. 'You have to kill a wildling in a certain way. You have to cut out its heart and burn the rest of it. And the parent has to do it.'

'Holy shit.'

He grins, visibly pleased that he's succeeded in scaring her. 'I saw them do it, you know.'

She studies him. 'Do what?'

He steps towards her. 'Kill a wildling. I was four. I hid behind a tree and watched it all. The heart cutting, the burning.'

She swallows hard, imagining him as a child witnessing such a horrific thing. She moves backwards. Her heel catching on something. She stoops to see what it is. A piece of frayed rope is visible there, hidden amongst the leaves like a snake. She lifts it up and runs her thumb along the fibres.

'The last thing that rope touched was a wildling,' Brodie says, and she drops it like she's been burned. He laughs and steps closer as she examines the hand that held the rope.

'Aren't you scared?' she asks Brodie, looking up into his dark eyes. 'Living somewhere like this?'

He bends to pick up the rope. Shows he's not afraid to touch it. 'Aren't *you* scared?' he says. 'You're just a wee lass.'

'Fifteen,' she says, straightening. 'I'm fifteen.'

'I'm fifteen,' he mimics, laughing. 'I bet it's a shock to the system, this place. So different from London.'

'York,' she says. 'I've never even been to London.'

'Yawk,' he repeats, mimicking her accent.

'Sorry, I meant "Yark",' she says, teasing him back.

He reaches out to place the rope back in her hands, daring her to hold it, and his fingers brush against hers. It's only a momentary connection and yet it feels like she's touched raw lightning. She raises her gaze to his. He stares back, nailing her to the spot with those eyes of his, filled with danger. She can tell, in a way that is cellular, that he is taking her in, layer by layer. She craves to be wanted.

'Maybe I could show you some other trees,' he says, the

corner of his mouth lifting into a half-smile. 'Ones that didn't involve murder.'

'I'd like that.'

Something flickers at the fringes of Saffy's vision, and she turns to see Rowan standing between the trees, watching them uneasily.

'Hey,' Brodie calls to Rowan. Saffy gives a big, friendly 'hey there' wave, as if she'd fully expected Rowan to manifest like a dark cloud. Rowan doesn't respond. She has her hood up, and eyes them both with a scowl. Brodie reads the mood and walks towards his girlfriend while Saffy busies herself by studying the rope in her hands. Her hearing is fully tuned in to the conversation.

'You OK?' Brodie asks Rowan. She responds, but it's in Gaelic. Angry, hissed words.

'Of course not,' Brodie says, then something else in Gaelic. Rowan arches her face up to his and he leans forward, pressing his lips against hers. Saffy tries not to look, but she sees and feels it all, the handful of seconds that he kisses Rowan stretching through time, glaciers melting, the earth burning and turning to dust. She imagines that this is what it must feel like to be impaled.

She crumbles the dry leaf in her palm, turning it to fragments.

LIV, 1998

I

Finn apologized for his comment that afternoon. I'd gone back to the bothy and made myself something to eat, though I couldn't eat at all. He looked shamefaced, his hands in his pockets. I let him in.

'I really didn't mean to offend you,' he said. 'Sometimes my sense of humour rubs people up the wrong way. This isn't the first time . . .' He cleared his throat. 'For what it's worth, I actually wasn't being serious when I said you were running from something.'

I folded my arms. 'I don't follow.'

'Thought we were having a bit of a laugh, that's all,' he said. 'But I know I go too far sometimes. People have told me.' He bit his lip. 'I'm sorry.'

I softened. 'You've nothing to apologize for. I was just being a bit . . . oversensitive.'

The truth was, I *was* running. But this time, I thought I'd managed to hide it from everyone, including myself.

Just twelve days ago, I had fled in the middle of the night with just my girls and whatever essentials we could pack into bin liners. My relationship with Drew had long gone sour, but it was a phone call I'd received the day before that had made me bolt. I'd had a smear test that showed some abnormal cells. They'd called me back for a colposcopy and blood test, which had left terrible bruises all over my arms when they couldn't find a decent vein.

The next day, the phone call came. It was a doctor at the hospital to let me know the scan results were in. They'd found a solid mass, around five centimetres in length, and she wasn't sure if it was in my cervix or ovary. She wanted to speak to me urgently about getting another scan.

For the rest of the day I was in another realm, outside time, floating above my body. I knew all too well what the outcome was. Mum had died from cervical cancer. And Aunt Lynne. And my grandmother. All of us, born with a gene that prevented the women in my family growing old.

Mum had four rounds of chemo. She grew thinner and weaker, less and less like herself. They tried surgery. We celebrated the news that it *did* work, only for the cancer to return. She died two weeks after the news.

I had three girls to care for. Three fatherless girls. Who was going to care for them, raise them? Not my father. Not Sean's family. They had hearts of gold, but his parents were too old and his brother was an alcoholic.

What if my girls were born with this gene?

I ran. I thought that if I kept moving, we might outrun this terrible disease.

I drove us all the way to Newcastle before the fuel light came on and I was forced to pull into a petrol station. I filled up with petrol, then bought us all some cold water and crisps in the services station. I spotted a small internet café in the corner of the station. I needed to check that email from Anna Taylor, the one about a commission. Some kind of mural she'd been asked to do but it clashed with her wedding.

Hello my lovely, how are things?

Sorry for the delay in getting back to you but I've been busy, as you can imagine! Are you able to do the commission? It's well paid and I recommended you very highly (I don't know if you're doing many murals these days? The one you did for St Mark's hospital was incredible. Still the best one I've seen!)

Patrick is very keen for you to take it up but he doesn't do email. Please can you think about it? I've forwarded you the info by email. Let me know as soon as you can!

The venue was a decommissioned lighthouse with the bizarre name of 'The Longing'. It was situated on an island, Lòn Haven, off the coast of Scotland. The owner wanted an artist to create 'a stunning and inspiring mural' inside the lighthouse, which was being transformed into a 'writing studio'. A handful of images showed rugged coastline fringed with turquoise sea, a tall white lighthouse overlooking cliffs. Five thousand pounds plus expenses for just over a month's work.

I'd already emailed Anna to say that yes, I'd be happy to do it, but now I emailed to say I could arrive earlier than planned. Tomorrow, in fact.

Anna replied straight away.

Thank you!!! I'll email them now. OK to pass on your number??

II

Right up until I arrived in Lòn Haven, I'd had no symptoms. Nothing at all to indicate that something might be wrong. And yet, the day after we arrived, I started peeing blood. It started off pink, with cramping, like cystitis. By the time Finn made the comment, I had back pain. I called at the island GP and asked for antibiotics.

'I have a tendency towards UTIs,' I told her. I was wary of being pulled into the surgery and confronted with the full facts of my diagnosis. I knew how stupid my own thoughts were, but it didn't make them any less compelling – the idea that, if I simply ignored it, if I point-blank refused to face up to the fact that the cancer that had stalked my family had finally found me, it would go away.

Distraction was key, especially now that I was showing signs of the illness taking hold. I took painkillers regularly, both paracetamol and ibuprofen. I wore pads to collect the spots of blood that ruined my underwear, and asked Isla if I could borrow a hot water bottle for back pain. I tried to force myself to enjoy every detail, every second of time.

When I looked out at the beach, I imagined each grain of sand like a measure of time that I'd been allotted. I could either let them run through my hands or I could stop and pay attention.

I started waking at dawn to walk along the coastline, immersing myself in the textures, colours, and sounds of this place, trying to summon the stories I'd need for the mural, something to add story and colour to Patrick's diagram. I noticed chartreuse lichen scabbing the rocks, the lick and suck of tide against sea-smoothed stones, how every single one of the shells in the bay was different; white limpet shells and ear-shaped mussel shells; kelp fronds, the ones like bronze ribbons, and cream ones like bandages, their stems like bone joints; and, of course, the ocean, that perpetual shapeshifter: one day a disc of hammered gold, the next wild and rearing, like a thousand white horses. I noticed how the ocean had moods, just like a person.

Every morning Clover made a point of running to the edge of the rock and calling out to Basil. More often than not his dorsal fin would be visible above the water, and I began to join her in calling 'good morning' to him.

I began to wonder if we might stay longer than the autumn. If we might make a life here, start over. If I could somehow will the cancer away, or at least find a solution to this impossible situation.

How could I leave my daughters without anyone to care for them?

LUNA, 2021

I

'Luna?'

Ethan is kneeling in front of her, his face full of concern.

'I'm all right,' she says, trying to blink away the white lights in her vision.

'Do you want to lie down?' the nurse asks. 'There's a free bed on the ward. An hour's rest won't do any harm at all.'

'Honestly, I'm fine,' she's saying, but it's a prayer instead of the truth, an effort to will the white lights away from her vision and restore her strength. Ethan takes her hand and watches anxiously as a nurse checks her blood pressure, then uses a stethoscope to check the baby.

'Heartbeat's nice and regular,' she says, smiling. 'Still, we don't want to take any chances. You've had quite a journey travelling up here, and a shock finding your sister, too.' Luna nods. Yes, shock. That's what it is. She isn't miscarrying. Behind the nurse she can see the detective, her arms folded impatiently and Clover's file in one hand.

Maybe this distraction isn't such a bad thing after all.

* * *

It's dark outside now, rain pattering against the window. Ethan is snoring in the chair next to her. She must have been asleep for most of the day. On the table there's a white envelope and what looks like a test tube with her name printed on one side.

Ethan rouses, rubs his eyes. 'How're you feeling?'

She blinks hard. The white lights are gone from her vision, as has the weird smashed-mirror effect that suddenly descended upon her before. The headache has lifted, too.

'Where's Clover?' she asks.

'She's fine. A psychiatrist came to speak to her. I think she's just left.'

'And the detective?'

'She said she'll be back in the morning.'

'Are you nervous?' Ethan says.

She swallows. 'Very.'

He smiles. 'You've been searching for your sisters for as long as I've known you. And that test tube might come back as negative. I'm just wondering what happens if it does.'

She lays a hand on her stomach, rubbing where she feels the baby's foot must be. The insistent pulse of that little heel.

'Why don't you get a train back home?' she says. 'Ryan'll be wanting you to get back to work.'

'I can't leave you here,' he says. 'You and the baby.'

'I'll be fine,' she says. 'I'll drive back as soon as they discharge Clover. I promise.'

He leans forward and kisses her on the forehead. 'No.'

'You won't have to cancel any classes. You know it makes sense.'

He runs a hand through his long hair, hesitant. 'You're sure this won't be another strike against me?'

'Don't be silly.'

II

He's on a train home first thing the next morning, leaving her the car. She stays at the hospital, both to be with Clover and to be close to help if she goes into labour. The nurses make up a bed in a side room. Luna sleeps solidly, not stirring until the breakfast trolley rattles into the room at eight o'clock the following morning. She notices that the envelope is gone from the side table.

'Morning,' Eilidh says, ducking her head into the room. 'Everything OK?'

Luna sits up in bed and fixes her hair. 'Much better, thank you.'

Luna gets up and washes in the small bathroom, then heads gingerly along the corridor to see Clover. She's out of bed and sat cross-legged on the floor, making what looks to Luna like an obstacle course for Gianni out of plastic cups and pillows. Luna sits in the chair next to her, noticing how much stronger she looks.

'Are we going to see Mummy today?' Clover asks. She doesn't make eye contact.

Luna bites her lip. 'If they discharge you, I can take you back to my flat. It's quite a drive from here. I don't have a child seat, though. I'll need to find one before we go.'

'And Pop Tarts,' Clover says. 'They don't have Pop Tarts at this hospital. I already asked.'

Luna feels her breath catch. She'd forgotten all about her and Clover's love of Pop Tarts. How the mention of such a small detail summons so much of their past. In an instant she is back in the kitchen of their little flat in Bristol, the one they lived in before Liv moved in with Drew, the smell of warm, sugary strawberry Pop Tarts fresh from the toaster filling the air.

III

Luna didn't use to believe in miracles. But now, as she walks with Clover to her car in the hospital car park, she could be persuaded that anything is possible. The social workers have granted her permission to take Clover home. She's sure it was Eilidh who made this possible. Shannon, the other social worker, was definitely not so keen. She'd heard low voices from the side room in heated discussion. She was sure they'd been discussing her and Clover.

Later that afternoon, they'd asked Luna to go for a walk around the hospital grounds while they chatted with Clover. On her way out, Luna heard Eilidh's voice. 'Are you happy to go home with you sister, Clover?' She'd strained to hear Clover's response but it wasn't audible.

When she returned fifteen minutes later, it seemed that Clover had said she was happy to go with Luna, and the decision had been made. All she had to do was procure a car seat and they could leave.

But things weren't as final as Luna hoped. 'I'll call and check up on how things are going,' Eilidh said. 'I'll not discharge wee Clover from our services just yet. Just gives space for you to access our support and . . . see how things go.'

See how things go.

Luna doesn't like the sound of Eilidh checking up on her. What if she decides to take her back?

At the car, Luna reaches past Clover for the seat belt and clips her in, noticing the large freckle just above her right thumb. God, it really is Clover. Twenty-two years of searching, hoping, fighting fears that said she was dead. And now she's here.

She turns the key in the ignition and puts the car into reverse, letting out a breath she hadn't realized she was holding as they exit the hospital car park. She daren't believe this is happening.

But, as with all Luna's wishes, it doesn't seem to last. The mood seems to unravel as they turn on to the road that leads to the Airbnb that Ethan has booked for them. A storm has whipped up out of nowhere, creating winds of fifty miles per hour and dumping a month's rain. A different kind of storm seems to be brewing in the car, for Clover has fallen silent in the back seat. Luna can sense she's upset.

'Are you OK back there?' Luna asks, feeling awkward. Silence.

'How about we get some ice cream?' she asks. 'Yeah?'

A glance at Clover's reflection in the rear-view mirror shows her face turned to the window, glancing back as though she's trying to find her way back to the hospital. Her jaw is tight and her eyes are hard.

Luna always knew it would take time to build the relationship she had with her sisters, if she ever found them.

Actually, this had only been a passing thought – what she *believed* was somehow they'd click right back into place, as sisters did, and the sudden shift in gears throws her. She draws upon her professional training. Clover's a traumatized child, after all. Her trauma has frozen her in time. She has to speak to her just as she'd speak to any of the kids she works with.

'Clover, I know this is difficult. It's very hard for you, being with a stranger like this.'

She speaks slowly and gently, watching Clover's reaction. Nothing. She must be patient.

'I know you're scared. But I can promise you, you're safe now. From this moment on, you're safe. We're together again.'

Clover's face reveals nothing, no hint of having heard or considered anything. Luna bites her lip. So much harder when the traumatized child is a blood relative. Entirely different applying her training to this situation, with so much skin in the game. It's only been ten minutes and already she feels completely out of her depth.

She watches the profile of Clover's face, the curve of her jaw, her small ears at a slight tilt from her head. Yes, there is something different about her. There's the glaring fact that she's about twenty years younger than she should be. But also something else.

Something that's harder to place.

IV

The Airbnb is a small cottage in Drumnadrochit, a village on the shores of Loch Ness. As they pull up outside, heavy rain starts to swallow up the horizon, smudging the outline of hills to obscurity.

The two-storey cottage is cramped and glum, the walls busy with dusty mounted plates. There's a well-used sofa, a frayed rug, an ancient wood burner, and a TV. It'll do. 'We're just staying here for a while, until the storm passes,' Luna tells Clover as they look over the room. Silence follows. It strikes her that she's forgotten how to entertain a child. Despite wanting one for as long as she can remember, she has never babysat. She was only two when Clover was born. None of her friends have had children yet. She works with children, but usually they're in their teens. The presence of this little girl – *my sister*, she reminds herself – is daunting.

'Shall I put the TV on?' she says.

Clover seems nervous, backing into the corner of the room. Luna throws her a wide smile, which only serves to make her stiffen like a frightened animal. She hugs Gianni protectively to her chest. The silence in the cottage is heavy, and Luna mentally kicks herself for not finding a park or play area to visit before returning to such an enclosed and foreign space as this. She moves to the small kitchen and finds two glasses which she fills with water. When she turns to give one to Clover, the room is already empty. The sound of feet upstairs tells Luna that Clover's exploring the space.

Give her time, Luna thinks. *This is completely strange for both of us.*

A moment later, she hears Clover's voice. *Not like that, Gianni. Like this.*

She sighs with relief. Playing is a good sign. It's an excellent sign. She finds fresh eggs and homemade bread in the welcome package, which she cooks and eats with a pot of tea at the old dining table with barley-twist legs.

With Clover occupied, Luna turns to Google for information about ageing disorders. She learns about Werner Syndrome, which causes accelerated ageing. She reads about chromosomes, amino acid proteins, DNA stability and exonuclease domains, hard-to-pronounce phrases that mean nothing to her but seem to mean everything to those children whose bodies hurtle into old age.

She finds little about regressive ageing. Information on cognitive and mental regression is abundant, and there are some news articles about gene experiments to reverse ageing.

Perhaps Clover has been used as a lab rat, she thinks. Her mind turns to the digits carved into Clover's hip. *They had to have been made by a human*. Those were the doctor's chilling words, confirmation that Clover has experienced some kind of branding. She types 'numbers carved in skin' into the search bar. Google brings up fifty thousand pages on cults, devil worship, human trafficking – and gene experimentation.

Her stomach roils. The reasons for the numbers on Clover's hip are too terrifying to think about.

The storm has reached Drumnadrochit. It drums the roof of the cottage and taps at the windows, and every so often distant thunder groans above the clapping of the rain. The sky blackens. There is wood for the fire; she stacks it as high as she can, then gives in to the urge to curl up on the sofa and pull a blanket around her. Upstairs, she hears Clover's voice, still talking to Gianni. She's laughing, but it sounds odd. Hysterical, cackling laughter. It doesn't sound like the Clover she remembers.

She catches the contradiction of her thoughts: she doubts that this is Clover. It's a small doubt, but it's there, a ball bouncing around the surfaces of her mind. There is one explanation, but it makes no more sense than her theory of age regression. The word has been cartwheeling across the floor of her mind since she laid eyes on Clover, brightening when she saw the mark on Clover's hip.

Wildling.

She pushes the thought away. She came across the word when she looked into the online coverage from the time she lived on Lòn Haven. On her phone, she brings up the digitized article from *The Black Isle Bugle*.

14 November 1998

The small population of Lòn Haven has been plunged – yet again – into shock and terror over the recent disappearances of four females. Although not members

141

of the local community – the Stay family was lodging temporarily on the island – the mystery surrounding the disappearances holds the residents in terror, with some claiming that the wildling myth has come to pass.

'We've witnessed a lot of tragedy on Lòn Haven,' the resident – who wished to remain unnamed – said. 'For such a small population we've had our fair share of folk going missing. Previous generations put these down to wildlings. I'm inclined to say that's what happened here.'

The family, consisting of Olivia Stay (36), and her three daughters Sapphire (15), Luna (10), and Clover (7), only arrived on the island in September. And now, it appears that all four females have vanished. It is understood that a widespread search has yielded few clues.

Anyone with any information should contact Chief Inspector Bram Kissick at Inverness Police Station.

She clicks away from the page. *Fuck,* she thinks. The mention of her own name there pulls a gamut of emotions to the surface, and she suddenly feels nauseous. What if Eilidh or Shannon starts digging around the internet and comes across this? She looks at her phone, suddenly nervous that it might ring. That they might have her arrested for lying.

She slides into a deep sleep brimming with dreams soaked in memories. She dreams that she is standing on the edge of a dark hole that falls down, down to the core of the earth, its fiery heart. On the other side of the hole, there's another woman. It's her. She watches herself climb down into the hole.

'Don't,' she says, but the other version of herself goes ahead anyway, heedless, sinking into the dark.

V

She wakes when the storm is at its peak, the gutters gurgling and rain streaming down the windows.

The lamp has gone off, and when she tries the switch it doesn't work – the storm has knocked off the electricity. Using the torch on her phone she moves to the sink to get another glass of water, and as she drinks from it a splash of water hits her head. She glances up; there's a small skylight overhead. It must be leaking. The water drips again. It doesn't seem to be coming from the skylight.

Luna sets down the glass and heads upstairs to check on Clover. The bedclothes in the smaller bedroom are ruffled, and she sees a foot hanging off the end of the bed. Clover must be fast asleep. She heads into the other bedroom.

Her torchlight falls on a shape on the bed. It's Gianni, Clover's fluffy toy. Only, his head has been cut off and set neatly beside his body. As she moves the torch across the body, she sees his belly has been slit, all the stuffing pulled out and thrown across the room.

A creak from the doorway makes her start. She turns her torch towards the sound – the light falls on Clover, who stands there silently, arms by her sides.

'Did you do this?' Luna says. She's trying to stay calm, but her emotions are getting the better of her. She picks up Gianni to show Clover, more stuffing spilling out to the floor. All these years she's kept him like treasure, the one link back to her sister, and she can't help but gasp at the damage. Why would Clover do this?

Clover merely stares at her, her face completely blank. It's then that Luna hears it: she'd thought the rushing sound was rain, but it's louder up here. It sounds like it's inside the house.

'What is that?' she says.

A second passes before she locates the whereabouts of the sound, then races to the bathroom and pulls open the door. Both taps have been turned on in the bathtub, and it's brimming with water. It slops over the side, pouring on to the floor. She's standing in about an inch of water that now seeps out into the hallway and down the stairs.

There's a moment where she can barely think of what to do. Without the lights on, the scene is revealed only in the small pools of light afforded by her phone. She has to set it on the windowsill and fumble for the taps. Finally, they're off, but the floor feels soggy underfoot – it isn't tiled. Just cheap lino rolled unevenly over ancient floorboards that are now giving way under the weight of water, pouring into the kitchen.

VI

Luna hates the rain, and this fucking cottage, and it's dark, and why the fuck did she send Ethan home again?

Enough self-pity – right now she needs to find buckets to catch the water that's gushing into the kitchen. She finds a couple of pots – barely big enough to boil an egg – and positions them under the drips before turning back to the cupboard with her phone light and rummaging for something else to catch the water. The water damage is going to cost her a kidney, she knows it. But she has no money.

There is one small mercy, however – Clover has curled up on the sofa, right on the spot warmed by Luna, and fallen asleep.

It's a good thing, too, Luna thinks. Otherwise she'd be tempted to throttle her.

Of course, this is bravado. Deep in her belly is a knot of confusion, which the baby must sense because he kicks and squirms wildly now. It doesn't help that she's in a strange house in the pitch-black of night with a child who is meant to be a grown woman, a grown woman with whom she otherwise should have been having a weepy reunion over pizza and mocktails. It doesn't help that she seems to have forgotten all her training in the face of this emotional and deeply strange situation.

Finally, the flooding is staunched. The bathtub gurgles loudly upstairs, and once the water level has dropped she uses a large beer glass to scoop up the remaining puddle from the floor, to pour it back into the tub and into the sink. Downstairs, the pots are full – she pours out the contents and returns them to their places on the floor to catch the remaining drips from the bathroom above.

It is after midnight by the time she's able to sit down. Her back aches and she's ravenous. Her phone is almost dead, too, the battery having been drained by the torchlight. She considers using the last of her battery to phone Ethan, but it's too late – and also, she has no idea how to explain what has just happened. *Hey, so Clover dissected Gianni and tried to drown us both. How are you?*

She spots two candles on the mantelpiece and a box of matches. She moves slowly to light them – the thought of spending the night in total darkness with Clover is a little unnerving – and as she strikes the match against the side of the box, Clover rolls over. The light of the match falls on the dressing that covers the mark on her hip.

Luna studies it carefully, a thousand questions rolling through her mind. She wants to reach out and peel back the dressing for a closer look, to check if it is numbers there, or perhaps just a wound that resembled numbers. But no – she remembers seeing it through the lens of the magnifying glass. The odd vertical positioning of the digits. Someone did that to her sister.

There has to be a reason for it.

As she stares down at the dressing, a flash of something brightens vividly in her memory. A knife. Blood flying through the air like a dark ribbon.

Instinctively, her right hand reaches for the white line on her left forearm. She has no idea how she got this scar. But now, the thought of Clover's wound summons a memory. A girl, about ten years old, standing in front of her. A worried look on her face.

She held out a hand.

We have to take hands, she said.

It only works if we hold hands.

SAPPHIRE, 1998

I

Saffy is fully dressed beneath the bedclothes. Every thirty seconds she glances at her wristwatch, sighing with frustration. Why did Brodie want to meet so late? She knows why – he's waiting until his parents are asleep so nobody asks any questions. But *still*. If the wait doesn't kill her the apprehension will.

In the meantime, she reads. When Liv told them all to pack their gear and leave York in the middle of the night, she'd been so out of it that she'd not packed a single one of her many books. She hates that she didn't bring any. Drew, her mum's vile boyfriend – or ex-boyfriend, she figures – will probably chuck them all out. She's an avid reader. The small selection of books in the bothy aren't exactly thrilling, some from the seventies on shipping routes and seabirds, but she is fast making progress through the strange handwritten book bearing the name of her mum's commissioner, Patrick Roberts. His grimoire.

C.J. Cooke

The GRIMOIRE of Patrick Roberts

I will never know how many women Duncan accused, and how many were accused by his wife and sons. Following this accusation, the Laird of Lòn Haven had applied to the Privy Council for a Royal Enquiry into the practice of witchcraft on the island. About twenty of the accused didn't get charged – folk said they'd bribed their way out of it – and in the end, twelve women and girls from the village were taken from their homes and thrown in the hole beneath the broch, where they were imprisoned until the trial. Among the women were my mother, as well as Jenny, Amy's older sister, and her mother, Finwell.

Amy stopped speaking. I believe she stopped eating, too, because she quickly grew so thin that her green eyes seemed to bulge out of her head and her knee bones looked like they were going to explode out of her skin.

My father was still gone, and I had to look after my little brother. My uncle lived nearby but didn't help, and I could understand why – folk were already distancing themselves from me and my brother due to our being the children of a witch. It didn't matter that the trial hadn't taken place. Women couldn't present evidence against their accusers, so to be accused was as good as being guilty.

Still, I held fast to the thought that the judges would find my mother, as well as Jenny and Finwell, innocent. It was wrong, so very wrong – I knew Duncan deserved what he'd got, and he was still gravely ill, but he had violated my mother. The only person who belonged at the bottom of the broch was Duncan.

And none of us, not the gifted healers nor Amy, with her stones and powers of bringing fish back to life, could do anything about it.

But then Duncan died, and the whole of Lòn Haven was set alight with terror and intrigue. He was buried the day before the trial. It had been two months since my mother and the other women and girls were taken into the broch by the sea.

The trial was held in the kirk. Amy and I were present, covered as best we could with shawls so as not to draw attention from the villagers.

Each woman and girl was presented in turn, silent and weak, as the charges against her were read before the crowd, as well as her confessions.

'Finwell Hyndman,' a judge called out. Amy stiffened and gasped as she watched her mother brought out to the court. Finwell was strong and stout, with thick black hair like Amy's, but she had changed so much that at first I was sure they'd brought the wrong woman. The figure before us was thin, her hair shorn and her clothes replaced with rags. She was barefoot and her face bore black marks that were either dirt or bruises.

Duncan's oldest son Calan took the stand to state the way Duncan had died. Calan was a tall, loud-voiced man with a flair for drama, which he used to regale the court with a long, drawn-out depiction of the way his father died. He said that Duncan's death was painful and horrifying in its physical elements, which I already knew, but new to the tale were visitations from the spirits of his tormentors. He said that Finwell and the eleven others had all swept into the room on regular occasions, invisible to everyone but Duncan, who begged them to remove the curse. Kit said a black cat had appeared in the rafters of the roof, and watched while Duncan writhed in pain.

Others were called forward to give evidence against Finwell.

Margaret McNicol, a wet nurse who had lost all four of her children in childbirth, said that she had often spied Finwell venturing out late at night, headed for Mither Stane on top of the fairy hill. We all knew Mither Stane, an ancient stone, brought good or bad luck, depending when you visited it, but Margaret charged Finwell with going there to converse with the fae.

'Finwell Hyndman,' the judge boomed. 'You are charged with the practice of witchcraft upon the Council of Lòn Haven in the Year of Our Lord, 1662. What is your confession?'

The crowd fell silent as the confession was to be heard. Finwell struggled to speak, but couldn't, and so the judge called out again.

'I have before me written evidence of your confession, which I shall present to this court. You will assign your agreement or disagreement by nodding or shaking your head. "I, Finwell Hyndman, confess to renouncing baptism in servitude of the Devil, and acting alongside my coven to bring about the sickness and subsequent death of Duncan McGregor."'

The crowd erupted into chatter and whispers. I saw Amy lift her head and stare at her mother, who kept her face bowed to the floor. What coven? I thought. Why isn't she refuting this charge? Why isn't she shaking her head?

The judge stared at Finwell. 'Speak yay or nay to these charges, woman.'

My heart was pounding in my chest as I watched Finwell for her response. Finally, with a whimper, I saw her nod. The crowd burst into jeers.

I felt Amy sway beside me. The sight of her mother being led away, charged with terrible crimes, had made her legs weak. It was the sight of her sister, Jenny, being brought to the court floor, that made her sharpen her focus again.

Jenny looked stronger than her mother, though she wept openly and her head was shorn like Finwell's had been. Elspeth Mair, a widow who Jenny had often assisted at the market, brought forth her evidence, sweeping to the stand and proclaiming to a rapt audience that she had seen Jenny speaking with the fae at Mither Stane. The fairy hill, she believed, was where the coven gathered to plot their foul doings. She had chided Jenny for this, she said, and as a result one of her cows died.

The judge told Jenny to nod or shake or head if she agreed or disagreed with her charges. She nodded.

'I have here your confession,' the judge said, 'which I will read before the court. "I, Jenny Hyndman, confess to performing acts of perversion with the Devil in the forest, whereupon he did turn me into a cat, instructing me to roam upon the rooftops of those I wanted to curse."' He lowered the scroll and stared at her. 'Nod or shake your head.'

The crowd gasped as Jenny nodded.

Amy and I shared a glance. We knew this wasn't true. Why, then, was Jenny confessing to such acts?

She knew the penalty for witchcraft was death – why would she lie?

But she wasn't the only one to confess – every woman and girl, the youngest only two years older than Amy, claimed to have made a pact with the Devil. The confessions turned my stomach and hurt my head. I didn't believe that any of them did these terrible things, especially not Finwell and Jenny, and yet each of them confessed readily.

Finally, my mother was called to the court.

She was painfully thin, the bones of her neck and cheeks visible from a distance. Her hair was shorn. She wore chains around her ankles and seemed to have trouble standing, so they brought a chair.

I looked up at the judges, seated on the balcony above. They were chatting and pouring water into their cups, laughing about something. Someone in the crowd threw something at my mother. It hit her head and drew blood. I moved to strike the person who did it, but Amy grabbed my arm.

'No,' she hissed. 'Do you want to be charged, too?'

'Order!' the judge shouted. An elder attended my mother to offer a cloth for her wound, but she seemed too weak to hold it to her head, or to speak.

One by one friends and neighbours told high tales of how my mother had been seen conversing with the Devil, had planned to sink ships and fail crops, had caused cattle to drop down, dead.

'I shall read the confession,' the judge said finally. '"I, Agnes Roberts, confess to leading my coven in servitude of the Devil, who appeared to me as a black wolf in the forest, insomuch as I served as his whore.

I confess to cursing Duncan McGregor to his death, and to cursing the villagers of Lòn Haven by sending a plague upon the crops hereafter."'

I watched, my heart pounding, as my mother gave a nod of her head to signal she agreed with the confession, the crowd exploding into cruel jeers.

II

Saffy feels someone coming into her room, the door creaking open and footsteps thudding across her floor. She stirs, sees it's dark outside, and before she can shout at the intruder to get the hell out of her room she feels the covers shifting off her, an icy cold hand reaching beneath the bedclothes.

She finds she can't scream. The fear is so powerful it renders her frozen and breathless. All she can do is lie there, immobilized with horror, as someone crawls in beside her, icy limbs wrapping around her. But then she realizes who it is: it's Clover, and she starts shouting at her out of sheer relief.

'Clover! What the hell are you doing? You scared me half to death, you little shit!'

'Hold me,' Clover whimpers. 'I'm frightened.'

Saffy softens, her heart still pounding in her chest. She lets Clover bury herself into the warm pit of her chest, rubbing her little arms with her palms in a bid to warm them both up.

'You're like an icicle. Why are you so cold?' she whispers. 'What time is it?'

Clover's teeth are chattering and she doesn't make sense. 'The . . . Longing . . .' she says.

'You were inside the Longing?'

'Mmmm-hmmmm.'

But it's the middle of the night, and a glance out of the window tells her that the waves and the wind are vicious. 'Clover! You could've been injured. You could have fallen or . . . why did you do that? Did you sleepwalk?'

Clover makes a noise that sounds like 'no'. She's shaking so hard that the bed is creaking, and she's so, so cold. Saffy's mind races with worry. Did Clover try to swim out to the basking shark? It would be just like Clover to do something like that. But she's not a great swimmer. She'd have drowned in the attempt. It must have been the rain. It's pouring out there, like usual, drumming on the bothy roof and howling against the windows. Saffy reaches for her mohair jumper on the chair by the bed and wraps it around Clover's little body beneath the blankets, then rubs her bare arms briskly to warm her up.

'If I tell you something,' Clover says when the shivering has died down enough for her to talk, 'do you promise to keep it a secret?'

Saffy nods, drawn in by this sudden sharing of a secret. 'I promise.'

'I saw a wildling.'

'A wildling?'

'Yes.'

'Where?'

'In the Longing.'

'Don't be stupid.'

'But I did.'

'You were sleepwalking, Clover. And anyway, they don't exist.'

'But they *do*! That's the thing.'

'Describe it, then.'

At school, a boy in Clover's class – Thomas McKee, a know-it-all who liked to one-up her at every opportunity – had told her that wildlings lived in the lighthouse right by her house. She told him that this was stupid, and that wildlings didn't even exist, but he insisted, blethering on about soul-sucking fae that were going to kill her whole family. Worse, the other kids had agreed with Thomas. She needed proof to convince them that it was nonsense.

Clover waited until her mum and Luna had fallen asleep. Then she wrapped herself up in her mum's coat, pulled on her wellies, and found a torch from the side of the front door.

Outside, the night was still. The ocean looked different in the dark, like a black planet that she might step on to and walk until the end of forever. The sky was thick with stars, and the rocks were like shadows.

She pushed open the door to the Longing. It hardly budged, and she had to lean all her weight against it to get it open. Inside it was dark and smelled toilety. She could feel her heart fluttering in her chest like a butterfly in a jar. Quickly she turned to leave, but the heavy door had already closed behind her, jammed shut. Somewhere above her a *caw* sounded, and there was a shuffling noise, like someone moving across the room.

With trembling hands she shone her torch into the gloom and called out, 'Who's there?' Her heart was jackhammering in her throat. She whimpered, stepping up against the door, praying that Luna would wake up. *Luna, please! I'm in here. Come and find me.*

The shuffling sound continued. She tried so hard to be brave, but it definitely sounded like something was dragging itself across the floor to get to her. Her torchlight fell on the stairs, and when the shuffling and dragging started again she raced up them, terrified.

By the time she reached the second flight her heart was pounding so hard she thought she might pass out. There was a window there with a very thick stone ledge, and she climbed inside it, tucking her knees up to her chin. Then she cried, as quietly as she could.

She'd only been there a few minutes before she realized something very odd – all the sounds had stopped. Not just the shuffling sound on the ground floor, but howl of the wind and the roaring of the sea. The chittering of the bats had stopped, too, and the creaking of the window frames. Everything was completely *silent*.

She sat up a little, wondering what had happened. Had there been some secret signal that she'd missed? It felt like the lighthouse was holding its breath.

But then, she heard it, a little ways below. Maybe the first turn of the stair.

A clicking sound.

She pulled back inside the window ledge sharply, terrified in case it really was a wildling. A horrible thought had slid into her brain – what if a wildling *did* live in the lighthouse, and it had smelled her? What if it came upstairs after her? There was nowhere for her to run.

She looked up above her and saw only the lantern room. There was nowhere beyond there, nowhere at all to hide. She was trapped.

Click-click.

She had to face it. She had to see what was down there. Maybe it was Luna, looking for her.

With her heart in her mouth, she raised the torch like a weapon, found the 'on' button with her thumb, and pointed the beam downward.

The light pooled on an empty floor – just her mum's paints and equipment for the mural visible, covered up with dust sheets. Clover gave a huge, lung-squeezing sigh of relief. She'd been *so* scared. But as she did, she saw it. From beneath one of the sheets, a thin, grey arm reached from the shadows, a hand retrieving something from her mother's paint supplies.

Clover screamed at the top of her lungs. She dropped the torch with a loud clatter and raced blindly downstairs, pulling with all her might at the front door until a crack of moonlight appeared, letting her escape.

'Do you think it could have been a badger?' Saffy asks, once Clover has finished telling her tale. 'Or a fox?

Clover hesitates. 'I don't know.'

'But you didn't see a *creature*. Or a . . . wildling. Just an arm of something?'

Clover nods, shaking all over again at the thought of it.

Saffy is struck by how convincing Clover's tale is, and for a moment she glances out the window at the Longing and feels afraid. She feels a sudden rush of protectiveness towards her baby sister. Clover and Luna have such a tight bond that she's been pushed to the margins. And it isn't cool to be all cuddly. But now, in this unfamiliar bed, with the rain pelting the roof like frozen peas, she's glad of Clover.

'You can't just run off like that,' she says, feeling Clover's legs warm against hers.

'Why not?'

'Well, you could have slipped and hit your head. And then what would we do?'

'But I didn't slip.'

'If I went missing,' Saffy says, 'would you miss me?'

'No, because you'd already be missing.'

'You know what I mean.'

'You said "miss" twice. That's like a double negative.'

'All right, smarty pants. Would you look for me if I went missing?'

Clover thinks about it. 'Yes.'

'Why?'

Clover shuffles closer to her oldest sister. 'Because you're so warm.'

III

It's time. Saffy slides out of the bed, careful not to disturb Clover, who is fast asleep. She treads lightly on her feet, rolling through her heels to her toes as she takes the stairs, aware of how a creaky floorboard could bring her mother darting out of her room and discover her headed out into the night.

She holds her breath the whole time. As she slips her coat across her shoulders. As she turns the doorknob, centimetre by centimetre, the spindle turning the old latch in the latch plate, springing the door free.

And she's out. Her breaths are quicker now, but still she forces herself to keep her movements slow, just as Brodie taught her: pull the door behind her, quiet as a cat, let the latch slip back. Her steps away from the bothy to the meeting point are as slow as she took the stairs, until she knows that the angle of her mother's bedroom no longer permits sight of her.

Outside, she feels a sudden elation at the wind on her face and the unloosed surf and the stars with their untram-

162

melled light. She heads to the meeting point and sits down, letting her legs swing loose over the rocks. Gold houselights glitter on the other side of the bay. She knows which of them is Brodie's house. In her bedroom she has turned all the shells and pieces of driftwood he's gifted her towards his house, as though it's a kind of Mecca. She's sure her heart even moves around her chest cavity these days, like a rose seeking the sun.

But where is he? She turns her head from side to side, taking in the velvet expanse of the ocean on her left and the rocks and beach on her right. Ahead, surf furls into the bay. Something there catches her eye, and she wonders if it's the basking shark, Basil, with his weird two fins. Something bobbing in the water. Seals, probably. Except, it's the wrong colour. It's pale.

She squints at the object. It's about thirty feet away, moving on the waves. A cloud shifts from the moon and for a moment the light finds the object. It's a face. A human face, its mouth open in a howl, someone in the water and, oh God, she opens her mouth to scream but suddenly there are arms around her and a warm mouth on her cheek and she turns to find Brodie there, and when she turns back to the person in the water they're gone.

'Miss me?' he says, careful to keep his voice low.

She finds she can't speak, she's breathless and dizzy with confusion. She points wildly in the direction of the head she saw just a moment before, she saw it, someone was in the water, she saw their face and their hair, it was a man, but Brodie isn't paying attention and within a moment he's pulling her across the rocks to the beach.

IV

They sit holding hands in a cave that's situated further along the bay. Like an optical illusion, it's hard to see on account of the striations of rock. The first time Brodie showed her the cave she thought he'd vanished.

'Perfect smoking spot,' he says, lighting a cigarette. She lights hers, and they watch the tide push forward and drag back just a few feet away. She loves how safe she feels with him. Just minutes ago she was terrified, wrung out with fear. And now, he is here, and she is shielded from all the monsters in the world, emboldened by his desire for her.

He's a couple of years older than her and has the body of a footballer, she thinks. The body of a man. He's over six foot tall, has dark black hairs on his belly and has to shave his face every day. She loves his voice, his hands, the planes of his face, the back of his neck. His smell.

They sit on a ledge in the rock, smoking and kissing. She tells him about the human head she saw bobbing in the waves and he laughs so hard that she laughs too and suddenly the whole thing is hilarious. The fear leaves her, and they talk about music (Marilyn Manson, Massive Attack, and Rage Against the Machine are mutual favourites), films (both liked *Reservoir Dogs* and *Reality Bites*), and their families.

'My mum's last boyfriend was a pig,' she says. 'But she's left him now and flirting with this new guy. Finn.'

'He a good guy, Finn.'

She frowns. 'Really? My mum always goes for assholes so I figured he was part of the club.'

'He's got this rewilding project going on, it's pretty major.'

'Rewilding? Is that something to do with those evil fairies that people apparently tied to the sycamore trees and cut their hearts out?'

She says it in a dry tone, and he grins. 'No, he's restoring the old forests that used to grow on these islands.'

'What do you mean, "restore old forests"? A forest can hardly disappear, can it?'

'Anyway, we were talking about something else.'

'Assholes?'

'Ah, yes. Parents. Mine argue all the time. Think they'll split soon.'

'Who would you live with?' she asks. She's guessing he'll say his mum. She's met her. Overweight, always tired.

'Dad,' he says without hesitation.

'Really?'

He nods, stares into the darkness. She senses emotion gripping him.

'What about you?' he says. 'How come you chose to live with your mum?'

'Oh,' she says, not realizing he isn't aware of this whole chapter of her life. 'My dad's dead.'

'Sorry.'

She tells him about Sean, how nobody seemed to recognize that his death might affect her, like, *at all*, because he wasn't her biological father. 'But he *was* my dad,' she says, her throat burning with anger and tears pricking her eyes. 'I called him Dad. He was going to adopt me. But nobody gets it. They were all *so terribly sorry* for Mum, Clover, and Luna. But not me.'

He shifts closer to her until his hip is touching hers, wraps his arm around her.

'People are bastards,' he says, kissing her forehead, and she breaks involuntarily into a snigger, glad of the opportunity to shift her mood. She hates talking about her dad. It always makes her chest tight and opens up all the old wounds.

V

She wants to photograph him, or sculpt him. Velvety pale skin, bee-stung lips that she imagines against her neck, her wrist, her thigh. Dark hair worn slightly long and messy, and his hands . . . Michelangelo couldn't have sculpted better hands. The kind that can wield a broadsword or tear the heart out of a dragon. She glimpses the bare skin of his knees through slashes in his black jeans. He has perfect knees. An image of her kneeling before him, licking the skin of each knee, startles her with its sudden eroticism.

When he kisses her again, his hand slips to her breast, and she pulls away sharply.

'What's wrong?' he says.

She feels embarrassed. 'It's just . . . I don't know.' She wants to say it's too early for that, she feels it's much too early, but then he's seventeen, and maybe for seventeen-year-olds it isn't too early.

'You don't like me,' he says. 'That's it, isn't it?'

'No!' she says, straddling him, cupping his face with her hands. 'I do like you.'

He fixes his eyes on hers. 'Then why not?'

Slowly, she moves his hand under her shirt. It feels uncomfortable and not nice. Something in her wants to run away but she grits her teeth and pushes the feeling down into her stomach.

'You can touch me, too,' he says.

'OK.'

He guides her hand to his crotch, unbuttoning his jeans and slipping her hand down his pants. She forces a smile on to her face as she touches it, the foreign hardness. She's only ever done this with Jack, and that was after dating for four months. She and Jack are both virgins, but she still feels much less comfortable with Brodie than she did with Jack. She's scared of being useless and disappointing.

It literally lasts a minute, maybe less. She yanks her hand away, trying not to show her disgust, as he strokes her face and buttons himself up.

'When are you going to break up with Rowan?' she says, wiping her hand discreetly on a clump of grass. She didn't intend to say it, and she feels him flinch.

'Actually, it's been on my mind,' he says, lighting up a cigarette.

'It has?'

He blows out a puff of smoke. 'Timing has to be right, though. Her dad's a policeman.'

She nods, but she doesn't understand what this has to do with dumping Rowan. But then, a voice inside her reminds her that she's only here until the end of the month. She's only fifteen. She can hardly just stay on the island. She'll have to go home, and he'll be here, alone. No. Not alone. With Rowan. The girlfriend he's had since he was fourteen years old. Three and a half years against five stolen nights.

'I liked the photo you gave me,' he says as they walk home. It's four in the morning, and she can't help but yawn into her hand.

'Thank you.' The photo was a Polaroid of herself that she took in her bedroom.

'Do you think you could give me a few more?' he says. She turns. 'Maybe some sexy ones?'

She searches his face, realizing at once that her understanding of what 'sexy' means doesn't match his.

'Would that be OK?' he says, faux-sincere. 'Or is it too *early* for you?'

He slips a hand under her shirt, touching her breast, and she squeezes her eyes shut, pushing away the urge to remove his hand. *Why doesn't it feel nice?* she thinks. Why does it feel like he's taking something from her?

'No,' she tells Brodie. She wraps her arms around his neck and forces herself to smile. 'Not too early at all.'

LIV, 1998

I

The days passed in a whirlwind of paint and school runs. The project of painting the lighthouse quickly proved to be the distraction I'd hoped for. I didn't have time to think about the phone call from the hospital, or about what another cervical scan might reveal. My days were carved up neatly by paint colours and sections mapped out by the mural, which I'd transcribed to several pieces of paper fixed in a circular shape and sellotaped to the dining table in the bothy, along with Polaroids of the sections of wall where they were to go painted. Each week day I dropped the girls off to school at eight am, then worked solidly until I collected them from afterschool club at five-thirty, often returning to the Longing once they were in bed. I enjoyed Finn's conversational tour of Lòn Haven, and occasionally his death metal tapes. Here, on Lòn Haven, I was untethered from the past. Everything I'd carried for the last fifteen years – the shock of my pregnancy with Saffy, the grief at losing Sean, and now, that terrifying phone call – was gobbled up by the ravenous tide. And witnessing the

Longing transform, stroke by stroke, into something a little less knackered, its former glory beginning to creep back, was rewarding. I felt that, maybe, I could start again, too.

One night, when I'd decided to give myself the evening 'off', there was a knock at the door of the bothy. I thought it might be Finn, eager to get going at the new section he'd finished plastering that day.

But it wasn't Finn. It was a group of chatting, excited women. Isla stood at the head of them.

'We've come to show you the mareel,' she said grandly.

'The what?'

'See for yourself,' one of the other women said, sweeping a hand towards the bay. I stepped outside to see what she was referring to. The tide was shimmering with an astral blue light, as though it was filled with fireflies.

'The mareel, also known as sea sparkle,' one of the women said. 'Scientists know it's caused by bioluminescent microorganisms.'

'It means good fortune for those who see it,' said Mirrin, a short, stout woman with a mane of gold hair, 'and even more for those who swim in it.'

Isla held up a wet suit and winked. 'Well now, isn't it lucky I've got a spare? Come and join us. I insist!'

I got changed quickly and followed the group to the beach, where the ocean greeted us with softly rolling waves, iridescent with trapped, glowing light. There were eight of us in the group. Mirrin worked part-time at the grocery store in the town and sold paintings in the small art gallery owned by her partner, Greer, who was also there; Ruqayya was a widow who ran the island's mobile library; Ling was a shaman, yogi, and sculptor; both Ailsa and Louisa were

171

veterinarians who had relocated from England twenty years ago to run a small animal sanctuary on the west coast of Lòn Haven.

'How often does it happen?' I said, clasping my arms across my chest. The icy water was only up to my ankles but I was shaking from the cold.

Ruqayya stood next to me as she tucked her long grey hair into a swimming cap. 'Once or twice a year,' she said. 'We always make sure we try and swim in it. The Vikings believed it was a healing tide. That if you had an affliction, mental or physical, and you swum in it, you'd be healed.'

'Do you believe that?'

'Not when I first moved here,' she said. 'But I had terrible arthritis. My fingers were all twisted. And now look.' She held out her hands. They looked strong and perfectly straight.

She stepped forward and lowered herself to swim. As her body moved, the water responded, each stroke of her arm streaking the water electric blue.

'Come on,' another woman urged gently from my left. Ailsa. She threw me a bright smile, her face lit up by the glow. 'You don't know how long it'll last. And you'll miss your chance.'

The cold water felt like a bite, fierce and swift. Isla cheered and clapped as I pushed my arms out in breast-strokes that created vivid neon arcs in the water, as though I was writing on the waves, imprinting the sea with my body.

I was mesmerized by the mareel. The ocean, it seemed, had become conscious, mimicking the northern lights. Some of the women were dressed only in a cap and swimsuit, yet braved the water without hesitation. I tried to think of the last time I'd been in the sea – it had been at least twelve years. I hadn't laughed with a group of women like that in a long time. Having a child so young had ostracized me from my friend groups. And who has time for a social life when you're eyes-deep in nappies and teething?

I stayed in the water for as long as I could, secretly pleading with it to heal me. Any other time, I'd have rejected the idea of a 'healing tide', of anything but medicine having the power to cure. But belief is a powerful thing. Maybe, I thought, if I put aside my scepticism and willed myself to believe that the cancer could disappear, it would.

II

In the days after that night, I felt a lot better. The blood in my urine cleared up; I stopped getting backaches. I didn't dare believe that it had anything to do with swimming in the mareel, but I was delighted all the same.

I took to joining Mirrin and Isla for a swim first thing every morning before the school run. Even in brisk winds, the icy sleeve of the waves around my body was exhilarating. I felt like I'd discovered a rare secret, the thrill of immersing myself in the thrashing wilderness of the Atlantic Ocean. Maybe, I thought, the diagnosis was wrong. They get things like that wrong sometimes, don't they?

Isla invited me and the girls to join her for dinner. We ate in the dining room, which was the size of all the rooms of the bothy combined, with an oval oak table in the centre and a fireplace that I could easily stand up inside. Rowan and Saffy sat next to each other. I'd hoped they'd be friends, but now I could see the reason why they hadn't clicked. They were like chalk and cheese. Rowan wore a vial containing wolfsbane – 'It kills werewolves, and you never know' – and a floaty purple dress embroidered with mystical symbols. Her fingers were covered in heavy silver rings and she talked in her high-pitched voice about tarot and a retreat to Iceland she wanted to take to meet with a coven. I spotted Saffy rolling her eyes more than once. She was dressed in a thrift store lumberjack shirt and ripped jeans and nine-hole Doc Martens with yellow laces. Her blonde hair hadn't been washed in a week and she'd piled it up on the top of her head with a pen spiked through the nest of it. She stifled a yawn, and I realized suddenly how tired she looked.

'And how is school, my lovelies?' Isla asked Clover and Luna when the conversation began to flag.

'I don't like it,' Clover said flatly. Always to the point.

'How come?' Isla said.

'We don't do *any* science, just collecting leaves and building dens in the forest.'

'Well, that can be scientific, can't it?' Isla countered.

'By "science", I think Clover means they don't set stuff on fire,' I said. Her school in York had a science lab, and Clover had shown a slightly worrying interest in exploding things.

'I like the school here,' Luna said. 'We made puppets yesterday.'

'What about you, Saffy?' Isla said. 'Rowan said you've settled in well?'

Saffy's cheeks reddened. 'It's OK,' she said to the plate.

'Will you be taking the girls guising, Liv?' Rowan asked.

'Guising?'

'Trick or treating,' Isla translated.

'It is *not* trick or treating,' Rowan said, mock-offended. She shook her head at me. 'Guising's a very different matter. You dress up to disguise yourself so the spirits think you're one of them. And you perform for your neighbours to bring them good luck.'

'So you don't get sweeties?' Clover asked.

'You might,' Rowan said. 'But if the neighbours give you something, it's to ward off bad luck.'

'Can we still dress up as Egyptian mummies?' Luna asked.

'If you like,' Rowan said lightly.

'What about bobbing for apples?' Clover added.

'It's a pagan ritual,' Saffy said, and Rowan turned to her in surprise.

'Dookin' for apples is a pagan ritual?' Isla asked. She cocked an eyebrow at Rowan. 'Did you know that?'

Rowan's cheeks flushed. 'Course I did,' she said, but she'd hesitated a second too long for it to be convincing. Saffy threw me a quick smile, proud of herself for one-upping Rowan.

Isla's husband Bram came in then, late from work – Isla said this was usual – and sat down at the head of the table. I said hello, but he didn't answer.

'Remember Liv?' Isla said, trying to get his attention. He was busy pulling off his tie and adjusting his shirt sleeves. 'We met her at the bothy. You've already met Saffy, and the younger ones are Clover and Luna.'

Bram merely raised his eyes and gave us all a disinterested stare. I wondered if we'd come at a bad time. He was a good deal older than Isla, mid-sixties, with a ruddy face and heavy-lidded, unimpressed eyes that flicked at me from beneath woolly eyebrows. Isla brought out his plate and set it in front of him, and immediately he said, 'Are you trying to kill me?'

'What's wrong?' Isla asked. He was looking at the plate as if he'd been served a human head.

'Are you blind?' he said, gimlet-eyed.

Isla looked puzzled, then seemed to realize her mistake and tutted. 'Sorry. Forgot you're off meat at the moment.' She rose from her chair and whisked the plate away. Rowan picked up her conversation about Samhain – Halloween – and the conversation moved on.

I thought it odd that Bram was so rude, especially with company present. I knew he was Chief Inspector on the island; perhaps he'd had a bad day. Isla never mentioned it afterwards.

Rowan came to the lighthouse the next day after school to 'cleanse' the place. Isla brought her as well as a flask of hot tea to share with me while she indulged Rowan's lighting of a piece of sage and wafting it around the place while chanting something in Latin. I'll admit, I felt better once she'd done that, and yet I usually wouldn't have given heed to such things. Fear, combined with a touch of desperation, makes you much more open to buying into otherwise crazy practices.

Later that night, once I'd put the girls to bed, a knock on the window made me jump. Isla and her ladies, I thought, come to collect me for a night swim. It was dark, and I could only see a shadow falling up the garden path. It didn't seem the caller was Isla and her ladies after all. Three more knocks at the front door.

'Mummy?' Luna called out drowsily from her bedroom. 'Is that you?'

I stood in front of the door and took a deep breath. Maybe it was Finn.

'Go back to bed,' I called to Luna. Then I opened the door.

Standing on the front porch was a little girl, about four or five years old.

Her pale hair was wild and matted, and her face was covered in mud and scratches, as if she'd fallen.

It was pitch-black, but from the glow of the light of my living room I made out that she was wearing nothing more than a filthy rag wrapped around her waist and that she was barefoot, overgrown toenails black with dirt. Also, she was shaking with cold.

'Are you all right?' I said. 'Come in, come in. It's freezing out there. You'll catch your death.'

Her teeth were chattering and I could see her eyes were glassy. I placed a hand on her bare arm, frail as a twig. I realized she must have been the child I'd spotted in the Longing. That child had this same white-blonde hair to her shoulders. But that was weeks ago. My mouth ran dry at the thought of her being out here alone all this time.

She spotted the fire and lunged towards it, holding her hands close to the flame. The rag that was wrapped around her waist loosened and fell to the ground, and I saw something between her legs. A penis. She was a boy.

I tore the throw off the sofa and wrapped it quickly around him.

'Where do you live?' I said. 'Are your parents nearby? Did you get lost?'

He answered me at length, but it was in a language I didn't know. German, or perhaps Dutch. Slowly, understanding crept upon me. The boy was from overseas. Perhaps he'd fallen off a boat, or escaped from traffickers.

He sat down on the floor then, the flames bringing colour back to his pale skin. I knelt by him and swallowed back a gasp at the smell. For such a delicate child, he smelled revolting.

'Your mum and dad must be very worried about you,'

I said, crouching down beside him. He flinched, and I moved back a little to reassure him I wasn't going to harm him. 'I'm going to call the police to let them know you're here. And I'll get you some hot tea and a sandwich.'

He didn't answer, and I decided he must not speak English. I was at once alarmed and relieved. For a while, I'd thought I was going out of my mind. And yet here he was, in the cottage. Proof that I *had* seen a child.

I rose and moved to the kitchen, quickly pouring a glass of water and making him a sandwich. Then I brought it through, intent on calling the police while he ate.

But the boy was gone. The rag that had been wrapped around his waist lay on the floor, and the front door was ajar. I raced out, calling 'Come back! Come back!'

But there was nothing but a long strip of moonlight where he had stood only minutes before.

III

My mother, along with Jenny, Finwell, and the nine others, were walked in chains back to the broch where they had been imprisoned for two months before standing trial. The judge explained that the stake should be placed in the grounds of the church, as per the wishes of the Royal Enquiry. But as the ashes of the witches would possibly be carried by the wind across the home of the man whose life they had taken, it was inappropriate. So, they would be burned by the broch, where naught but the sea would be touched by the ashes.

The day was bright, the sky clear of clouds and the blue sea gently swaying. Four stakes had been erected in front of the stone broch. I'd seen some villagers hauling the trunks from the forest a few days before – it was good quality wood, tall lengths of it forming the spine of the stakes and thick branches propped up at angles against it to catch the flames. I wanted a storm to rise and send lightning forking down, or the sea to rear up over the rocks and sweep away the stakes. Surely if the women really were witches, the Devil wouldn't let them be burned?

The guards from the Privy Council led the women and girls close to the stakes and began to remove their chains. The whole island had turned out for this terrible scene and I hated every one of them. Familiar faces greeted me at every turn; the women whose babies Finwell had delivered, who had sung her praises every day since; the men my father had worked with, and the children I played with often. They knew my family, and they knew my mother to be the sort of person who would never do the kinds of things she confessed to. I saw Duncan's sons and his wife, who must have known what a black-hearted bastard he was. What cowards they were, to watch on as the accused were pulled by ropes around their necks to the stake, bony and obedient as mules.

My mother was innocent, as were Jenny and Finwell. I knew she had only confessed to those things because she was scared.

Father Skuddie stepped forward towards the woman, and I thought for a moment he might announce that God had forgiven them and they were to be set free. But he simply crossed himself and prayed that their souls wouldn't be left to linger in Hell.

The guards began to tie the women to the stakes, three to each one. When a guard tried to separate Jenny and Finwell, Jenny began to scream. 'No! No! Let me stay with her!' she shouted, and the guard relented, shoving her roughly against the stake so that she banged her head. She started to slump as they tied her, and I realized she'd blacked out.

My mother was tied to the stake opposite me. She was scanning the crowd, and I waved until she saw me, and her face brightened.

I will never forgive myself for what I did then.

I froze.

There were too many words I wanted to say to her. I wanted to pull her away from the stake and save her and I wanted to push all the guards and the judges and tie them to the stakes, and at the same time I wanted to run away and hide in a cave and pretend none of this was happening. But instead, I froze and stared blankly at her, and she stared back at me, terror laid nakedly on her face.

The guards tossed gunpower around the stakes and threw in the torches. In seconds, the flames were creeping up the wood, sending black clouds of smoke whirling into the air. The noise of the sea and the crackling wood grew louder, but suddenly a loud voice sounded from the front. I looked up and saw it was Finwell, her head reared back and her mouth open.

'I curse you, sons of Duncan, and your sons' sons, and all the people who stand before me now. I curse you that Lòn Haven will atone for our blood, and that there will never be peace on this island until our innocence is spread throughout the whole of Scotland!'

The other women started shouting their own curses, calling up the fae, conjuring the powers of darkness on the island, a chorus of rage rising up amidst the flames. It was an astonishing sight, and the crowd were shocked into silence. And as the women started to fall unconscious, consumed by smoke and flame, one voice in the crowd sounded loudly.

'I curse you all, people of Lòn Haven! I curse you to burn your own children just as you've burned my mother!'

It was Amy, shouting at the people around her.

The crowd moved back, wary of the cacophony and the

flames, which were being driven by the wind towards them. The sky darkened and the waves lashed at the rocks. In a moment, I watched as a guard grabbed Amy by the hair and started to drag her towards the stake, apparently with the intention of burning her with the others. My mouth was wide in horror, and I was still rooted to the spot, nailed down by fear and the strange, weightless sensation that this wasn't real, that it wasn't happening.

A judge shook his head at the guard, who gruffly shoved Amy to the ground. I would learn later that the only reason her life had been spared was because the Royal Enquiry had a strict judicial process in place for witches – a barbarous process, yes, but one that had order.

In a moment, the rest of the women's cries died out, their voices quenched by the flames. The crowd began to tire of the scene; children grew restless, babies cried for milk. I stayed until Amy rose up from her spot on the ground and huddled close to me, both of us watching our mothers and Amy's sister consumed by the fire, black smoke rising into the darkening sky.

LUNA, 2021

I

It's morning; Luna wakes with a drumming headache and a strange euphoria at having survived the night. The sun is shining, the loch a bright lens and the hills proud and purple with heather. Last night's torrential downpour is a distant memory, save the pans full of water on the kitchen floor and the wet patch on the ceiling. Mercifully the electricity seems to be back on again, so she's can charge her phone. She plugs it in then stares up at the ceiling and sighs. She'll have to message the owner. There will be money owed for repairs. But first, she needs to deal with Clover.

Luckily, Clover seems a little less hell-bent on destruction this morning. She asks for Pop Tarts – which Luna bought on request – and they eat those together at the dining table, both in their pyjamas. For a moment, Luna considers not mentioning the overflowing bath episode. But she knows, from her training, that Clover needs to talk about this. Silence never works.

'How are you feeling?' she says.

Clover shrugs. She's focused on her Pop Tarts, and the

skin beneath her eyes is mauve and sunken. She's slept in her day clothes, and strands of brown hair have loosened from her ponytail, hanging around her face.

'Can you tell me why you left the taps running in the bathroom?' Luna says gently. 'Did you want to take a bath and simply forgot?'

Clover keeps her eyes on the plate, her lips tight.

'And what about Gianni?' she presses, careful not to speak too fast, to keep her tone gentle. 'I saw you cut him up. Did you decide you didn't like him any more?'

'He needed to die,' Clover says, raising her eyes to Luna.

'Why did he need to die?'

Clover shrugs.

'You know, if you wanted to have a bath, you could just tell me . . .'

'I didn't,' Clover snaps.

'I see. So why did you run the taps to flood the bathroom?'

'To flood the *house*, dummy,' Clover says crossly.

Luna takes a breath. She can feel her nerves ringing, her heart pounding. She has met many, many children with behavioural problems. She was one of them, once upon time. But she never expected a reunion with either of her sisters to turn out like this. How naïve she was to think things might ever return to how they were over twenty years ago.

'I was thinking we could go somewhere fun today,' she says brightly, changing tack. 'Just the two of us.'

Clover looks puzzled. 'Why?'

'Well, to get to know one another again. To . . . spend time together.'

'*Why?*' Clover demands again.

Luna stares at her plate of half-eaten Pop Tarts. How did she ever find these remotely edible? She needs to find a Starbucks or Pret for breakfast. 'Would you like to go to a park?' she says.

Clover looks restless. She looks around, taking in the room. 'How long do I have to stay here?'

'We can leave anytime,' Luna says. 'We can go to my flat today if you like.'

'Where's your flat?'

'I live in Coventry. Do you know where that is?'

She shakes her head.

'It's quite a drive from here. We can take it in stages. Spend a night in Edinburgh, maybe? And then drive down the next day?'

'I want to go back to the Longing,' Clover says.

Luna stares, a sudden wave of panic washing across her. *The Longing*. The name conjures such terror, such complex memories. They're so close to it now, just a short drive and a ferry away. She can almost feel it calling to her.

She tells Clover to brush her teeth and get ready. She has no plan, but right now she needs to be alone. She needs a moment to think about what to do next.

Ethan calls, and she's relieved to hear his voice.

'Everything OK?' he asks. She tells him about the events of the night before. It's a relief to confide in someone.

'Fucking hell,' he says. 'I knew I should have stayed.'

'What could you have done?'

'I don't like the sound of this. You had labour pains in the hospital. What if the stress of this kicks that off again?'

'I'm fine.'

'Please come home today. *Please.*' A pause. 'Though

can you imagine Margaret's reaction if Clover flooded our flat.'

'She'd go mental.'

'We'd not hear the end of it for decades. We'd literally never be able to sell the place.'

She hears something in his comment. He's thinking they're going to sell the flat. They're still splitting up.

She ends the call by telling him she'll come home as soon as she can. Clover comes downstairs in the clothes she was wearing the day before, a white T-shirt that looks dirty and boy's jogging bottoms, donated by the hospital.

'I have an idea,' Luna says. 'Why don't we go get you some new clothes?'

Clover's eyes light up, and Luna remembers how much she and her sister loved dressing up as children. It's a reassurance, a tenuous one. But she can't help but feel hopeful.

She's uncertain where to go for toys or clothes befitting a child, least of all in somewhere as rural as Drumnadrochit. This is not something she's ever done before, and she hasn't even started shopping for the baby yet. They drive to Inverness, where the busy city and bustling mall are a comfort. A false one, she knows, but it's a relief to be amongst crowds.

They find a Starbucks – *thank you, God* – where she gets a decaf latte and a croissant. The presence of familiar chain store names is a balm. They find a Next store. Clover's face lifts at the bright lights and the mannequins dressed in colourful clothing, the racks of sequinned and printed T-shirts and dresses.

'Can I try on this one?' she says, lifting a tulle dress in vivid pink ombre.

'I'm afraid that's only for babies,' Luna says. 'See? It's

too small. The label says it's only for children aged eighteen to twenty-four months.'

Clover is crestfallen.

They head to the section for children aged seven and over, where Clover delights in the range of outfits, the velvet headbands, trainers with pom-poms, and dinosaur-shaped handbags. The mystery of Clover's age aside, her reaction is heartwarming; the angry, sullen child from last night is gone, and in her place is a chatty, funny child completely in her element amongst fashion.

Clover picks out leggings with a unicorn print, dungarees embroidered with roses, a dress with pink and blue tassels, and a handful of shoes, including wellies with a dolphin fin on the back seam. In the baby section, Luna can't help but look over the beautiful babygros and dungarees. Would it be jinxing things if she bought something for the baby? She lifts a panda-print onesie in size 'newborn' and thumbs the soft fabric. She tries to imagine a baby wearing it, *her* baby, slipping the tiny legs and arms inside and holding him lengthwise along her arm. Will it actually happen?

In the changing room, Luna waits outside while Clover tries on her selection. She calls out, 'Luna? Would you help me, please?' The curtain moves, and Clover's head appears there. She gestures for her to come in.

Inside the cubicle, Clover is naked save her underwear, and instantly Luna's eyes fall on her little body reflected in the triple mirror. The smooth, unblemished skin, the round belly and flat, undeveloped chest. How little she is, Luna thinks. And how vulnerable. Just this morning she'd wanted to strangle her. Well, not quite – but putting her on a time out for sure.

The square white dressing on Clover's hip stares back at her.

'How's the ouchie on your hip?' she says, as she bends to unzip Clover's outfit. 'Do you need a new dressing on it?'

She glances at it in the long mirror. Clover follows her gaze and twists to inspect the dressing. 'It hurts a little,' she says, her fingers tracing it.

'How did you get that mark, Clover?'

She shrugs. 'I don't know.'

Unease grows in Luna as she studies the mark. A memory rises up: she's in a police station right after she'd been found in the forest, after her mother had left her there and she'd apparently tried to find her way home, but got lost in the process. There's something on her leg that the police were concerned about. They ask her about it, over and over. *I don't know how it happened,* she hears herself saying, just like Clover is saying now.

Clover takes off her outfit and pulls on a navy sequinned dress. She looks in the mirror at her reflection, hand on her hip, one knee bent in a sassy pose. 'This one's gorgeous. Can we buy it?'

Luna tells her yes, and as she reaches to move the price tag her fingertips brush Clover's skin. Instantly she feels the snap of an electric spark, then the punching strike of that pain behind her eyes, deep in the bones of her skull and the grooves of her eye sockets, all the way to the back of her neck. Luna sinks to the floor, gasping with the pain and shock of it. Her vision is like a smashed mirror, and the lights are there, six white lights in a row.

As she lies on the floor she can just make out Clover standing over her. Luna tries to open her mouth to speak, to tell her to get help, but then she notices Clover's expression.

Her face doesn't betray a hint of fear or concern at Luna's state.

It's a look of satisfaction.

II

'Feeling any better?'

Luna looks up at the shop assistant and nods, grateful. 'Yes, thank you.'

'I had dreadful fainting episodes when I was pregnant,' the woman says. 'Passed as soon as I gave birth. Hopefully yours'll be the same.'

Luna gives a weak smile. She's sitting in a chair in the storeroom clutching a cup of sugary tea that the shop assistant made her. The thunder in her head has retreated to a dull throb at the back of her left eye, but she still feels worryingly nauseous and dizzy. Clover stands nearby. She looks anxious. Luna looks down at her hand, where she touched Clover. She had felt a small electric shock, then the bang of a headache that seemed to roll in out of nowhere. At the time it had been frightening, but now that the pain has diminished she can see her reaction must have alarmed Clover.

'I'll buy you the clothes you liked,' she tells her gently. 'Do you want to pick out a new pair of shoes?'

Clover reaches out to take her hand, but Luna draws back, nervous. Clover's expression changes – she's hurt, and frightened, but Luna is still too hesitant to touch her.

Back at the Airbnb, Luna slides the ready meals she picked up at the Co-op into the oven and sinks down into the armchair. She still hasn't contacted the owner about the water damage. There are other, infinitely more terrifying things on her mind. Like why touching Clover seemed to bring on a horrific headache. Like why Clover is a child of seven and a half instead of a grown woman. Whether having Clover back in her life is a good idea or if it's putting her and her unborn son at risk.

At risk of what? she thinks.

Death, answers a small voice from the corridors of her mind.

She watches Clover carefully, weighing up her thoughts. *Is* she Clover? A voice tells her that she can't be. Nothing that Luna has found online can answer why Clover remains a child. Yet she looks and sounds just like Clover.

And there's the mark on Clover's hip, the horrible burn with numbers sliced into her flesh.

She checks that Clover is occupied before heading to the bedroom, using her phone to try and take a photograph of the area behind each of her knees. It's the only way she can see if anything is there, though it's possible that such a mark would have long since faded.

It's an awkward area to photograph, especially with a flash. The first three images are blurry, the next too far away. She's about to give up when she sees something in one of the shots of her right leg. A tiny mark.

She zooms into the image. It's grainy, and very faint, but

she can just make out a shape. No, not a shape. With a gasp, she realizes it's a number.

8

She covers her hand with her mouth, zooming further into the figure on her screen.

All this time, the mark has been there.

Just like Clover's.

III

That night, Luna's dreams are memories filtered through imagination. She's back in the bothy on Lòn Haven, a boisterous grey sea visible through a small window. Her mother is there, telling her to put on her trainers and fleece jacket so they can go out walking together. The air in the room feels wrong and her mother's face is tight, but she doesn't know why.

And then, she's in a forest. The wind is swaying the trees, their long black branches twisting overhead. She can see faces in the distance, watching her and her mother as they walk.

They stop in a clearing. Isla is there, strands of red hair falling down from beneath a yellow beanie like red snakes. She smiles down at her, but there's a rope in her hand.

Be a good girl.

Her mother's tying her to the tree with the rope, wrapping it around her legs and arms the way she once bandaged her wrist when she sprained it. Her mother ties the rope in knots, fastening her in place. Luna's heart is racing. She can feel the rough bark against her hands, the rope digging into her shins. Her mother is sobbing.

And then, she sees the knife lifting in the air. She feels the sting of it against her arm. The blood hitting her mother's face.

She wakes up gasping, her throat dry from shouting out. In the moonlight she can see a figure in the doorway. Clover.

'You were yelling,' she says. 'About someone trying to kill you.'

Luna rises, takes Clover back to her bed. She sits beside her until she falls asleep, running a finger across the small white scar on her own arm.

The scar caused by the blade.

She shivers, her stomach dropping. Liv did this.

Liv tried to kill her.

SAPPHIRE, 1998

I

'What are you reading?'

Saffy jumps at the sound of Luna's voice. She looks up angrily and sees her younger sister standing in the doorway of her bedroom.

'What do *you* want?' she says, turning the page in her book.

'Nothing,' Luna says, shrugging, but it's obvious she wants *something*. Saffy sets down her book and signals reluctantly for Luna to come in.

'I can't sleep,' Luna explains. 'What are you reading?'

'What does it fucking look like I'm reading?'

Luna shrugs. 'A book?'

'Whoop de bloody doo.'

'It looks like a very old book.'

Saffy sighs. Why does her younger sister have to be such a moron?

'Look, just sit on the floor and shut up.'

Luna obeys. Their mum is busy in the Longing and she hates going in there.

'What's the book about?'

'Witches.'

'Like *The Worst Witch*?'

Saffy sneers. 'It's not a stupid kid's book. This is a history book about all the witches that they burned on Lòn Haven.'

Luna looks up at her as though she's not sure whether Saffy's pulling her leg or not. 'Why did they burn witches?'

Saffy shrugs. 'Lots of reasons. Misogyny. King James VI's massive ego. Probably overcompensating for something. Also, religion – King Jamie wanted everyone to conform to his belief system and there were still a lot of pagans knocking around. They still kill people for practising witch-craft in some countries. Did you know that?'

'There are witches, still?' Luna says, wide-eyed.

'They *aren't* witches, silly.' She holds her younger sister in a long stare. 'Or at least, not all of them. Do you know what a grimoire is?'

Luna shakes her head.

'It's a book of spells. Look.'

She shows Luna, who looks puzzled.

'What's this one?' she says, pointing at a set of triangles. 'It looks like the one Mummy painted in the Longing.'

'It is,' Saffy says. '"*Rune to call a loved one home from afar.*" But it only works if you cast the spell.'

'What's the spell?'

'"Living bones," it says. Look.' She points at the archaic handwriting.

'Bones that live?' Luna says, screwing up her face.

'No, you dimwit. Bones taken from a living creature. As in, one that's still alive.'

'Gross.'

'You're gross.'

'Is there a spell for Mummy?'

Saffy gives her a puzzled look.

'What, to make her disappear?'

'To give her money and make her happy.'

'Money wouldn't make Mummy happy,' Saffy says sourly. 'Getting rid of me would, though.'

'Money would make her happy. And getting Daddy back.'

'There are spells here to bring people back. But they won't work on Daddy.'

'Why not?'

She lifts her eyes to Luna's and looks gut-punched. 'Because he's dead.'

II

Saffy takes one last look behind her before tugging the door of the Longing and stepping inside.

It is freezing cold, and already she's starting to regret this. Why is she doing this again?

It's about one in the morning. She can hear the sea exhaling against the rocks, and she's pretty sure there's a seal or a dolphin or something at the bottom of the cliffs, a low, guttural sound marking its presence within the tapestry of this wild place. She fingers the skeleton key that she's tied around her neck with a leather shoelace, sitting low between her breasts so that her mother doesn't spot it. It's cold against her skin and she wants to take it off.

But first, she thinks. But first.

She has it planned. She borrowed her schoolfriend Machara's make-up and has spent a long time putting it on, coating her eyelashes with mascara, drawing in her pale brows, shading her eyes in dark brown and copper. Inside the Longing the darkness is thick as soup, but she clocked her mum's work lamps the other day and figured the lighting would be perfect. The lamps come with a filter and a remote control that lets you dim the light, which is perfect as she doesn't want anything too bright. She'd draw attention to herself if the light is too bright.

For one, she's naked beneath her coat, and she can well imagine her mum's face if she barged into the place and found her oldest child lolling against the staircase of the Longing in her birthday suit. Saffy hates her body. She thinks she's too tall, her hips too big, and she hates that her left boob is slightly bigger than the right. She hates her arms, and her ankles, and her feet, and her knees. Her bum is long and square, not pert and round, as it should be. That said, she's well aware that her body seems to exert a particular effect on men. And if Brodie wants sexy photos, he'll get them.

She closes the door behind her and looks fearfully around. It smells of paint and dead fish, and a quick flick of her torch shows where her mum has already started the mural. The plasterwork helps it look a little less like a ruin and more like a work-in-progress. She finds the round light, plugs it in, dims it down low, then searches for her mum's Polaroid camera. There it is, on top of the wallpaper table.

She removes her coat and wellies. She wears only the old heavy skeleton key that she found in the bothy, tied around her neck with a shoelace. It looks like something you'd find on a pirate ship, which she thinks is appropriate for the tone of the pics.

She sets the camera timer and poses, rolling her shoulders back, looking back over her shoulder, pouting her red lips, opening her mouth, and showing her tongue. She unties her hair and lets it hang long and loose, trying much more overt pictures in case the ones she's taken are too tame for someone like Brodie. She opens her legs wider, lets her hands roam across her skin.

She tugs on her coat and looks over the prints that are coming into view on the small white square. The prints are startling – she doesn't look like herself.

She looks like a porn star.

Hopefully Brodie will like her now.

As she tugs the zip on her coat, the shoelace from which the skeleton key hangs comes loose, sending the key to the floor with a sharp clang. She tenses, worried in case someone outside will hear. The noise sends bats flittering above, and she's about to grab the key and race outside when she notices something. On the floor by the stairs, there's an old lock peeking out from beneath a slab of wood.

Quickly she pulls the wood slab aside and fingers the lock. It has a similar insignia on the side of it to the one on the skeleton key; a snake eating its own tail, so it looks like a circle. An ouroboros.

She slips the key inside the lock and is amazed when it clicks open, smooth and unhesitant. She pushes the wood slab further and finds that it was covering a strange metal grille that is now unlocked. She opens it to find nothing but a deep, dark hole. No secret treasure chest or room full of secrets. Just a weird old hole. A deep one, by the looks of it.

She locks it and ties the key around her neck. It will be her secret.

III

My mother was dead. There was no burial, no grave for me to visit and pay my respects. I could not speak of her to anyone. She was not missed, or remembered with fondness. The site where they burned her body was a black stain on the cliffside, the ashes of the bodies and the stakes swept away by sea and wind but somehow, the stone that had stood there since the beginnings of the earth retains the mark of the flame, scorched into it like grief.

I understand now that this was the beginning of my current mental state. Missing someone you love for an extended period of time can and will lead to madness, every bit as much as a wound that is not cleaned will lead to a festering sore, and thence an illness that spreads throughout the body. The only boundary between desire and obsession is time; if you crave someone long enough, it becomes a need. It becomes your ever-waking thought. The only thing you live for.

Not long after my mother was burned, my uncle fetched away my brother, and I was alone, orphaned and unwanted.

Amy persuaded her father to take me in, and so I kept myself scarce, trying to earn every scrap of bread he fed me by tending to the fields and caring for the animals. This helpfulness earned me both her father's admiration and her brothers' jealousy. They beat the living tar out of me almost daily, and while her father stopped it at first I think he grew tired of having to defend me. It was extra work, and perhaps he questioned whether I didn't deserve it.

Tavish was the strongest of the two and driven mad by his mother and sister's deaths, for he liked to make a little stage play out of my beatings. He'd pretend I was a heretic, or accused of witchcraft, and he'd pull out a bag of stones and have me kneel while he cited scripture and stoned me.

Amy never spoke a word about her mother and sister, but she didn't have to; I knew her thoughts as intimately as I knew my own. She barely spoke, never smiled, and I knew she blamed herself for what had happened. Had she never cursed Duncan, there would have been no trial. Twelve women had been burned to death. And in the weeks thereafter, three more women and their babies died in childbirth. Had Finwell been alive, it is likely they would have lived. And Amy knew it.

The curse that her mother had uttered was not forgotten. People were wary of everyone associated with the accused, but none more than Amy. She was yet a child, only twelve years old and small enough to pass for nine, but I saw people avoid her like a pox. I waited for the Privy Council to come and take her away for what she'd shouted at the execution, but it didn't happen, and Amy threw herself into practising her magic.

She was determined to bring her mother back.

One night, I saw her creep out over the fields. I followed her, careful to keep a distance. I wanted to see where she was going, yes, but above all I wanted to protect her.

I saw her move towards the bay, and my heart ached for her – she was going to the site of the executions.

I thought she might be going to pray where the stone was scorched, but as I drew near she was nowhere to be seen. The lip of the broch shone silver in the moonlight, the stones washed smooth by the ocean over centuries. I climbed over the smallest section of the ruin and looked around, and it was there that I saw the iron grate that led to where they'd held my mother. A dungeon deep in the earth.

I knelt down to inspect it, running my hand over the grate. I felt tears creeping to my eyes. My mother had been thrown down there and tortured into making a false confession. And if it wasn't bad enough that she was murdered, they'd ensured that she was forever remembered not for her goodness, but as a witch who had fornicated with Satan and cursed an elder to his death.

As I was looking, an outstretched hand reached up through the bars of the grate. I screamed and fell back, convinced it was a ghost, or a demon. But then I heard a voice.

'Patrick? Get down here!'

It was Amy's voice. Slowly, I crawled towards the grate and looked down. Her face was angled up at me, her eyes wide.

'I saw you following me,' she hissed. 'Come and see what I'm doing.'

For no other person, alive or dead, would I have removed the grate and entered that terrifying place, a place where only death and the horrors of hell lingered. But Amy was down there, and I was concerned for her wellbeing. Truth of the matter was, even at that young age, I was prepared to die with her, or for her – whichever came first.

What Amy showed me in the cave, the place that villagers were beginning to call Witches Hide, was carvings, elaborate runes etched into the rock.

'I recognize them,' Amy told me, excited. She ran her hands over the shapes, fingering the grooves. 'My mother did these while she was down here.'

I felt sick at the thought of it – twelve starving, tortured, and terrified women, my mother among them, clawing at the rock with their bare hands. But Amy knew something I didn't.

'Is it magic?' I asked her, and she nodded.

'The curse my mother shouted before she died. This is part of it.' She frowned. 'But I don't understand how to use it. Not yet, anyway.' She turned to me, her jaw set. 'But I will.'

LIV, 1998

I

After the child turned up at the bothy and ran out, I went looking for him. I searched the Longing, then walked up and down the bay with a torch, searching the caves and the road. I worried that he'd drowned in the sea or died of hypothermia. I couldn't stop thinking about his little cold hands and his terrified eyes. I felt responsible. I should have kept an eye on him, stopped him from running outside.

When I couldn't find him, I lifted the handset of the old rotary-dial telephone in the hallway of the bothy and rang the police to report a missing child.

'I'll be honest with you,' the officer said. 'That doesn't match the description of any children on the island.'

I held back from asking whether he personally knew every single child on the island. He probably did.

'We've had no calls from any parents, no missing persons reports filed. But we'll send a dispatch unit out to the bay within the hour. OK?'

'Will you let me know when he's returned home?'

'Of course.'

I'd waited by the phone. But they hadn't called to let me know they'd found him and he was all right.

I'd made three sketches until I was satisfied that I'd captured the child's likeness. I recalled that he had a heart-shaped face with a high forehead, fine, white-blonde strands of hair falling silkily down either side of his face. His eyes were large, the colour of the mareel, and there were deep shadows underneath, though I conceded this could have been an effect of the porch light. I had touched his arms, felt the goose bumps there from the cold. And I'd seen his feet, and his toenails – long and filthy, like he hadn't been cared for.

The morning after, I waited until midday until I went to the police station in person. Located inside a small shop in the village, close to Isla's café, the station was tiny. An officer at the front desk took my details and didn't seem to know anything about the call I'd made, or the child. He told me to take a seat on one of the plastic chairs while he located the sergeant.

'Detective Sergeant Kissick at your service,' a voice boomed. 'What can I do for you today?'

I stood and saw that DS Kissick was Bram, Isla's husband.

'Oh, hello again,' I said, but he met me with a cold, flat stare. I couldn't tell if he recognized me. 'I called yesterday to report a missing child,' I said. 'I was wondering if he'd been reunited with his family.'

Bram thumbed through a notebook on the front desk, then turned to the computer. 'I have a note of your call here,' he said, squinting at the screen. 'Nothing about a child being found. And no reports from any families on the island about a missing child.'

'No reports?' I said. Surely someone was missing their baby boy this morning? I'd envisaged a mother finding her son's bed empty this morning, her frantic calls to the police for help.

'This was the boy,' I said, spreading my sketch across the desk. He made a big show of digging a pair of spectacles from his shirt pocket and squinted crossly at the drawing.

'Don't recognize him. What was his name?'

'He didn't tell me his name.'

He raised his eyes to mine. 'Did he give details about his parents? His address?'

'He was so cold he could barely speak,' I said. 'He didn't appear to speak English, actually. He ran outside. I'm worried he might have hypothermia.'

Bram turned back to the notebook and tapped the page with a finger. 'You said he ran out. A child with hypothermia wouldn't be able to do that.'

'I meant that he might have developed hypothermia when he ran back outside,' I said.

'Well, as I said,' Bram said, with an infuriating smile, 'you're the only one to have seen this boy. Until we get a report from the parents there's nothing more can be done.'

'There's a hole in the ground floor of the Longing,' I said. 'Last time I checked, the grid had been opened. What if he's fallen down there?'

'The matter's closed,' he said, turning away from the desk and gesturing to a colleague. He wouldn't make eye contact.

'Can't you at least send a few officers down there to check?'

Bram turned his back on me and walked away. I gritted my teeth. I'm not normally an outspoken person, but this was too important, and I wasn't going to be ignored.

'I think I'll file a complaint,' I said loudly. 'I'm sure your boss would be pretty outraged to hear that you didn't act on a report about a missing child.'

He turned then, his eyes blazing. 'You think I'm going to send my officers down *that* cave?'

I stepped back, wiping my face. He was so angry he'd spat on me, and his choice of words – the emphasis on 'that' – was telling.

'You're a fucking detective!' I shouted back. 'I saw this child with my own eyes! It's your *job* to find him!'

Another two uniformed police officers entered the reception area. They stood behind Bram, eyeing me coldly. I could see they agreed with him, not me.

'I think I'll be the one to decide what my job involves,' Bram hissed. 'Now get out of my station before I have you arrested for disorderly conduct.'

II

I spent the rest of the day in a daze, completely confused. And furious.

At the Longing, Finn hadn't turned up to sort out the bats, and I couldn't paint the upper levels until he'd moved them. Right as I was thinking of finishing for the day, I heard a car pull up outside.

Isla came running across the rocks towards me, her face drawn.

'The child you saw,' she said when she caught her breath. 'Did he have a mark on him? A set of numbers on his skin?'

'Numbers?' I said, astonished by her appearance. She was electrified by fear, her eyes wide and her voice loud.

'Did he hurt you?' she said. 'Did he threaten you with anything?'

I reeled. '*Hurt* me?'

She drew a hand to her mouth, and I saw she was becoming upset.

'Isla, what's going on?'

'I was just so worried,' she said, gripping my arm. 'When

Bram told me what had happened I had to come straight to see you.'

'Has the boy been found?' I asked. 'Did the police find his parents?'

She shook her head. 'Come over to the café tonight at seven,' she said. 'There'll be a group of us. We need to make sure this is dealt with, and fast.'

'Make sure *what* is dealt with?'

'Trust me.'

She gave me a long look before turning to run back towards her car.

I went to Isla's café at seven, still baffled but determined to find out what was going on. Of all people, Isla would know who the boy was, and why he was roaming the bay on his own. She would know if he was safe.

The café windows were dark, the blinds down. I opened the door and called 'Hello?' before spotting a dozen candles flickering in the center of a circle of women, all sat cross-legged on cushions. It looked somewhere between a yoga class and a séance.

Isla appeared in front of me. She'd put on make-up and pinned up her hair, and I saw she was wearing a long black dress.

'Come in,' she said, a pleased glint in her eye. 'Lock the door behind you.'

I saw that the women in the circle were all the women I'd swam in the mareel with – Ailsa, Ruqayya, Louisa, Greer, Mirrin and Ling. Niamh was there as well, a great-grandmother who I'd often spotted walking her sheepdog, Ginger, along the bay. She ran a croft just outside the village and was related to Isla. The room was charged with anticipation, as though we were celebrating something. The child, I thought – maybe the boy had been found.

'Have a seat,' Isla told me. There was an empty seat cushion on the floor between Louisa and Ling. I sat down, and Ling reached out and gently took my hand.

'I can imagine this all looks very strange,' Isla said. 'Perhaps this will help us all feel a little more . . . at ease.' She picked up a tray from a nearby table. Balanced on it were three bottles of wine, and nine glasses.

Isla poured each of us a glass and held it up in a toast. 'To protecting the ones we love,' she said.

We toasted, and I drank.

'I've told the ladies about the child you saw,' Isla said, turning to me. 'We're all persuaded that this isn't a child from the island. Not a *human* child, at any rate.'

I looked from Isla to Ling, who sat next to me. Had I heard her right? 'I don't follow.'

'We've each of us studied the sketch you provided of the little boy,' Greer said gently. 'And he's definitely not one of the children from the island.'

'Perhaps he's a tourist,' I said. 'He didn't speak English. There could be a family staying on the island. Or perhaps they sailed here.'

'I've already asked,' Ruqayya said. 'My neighbour Allie works at the tourist office. Nobody has reported a missing child. Not for years, now.'

It didn't make sense. I had seen him, *touched* him. He'd been inside my home.

'Remember I told you about the history of this place?' Isla said. 'About the witches who were burned near the Longing?'

I turned to her. 'Yes?'

'I told you about how the witches put a curse on the island,' she said, tilting her head. 'This child you saw – we believe he's part of that curse.'

A finger of ice crept up my spine. I'd read the situation wrong: this wasn't about helping find a little boy who was lost. They were pulling back the curtain on a world I didn't know, a world of whispers and fear, inviting me in.

I set down my drink, my mind racing. 'You remember I told you my brother went missing?' Isla said. 'Right before he disappeared, my mother had an encounter exactly like yours. She heard something at the door, and when she opened it, she found a little boy looking up at her. She assumed he was lost, and she said she noticed he looked like he'd had a fall, for he was covered in dirt. She said she tried to bring him inside, but as soon as she turned around again the child was gone. Not a week later, my brother went missing.'

I looked around at the women in the room. Did they all believe in this?

'What are you saying?' I asked.

'I told you my brother went missing,' Isla said. 'But that wasn't the whole truth. What actually happened was, he went missing, but another boy was found a year later. A child who looked exactly like my brother.'

'*Not* a child,' Ruqayya added. 'A wildling. One of the fae in human form.'

'One of the fae,' I repeated, confirming I'd heard her correctly.

'Remember, I told you about the curse,' Isla said.

I gave a nervous laugh. 'You can't reasonably expect me to believe . . .'

'My mother didn't believe it either,' Isla cut in, undeterred. 'She'd been born and raised here on the island so she'd heard the tales of wildlings, and she knew what to do if she saw one. And then, when a boy appeared, in every way similar to my brother save the mark on his neck of a set of numbers, she couldn't believe it.'

I was confused. They'd found her brother. So what if he had a mark on his neck? 'OK. So what did your mother do?'

'It wasn't just the mark,' Isla said. 'They knew he was different. A parent knows their own child, right? My father told her that she *knew* in her heart of hearts that the boy wasn't Jamie. He had the mark. Beneath the disguise of blood, bone, and flesh, he was faery in disguise, sent to kill every member of our family until the bloodline was destroyed.'

I'd heard enough. I made to get up, but Ling squeezed my hand. 'What until you hear what happened,' she said, a little forceful.

'My mother hesitated,' Isla said, continuing the story. 'Like any decent woman, the thought of killing a child, or what she believed to be a child, her own son, was a brutality of which she wasn't capable. But not twenty-four hours later, Lòn Haven had its worst storm in living memory. Boats sank at the port, and several homes were underwater. There were deaths. My grandfather . . .' There was a catch in her voice, and she took a moment to recover. 'My grandfather's car got pulled into the sea. He was inside it. He drowned.'

'I'm so sorry,' I said, and I was. To have lost her brother and grandfather . . . I knew intimately how devastating it was to lose someone you love, how your entire life can change – or end – in the blink of an eye. But still. What did they mean by wildlings destroying bloodlines?

'The fae have all kinds of powers,' Greer explained. 'In human form, they have fae *and* human power. They can get close to folk. Their curses are more potent.'

'Perhaps this might offer another example of how wildlings have driven scourges on these isles,' Niamh said, producing a long tube of something and unrolling it in the center of the group. 'Seeing how you're an artist, I thought you'd appreciate this.'

I watched as she delicately opened an old scroll, about six feet in length. The lights were low, but I could make out that the paper was brittle with age, the edges rough and the ink faded. The scroll seemed to be a story, or a medieval kind of comic strip, with scenes and close-ups of people, animals, and trees. I made out a drawing of a house on fire, another of what seemed to be a haystack but turned out to be an enormous pile of bodies.

'What is this?' I said.

Mirrin pointed at one of the close-ups. A demonic face, with pointed teeth, crescent moon eyes, and horns, the mouth open in a cruel laugh.

'The fae are as old as the hills,' she said. 'This scroll belonged to my great-grandfather. All of us have been disbelieving, at some point, but it's hard to argue with history. The witches that were burned here cursed the island to have wildlings. Whole islands have been left without a single man, woman, or child due to these creatures. Scotland has just shy of eight hundred islands. At one point in history, all of them were inhabited. And then the wildlings came. You know how many of those islands are without a single human on their shores?'

I shook my head. 'I've no idea.'

'More than seven hundred.'

'You've heard of shape-shifting?' Ruqayya asked. 'Metamorphosis?'

'Yes, but . . .'

'In Greek myth,' Louisa said, 'Zeus turns himself into a shower of gold, a cloud, a swan. In Norse folklore, Loki shape-shifts into anything and anyone, even giving birth a few times when he shape-shifts as a female. The Navajo know very well about skin-walkers, and the Irish have their púca, or Puck, as Shakespeare called it. And we have our own shape-shifters in the form of faeries, pixies, and goblins, to name just a few.'

'But those are myths,' I said. 'They're not *real*.' I looked at the scroll, astonished that they thought it was going to convince me. I didn't care how old it was – were they really treating it like a serious historical record, this series of horrific portraits?

'Stories, yes, but very real indeed,' Ling added, resting a hand on my shoulder. 'People have told stories about the natural world since the beginning of time. For hundreds of years, nature held dominion over humans. It was truly *wild*. We've spent centuries creating stories about our place in that wildness. You know how much of the world's land remains wild right now?'

I shook my head.

'*Five* percent,' she said. 'That's a huge human impact. And look at our stewardship. We're destroying it.'

'I agree with you,' I said, treading carefully. 'But that has *nothing* to do with this child . . .'

'Liv, I implore you to put aside what you think you know and listen to those of us who have suffered,' Mirrin shouted then, throwing her hands up. The room fell silent, and Mirrin fixed me with an emotional stare, her eyes wide and glassy with tears. She lifted a hand and pressed it to her chest. 'I lived on an island called Mulltraive,' she said, her voice trembling. 'I had four brothers and three sisters. My parents ran a farm. My mother found a child wandering along the riverbank, a wee boy. My mother took him in and set about finding his parents. I remember my brother Ian forcing us all to play with the child. Said he'd want to make sure the wee boy didn't feel too scared while his parents were found. Not long after, I went to visit my aunt Shauneen in Fort William. By the time I returned to the island, my family was dead.' She hung her head, overcome with emotion. 'All my brothers. All my sisters. Both my parents. And not a month later, we had floods. Hundreds of livestock killed, twenty crofts underwater. Crops destroyed. It took a government intervention to keep the community from starving. But no one ever claimed that boy. And he was never seen again.'

I was reeling from what she told me. From the connections they were all drawing between terrible, gruesome events, and innocent children. 'I'm sorry for you, and for your family,' I said carefully. 'And I'm sorry about your brother,' I said, turning to Isla. 'But . . . the risk you run in telling such stories is that you persuade people to do terrible things.'

'There is a way to distinguish between perfectly innocent children and the wildlings who mimic them,' Ruqayya said. She moved forward, on to her hands and knees, staring down at the scroll. 'There,' she said, pointing at an image of numbers. 'A red mark, a burn, with scratches in it. If you look closely enough you'll see they're numbers. Always numbers.'

I looked at where she pointed. There was a large set of numbers drawn in a row.

217

'My mother wouldn't hurt a fly,' Isla said. 'But the mark she found on the wildling was undeniable. It had four numbers, just like the curse said. The wildling cried for her, and her heart was broken, but she went through with it. She dragged that *thing* to the burning trees up by the Brae and did what was needed. She never spoke of it until many years later, and only then it was to warn me. She took no pleasure in what she did. But she'd had to bury my grandfather because she'd hesitated. And the day after, the storms stopped.'

My stomach dropped as I realized what she'd said. Isla was telling me that her mother murdered her little brother. And if that wasn't bad enough, Isla believed what she did was *right*.

Carefully, I set down my glass and stood up, measuring my words carefully. 'Ladies, I appreciate you telling me all this. But really, there is no need. If I see the boy again, I'll call the police.'

They all looked up at me from their circle as I stood to leave. I didn't want to offend them. I didn't want to lose their friendship. But I could take none of it seriously, and I needed to process what Isla had revealed to me.

As I went to walk out, I felt someone grab my hand. It was Isla.

'You should consider leaving the island,' she said, her eyes stern and her grip hard. 'There might still be time.'

I pulled my hand away and forced a smile on my face. 'Oh, I bet we'll be fine,' I said, and walked quickly out of the door.

III

I don't think I've ever felt as alone as I did that night.

Once the girls had gone to bed, I sat in the armchair of the living room in the bothy, looking out the window at the moon streaking the back of the sea with a white stripe of light. I had spent some nights here feeling increasingly at home, soothed by the waves and the vast spread of the horizon. But now, I felt sick to my stomach. The thought of Isla's mother murdering her little brother played over and over in my head. A helpless little boy, his life taken in the most brutal way because of some ridiculous superstition. No justice for him. And the superstition persisted, even now, in 1998. It made me so angry.

No call had come from the police about the missing child, and I felt worried. I had made a nuisance of myself, calling again and again and pressing each officer who answered about whether there had been a report of a missing child from the parents. No, they said. No one had reported a missing child.

The boy was still out there. And the women I so admired,

my new group of friends . . . they'd suggested that the boy I'd seen and comforted wasn't human. That he was some kind of creature, a fae. And that if I saw him again, I was to kill him.

I tried to put aside my disgust at Isla's story to imagine how a history like the one experienced by the community of Lòn Haven might filter down to the present day. Everyone believed in one false narrative or another, I reasoned. I remembered my mother telling me that for every child that was born, someone close to them had to die. I remembered that every time someone died, I linked it to someone who was pregnant, or who had given birth, and the narrative began to make sense to me. Even when Saffy was born I started calling my grandparents more often, worried that her birth would cause one of them to die. And when my grandfather *did* die a year later, I told myself it was related to Saffy's birth. That he'd just clung on a little longer.

Such bullshit.

A wild place with a Viking soul, Lòn Haven's violent and tragic history had clearly infected the minds of its inhabitants, creating beliefs rooted deeply in fear. And they were prepared to slaughter innocent children in order to protect their community.

I couldn't get past what Isla had told me. I was fast learning that Lòn Haven was an island of two halves.

I was just about to go to bed when I spotted something outside, moving towards the Longing. A figure. The boy.

This time, I didn't hesitate. I raced outside and ran after him, slipping on the rocks, my voice carried off by the wind. I pulled open the door of the Longing and went inside, shouting 'Hello! Hello!'

My own voice answered, echoing again and again as it

spiralled up the walls of the building. Then I took to the stairs, moving quickly to the lantern room. If he was there, I'd find him, and bring him home.

He wasn't there. I looked down at the bones on the floor. Angrily, I scooped them up and threw them out the window.

Whatever secrets the community of Lòn Haven was hiding were long past being brought to light, and I swore then that I'd no longer stand for anything based on fear or hearsay. No matter how much it terrified me, or left me friendless.

IV

I was desperate to make sense of what Isla and the others had told me that night at the café. About the history of Lòn Haven, about the curse the witches had placed on the island. About wildlings.

I'd heard about a memorial to the witches who had been killed at the Longing. It was a plaque inside the auld kirk, or old church, in the south of the island.

I drove there the next morning. The church building was small and plain, the stonework blackened over the years and the graveyard filled with indecipherable tombstones that lay wonky and haphazard amongst mossy lawn, their script smoothed away by time. An old clock at the apex of the church had stopped. A Latin verse was carved into the stone around it: *Maleficos non patieris vivere*. Later, I'd discover its English translation:

> *You shall not suffer a witch to live.*

It was dark inside. Stained-glass panels depicted scenes

of Christ's life along the east wall. The pews were empty, and I noticed some shrines set up along the sides, paintings of angels on wooden boards shimmering in the faint light of candles. At one of the shrines, a small black and white photograph of a child was propped up against the wooden board. A little boy, his hand held up as though he was waving. I squinted at it. Who was he?

'Can I be of any help to you?'

I looked up and saw a man in a long black robe and a white collar standing there. The pastor. 'I was just . . . I was wondering about the memorial to the women who were burned during the witch hunts,' I said awkwardly.

He raised his eyebrows. 'I've heard about some work being done there recently,' he said. 'Are you the painter?'

I nodded. 'Yes.'

'Come this way.'

I followed him to the back of the church which was laid out as a cross, with three sections set up as shrines. I supposed one of them to be set up to commemorate the women, but he walked past them to the far wall, stopping at a small rock sticking up out of the ground. He knelt by it and blew some dust off one of the faces.

'This is it?' I said. Surely he was wrong?

He nodded. 'If you look closely, you can see the dates of the burnings.'

I knelt down and looked harder. It was faint, but I could make out a year, etched in old script. *1662.*

'You were expecting something more, I take it?'

I nodded. 'How do you even know this is the memorial to the witches?'

'It's in the parish history books,' he said. 'I can tell you their names, if you like?'

I straightened. 'I'd love that.'

He took me to a small reading room installed in a modern extension at the back of the church. On a microfiche viewer, he toggled the magnifier until an old, hand-written document came into view. *The Lighthouse Witches*. And beneath it, the names of twelve women.

1662

Elspeth Alexander	*Jean Anderson*
Margaret Barclay	*Helen Beatie*
Catherine Campbell	*Margaret Fulton*
Finwell Hyndman	*Jonet Hyndman*
Marie Lamont	*Agnes Naismith*
Agnes Roberts	*Jane Wishart*

'Is there information on why they were accused of witchcraft?' I asked.

He shook his head. 'To be honest, the fact that we know the names of these women is considered substantial, given the dearth of information about the witch hunts. You might find the name of the commissioner and perhaps the method by which they were put to death if you go to the National Library, but it would take some digging around.'

I nodded. 'Thank you.'

I think it was the fact that there was so little information about, and such a sorry memorial for these women that I wrote down the names on a scrap of paper, clutching it tightly as I walked out of there.

That afternoon at the Longing, I asked Finn about the wildling myth, and the boy I'd seen.

He straightened and gave a stretch, having spent half an

hour on his hands and knees to finish plastering a lower section of the Longing. 'Maybe you saw a ghost.'

'A *ghost*?'

He cocked an eyebrow. 'Aye. Lòn Haven has a bit of a track record of folk vanishing into the ether.'

'Don't tell me you believe in ghosts, Finn.'

'Ghosts, not exactly. Traces, yeah. Sort of.'

'Traces?'

'Here's my theory. Everything is energy. We all leave something behind. Now, there's folk who'll swear on their granny's last breath that they've seen a ghost. And I reckon some of them *have*. Or rather, they've seen traces of a past energy.'

My face was screwed up, because after that night at Isla's café I was way past tolerating nonsense. And when I got back from the church, I found I'd started spotting again. I was tired of the bullshit.

But Finn was talking with his hands now, trying to make some sense. 'We think that time moves forward, in a linear fashion. Yeah? But sometimes you get déjà vu, or there's some mad coincidence that you can't explain. I think time *doesn't* move in a linear fashion, but in a spiral, and sometimes there's echoes from the past. And a ghost is just an echo of someone.'

'And why would I see such an echo?'

He shrugged. 'Now *that*, I've got no clue about. Maybe he was trying to tell you something.'

'He wasn't a ghost, Finn. I touched him. He was a little boy.'

He lifted another wedge of plaster and dabbed it on the stone. 'I've experienced odd things in my time. Stuff I couldn't explain. I'll tell you one coincidence that's never left me.'

I sighed. 'Go on.'

'Well, when Cassie was ill, and the doctors said they couldn't do anything more for her, I got a call out of the blue from an old friend of my father's. He needed me to do a bit of plastering for him. And even though I had to be around for Cassie, I said aye, I'll do the job. It made no sense. The job was on Skye. I'd have to leave Cassie for three whole days. But I had this feeling in my gut that I *needed* to do this job.' He looked up at me. 'I felt guilty the whole time I was there. The man just wanted his downstairs loo redone and knew I'd give him mates' rates. I thought, what am I doing? I'm miles away from my wee girl while she's knocking on Death's door, and all because this guy wants to save a few pennies on a toilet.'

'And what happened?' I asked, wondering where the story was going.

'So I'm packing up, about to leave, and he asks about Cassie. I tell him she's got leukaemia. Doctors have washed their hands of her. The guy makes a call to someone. Next thing I know I'm on the phone to a doctor in Los Angeles who says he can help.'

'And he was the one who saved her life?'

He nodded and dabbed his forehead with a rag. 'Now, I'm not a religious guy, but that wasnae a coincidence.'

'Intuition, maybe?' I said.

'More than that,' he said firmly. 'When I said I had a gut feeling about it, it was . . . like something kept badgering me. In the end I only gave in to make it stop. And once I was on my way to Skye, I felt like . . . something left. The *thing* that had been bugging me wasn't there any more. Like it had done its job.'

He said this self-consciously, earnestly, and I bit my

tongue. He was talking about his daughter, and how her life was saved. I thought about my mother's false narrative. *For every birth, a death.* We form stories about our lives to create meaning out of them – without meaning, they feel shapeless, and without purpose. When something lies beyond the realm of meaning, it's terrifying.

'But surely the police don't believe in that?' I said. I'd told him about my visit to the police station and how Bram dismissed me. 'They have a duty to investigate a reported missing child, surely.'

Finn's face darkened. 'Ah well, that's a whole other level of batshit crazy, that is.'

'What is?'

He stepped closer, wary of his words carrying to other ears. 'The problem with an island like this is that everyone knows everyone else. And that causes problems when, say, the Chief Inspector is married to someone who *does* believe in wildlings.'

I frowned. 'But surely his wife's belief systems don't override his professional obligations.'

'Ah, *now* you sound like a townie,' he said ruefully. 'Did you know we're the only island in the small isles to have our own police department?'

I shook my head, unsure of his meaning.

'Bram was stationed in Inverness, apparently made a big fuss until he got stationed out here and made Chief Inspector. And you know all Isla's crew are shamans and witches and what have you?'

'And?'

'Professional obligation is one thing. But when you have a small community, especially one that's cut off from every-where else, you have another set of obligations. And I'm telling you now, law and order works differently when everyone's related to each other. And speaking of Isla . . .'

I wondered whether I should tell him what Isla had revealed about her brother. 'What about her?'

He pulled a face. 'You must have worked out for yourself what Isla's about.'

'Which is?'

'Self-appointed queen of the island. Knows everything about everyone, stretching back centuries. I'm not kidding. It's the only reason she runs the café, and her cleaning business. Has to keep tabs on everything. Knowledge is power, as they say.'

'Plenty of people are nosy,' I said carefully. 'Is that the only thing she's about?'

He grabbed a cloth from the wallpaper table and wiped his trowel. 'She's a shite stirrer.'

I looked up. 'What?'

'Whatever info she has on folk, she uses for her own agenda.'

'You mean, she spreads lies?' This made sense. I hoped that the story of her brother wasn't true. Just a lie she'd told to scare me.

'More like, she suppresses information,' Finn said. 'There's an unofficial wildling committee on the island. Did you know that?'

'Shut up,' I said, aghast.

He chuckled. 'Serious. Not kidding. I'm pretty sure Isla is the Chairperson, or Vice-Chairperson of said Committee. What I do know is that over the last ten years, there have been sightings of at least two wildlings.' He pointed his trowel at me. 'And you'll know by now what you're meant to do to a wildling.'

I took a deep breath. 'If I tell you something, you promise not to tell anyone?'

He nodded. 'I promise.'

'Isla said her mother killed her baby brother. That he turned up a year after he went missing and her parents believed he was a wildling. So they killed him.'

'Fucking hell.' He stared, appalled. 'That's a new one.'

'You didn't hear about it?'

He shook his head grimly. 'I'm not part of the insider group when it comes to those things. My family never got involved with that stuff. And I've lived here long enough to avoid it being too much of an issue.'

He filled his bucket with fresh water from a barrel and scrubbed it out. 'There's this guy I worked with, Malcolm – he was having an affair. Not an easy thing to do in a place like this. Definitely not a smart move, either. He swore he saw Isla and her crew taking a child to the woods. Says he heard screaming.' He lifted his eyes to mine in a meaningful glance, and I pressed a hand to my mouth, horrified. I wanted so badly to believe that Isla would never do that. Maybe she believed her mother was right, but to think she was capable of doing the same thing . . .

'What happened?' I asked.

'Malc went to the police about it. Next thing, Isla's on his doorstep, all friendly neighbour, your average smiling assassin. Basically she told him if he wasn't careful, his wife would hear all about his affair.'

I wondered what would happen if the boy I'd seen turned up. Would she kill him, too?

'Anyway, that's me done now,' Finn said after a while, stretching his arms.

'I think I'm done for the day, too,' I said, winding up the cable for the cherry picker. 'You here again tomorrow?'

'No. I mean, the job's done.' He grinned, then looked over the place. 'All the plasterwork, *finito*. Looks good, doesn't it?'

I stepped off the platform and hit the 'off' switch. 'You're finished?'

I couldn't conceal how sad I was about this. I'd grown to enjoy Finn's company, even look forward to it, and I felt he enjoyed mine. I watched him pack up his gear, floundering for a way to maintain a connection. It seemed wrong, somehow, that this should be the end of us spending time together.

'Actually, how about you and Cassie come over for a celebratory dinner?'

He closed the lid on his toolbox and lifted it by the handle. 'Celebratory? What exactly is it that we're celebrating?'

I felt myself blush. Maybe I'd read our dynamic wrong. Maybe I was forcing a friendship that didn't exist. 'Well, you're done, I'm almost done . . . and we've been to your house so often it's only fair that we have you round to ours.' It struck me that the bothy we were staying in *had* been his house, and I faltered. 'I mean, unless it's too uncomfortable . . .'

He threw me a reassuring grin. 'I would be delighted. And I know Cassie would as well.'

V

They came over the following evening, Cassie in a green velvet dress and Finn in a shirt and a tartan waistcoat with a thistle brooch, his beard oiled and his hair slicked back. It felt good to do something normal, to distract myself from the thick web of myth and murder that I seemed to have fallen into.

'Look at you, all spiffed up,' he said. He'd only ever seen me in a paint-splattered boiler suit, or in sopping wet jeans covered in kelp, but I'd found a pretty floral dress amongst Saffy's things and borrowed it for the occasion. I'd also borrowed her lipstick and some mascara, and blow-dried my hair.

'You look pretty,' Cassie said.

'Thank you,' I said. 'And look at you in your lovely dress.'

She gave a little twirl. 'I can almost put my hair in a ponytail now. See?'

She pulled a blonde strand out to the side.

'It's beautiful,' I told her, and she bounced off to find Luna and Clover.

231

Finn handed me a bottle of wine and a bouquet of pink flowers wrapped in brown paper.

'These are machair orchids,' he told me. 'I grow them on my land. They're native to the western isles, where my mother was born. They're fragile as soap bubbles, these things. I grow them in a greenhouse.'

I rinsed out an empty milk bottle and arranged the orchids inside. 'They're beautiful. Thank you.'

He glanced around the bothy. 'You've made this place very homely, haven't you?'

'Thank you,' I said. 'Did you . . . live here in the bothy?'

'No, but my grandfather did.' He nodded at the old armchair by the fire. 'That's his chair.'

He glanced at the book of Scottish fairy tales on the side table and I wondered if I should ask him about the old sketchpad I'd found amongst its pages, with its drawings of runes.

'Can we play in the Longing?' Clover ran in and was bouncing on the balls of her feet.

'No, sweetheart,' I said. 'It's too dangerous for you girls.'

'Outside on the rocks, then?'

'You can play in your bedroom until dinner's on the table, OK?'

She rolled her eyes and slouched off. I turned back to Finn, who'd picked up the book of fairy tales. 'Swotting up on your folklore, I see.'

'The girls did a project at school and wanted to know more about selkies and such like. And I was trying to work out how to make the mural for the Longing a little less . . .'

'Weird?' he offered.

'Well, yes. But I was trying to figure out what all the

drawings meant. I asked around in case they were from Scottish folklore but nobody appears to recognize them.'

'If I know Patrick Roberts, it'll either be some kind of corporate logo or a Satanic symbol.'

'Is there a difference?'

He grinned. 'Touché.'

'You don't like him very much, do you?'

'Oh, you picked that up, did you? I thought I'd done a fine job of hiding it.'

'Why don't you like him?'

He screwed up his face. 'It's nothing personal. He's just a bit of a bawbag.'

In the kitchen, I set about opening the bottle of wine and poured us both a short glass each.

'Smells nice,' he said, nodding at the oven, taking a glass from me. 'I'm surprised it works. Patrick didn't exactly bother to upgrade the amenities in the place, did he?'

'I suppose he doesn't live here, so why bother?'

Finn grimaced. 'I think it's fair to assume that he holds that attitude for everything he buys.'

'What do you mean?'

He sipped at his wine. 'Well, just look at the Longing. Doesnae even fix the place up. Hires you to paint some weird graffiti on it. He owns most of the island. Did you know that?'

'Most of Lòn Haven? Isla said he owned some properties . . .'

'About twelve houses, I believe. Also land. Twelve thousand acres, and counting.'

'What on earth does he need all that land for?' I asked.

'That's what me and the team have been asking ourselves for months, now.'

'"Team"?' I said, folding my arms.

'Aye, it's just a side project,' he said. 'Me and a few of the boys from the village got together a few years ago, decided we'd like to rewild a bit of the island. Replant some native trees, that kind of thing.'

'Is this another "on-the-side" job?' I said with a wink.

He smiled. 'Aye. Something like that.'

He told me that the ancient forests that once spread across the island and the rest of Scotland had been wiped out by timber companies, and that many plant and animal species had been obliterated as a result. 'So it's not just about the trees,' he said. 'Though it's no secret I'm quite a fan of them.'

'I don't think anyone can be neutral about trees, can they?' I said.

'Aye, you'd think that was the case, given how they provide, oh, oxygen, wood, paper, and a few other things. But folk like Patrick Roberts aren't so keen. One of the first things he did when he bought Haven Forest was raze half of it to the ground and sell the timber to a merchant.'

'I bet the islanders had a thing or two to say about that.'

'Yup, they did. But it made him money. The fella has more money than all the rest of us put together.'

'Is that why he keeps buying so much land? To sell it off for profit?'

Finn shut the kitchen door quietly, then stepped closer to me. 'The archaeologists are all but digging the whole place up. They're always rooting about the place, finding Neolithic tools and bracelets and what-have-you.'

He'd lost me at this point. 'And . . . what has that to do with Patrick buying the land?'

'Ach, it's just a theory.'

'Which is?'

He stroked his beard. 'Well, with kids going missing and all that . . . Some folk say that archaeologists are going to dig up murdered bodies. And that's why Patrick's buying so much land. To control where they dig.'

I followed his train of thought. 'So he doesn't get caught for murder?'

He turned to me, the answer written all over his face. I recalled what Isla had said. *He's an odd one, that Roberts. I work for him to keep an eye on him.*

I said, 'But if everyone thinks he's a murderer, how come he hasn't been picked up by the police?'

'Well, Bram's head of police,' he said. 'And who is Bram married to?'

'Isla,' I said. But Isla had told me she found Patrick to be odd. What could her motive be for keeping an investigation away from him?

'Anyway, enough conspiratorial talk,' he said suddenly, waving a hand in the air to disperse our speculations. 'How's about I propose a toast?'

'To?' I said, lifting my empty glass.

'You, Ms Olivia Stay.' He raised his glass. 'For all the work you've put into making the Longing a little less crap.'

I laughed. 'Cheers.'

The timer on the oven buzzed. I set down my glass to retrieve the quiche I'd made. I could never cook very well, but quiche I could do, having learned at art school that eggs tended to be heavily marked down at supermarkets close to student digs because no student could be bothered with the faff. We called the girls to the dining table and I lit a candle.

'One minor detail,' Finn said, biting his lip. 'I'm allergic to eggs. Sorry.'

I looked from the quiche – which had turned out beautifully – to him, and then both of us burst out laughing.

'Shit. I should have checked.'

'I *love* eggs,' Cassie piped up. 'I'll have Daddy's portion.'

I stood and rummaged through the cupboards. I'd avoided the supermarket in Strallaig so thoroughly since that weird night at Isla's café that all I had in was a half-packet of crackers and a can of baked beans.

'Can I interest you in . . . six crackers and some baked beans?'

'Yum,' Finn said, holding up his plate. 'Get in my belly.'

Despite its rocky start, the evening was relaxed and fun, with the three girls chatting and laughing and Finn joining in with their banter. Saffy's absence both relieved and concerned me. She was free to go as she pleased so long as she adhered to a curfew and let me know where she was, but since we'd arrived she'd abandoned the second part of that rule, and my nagging hadn't seemed to have achieved much. When Cassie started to wane, I saw Finn become anxious to get her to her bed, so I suggested to the girls that we say goodbye. Nobody wanted to.

'We can do this again,' I said.

'When?' Clover insisted. 'Tomorrow?'

I laughed. 'We'll see.'

Finn scooped Cassie up and carried her to the car parked by the road at the end of the causeway. I told Luna and Clover to stay indoors while I carried Cassie's shoes, which she'd taken off in the bedroom.

'Thanks for a lovely night,' Finn said, closing the passenger door and straightening before me.

'You're welcome,' I said, and then neither of us said anything, because it seemed that something had grown between us over dinner. Perhaps it was just friendship, I told myself. We'd certainly grown closer. Friends did that. But as he took a step closer, kissing my cheek softly, I realized it was something more.

I felt immediately guilty. I hadn't told him yet that I was ill. I knew that, like me, he was ferociously cautious about romantic relationships. But Finn was standing in front of me, so close our noses almost touched, a look in his eyes that seemed to say everything I was thinking and feeling inside. And then, a bang on the car window.

'Kiss her, Dad! Kiss her!' Cassie screamed.

Both of us laughed and took a step back.

'Aye, thanks for that, Cass,' he said, embarrassed.

'Thank you for coming,' I said, smiling. 'Maybe we can spend some time together. As friends.'

If it's possible to describe the look he gave me in the half-second before he answered, I'd say he looked a little crushed, and instantly I knew I'd said the wrong thing.

'I mean . . .'

'Yes,' he said, rallying. 'Actually, maybe I could show you the rewilding project.'

I told him I'd love to, and we made plans to see each other a couple of days later, with the girls of course.

He drove us all in his truck to the plain that he was rewilding with his 'team', which turned out to be his friend, Willy, who had fitted the windows in the Longing, another man, Kirwin, who worked at the ferry port, and Finn's brother, Leo, who was an older, rounder version of Finn. He lived with his wife and three kids on the south side. The trees were little more than saplings, but haste wasn't the objective, Finn said. 'In fact, haste is the enemy,' he told the girls, who all mouthed 'Haste?' at each other. 'A project as important as this one demands considered planning and patience.'

'And plenty of trips to the pub,' Leo added.

'Speaking of which,' Finn said, 'shall we adjourn to the island's one and only pub? They serve fabulous chicken nuggets.'

VI

He took us through the mountains to the west side of the island, where the ferry port was. The west side was noticeably more populated than the east, with white-washed croft houses dotting the landscape. The beaches were like the Bahamas in appearance, with a bow of pristine white sand and turquoise blue water, green cliffs on either side.

'You'll sharp know you're in Scotland and not the Bahamas when you swim in it,' Finn said. We parked up and I stepped outside to take in the scene, wishing I'd brought a sketchpad to paint it. It had been a long, long time since I'd seen a view quite as incredible, and I felt moved by it. I wanted to absorb it, be in it. The girls all ran off to paddle, and before I knew what was happening Finn had cupped my face in his hands and was kissing me, a sensation at once startling and welcome, the closeness of him so natural that all the fear I'd had about men and love and relationships managed to subside, just for that moment.

'Can I come over tonight?' he said in a low voice when

I pulled away. Then, when I flinched. 'I'm not suggesting . . . I mean, just to spend time. I'm not wanting to rush anything . . .'

'I was just wondering whether you meant you had a babysitter,' I said.

'Well, that there's a bit of a conundrum,' he said. 'Seeing as we're each other's babysitters, in effect.'

'Bring Cassie. She fits right in with Luna and Clover.'

He kissed me again, and this time the girls caught sight of us from the shoreline and laughed, pointing and making 'wooo' noises.

'Nothing like pre-adolescent girls to keep you humble,' Finn said.

Later, once Finn had dropped us off to allow Cassie time for a nap at home before dinner, I stood in front of the small mirror in the bathroom of the bothy. I had started bleeding again. The cramping had started in my lower back and deep in my pelvis. It wasn't my period. I knew this wasn't going away. No matter how much I tried to run from it, or deny it, this illness was here, inside my body. Stitched into my DNA.

I needed to see a doctor. I needed to be upfront with Finn, and with my daughters.

After all, they were at risk of inheriting it, too.

I was wearing another of Saffy's dresses and a touch of red lipstick. I looked nice. I even liked my hair. I felt like I had been in hiding for years, and now, for the first time, I felt I was coming out of the cave. Right as my time was running out.

The doorbell rang. I took a breath, tried to position the words on my lips, and opened the door.

But the man who stood there wasn't Finn. He was young, late twenties at a push, a black beanie tugged down over black hair to his jaw and a hoodie worn under a denim jacket.

He did a double take when he saw me, so much so that I wondered if we knew each other.

'Patrick,' he said, expectantly. 'I'm Patrick Roberts.'

VII

'Patrick Roberts?' I said, uncertain if I'd heard correctly. This . . . was Patrick Roberts? *The* Patrick Roberts?

'Yes,' he said. 'You're Liv? The artist?'

'I am,' I said, clearing my throat. I hesitated, expecting him to say he was the son of the owner of the Longing. But he didn't. He *was* the owner. I held out a hand. 'We finally meet.'

He was slender with searching eyes and a soft voice, barely more than a whisper. I looked him over, taking in the tatty black jeans and Adidas trainers, trying to reconcile the image I'd carried in my mind of this man with the one in front of me. I'd always pictured an older man, the kind who wore a tie and played golf, who talked too loudly and maybe drank too much. This was a . . . boy. A gentle, slightly awkward, rakish twenty-something, with a whiff of nerves and body odour. A Keanu Reeves circa *Bill & Ted* kind of boy.

He spent a moment wiping his feet on the doormat – laughable, really, given how old and worn the carpet was

– before stepping inside. His eyes fell on the dining table, set for six – my girls and I, as well as Finn and Cassie.

'I'm not disturbing you, am I?' he said.

'Not at all,' I said, lying. The fact that Finn and I had just been talking about him made me self-conscious, as if our words lingered in the air, incriminating us. I scanned the road outside nervously. It occurred to me, a moment too late, that if Finn arrived to find Mr Roberts here it would be an awkward start to the evening.

'I'm sorry I wasn't here when you arrived,' Patrick said, glancing around. 'Did Isla tell you I was on a sailing trip?'

'She did,' I said. 'Shetland, I think she said.'

He nodded. 'You've settled in OK?'

'Yes, thank you.'

His eyes fell on a pair of Clover's knickers, which she'd inexplicably left on the armrest of the sofa, and he gave a nervous laugh.

'My daughters are with me,' I said as an apology.

'Sapphire, Luna, and Clover,' he repeated with a smile. 'Isla told me. Are they here? I'd love to meet them.'

Just then, Clover came into the living room, dressed in nothing more than a swimming costume, a pair of goggles strapped to her forehead.

'Hello,' she said, looking up at him. 'Who are you?'

'I'm . . . Patrick,' he said. I could tell he wasn't used to kids. 'How are you?'

'Why are you wearing a swimming costume, Clover?' I asked.

She toggled the goggles over her eyes. 'Just to look fabulous.'

Patrick grinned. 'I like your style,' he told her.

'Thanks,' she said primly. Then: 'I like your shoes.'

243

He looked down at his shoes and smiled. 'Oh. Thanks.'

'Who is this?' another voice said. Luna, studying Patrick with a serious expression.

'This is Patrick Roberts,' I told her. 'He owns the Longing.'

She looked him up and down. 'You own the Longing?'

He grinned, still nervous. 'Uh, yes. I bought it last year.'

'Why did you buy it?' Luna persisted. 'It doesn't work, you know.'

He ran a hand through his dark hair. 'I know . . .'

'You have the same name as Saffy's book.'

'Do I?'

'The one with Icelandic words in it,' she said. 'I'll show you.'

She ran up into Saffy's bedroom in the loft, returning with the old book I'd seen Saffy reading the day after we arrived.

'I've told the girls to take extra special care with that,' I told him, apologetically. 'I can tell it's very old.'

Patrick took the book from Luna and looked it over, his long fingers turning the pages carefully. I could see there were some runes in the book, similar to the ones in the Longing. 'You said it has Icelandic words?'

Luna nodded.

He bent down to her eye level. 'Do you know what Iceland used to be called?'

She shook her head.

'Snowland.'

She raised her eyebrows. 'That's a much better name.'

He brightened and flicked through the book. 'Do you think so? It's had a lot of names, actually. Gardarsholmur was one. The Norse used to call it Saga Island.'

'A saga's a story.'

He smiled. 'A particular kind of story, but yes, a story. Do you speak Icelandic?'

'Well, not yet,' Luna said bashfully. 'But Saffy looked up some dictionaries at school.' She craned her head to see the page he had opened. '*That* word means "bird",' Luna said proudly, pointing at one of the scribbles. 'And that one means "human".'

'Human?' Patrick said, puzzled. 'I don't think so.'

Luna nodded, adamant. 'Saffy checked it.'

He smiled at her. 'Oh. I'll check it again, in that case.'

'Go to your room, girls,' I told Clover and Luna. 'I need to discuss the project with Mr Roberts.'

'You got my instructions, then?' he said, once we'd sat at the dining table. 'For the mural?'

I nodded, noting the word 'instructions' – a generous description of the sheet of paper bearing a scribble that I'd received. 'I did,' I said. 'I'm almost finished.'

His face lit up in surprise. 'I'd love to see it.'

VIII

I left the girls in the bothy while Patrick and I headed to the Longing to look over the mural. I felt nerves setting in as I turned the key in the door. I had to remind myself he was the owner of this place, despite looking so insanely young. What if he didn't like it? This was the moment of truth. I was finished with the rune design, but there was a lot of 'filling in' to do, and I worried that he expected me to be a lot further on.

Inside, I flicked on the work lamps, flooding the place with bright light. The raw patches of stone had been covered with fresh plaster, and the residue of dirty water that I had sloshed through the first time I stepped inside had been pumped out and cleared up, and with it, that awful dead-fish smell. My equipment was still in place, the work lights shining on the chrome legs of the cherry picker and pooling on the empty paint tins I'd stored under the staircase. I'd painted the mural in oceanic colours to make it a little more themed, and more appealing to the eye. I turned the light to pick out the shades of blues and greens that I'd used as a base colour for the overlapping triangles, and the lines that fanned outwards to the other symbols.

As I watched Patrick's expression shift to one of surprise, then delight, my nerves melted away, and I felt proud.

When he spoke, his mouth had an odd tremor to it. 'It's . . . out of this world,' he said. 'Simply out of this world.'

'You like it?' I asked.

'I do,' he said, his gaze roving across the runes. 'It's a lot prettier than I imagined it would be.'

'Really?'

'I'd honestly thought you would just paint the runes in black lines.'

'Well, you could have done that yourself,' I said lightly.

He looked blank for a moment. 'Oh, right. Great idea.'

I had the weird sense that we were imagining the project from entirely different viewpoints. But that was my job, I reasoned. I was the artist. He'd hired me to imagine it for him, as well as execute it.

I told him to follow me on to the cherry picker platform for a better view, explaining that I'd used it to reach the highest parts of the Longing and that he'd be safely harnessed on it. I moved the platform slowly upwards to the apex of the painting, explaining how I'd sometimes had to redo some of the symbols to accommodate the sections of plaster that Finn had added to smooth out the surface, or had embellished them to make them stronger. I'd painted the symbol of a flame, for instance, with the colours yellow, red and orange, but I'd decided to paint it quite large as that section of wall got less light from the windows. 'I had to think about the shape of the building,' I explained. 'Obviously the walls are curved, which means that perspective is a little different. Especially from the floor. I painted it so that when you look up from the bottom of the lighthouse you can see the mural almost as it appears on the page. Does that make sense?'

He kept his head tilted back, his eyes on the mural and a hand to his mouth in contemplation. 'It makes complete sense,' he said, though I caught him stifling a yawn.

I lowered the platform gradually, spending a minute or so at each section to talk over the colour choices and suggestions I had for developing it.

'I was wondering if you had any ideas on how we could incorporate scenes or patterns around the mural,' I said, in an attempt to draw him into the process. He didn't appear to hear me, so I pointed at a section that was unfinished. 'Here, you see, I thought of maybe incorporating some elements from Scottish folklore.'

I went to say more, but beneath the burr of the platform he had whispered something. A name.

'I'm sorry?' I said loudly. 'I didn't quite hear what you said.'

We were still on the platform, his face close to mine, his eyes searching me and his lips moving, though I still couldn't hear what he was saying. I stepped back, backing into the metal barrier. The lights were bright, but it was just the two of us in the Longing.

'Are you . . .?' he said, his mouth open and his eyes searching my face.

'Am I what?' I said.

He lifted a hand to his mouth, and for one unnerving moment I thought he was going to cry.

'Sorry,' he said, seeming to right himself. 'For a moment there, I thought you were someone else.'

I stepped off the platform and busied myself by tidying

away the cable. 'It's all right,' I said lightly, though my heart was racing. 'It happens to the best of us.'

'Does it?' he said. He was still standing on the platform, looking up over the mural. 'I get so lonely. It can do things to you. Loneliness, I mean.'

I rose to my feet, feeling slightly sorry for him now. 'Do you have any friends or family here on the island?'

'Not anymore.' He lifted his eyes to mine, and that weird moment was back, his stare boring through me. 'You do look very . . . familiar,' he said.

I didn't know what else to tell him. 'Shall we go back to the bothy?' I started to say, but he cut me off.

'When you were painting the runes, did anything come to mind?'

I looked at him, puzzled. 'Like what?'

'Maybe you remembered something?'

'*Remembered* something?' I said. I was lost. What on earth did he mean?

'It doesn't matter,' he said after a long silence. He smiled, breaking the tension. 'Forget it.'

IX

I was glad to get back outside into the cool air of the bay, where the seals were barking and the ocean was sweeping up the bay – both good distractions from what had transpired with Patrick inside the Longing.

'I've left my jacket in the bothy,' Patrick said, striding to keep up with me as we walked across the rocks. 'Would it be OK if . . . ?'

'Of course,' I said brightly, glad to be ending the night. I made sure to leave the front door ajar as he came inside and plucked his denim jacket. But as he made to leave, Finn and Cassie appeared in the hallway.

'Mr McAllen,' Patrick said nervously. He looked a little surprised, then seemed to realize that Finn and Cassie were coming to see me.

'Patrick,' Finn said. 'Always a delight.'

Patrick gave me a last nod goodbye as he brushed past Finn into the night.

'Where are Clover and Luna?' Cassie asked loudly.

'In their bedroom,' I said, closing the door, and she

scampered upstairs to join them. Through the glass I could see the blurred shape of Patrick outside, moving slowly towards the road.

'I can see there's no love lost between you two,' I told Finn.

'Aye. You arranged for him to come over tonight?'

I bristled. 'He just called by. He wanted to chat about the mural.' Why was I having to explain myself?

Finn wouldn't make eye contact. Part of me felt his mood was unfair – this *was* Patrick's bothy by right. It wasn't my fault he called, and I was irritated by Finn's question – or was it an assumption? – about whether or not I'd arranged for Patrick to come over. But then, he produced something from a bag and told me it was a gift, and the mood shifted again.

'What is it?' I said, pulling out a round glass vase half-filled with water and a web of orange roots, and a thick green shoot winding upwards.

'This is a gift,' he said. 'It's an oak tree. Or a seedling, as you can see. But it's not just any oak tree. It's a seedling from the Birnam Oak on the River Tay.'

'Birnam,' I said. 'That name sounds familiar.'

'You must know your Shakespeare, then. It's from Birnam Wood in *Macbeth*. The Birnam Oak is the last survivor of that wood.'

I set the glass container carefully on the windowsill behind the kitchen sink, watching the light play amongst the roots tangled in the glass. My chest was still tight from the stand-off between Patrick and Finn.

'I thought you could take it with you,' he said. 'When you go back to . . . wherever it is in England you live.'

'Ah, that *is* the question,' I said.

'What do you mean?'

I bit my lip. I wasn't sure whether or not to say anything. If I told Finn I technically had nowhere to go, that the girls and I were without fixed address, I'd wind up mentioning that I was sick. It just seemed easier to keep it all locked away. But Finn could tell that I was doing precisely that, and I could see him attempt to gently coax my secrets from me.

'You're considering not going back?' he said lightly. 'Well, I have to say, I'll be only too glad to tempt you into staying on Lòn Haven. What we lack in the way of theatre and art galleries we make up for in myth and murder . . .'

'Thank you,' I said, laughing. 'I don't know what my plans are, to be honest. I'm somewhat adrift at the moment.'

He stepped closer and moved a strand of hair from my face. 'I'm pleased to hear you're not rushing off in a few weeks' time. There's a lot more of this place to see, you know.'

'Is there?'

'Oh, aye. Hidden coves to explore, hidden treasures to discover. You might even find a handsome, red-bearded Scotsman with a fine set of abs who makes you want to stay longer than you thought.' He sucked in his gut. 'Well, a red-bearded Scotsman. Forget the abs part.'

I laughed. His face was close to mine, and he kissed me, lightly at first, then deeper. I pulled away, and he looked embarrassed.

'Sorry,' he said. 'I didn't mean . . .'

'I want to stay,' I said. 'I want *this*. But . . .'

I couldn't bring myself to say it. *I think I have cancer. Every woman in my bloodline has died from it.*

'Och, it's fine,' he said, and I realized I'd stood there, staring and silent, for a long time. I could see he was upset.

'No, no,' I said. 'It's not you.'

He closed his eyes and took a deep breath, stung. 'Ah, OK,' he said. 'It's not me, it's you. I get it.'

'*No*,' I said, but I already knew I'd made the situation worse.

He bit his lip, his eyes on the ground. I didn't want to upset him, and it struck me then how much I really did care. No, he wasn't my type. His dress sense was terrible, and his taste in music was beyond my comprehension. But he was gentle and big-hearted, and I loved his eyes and his tattoos and he made me laugh. He could fix anything. Just not me.

I'd expected him to turn and walk out at this point, but he was already talking, uncharacteristically tripping over his words. 'Look, I haven't . . . I haven't meant to come on too strong,' he said. 'If I have, I apologize.' He took a step back, as if to create a more neutral space between us. A distance that marked friendship instead of romance.

'I wasn't lying,' I said. 'The thing is, I'm sick.'

'Sick of what?' he said. 'Me? Men, in general? What?'

I sighed and covered my face. The truth was, I didn't even know how to begin to tell him. I hated being vulnerable, and I knew I'd start crying the minute I said it out loud.

Just then, he said, 'I thought we were honest with each other.'

He sounded wounded and self-righteous, and I bristled. 'I don't think I'm the only one who isn't honest.'

'I'm honest,' he said.

'Oh yeah? Why did Cassie's mother leave?'

He looked down and clasped his hands, as if he didn't know what else to do with them. 'We . . . drifted apart. And she struggled with it.'

'Struggled with what?'

He looked down. 'Motherhood.'

'Do you want to talk about it?'

He glanced towards the girls' bedroom, where laughs and chatter could be heard. He opened his mouth, then closed it. 'I don't . . . I don't talk about it very much.'

'I know.'

He lifted his eyes to mine and sighed. He was reluctant to talk about it but did all the same. 'Cassie was two. Jane just left. No note, no warning. She'd taken a suitcase so I knew she'd not been kidnapped or anything. We didn't hear from her for about a year. And then, I heard through the grapevine that she'd got married and was living in Brighton.'

'That must have hurt.'

He nodded and chewed his cheek, his eyes on the floor. 'She had problems with depression. I didn't realize how bad it was. When she found out she was pregnant, I was over the moon. It was an accident but I was thrilled. Looking back, I can see she was devastated.' He looked up, gave a sad smile. 'I think she only went through with it because I was making such a big fuss. I should have given her space to . . . speak up about *her* feelings.'

He spoke hesitantly, as though these were words he'd never said aloud, maybe not even permitted himself to think. I felt moved by how honest he was in sharing this with me, laying himself bare.

'When Cassie was born, I tried not to work too much,' he said. 'You know, to be supportive. Night feeds, and so on. But it was easier said than done. And I could see Jane was sliding back into that dark place she'd been in before. I just kept thinking she'd get through it.'

I nodded. 'And how is Cassie about it?'

'For years she asked if I was leaving her. Every single day, I couldn't leave her at nursery or school without her worrying that I'd not be coming back.'

'Does she ask about her mother now?'

'Now and then. I think it would have been a lot easier if Jane had left before Cassie was old enough to talk. If she'd left when Cassie was an infant she'd likely have no memory of her. But she does. She remembers what Jane looks like, things they did together. It's scary, actually, how much she remembers. I sometimes wish I could put a spell on her, take away her memories of Jane.' He looked up at me and cleared his throat, righting himself. 'Anyway. It is what it is.'

'Luna and Clover's dad died four years ago,' I said. 'He'd been a father to Saffy, too. They were all destroyed by it. So yes, I wish I could erase their memories, too. It would certainly take a lot of pain away, wouldn't it?'

'A lot of good too, I suppose,' he said. 'Cassie's asked more than once if Mummy left because of something she did.' His voice shook, and I reached out to touch his arm.

'It must be heart-breaking to hear a child ask if she made her mum abandon her.'

He nodded, dabbing his eyes.

'What about when Cassie got sick?' I said. 'Didn't her mother want to see her then?'

'I passed on a message through Jane's brother. We got a teddy bear through the post. I don't even know if it was from her.'

'I'm sorry.'

He cleared his throat loudly. 'So, then,' he said, rallying. 'Now that I've revealed that I'm really a big softie underneath my extremely muscular exterior, what do you think of all that?'

'What do I think?'

'Yeah. It put you off?'

I sat down next to him. 'When I said that I was sick, I meant that I've got an illness. And I'm not sure how bad it is.'

I told him about the phone call, and the diagnosis. How I didn't want to hear it, *couldn't* hear it, actually, on account of my three daughters who'd already been through so much.

He clasped his hands to his face. 'You already know what I'm going to say.'

I nodded. 'I need to speak to a doctor.'

'Like, yesterday,' he said, his voice pierced with alarm. 'No more procrastinating. I'll come with you. I mean, only if you want me to . . .'

I nodded. 'Yes. I promise I'll see someone.'

X

The day after Amy and I discovered the markings in the cave left by her mother, fate took another wrong turn for me. Her brother, Tavish, subjected me to another beating the day after. I was so tired from the night before, and quite honestly sick of his mindless brutality, that I stood up and threw the stones back at him, hitting him square between the eyes.

'You're a lunatic!' I shouted at him, or words to that effect. 'You deserve to be stoned, not me!'

He cowered on the ground, his hands up and his big blue eyes wide with terror. He'd forgotten that despite how skinny and small I was, I was fit as a butcher's dog, what with spending twelve hours a day hauling rocks for his father and tending the fields. Once I knocked him down I couldn't stop kicking. I was yelling and shouting, and Tavish was unconscious, blood splattered across his pale face. I hefted a huge rock from my pile of boulders and was about to bring it down on his head when someone grabbed me.

'Patrick, stop!'

257

I dropped the boulder and clamped my hand around the gullet of whoever had intervened, only to find that I was squeezing the life out of Amy. Her face was all crumpled and her skinny hands clawed at the one I was digging into her windpipe. I let go, as startled as though I'd been hit by lightning. I couldn't speak; neither could Amy. She collapsed against a tree, coughing and hacking. I looked from Tavish to his sister, my awareness coming back in heavy, terrible increments. It was if I'd somehow been lifted out of my body for a few minutes, my skin inhabited by a bear, while I drifted off in a dream.

'Amy,' I mumbled. 'Amy.' I placed a hand on her shoulder and she pulled away.

'I'm sorry,' I said, and then I didn't say anything more, because Tavish had regained his strength and clouted me over the head with a rock.

When I woke up I was in the barn with a terrible headache and surrounded by hens and sheep. I could sense someone nearby, but my vision took a while to catch up with my other senses.

'Amy,' I called out. 'Is that you?'

'Here,' I heard her say. 'Lean forward.'

Now it was my turn to hack and cough, only I was spitting up blood and bits of teeth. She'd brought me a drink of water. I didn't realize how weak I was with thirst until I started drinking.

'You shouldn't have done that,' I heard her say.

'I didn't mean to hurt you,' I told her. 'I love you.'

She said nothing, and when she moved away I saw the reason why. Her father was behind her and in earshot.

'On your feet,' he said, casting a grim look over me. I got up stiffly and kept my eyes on my toes, expecting

another beating for what I'd done to Tavish. He took three heavy steps forward, his boots squelching in the mud and his breath clouding in the cool damp air. He looked me over, cursing at the smell.

'It's a crying shame,' he muttered. 'You'd become a good farmhand. You're to get your things. Lockie'll take you to the boat.'

Not long after I was aboard a huge ship set for Ireland, wedged inside a filthy, lice-ridden cabin with fifty other men and boys, about half of whom were puking their guts out with seasickness. The smell was almost as bad as the noise, and I don't think I've ever been as miserable in my life as I was then. The boat rocked so violently I didn't expect to survive the night, but that wasn't the worst of it. No, the worst of it was knowing that I'd drown not in seawater, but in the pool of bile sloshing up and down the deck beneath my hammock.

But that night, as I opened my small bag of belongings, I found a flat stone tucked in between the pages of my Bible. It was from Amy. In blood, she'd painted a rune on the back, one that I recognized.

It was a love charm from a woman towards a man, and it offered protection. With my knife, I skewered a hole through the top and fed a piece of string through it, tying it around my neck. I might otherwise have supposed that I'd never see Amy again, not with an ocean between us and her father's will against me.

But like I said, Amy had a gift.

The rune would bring us together again when the stars were in our favour.

I was gone for five years and put to work in a butchery. I acquired an inadvertent but extensive knowledge about anatomy, which came in useful towards the end of my tenure.

My mind continued to loosen. I would wake up sometimes completely naked and drenched in blood, clasping an axe, without knowledge of why I was thus nor whose blood it was. I was no longer certain that I would ever see Amy again. Or, if I did, that she would want me. I was not who I had been.

I had just turned seventeen when the guild took action against my employer. There were thirty reports of him selling rotten meat. After a brief trial, it was William O'Daly alone who was dragged through the streets and smeared in horse shit by the peasants, before being hauled into the stocks. His business finished, I was sent back to Scotland with a bag of coins for five years' work and no plan for my life at all, except finding Amy.

And find her I did, or at least a version of her, for she was forever changed. And it was entirely due to Witches Hide.

LUNA, 2021

I

The smell wakes Luna up. The bitter smell of smoke hits the back of her nose. She bolts upright in bed and calls out.

'Are you OK, Clover?'

No answer. Luna scrambles out of bed and on to the landing, where a thick plume of grey smoke is trailing from Clover's bedroom.

Clover is standing beside her pile of new clothes, but they're on fire. Bright orange flames dance above the dresses, sparking on the lace fabric. Clover looks up at her, the blaze revealing menace on her face.

Luna darts into the bathroom, where it seems to take an eternity to find something to fill with water. All the pans are downstairs collecting the drips from the ceiling that Clover drenched with bathwater. The room is thickening with smoke, stinging her eyes and the back of her throat. She spies a small bin beside the toilet and grabs it, filling it quickly with water. Then she runs into the bedroom and throws the water over the pile, but it's not enough to damp out the flames completely. They curl dangerously towards the bed, and Luna has to pull Clover out of the room and order her out of the cottage while she races back into the bathroom for more water.

Mercifully, the fire dies down, though thick black smoke clings to the air. Luna covers her mouth with her hand as she rushes outside, gasping. Clover is in the garden of the cottage wearing only her nightie and a scowl. Luna sits down on an old garden bench, utterly spent.

She sits a long time in silence, her elbows on her knees and her head lowered into the palms of her hands. It was a mistake to bring Clover to an Airbnb. Her training has taught her that children with traumatic backgrounds need to be watched carefully in case of dangerous behaviour, that the environment needs to be controlled. In her own home, she'd have put all sharps, pills, and matches in a locked drawer. She has no idea where Clover found the matches, but it's her fault that she did.

It was a mistake to take Clover from the hospital. A mistake that could have cost them all their lives.

After a while she feels Clover approach. She raises her head to look at her.

'Why did you do that?' Luna asks. 'Why did you set all those clothes on fire?'

Clover doesn't answer. She stands in front of Luna with her arms by her sides, her face blank.

'I'll take you back to Inverness,' Luna says sadly. 'I'll call Eilidh and take you to her. I'm sorry I brought you here.'

'No!' Clover says, stamping a foot. 'I don't *want* to go to Inverness! I want to go back to Lòn Haven!'

Clover's eyes fill with tears. She sits down on the grass in front of Luna and wipes her eyes.

'Who are you?' Luna asks gently.

Clover considers this. 'I don't know any more,' she says, plucking a daisy. 'Actually I do. I'm *lost*. That's what I am.'

'Well, that's a start.' Luna can see she's getting somewhere. It energizes her, the feeling that she's making a connection. That some truth is coming out, at last.

Clover's face softens. 'I miss my mummy,' she says in a small voice. 'I want to see Mummy.'

'Where is your mother?' Luna says.

'Lòn Haven,' Clover says. 'She's going to be so upset because I'm gone. I have to go back."

'What's your mummy's name?' Luna asks.

'She's called Liv. Her real name is Olivia, but everyone calls her Liv.' She looks up at Luna. 'And she looks like you.'

Luna nods, but she's struggling to make sense of this.

Clover sits down next to Luna, who flinches. She's still scared that Clover's touch will hurt her.

'Mummy's going to be worried about me,' Clover says.

'Is that why you burned the clothes?' Luna asks. 'Because you want me to take you to your mum?'

Clover nods.

'Clover, I want you to try and remember,' Luna says carefully, trying a different approach. 'Can you do that for me?'

Clover gives a heavy sigh. 'I'll try.'

'What do you remember last? Before I came to the hospital and found you. Who were you with?'

Clover takes a deep breath and squints her eyes. 'I was walking along . . .'

'Where?'

'On the grassy bit.'

'In a field?'

Clover shakes her head. 'The road was here . . .' She uses her hands to signal a road to her left. 'And the grassy bit was here . . .'

'Which road? Can you describe it?'

'Um, it had some stones. And sheep.'

'And . . . what happened? Did you get lost?'

Clover picks at the grass in front of her, threading it between her fingers. 'Well, I *was* lost for a little bit, but then the man took me in his car and we went to the hospital. And then you came . . .'

She's getting distracted, Luna thinks. 'Clover, I need to think back, right back to when you went missing. I know it was a long time ago . . .'

'Mummy's painting the Longing.'

'So, Mummy was painting the Longing. And then, what happened? Did someone take you away?'

Clover cocks her head. 'Why would someone take me away? Did they think I was a wildling?'

Luna reels. She bites her lower lip, trying to recall if she has mentioned this to Clover. She's sure she hasn't.

'Where did you hear that word?' she asks carefully.

'On Lòn Haven. Everyone said the wildlings lived in the Longing. I think they were hiding in the cave.'

Clover's telling the truth. Luna stares, her mind racing. 'Which cave?' she says. 'Do you mean Witches Hide?' The name comes rushing to her, a memory unloosening without her forcing it.

Clover cocks her head. 'The what?'

Luna doubts herself. That was what it was called, wasn't it? *Witches Hide*. Maybe she just made it up. '*Witches Hide*. That's the name of the cave. Tell me about this cave, Clover.'

'Well, first of, there were no witches in there. So whoever named it is *stupid*.'

'You went inside this cave?'

Clover nods, and she seems wary to reveal this. 'Yes. But only because I thought Saffy might be there. And I wanted to find her.'

Clover tells her it was dark. Night time. She went inside the Longing at night, looking for Saffy. She'd seen Saffy go inside there at night sometimes and she thought she might have been there. But she wasn't. And then Clover found a hole in the floor and fell down, and when she stood up she saw she was in a cave.

Luna's mouth runs dry. She remembers this cave. She remembers falling down a long drop into it.

'And then what happened?'

'I ran through the cave, trying to find Saffy. But she wasn't there.' She looks crestfallen.

'And did you climb back up the long tunnel?'

Clover shakes her head. 'I found another way, where the sea was. I jumped into the water.'

'So there was no one in the cave with you?' Luna asks. 'No one who . . . hurt you?'

Clover shakes her head. *She must have forgotten*, Luna thinks. The terrible wound on Clover's hip didn't get there by itself. Someone had to have hurt her.

'Do you remember what happened after you went in the water?'

Clover starts to look worried again. 'I had to swim. But when I was on the beach again I couldn't find mummy. I thought she must have driven away because the car was gone. And I must have fallen asleep because I woke up and it was daytime. Then I walked for a little while and then the man came and took me to the hospital.'

Luna considers this. *I woke up.*

So Clover had amnesia. She's forgotten – or blocked out – the bit in between entering the cave and being found by the farmer who took her to the hospital in Inverness.

'And . . . the ouchie on your hip. You don't remember who did that to you?'

Clover pulls up her nightgown to look at her wound, as though she'd forgotten it was there.

'No,' she sighs. 'I really don't know how I got that.'

II

It is decided – Luna will take Clover to Lòn Haven. Taking her to Coventry isn't an option. She'll go to Lòn Haven to the place they had once stayed, to find her mother. If she isn't found, then she has no other choice but to call Eilidh in Inverness and explain the situation.

At Cromarty they drive on to the ferry, watch the mainland of Scotland slip away from them, and gradually, the triangular shape of Lòn Haven shading in the horizon.

Luna feels another wave of vomit threaten. She's already had to pull over at the side of the dock and throw up. She never, ever thought she'd return to Lòn Haven, and even now, she feels caught in a fever dream; the only thing stopping her from turning around is the mad kicking that the baby has launched into, squirming away as if to signal he's still there. She feels the eyes of the ticket collector on her as she takes Clover to use the bathroom. He'd studied her credit card a moment too long when she passed it over to buy the ticket, and then he'd stared at Clover. She'd tried to tell herself that she was just being paranoid. But when she'd returned to the car, she'd spotted him again on the deck. He had his phone held up as though he was taking a photograph.

She lifts her phone and finds Ethan's last message, asking her permission to come and join her in Lòn Haven. She texts quickly back.

Can you leave tonight?

Clover is like a different child now that she sees the signs for Lòn Haven everywhere. She chats non-stop about things that Luna doesn't quite hear. When the ferry docks, she has to will her hand to turn the key in her car's ignition. And in a moment, she has crossed the threshold – her first venture on to the island in twenty-two years.

Lòn Haven is not how she remembers it. Luna recalls the white stem of the Longing sitting against the backdrop of the ocean on its rocky island, linked to Lòn Haven by a snaking causeway. She remembers the small village of Strallaig with its colourful row of shops, and the patchwork quilt of fields, green as algae and dotted with ancient standing stones, sombre as monks.

After driving up and down the road that runs along Lòn Haven's coast, she stops at the old signpost for Strallaig and looks out at the tide washing up against the cliffs. There's a dirt track that looks familiar, and a flat bank of rock. There *should* be a lighthouse here, she thinks, and a bothy with a garden at the front.

She parks up and tells Clover to stay in the car. She gets out and walks gingerly along the track towards the cliff edge. Below, there's an odd shape in the grey water, a rock that juts up out of the waves. But as a cloud passes from the sun, she sees it's not a rock. It's a jagged hollow.

The remains of the Longing.

She has to look three times before she'll believe it. There are scattered remnants of the Longing's lantern room at the bottom of the cliffs that confirms it has fallen. The staircase gone, her mother's mural obliterated. Only the base of it left. No sign of the bothy.

The destruction of the Longing disorients her so much that she drives through the village twice, looping around the east side and coming to a stop at the Neolithic site. There are new roads, new signs, a few expensive glass-fronted houses dotting the hillside. The Neolithic museum is still there, though much bigger than last time. Historic Scotland have evidently built a shiny new visitors' centre, with a driftwood sculpture of a deer at the front of the complex, a tarmacked car park with a play area for children, and a sandwich board announcing a new Italian restaurant. A long banner promises an exhibition of traditional island tapestries.

She parks up. A bright PVC board by the deer sculpture offers a map of the island and information.

In 2018, Lòn Haven began experiencing extreme flooding and coastal erosion. Historic Scotland and CCF are working hard to delay and prevent further damage to the island's historic artefacts, therefore some of the sites may be under construction and/or temporarily closed. Scan the QR code here for updates!

She feels woozy. Everything is staggeringly, painfully different.

They return to the site with the dirt track and the rocky bank. She pulls over to the grassy bank and looks out at the remains.

'I think we're on the wrong island,' Clover observes, squinting out to sea.

'We're definitely on Lòn Haven,' Luna says.

'No, we're not. The Longing and the bothy should be *there*. And you see that hill?'

She points to the right at the bell-shaped rise that Luna remembers sledding down on a tea tray.

'There should be a cairn on the top,' Clover says. 'Do you know what a cairn is?'

'It's a pile of stones.'

'Exactly. And *that* one was called Camhanaich. Or it would be, if we were on Lòn Haven.'

'It's there,' Luna says. 'Look. It's Camhanaich.'

She points to where the light reveals the outline of the cairn. Luna hears the confidence slide out of Clover's voice, feels the shock slide into her as she realizes that yes, this *is* Lòn Haven.

'But where's Mummy?' Clover says, her voice breaking. 'Where's the Longing, and the bothy?'

'Let's go and find out.'

III

They drive around the island for hours, searching out places that they both might remember. Clover brightens when they reach Strallaig, recognizing a shop front that she expects to be an ice cream shop and growing upset when it turns out to be a nail bar. They get out of the car and walk up and down the high street. There's a small Boots store and a 'Starbox' – someone's attempt to pastiche Starbucks, including the green signage – a deli, and an art gallery. A group of blue- and pink-haired teenagers walk along the street, chatting and laughing.

The back of Luna's neck prickles. She turns, and a woman is there. She's an older woman, Chinese, a heavy black raincoat and a pair of wellies. A blunt fringe hangs low over her eyes, and she frowns at Clover before lifting her gaze to Luna. It's only a half-second glance and yet it seems to pose a question.

Ling. One of Isla's friends.

But before Luna can approach her, she's gone.

Lòn Haven is at once familiar and foreign. Luna has

moments of recognition, but they are so fleeting that she suspects she's inventing them. Clover's mention of their mother, Liv, residing on Lòn Haven has awakened the old hope that, somehow, her mother is alive. That somewhere, she's searching for Luna. Waiting for her.

She goes to the police station and asks about the Longing.

'Burned down,' the officer at the desk tells her. 'Years ago. The sea claimed what was left.'

Luna's eyebrows knit together. 'Who burned it?'

The officer leans across the desk, clasps her hands. 'The owner, I believe.'

'Patrick Roberts,' Luna says, and the officer's silence confirms it. The man her mother was working for. The mural.

'Do you happen to know why?'

The police officer shrugs. 'I was only little at the time. Probably an insurance claim, that's what folk said.' She catches herself and clears her throat. 'Anyway. He died inside it.'

So he's dead, she thinks. The sense of relief that comes with this knowledge is short-lived. Patrick might have had answers.

She pulls out the photograph of Liv that her uncle gave her, then the Polaroid of Saffy, and asks the police officer if she's seen either of them.

'I'll check our database,' she says. 'But they don't look familiar.'

Luna buys Clover an ice cream as they wait. An hour later, she returns, and the police officer shakes her head. 'I've checked the last ten years. Nobody matches those descriptions, I'm afraid.'

The storm sweeps up again, waves towering against the harbour walls and storm clouds sending rain down like chainmail. The horizon darkens; Luna wonders if Ethan will make it up north as planned. She drives aimlessly, noticing how Clover seems consoled by being back on the island, however different it looks. Luna knows the calm won't last long. She has to figure out her next steps.

Darkness stretches across the sky, swift as a blind being drawn. Silver tendrils of lightning whip across the ocean, a low groan of thunder. In the distance, rain is racing towards them in sweeping chains. She drives back to Strallaig to find somewhere to stay for the night. A hotel, Lòn House, sits at the far end of the street, close to a car park and a new children's play park.

The room comes with Netflix and a menu for room service. She texts Ethan to tell him where they're staying, then orders soup for herself and chicken pie with chips for Clover, who has fallen quiet. The room swells with sadness and disappointment. Tomorrow, they will head back to Inverness, where she'll contact Eilidh.

The food arrives, the smell of it making her mouth water. She and Clover sit at the small round table by the window. She pours Clover a glass of water.

'Cheers,' Clover says, lifting her glass with a smile.

The scene is heartwarming, and Luna finds herself lifting her glass to toast Clover. 'Cheers,' she says, clinking Clover's glass with her own. It might be miserable outside, and she may not have found what she came for, but Clover is happier. As though she's getting used to Luna.

'What's that?' Luna says, right as Clover holds a forkful of pie to her mouth. Something doesn't look right. She lunges forward and takes the fork from her hand.

A sharp turn of the fork towards the light reveals it – a shard of glass sticking up out of the pie.

Quickly Luna pulls apart the pie and finds more glass. Smaller pieces. Less easy to detect. A minute longer and Clover might have swallowed one.

'Why is there glass in my pie?' Clover asks.

'I don't know,' Luna says, a chill running clean up her spine.

But she does know. She remembers the way the ticket officer ran his fingernail under her name on the ticket, then did the same to Luna's. The way he looked at them both.

Someone knows they're here.

LIV, 1998

I

I kept my word to Finn – I rang the island GP and booked the earliest appointment I could. Finn wanted me to drive back to England and go straight to the hospital, but I wasn't ready for that. I could not, would not leap that fast, but I *could* manage to speak to a GP locally. The GP only came to the island three days a week, and the earliest slot was the day after. That was good enough for me.

It was Halloween, or Samhain, as the Scottish called it. The girls had spent the day making costumes at school, transforming black bin bags, twigs, and pipe cleaners into witch costumes, replete with broom and cauldron. They carved out turnips, or 'neeps', for lanterns. They'd also learned a special Samhain poem off by heart to perform to the neighbours.

Finn brought Cassie over and we painted the girls' faces green before taking them in the car to the village.

'When are you leaving?' Cassie asked as I painted her face. She was sitting in the kitchen, swinging her legs and holding hands with Luna, who was next in line to have her face painted.

'We're leaving in about thirty minutes,' Finn said.

'No, I mean – when is Luna going back to England?'

'Oh.' I bit my lip and flicked my eyes at Luna. Both girls were looking very sad.

'Can you stay forever?' Cassie said.

'*Please*, Mum?' Luna said. Clearly they'd been discussing this, planning to petition me as a unit. 'We like it here. And I've been doing my homework every night.'

Finn folded his arms and raised his eyebrows in a you-should-say-yes gesture.

'This is a big conversation,' I said gently. 'We'll discuss it later.'

Cassie and Luna threw their arms around each other, and I worried – what *were* we going to do, after the commission ended? Where would we live?

In Strallaig, the streets were aglow with neeps lanterns and fire pits. Some of the locals had dressed up in white sheets, dragging tin cans behind and making ghoulish noises at groups of children, and the windows of all the houses and even the shops glowed with candles. The window of Isla's café had clearly been decorated by Rowan, with a line of gemstones along the interior windowsill and an elaborate pentagram drawn in glow-in-the-dark paint on the glass of the window. Around it, in a circle, she'd drawn skulls and bats, and the words of a poem in white paint.

> *The veil is thin*
> *The circle complete*
> *We honour the dead*
> *Who follow our feet*

Luna, Clover, and Cassie recited their poems to dozens of neighbours, all of whom rewarded them with baked treats, toffee apples, and sparklers, which they lit and used to write their names in the darkness. The air was filled with the bitter tang of fireworks and flame.

In the small square in the centre of the village, flames sprung from a bonfire, and a woman dressed as a witch had set up a large barrel of water where children were bobbing for apples. The girls raced off. Finn and I sat down on a park bench, bracing ourselves against the sudden cold.

'You feeling any better?' he said.

I nodded, though I wasn't. 'A little.'

'Hey, remember you wanted me to take care of the bats in the Longing?'

'Yes?'

'I found some black lamps. It's an effective way to get rid of them.'

'Black lamps?'

'UV lights. It encourages them to roost elsewhere. Worked in Ian Ewart's barn. You just plug it in and let them get on with it. Also insects. So, I got you two – one for the lantern room and one for the main building.'

'Cool.'

He kissed my head. 'Meant to say – I'd one of my hunches when you said you'd booked an appointment with the GP.'

'And what did your hunch say?'

A long pause. 'It said you're going to be around for a long while yet.'

I sighed. 'How long's a long while?'

'I think you'll see your grandkids.'

I squeezed my eyes shut. To see my girls reach woman-hood. That was all I wanted.

He put his arm around me, and I laid my head against his shoulder. In the distance, someone started to play the bagpipes, a plaintive ballad that drifted through the night.

I looked over at the girls. The woman dressed as a witch was handing out woollen dolls. 'Take your wildlings,' she said.

Then she instructed them to cut them up with a pair of scissors, and toss them into the fire.

II

Finn drove us home a little later. He made to get out but I stopped him.

'Where are you going?' I said, glancing at Cassie in the back seat. She was fast asleep.

'I've got to set up the black lamps,' he said.

I looked out at the scene in front of us. The black clouds that had bubbled on the horizon all evening had finally swept in, wind and rain battering the Longing. 'Leave it,' I said. 'You take Cassie home.'

He tried to insist, but I made him tell me how to do it and promised I'd do it myself. Two black lights, one for the lantern room – this was to deter insects, which had started to stick against the paint – and one for the top of the staircase to slowly encourage the bats to roost elsewhere.

I wrapped myself in the old fisherman's coat Saffy had found in the shed and lowered my head against the gale as I walked to the Longing. I was nervous about going into the lantern room again, but I told myself that I was so close to finishing the job. And now that Patrick Roberts was back in town, I didn't want to waste any more time waiting for the bats to leave. It would be a quick job, I thought. Place one UV lamp in the lantern room and one on the stairs, and that would be that.

I set up the first one at the top of the stairs. It sent a faint purple glow throughout the dark space, not unlike the mareel. I saw some of the bats begin to stir, and two flew outside. Encouraged, I moved to the lantern room. Quickly I set up the black light. And then I gasped.

In the vivid glow of the black light, something on the windows was revealed. Numbers. Thousands of them.

I turned around on the spot, my eyes adjusting to the light, taking in the sight of it, trying to understand what I was seeing.

It wasn't just on the windows, either – the writing continued across the floorboards, on the walls, a frenzy of numbers and words. The numbers appeared to be grouped in four, written vertically.

1	*1*	*1*	*1*
6	*7*	*8*	*9*
8	*1*	*9*	*2*
2	*6*	*9*	*1*

The hairs on the back of my neck stood on end. It looked like the work of madness, all the numbers glowing in the dark. A film of grime had grown over the numbers so it hadn't been done recently. Why would someone do this? It couldn't have been the little boy I'd spotted. He was far too young, and he could never have sourced the kind of paint that only showed under UV light. Tourists, I thought, hopefully, playing some sort of game. Or 'outsiders' – the same people Isla had blamed for the graffiti. A shiver ran all over me. First the bones, now this . . . it was deeply creepy. The writing was the same throughout, the same flick on the tail of the '9', the same exaggerated cap on '7'. One, maybe two people had written all of these. And they'd gone to the trouble to use paint only visible under blacklight.

On the floor, where the triangle of bones had been, I spotted a rune. A star inside a circle, or a pentagram. The bones had been placed in the centre of it.

So they hadn't been left at random. The frenzied numbers and words and runes looked Satanic, or the work of someone who needed help.

I raced down to the bottom floor, where I'd left my Polaroid camera. My heart was racing and I was shaking with fright, but I knew I had to go back up. I had to will myself, count to three in my head before forcing my legs to move. I went back up and took a handful of photos before racing back down again and into the night.

In the bothy, I started to dial Finn's number, but I stopped halfway and hung up. Why was I calling him? No – I needed to call Patrick Roberts. It was his property, and we needed to go to the police together. He answered after two rings.

'Hello?'

'Patrick? It's Liv.'

A silence. 'Hello, Liv.'

'Sorry to call you so late. It's just . . . there's something in the lantern room that I'm concerned about.' I told him about what I'd spotted. The numbers. The writing.

'I . . . I spotted a little boy in the Longing,' I said, tripping over my words. 'I told the police but they didn't believe me. I'm not sure he was the one who did all the writing but maybe this proves someone was with him?'

'Stay calm,' he said. 'I'll come straight away.'

'I took photographs. I thought we could take these to the police. As proof.'

'Don't do anything just yet,' he said hastily. 'I'll be there in ten minutes.'

I hung up, filled with a strange relief. Maybe this would force the police to search for the boy I'd found.

I spread the Polaroids I'd taken over the dining table, studying them in the light of the table lamp. I could make out words, too, but they were like nonsensical, a kind of delirious poetry, written in a scrawl.

AMY.
WHERE ARE YOU?
AMY. AMY. AMY.

A knock sounded at the front door. It was Patrick.

I turned back to the photograph, my heart racing. The words stirred something in my memory.

The night I'd met him, we'd had a weird moment when I heard him call me by another name. What was it?

Amy, that was what he'd said. He'd asked if I was Amy.

Patrick had written the frenzied numbers in the lantern room.

III

We stood together in the lantern room, and I kept my arms across myself protectively. Despite the cold, I could feel sweat gathering under my shoulder blades, my heart banging in my chest. I could tell he was trying to work out if I knew or not, a darkness in his stare that wasn't there before. It made my unease even worse.

'I see,' he said, bending to look over the numbers on the walls. We were in darkness, save the purple light of the UV lamp. He ran a hand over the word 'Amy', and I flinched.

He looked up. Had he seen me jump? I watched him carefully, turning every so often to look out over the bay for car lights. I hadn't called Finn. I should have, but I'd felt foolish. What was I going to say? That I'd found some writing in the lantern room? That I thought Patrick Roberts was out of his mind?

You should have called him.

'I'll change the locks on the door,' he said, straightening. 'And the door to the bothy. Perhaps look into some security system.' He stood, looked me in the eye. The nervy, awkward boy I'd met before was gone – he was sour, now, and the curl of his lips when he smiled contained a malice I'd not seen. 'Will that make you feel safer?'

I turned off the UV lamp, flooding the room quickly with the white glare of my torch. 'Yes,' I said, with the biggest smile I could muster. '*Thank* you.'

He smiled back. But the air between us was charged with a shared knowledge – he knew I knew.

We took to the stairs in silence. I walked quickly, chatting animatedly about the mural, about the paint quality and the weather – *anything* I could think of to spin the conversation towards the realm of normality and fill the terrifying space that had cracked open between us. Once I hit the ground floor I strode quickly to the door and yanked it open, never more relieved by the fierce winds outside that met me.

'Thanks for coming over,' I said, when he came outside. Big smile. 'I didn't mean to cause alarm.'

He swept my apology away with his hand. 'Think nothing of it.' He held my gaze. There was suspicion in his eyes. 'It's a beautiful night. Why don't I take you on a cruise of the island? You wanted to learn more about the history of this place, if I remember correctly.'

'I've no one to watch my girls,' I said, explaining that Saffy was at a friend's house and Luna and Clover were too young to be left alone.

'Bring them along,' he said. There was no denying his tone – it was insistent.

Say no.

'Think of it as part of your commission,' he added, and I swallowed hard.

'I'd love to.'

284

Outside, the wind was picking up, and once we'd collected the girls we headed quickly to my car parked at the roadside, and from there it was a short drive to the port along the bay to a large white boat. Clover and Luna had long forgotten their board games and were now enthralled by the prospect of going out on a boat. This will be good for them, I told myself, but inside my instincts were shouting at me, telling me to make an excuse and back away. But too late – he led us onboard and pulled up the gangplank.

Clover took the opportunity to tell Patrick all about Basil the basking shark, who Patrick surely must have known about but pretended he didn't.

'He must be *very* lonely,' she said. 'All the other basking sharks have gone home for the winter, but Basil just stays around because he likes it here so much.'

'He'll be heading on his way soon enough, I'm sure,' Patrick told her. 'If we see him while we're out, you can always give his back a good scratch.'

I was imagining Patrick's boat to be something like Mr McPherson's fishing boat. Instead, we were on a sleek, modern yacht, gleaming white with a shark-nosed bow. Inside were six bedrooms and a beautiful kitchen. I spotted a gym through one of the doors, too, and a glass-fronted cabinet filled with wine bottles.

'I have a games room,' he told Luna and Clover, who both immediately started pleading with me to let them go there. I relented, and Patrick took us to a room decked out with arcade games, a pool table and an air hockey table.

'The best views are from the cockpit,' he told me. There, two white leather seats looked over a digital console towards the front of the boat. In a moment we had pulled out of the dock and were headed back towards the bay. The sky had turned to a navy velvet glittering with stars and the boat rocked slightly against the waves that seemed to paw at us as we made our way into deep water.

'Would you like something to drink?' he asked. 'Wine? Tea?'

'A tea would be lovely, thanks.'

He headed to the kitchen at the other end of the room while I stood, still feeling too out of place to sit down. I noticed some intriguing keepsakes in a wall-mounted cabinet – a huge conch shell with a raw pink centre, a dried sea urchin, prickly as a hedgehog, a set of moss-green skeleton keys, and some bits of wood.

'I see you've discovered my Viking ship,' he said, returning with two wine glasses and a bottle of expensive-looking wine under his arm.

'A Viking ship?'

'I had no tea, so I brought wine,' he said. 'Shall I pour you a small one?'

I nodded. 'A very small one.'

He handed me a glass and popped the cork. 'I used to go deep sea diving. I did a dive in the Shetlands. Found a wreck on the sea floor.' He nodded at the splinters of wood in my hand. 'I spotted the snake helm and figured it was a Viking ship,' he said, marking the curved shape of the helm in the air with his hand. 'I contacted the National Library in Edinburgh and they sent some divers down to explore. Cheers.' He held up his glass, and I toasted him.

He stepped closer, slipping a hand in his trouser pocket.

'They were able to carbon-date it. Have a guess how old?'

'A . . . thousand years old?'

'Close,' he said, weighing one of the fragments in his hand like gold. '700 AD.'

I watched him carefully. He was a bit of chameleon, his moods shifting so ferociously that it was like watching him perform different personalities. The shy boy in the bothy had gone, as had the sinister, brooding man I'd encountered in the Longing. Even his form seemed different – when we'd first met I'd thought him thin and finely built, but his short-sleeved T-shirt revealed strong, muscular arms riddled with scars. The air was clammy with tension, and I figured that keeping the small talk going was the best way forward.

'What about the Viking ship?' I asked, my voice light. 'Did they hoist it out of the ocean?'

'No, too dangerous,' he said. 'Max, my diving partner, said we missed a trick.' He set the Viking ship remnants carefully back in place. 'He said we should have dredged an oar up or something, charged tourists to come and touch it.'

I cocked my head. 'You're . . . not keen on tourists?'

He gave me a look that said *definitely not keen.*

From a window I could see the silhouette of the Longing shrink against a purple sky, the gold lights of houses shimmering on the other side. We were moving steadily away from the shore. A flash of the writing in the lantern room came to my mind, and my stomach twisted.

Why did I agree to this?

'So . . . the mural,' I said, guiding the conversation to safe ground, keeping my tone light. 'Have you thought any more about how we could develop it?'

'Actually, it would help if you talk me through your work as an artist,' he said, turning the wheel to the right, shifting the long white glare of the moon across the helm. 'Do you just do murals, or do you do traditional art? Paintings, and so on?'

I told him that when I'd gone to art school, I was in love with Degas and Balthus, and my dream was to have an exhibition of my paintings in some upscale gallery in London, or even the Tate Modern. Until I realized how naïve that idea was and radically scaled down my goals. Back then I was obsessed with wolves, mostly because I had a second cousin who was in the newspapers for her attempts to reintroduce wolves to England. I'm not a natural realist painter – I didn't really try to paint wolves, but large abstract canvases full of colour and anarchy.

He lifted an eyebrow. 'You still paint wolves?'

I shook my head. 'No, no. And it wasn't so much the wolves that had my interest but the idea of . . . wildness.'

'Shame,' he said. 'Scotland used to be full of wolves. Even Lòn Haven.'

'I could add them,' I said brightly. 'It would be good to incorporate some of the older natural elements. Good idea.'

The lights of the island were growing steadily smaller, the line of the horizon drawing closer. 'Perhaps you could show me a little of the coastline of Lòn Haven,' I said carefully. 'It would be useful to see the Longing from the ocean.'

He thought about that, and for a long moment I held my breath.

'Of course,' he said.

But instead of turning the boat back to shore, he flipped a switch, and I felt the boat shudder to a stop.

'Is everything all right?' I asked.

His head was bowed, and the mood had shifted again. 'To be honest, I just thought you might remember,' he said.

'Remember?' I said, holding my cup tight. 'Remember what?'

He looked up. His eyes were dark. 'Who you are.'

'I'm sorry,' I said. 'I don't know what you mean.'

He moved a hand to touch me, and I flinched.

'Do you realize how long I've waited to find you? How far I've travelled to find you?'

I eyed the keys on the control panel in the cockpit, the helm between us.

'I'm really sorry,' I said, forcing a smile on my face. 'But I think you've mistaken me for someone else.'

'I've been searching for years and years,' he said in a low voice. 'I thought if I had the Longing painted with the runes, it would help me find you. And instead of leading me to you, it brought you back to me.' He took my hand in his and clasped it tight, and I didn't dare pull it away. I saw his eyes were wet with tears. 'I always knew you'd come back,' he whispered. 'I always knew it, Amy.'

Terror crept upon me. 'Amy?' I said, trying my best to sound measured and unafraid.

He is mad. Absolutely stark raving.

And dangerous.

He removed something from a strap on his ankle. A small, sharp knife.

'Remember this?' he said, and I let out a cry. He frowned. 'What's wrong?'

I took a full step back in the direction of the room where my girls were playing. The sight of them brought my courage back, sending adrenalin through me. 'My name isn't Amy,' I said.

I'll bolt us in the room until he turns us around. I have to protect them.

289

He shook his head with a smile, dismissing everything I'd said. 'The runes must have wiped your memories. It'll all come back to you eventually.'

On the wall behind me was an old wooden oar, mounted for decoration. Quickly, I lifted it down and held it in front of me like a baseball bat.

Patrick stared at me. 'What's going on, Amy?'

'My name is Olivia,' I said fiercely. 'Now I'm sorry, but you have me confused with someone else. Take us back to shore right now.'

His face dropped then, and he held his hands up. 'Please accept my apologies,' he said, righting himself. 'You have children. It must be their bedtime.'

When the engines roared back to life I felt a moment's relief. But I didn't let go of the oar, not even when he broke the silence.

He turned to me, and I was alarmed to see he was crying. 'I'm ever so sorry,' he said, and the nervous, awkward boy was back with me, dabbing his eyes. 'It's just been so long . . . sometimes you can miss someone so badly you just want to believe you've found them, you know?'

IV

And so, at the age of seventeen, I was shipped back to Lòn Haven. I had no home to return to, no family, and only a little money, but I hoped that Amy was still there, and that she hadn't forgotten me.

I walked from the dock to her croft, telling myself to keep my expectations low – she was likely married now, perhaps with a bairn. She might have moved away. She might have died.

In the distance, I saw a woman outside the croft, flinging out a blanket. She was tall and wore her long black hair in a plait. Finwell, I thought, astonished. But as I got closer, I recognized her movements. The turn of her head towards me, her gait as she started walking down the path. Then her voice as she shouted my name.

And in a second she was there, crying and shouting at me, her hands grabbing my clothes and pounding my chest.

'You left!' she shrieked. 'You never said goodbye!'

I was too overwhelmed to speak. I opened and closed my mouth but only sounds came out, and I was crying.

Suddenly she stopped pounding me with her fists and flung her arms around me, and I dropped my bag and held her, cupping her head to my shoulder. I had missed her so badly it had all but turned me inside out. I had missed her so badly that I hadn't wanted to live. And yet, now she was here, and I never wanted to let her go.

We were both different. I suppose we had been children when last we spoke and now we were adults. The scrawny, feral girl I'd known was now a woman, taller, beautiful, the wild daring in her eyes cooled to wisdom, and sorrow. She pulled me inside the croft before anyone else could see, so my return might stay a secret a while longer.

'The island has changed since you left,' she said, as she lit the fire. She served me oat bread and pottage as she told me what had happened. The year I'd been sent away, the sickness that Duncan had died from ravaged the island. Hundreds fell ill, including the laird, who was the first to die. All the judges who presided over the court that sent the twelve women to their deaths also died. Then Duncan's sons, and his wife.

Fifty men, women, and children died, and those who recovered bore scars from their illness. Rumours began to spread about an event that had preceded the plague. Mrs Dunbar, an old woman who had lost two grandchildren to the plague, spoke of a little girl that had come to her door. She was terrified; Mrs Dunbar knew the child was not from the island, and she did not speak Gaelic. She bore a mark on her leg, a strange burn with numbers therein. Mrs Dunbar persisted in trying to communicate with the girl, using charcoal and scraps of paper to have her draw where she had come from, so that she might be returned to her family. The little girl drew the cave deep in the broch that had become known as Witches Hide.

The child had disappeared, never to be seen again. The day after, the laird died. Mrs Dunbar informed the Privy Council, who placed notices of the child around the village. There was no doubt that the child's appearance was of the Devil, the witches' curse coming to pass.

I heard the fear in her voice, but I did not yet register the change that had swept across Lòn Haven. I was still stunned to be back in Amy's presence, and although she had wept in my arms I didn't dare ask the question that buzzed in my head.

'I'm not married,' she said then, as though reading my mind. She looked at me with caution. 'Are you . . . promised?'

I blinked. 'No.'

She took my hand in hers and gently drew her thumb across my palm.

'I missed you, Patrick Roberts,' she said softly. 'I hated you and I missed you.'

My heart all but burst inside me. Amy was everything to me – my kin, the other half of me. 'Believe me when I say I wanted nothing more than to come back.'

'Will you marry me?' she said softly.

SAPPHIRE, 1998

I

'I want to show you something,' she tells Brodie. 'But you've got to promise me you won't get scared.'

They push open the door to the Longing.

'Aw, man,' he says, frowning at the smell of paint. 'I hate this place. If I'd known you were bringing me here, I'd . . .'

She silences him with an ardent, hungry kiss. It sends white heat from her toes right up to her head, shooting through her skull in bright sparks. Then she plucks the skeleton key that's tied around her neck between finger and thumb and holds it up.

'Follow me,' she says, leading him through the dark across the floor of the Longing.

'It's creepy, this place,' he says. 'They used to kill witches here.'

'You've mentioned,' she said, enjoying the shift in power from him to her. She bends, a small torch between her teeth, and reveals the lock on the floor.

'Watch,' she says, slipping the key and turning it slowly.

'Do you even know what that is?' Brodie says in a low voice.

'It's our secret cave,' she says, pulling back the grille.

'It's Witches Hide,' he says. 'Everyone says it's cursed. You go through that cave and you never come back.'

She delights in his sudden terror. 'You're not *scared*, are you?'

She sits down on the edge of the hole and dangles her leg. The torch light reveals a drop of about ten feet. As long as she falls right, she should be fine.

'Saffy,' he says, warningly.

She jumps. A second later, there's a thud, then a light sigh. He looks down into the hole.

'You OK?' he says.

She looks up at him with a grin.

'Come on, then.'

In a moment he has lowered himself as deep as he can into the hole while holding on to the edge. And then he drops, bending his knees and rolling awkwardly in a bid to lessen the impact on his legs.

He finds his cigarette lighter and flicks it to life. The small yellow flame barely cuts through the gloom.

Mercifully, the sheer drop leads to a long underground chamber, that deepens further into something that reminds Saffy of a cathedral. There are stalagmites and stalactites and pools of murky water. About thirty foot ahead the cave seems to split in two directions.

Brodie looks wary. She smiles to herself, relishing the fact that he is trying to conceal his fear. The cave is kind of creepy, she thinks, but with Brodie here she feels safe. 'How far does the cave go?' she asks him, wondering if it cuts through to the other end of the island. If they might tumble out into the ocean without realizing it.

'I'm not sure,' he says. 'I've never gone through it. I'm not allowed.'

'You're not allowed?' she says, laughing.

'It's called Witches Hide for a reason,' he snaps. 'And if my dad discovered I went through he'd break my legs, I can tell you that. Here, have a look at this.'

He gropes the rock with his left hand while holding the lighter close to the surface. She sidles up to him and squints. 'There,' he says, running the light over the markings. Carved deeply into the stone are a dozen individual runes. Lines, circles, and geometric patterns, similar to the mural. Similar, but different.

'What do they mean?' she asks him.

'Apparently it's black magic,' he says. 'The witches did it when they were held here.'

'But weren't all the women innocent?' she says. 'Like, witches weren't actually real . . .'

'I'm only going by what the stories say,' he says. 'Look. Up there.'

He stretches up high and illuminates the ceiling. Four digits. *1662.*

She gasps. 'Is that the year these were made?'

'Apparently. They say there's other graffiti further on in, names and so on. But I think we've come far enough.' He turns to head back towards the entrance.

'Wait,' she says, wrapping her arms around him, pulling him to her for a long, ravenous kiss. As if he is hers and hers alone, forever and ever.

LUNA, 2021

I

She slides the key back across the front desk and holds Clover's hand firmly as she heads towards the street.

'Where are we going?' Clover asks.

Luna shushes Clover and keeps her gaze firmly ahead. A man appears in the corner of her eye, a name tag on his shirt indicating that he works at the hotel. She doesn't stop. They have to head to the car. It's too dangerous to stay here.

'But I'm *starving*,' Clover whines once they're in the car. 'Why was there glass in my pie?'

'We'll find a fast-food place,' Luna says, turning the key in the ignition. In the rear-view mirror, rain has transformed the windows into surrealist portraits of the streets. But she can make out a figure getting into a car, the lights flicking on as she pulls off.

'I thought you were taking me to see Mummy,' Clover wails in the back seat behind her. She grows more fractious with each second, kicking Luna's seat with each word.

Luna tries to keep the car behind her in sight as she pulls

out of the car park. She can see the headlights in her rear-view mirror moving quickly behind them. She heads on to the coast road, pressing her foot against the accelerator.

The roads shine with rain, the windscreen affording only a staccato glimpse of road before a fresh deluge obscures her vision. Luna's heart is racing. The road is empty, save her car and the one behind, the two headlights uncomfortably close. She presses a hand against her stomach. She should have called the police when she found the glass, she thinks. Driving was a bad idea. The person behind seems to be following her.

The only option is to drive faster. Her heart beating in her throat, she accelerates to sixty, eighty miles an hour, desperate to throw off the car behind.

'You're going too fast!' Clover yells. Luna grips the steering wheel and concentrates on the road ahead. There are small turns ahead, she thinks. A sharp turn might be the only way to lose him.

Clover is screaming in the back seat. At the side of the road ahead Luna spies the glint of a metal gate, leading to a field. A small opening, just big enough for her little car. But the glare of another set of headlights appears on the crest of the hill; she'll have to pull in front of the other car if she's to make it. She counts in her head, jerking the car left at the last second. There's a terrifying moment when the car on the other side of the road is too close, within metres of them, and a horn blares loudly. With a bang, she brings the car to a stop against the grass verge.

There is a horrible stillness from the seat behind her.

Luna rubs her stomach in panicked circles. 'Are you OK?' For a terrifying handful of seconds, the baby is still. Then he nudges, as if to say he's still there.

'Clover?' she says. 'Clover, are you all right?'

No reply. Luna can't turn around far enough to see if she's OK, so quickly she gets out of the car and steps into the rain, pulling the passenger door open. Clover has been rolled into the passenger footwell, curled up with her face into her knees.

'Clover?'

A whimper lets her know that she's conscious.

'Are you hurt?'

'I hurt my knee.'

'Let me see.'

She looks over Clover, determining with relief that she's fine, other than a few bumps from jerking forward. The seat belt caught her.

Suddenly, a bright light shines on them both. Luna turns to see a car heading straight for them, coming to a screeching halt at the side of the road. In seconds, a man has stepped out and is striding towards them.

He's tall and rakish, with greasy black hair to his jaw, a tattoo of a panther on his neck, a missing front tooth. A grin.

'You're Luna Stay?'

She frowns, confused by the shift to a smile. 'Yes?'

He steps forward and eyes her coldly. 'You're supposed to be dead.'

II

Luna tries to conceal her terror. A stint in juvenile detention taught her this – you show fear, you give away your power.

'Brodie,' she says, reading his name badge. 'Do I know you?'

He narrows his eyes. 'Isn't that why you're here?'

'Very modest of you to think I'm only here for you,' she says. 'Is that why you put broken glass in my food? So very brave of you.'

He spits on the ground. 'Look, I'm not here to start a fight.'

'You could have fooled me,' she says, her nerves jangling. 'Or maybe the car chase was meant to kill us outright.'

He steps forward, his hand raised, and she jumps back.

'Back off,' she says loudly. 'Or I'll scream.'

His face softens. 'Look, I'm not the one you should be worried about.'

She laughs. It sounds insane. 'No?'

He glances behind her. 'They know you're here. I came to warn you.'

She frowns. '*Who* knows I'm here?'

'All of them. As soon as you boarded that ferry, they were waiting for you.' He shakes his head. 'You didn't think to change your name?'

'What are you talking about?' she hisses. '*Who* was waiting for me?'

He looks her up and down. 'Are you really Luna? Saffy's sister?'

The mention of Saffy feels like a slap. 'What do you know about Saffy?'

Another glance behind her. 'They say your ma tied you to a tree and cut out your heart. When they said you were here, I had to come and see for myself.'

'Do "they" know where Saffy is?'

He turns to walk away. 'You'd better go,' he says. 'You're mad, coming back here.'

A sudden memory of Brodie and Saffy together clangs in her mind, and she takes three quick steps towards him, her eyes blazing. 'Did you kill Saffy?'

He stops, his back to her, then keeps walking, pulling his car door open.

'I'll go to the police,' she shouts after him. It's intended as a threat, but he stops and strides back towards her, his face dark with anger. She grits her jaw and stands her ground.

'Do you know what I've risked to warn you?' he says, his face close to hers. 'I've lived with what happened to Saffy all this time.'

'So have I,' she spits back, tilting her jaw up. 'I lost my whole family. And you can tell whoever put glass in my food that I'm coming for them.' Her words – their sudden, truthful venom – shocks her.

301

'You better watch that temper,' he says quietly. 'If you're still on the island in twenty-four hours, you'll be buried in it.'

He stares purposefully at her pregnant belly, then at Clover in the car, before getting back inside his car.

III

Luna drives straight to the ferry port, shaking with anger and shock.

'Who was that man?' Clover asks.

'No one,' Luna says.

'He looked scary. Did he want to rob us?'

'No,' Luna mumbles, pulling into the port.

How did he know it was me?

She allows herself to breathe out in relief at the sight of the ferry. It was a mistake to come to Lòn Haven. It has always been her biggest terror, and now that she's here, she's risked her life and her son's. And Clover's.

The only reason Brodie would know it was me is because he's been waiting.

They all have.

She pulls up at the ticket office and rolls down her window, covering her face when the ticket officer glances in. She doesn't know who to trust.

'No tickets for the rest of the day, I'm afraid,' he says. 'Wind's too strong for the crossing.' She gapes. The cars in front of her are all pulling back around and driving away.

She watches as the ferry sits dormant in the dock, swaying in the wind.

A text from Ethan pings on her phone.

Am at Cromarty. Ferries cancelled. Will try again tomorrow
morning.
Love you x

She covers her face with her hands and cries. She would give anything, anything at all right now for Ethan to be here.

A hand reaches for her shoulder. 'I'm sorry you're sad,' Clover says softly. 'When I'm sad, sometimes I sing a lullaby. It makes me feel better.'

She starts to sing 'Twinkle, Twinkle, Little Star'. Luna finds herself smiling at the gesture. In the stillness of the car, marooned on this godforsaken island, Clover's voice is a small spell, casting the terror far enough away for her to think clearly.

'See?' Clover says, smiling. 'It works.'

Hunger drives her to find a fast-food place – another pastiche, King Burger – where she buys enough food for a small tribe. She and Clover devour the meal in the car. The sky bruises with night clouds. She has no idea where to go. Brodie's warning has sent her mind reeling. Who is watching her? Why do they want to harm her?

Going to a B&B or hotel is out of the question. Perhaps, like her mother all those years ago, she'll have to sleep rough.

'Why do we always end up sleeping in the car?' Clover asks when she mentions this.

They drive towards the visitors' centre where she hopes

the trees will provide cover from the storm. And there's a CCTV in case someone tracks her down – though she remembers the way he laughed when she threatened to go to the police. Nowhere feels safe.

She remembers how it felt that night when she came at ten years old, her heart filled with hope that she might discover one of her sisters, or both. That one of them might leap out and say *boo!* And then they'd go home and the anguish that their mother was suffering every second of every day would be forgotten.

It had been a dry, still night, and she'd been afraid. Any other time she wouldn't have had the courage to be out on her own, much less venture into the Longing on her own, in the darkness. But the devastation of her sisters' disappearance diminished every other emotion, and the world had narrowed to the sight of her mother's gaunt, harrowed face. As though her soul had left her body and she was now shuffling around like a kind of hole with a human face. What Luna had wanted more than anything, more than a million Christmases all at once, was to see her sisters again. Even Saffy. And to see her mother smile once more.

She remembers that she went into the Longing. It was so dark inside that she'd wished she had thought to bring a torch. She'd leaned into the darkness and called her sisters' names.

'Saffy? Clover?'

She'd listened hard. The sound of the sea washing the shore, the far blare of a ship's horn. And then, a whisper.

She'd stiffened and listened again. This time, she'd located the source – the grille in the floor. Wind was rushing through it. Maybe that's where Saffy had gone. She'd opened it and jumped down.

It was a long way down, and she'd hurt her knee. But once she was there, she found the cave was wider than she'd expected, and much longer, too. It was scary, like the mouth of an enormous crocodile. Lots of spiky things coming down from the ceiling like teeth and bigger ones rising up from the ground, sharp as knives.

'Saffy?' she'd called. 'Are you here?'

Her fingers had reached for the wall to help steady herself as she made her way forward. A little further ahead there seemed to be light trickling through an opening at the end, and she could see markings on the cave wall. A pattern, of some kind. It was very big, and deeply carved into the rock. She remembers thinking a giant must have done it, because the rock was so very hard against her fingertips and it would have taken a lot of strength to leave so much as a scratch. As she thinks of it now, the pattern looked very like the mural her mother was painting. Interlocking triangles forming a star, with other squiggles and circles carved into the stone.

IV

They park up at the visitors' centre. The wind is howling and the temperature gauge reads four degrees Celsius – much too cold for a decent night's sleep. Shivering, she steps outside to find a blanket, or perhaps a jacket, in the boot of her car.

She's about to step back inside when a woman approaches.

'Sorry,' the woman calls over the wind. 'I'm afraid we're closed. I have to lock up the car park for the night.'

Luna opens her mouth to explain, engulfed with shame.

'The ferries are cancelled,' she says. 'I . . . we have to sleep here until the morning.'

The woman's face drops. Her eyes slide to Clover in the car. 'You can't stay in a hotel?'

'It's a long story,' Luna says.

The woman fixes her with a searching stare. It makes Luna flinch with embarrassment. 'I'm sorry, but I don't suppose I know you?' she asks. 'I think I recognize you. Your mum was painting the Longing?'

Luna stares, her eyes widening. The woman is faintly

recognizable, with short blonde hair teased into a quiff and a septum piercing. She recognizes her eyes. The same laughing eyes.

'*Cassie?*'

V

Amy and I were married on a Tuesday, in the church where our mothers were condemned to their deaths. I would never have believed that I could laugh and smile in that place, to which I had returned in my nightmares many times over the years, but that day, I did.

Her father had remarried, and his new wife, Aileen, had softened him, therefore the marriage went unopposed. Such was the loss of the community to the plague that had killed Duncan, and a blight the year after that, that I was largely unrecognized; our old neighbours had moved away, and the island community looked very different to the one I had known. I was hopeful, that day, but not a day thereafter.

That winter was the toughest the island had ever faced. Snows the height of a man wrapped the fields and crofts. And as the farmers struggled to keep the livestock alive, the elders sounded the alarm – a child had gone missing.

Little Blair Reid, all of seven years old, was known to play near Witches Hide, and now he was gone. The savage weather made searching difficult, but I joined the men who scoured the fields for fresh tracks. One evening, the church bells sounded – the lad had been found on the bay close to the broch. He was returned home, his parents overjoyed.

They bathed and fed him, but that night, his mother took ill. Her cheeks burned though she said she was cold, and the next day, she passed. That was when Angus Reid noticed the mark on his son. A mark on his hip, with numbers.

Folk said Angus had tried to conceal the mark, but eventually it had got out, and folk were scared. This was not a child, not Blair Reid at all, but a wildling, and if Angus didn't act quickly, the whole family would be wiped out. Maybe the whole bloodline, which stretched far across the island and into the south. The winter deepened, storms beating down on the houses and tearing apart fishing boats. We were faced with starvation. Angus had only just buried his wife. Now he was tasked with taking his oldest son, or the wildling that mimicked his oldest son, to a tree in the valley to be killed, as the elders had instructed.

We heard the cries. Angus was taking the boy to be killed in the valley, and the boy's grandmother was distraught, pleading for him to stop. As smoke drifted high across the village, rumours abounded that Angus had drugged the boy beforehand.

This time, I prayed the rumours were true.

I imagine that Angus' grief sharpened his memory of Finwell's curse. And he remembered Amy's screams alongside her mother, proclaiming that the islanders would burn their own children just as the witches had been burned. As soon as Blair was killed, the winter storms lifted, as though the weather had been turned by the actions taken upon the wildling. Gossip began to be spread about Amy, how she was to blame for the curse, how I was the son of a witch, and now our wicked powers were conjoined in holy matrimony. And so the cycle went, story after story being passed around the island like the changing of the moon.

LIV, 1998

I

When we arrived back at the bothy, I closed the door and moved a heavy chair against the knob.

'What's happening?' Clover wailed.

'Mummy, you're scaring us,' Luna said, her voice trembling.

I moved quickly to Saffy's bedroom, intent on telling her to pack her things. I knew it was late, and once again I was dragging my children out late at night, fleeing another home and driving them to who knows where. But the encounter on the boat with Patrick Roberts had terrified me, and that terror had leveraged a clean vision of what I needed to do – I needed to leave. I needed to see a doctor. I needed to focus on getting well; not by folklore and not by shamanism, but by science.

But Saffy wasn't in her bedroom. I squinted at the clock – it was after eleven o'clock. She should have been back from Machara's house. Where was she?

I looked at the list of phone numbers scribbled in pencil on a page that was Blu-tacked to the fridge. There was a number for Sibyl, Machara's mother. I called it.

'Hello?'

'I'm sorry it's late, but is Sapphire there?'

'No. I've not seen her for a few days now. Machara's here. I can ask her . . .'

I waited. She returned to the phone.

'Machara says she hasn't seen her either. Not since yesterday.'

'Are you sure?'

'That's what she said.'

I set the phone down carefully, trying to think about what to do, who to try. I called Isla to see if she'd been with Rowan. It was a long shot, and Isla confirmed that she wasn't. I tried other people, other school friends and acquaintances – everyone and anyone Isla could provide a number for.

But no one had seen her.

Finally, I called Finn. I hoped beyond imagination that maybe she'd walked to their home to see Cassie. Perhaps she'd fallen asleep, and Finn hadn't the heart to wake her. I was clutching at straws.

'She's not here,' Finn said, and I started to cry. 'When did you last see her?'

I couldn't think. My mind was a flurry of names and dates, the terrifying images in the lantern room still flashing in my brain.

I was still on the phone to Finn when Luna stepped forward, one arm across her stomach and her face full of guilt. 'I think she's run away.'

I grabbed her by the upper arms. 'What do you mean, Luna? What did you see?'

She broke down into tears.

'I'm sorry!' she shouted. 'I promised not to tell!'

II

Saffy was gone. She had been gone for days.

I felt like I was in a nightmare, a living, labyrinthine nightmare that I was having to drag myself through on my elbows. Saffy's teacher told us that she'd been off school on Friday; I had supposed she'd woken early and caught the bus herself, as she occasionally did. And when she didn't come home, I supposed she'd gone to Machara's house.

I wracked my brains; I had *thought* I'd heard her come in at night. I had even crept up to the loft and peeked my head around her door to see if she was in bed, and I'd seen the rumpled covers of her bed and thought she was there. Why hadn't I made sure?

I had been distracted by my work. So hellbent had I been on finishing the Longing that I hadn't even noticed my oldest child wasn't at home.

It was after midnight, but Finn insisted on bringing Cassie over while he searched the island in his car. Cassie proved a good distraction for Luna and Clover while I made more calls. To the police, to the coast guard. I made desperate calls to Sean's family, my father, Saffy's old school friends, even teachers from her old schools – anyone and everyone that Saffy might have contacted.

At seven the next morning, a black Range Rover pulled up outside and two men got out.

'Who are they?' Clover said warily, watching them negotiate their way to the bothy.

'Detectives,' I told her, and I felt a fleeting sense of relief, which dissipated when Bram walked into the bothy with a junior policeman, Police Constable Thomson, a short, dark-haired man in his twenties, both in plain clothes.

My throat was tight and my head bursting with noise. I hadn't slept, not a wink. Saffy was impulsive, and she was bullheaded and so downright hateful that sometimes I'd had to force myself to walk away from her so as not to scream in her face. But I knew my oldest daughter. She'd have contacted me by now. At the very least, she'd have wanted to know that her punishment had worked. She'd have wanted to know that I was beside myself, searching every corner and overturning every stone to find her.

Bram and PC Thomson searched her bedroom. They found some letters to her boyfriend, Jack, and some books she'd been reading. One of them had several pages folded down at the corners. The one by Patrick Roberts.

'Was she having a relationship with Mr Roberts?' Bram asked.

'A relationship?' I said, looking from him to PC Thomson. 'No! And in any case, Patrick Roberts has been away for most of the time we've been here.'

He flipped a Polaroid out of the back of the book. 'Did she take this for him?'

I took the Polaroid and gasped. It was a picture of Saffy,

but I almost didn't recognize her – she was naked, her red lips stretched into a seductive smile, one hand cupping her breast. My little girl. I looked up at Bram, unable to speak for horror.

He flicked a grim look at PC Thomson. 'Bring Roberts in for a chat.'

III

For several hours, I fell into the abyss of despair imagining what Patrick might have done to my daughter. How I'd neglected to keep as close an eye on her as I should have done. How I should have seen that she was desperate for attention, for love.

I had failed as a mother.

When Bram called to say they'd let Patrick go, my despair only widened. I had so many questions, and no answers.

Needless to say, I missed my GP appointment. I did not sleep, nor eat. Time passed in strange bursts.

Bram and PC Thomson insisted on interviewing Luna several times over the next few days. Even though I could see she was suffering with guilt and devastation, I allowed it. They said the slightest detail that Luna could remember – a throwaway phrase Saffy had used, some minor action that was in some way out of the ordinary – could point the way to Saffy. Boats docked and sailed away dozens of times a day; she might have been dragged off by anyone, halfway across the ocean in any direction. Or she could

317

have drowned. Or she might have simply decided to punish me for real and hitchhiked back to England, or further.

Isla and Mirrin came to the bothy with food and video-tapes for Clover and Luna. It was this last touch that warmed me to them. For a few moments after they'd put on *Barney the Dinosaur* the girls were glued to the screen, their crying about Saffy temporarily halted. Finn and I went out and waded across the causeway. Rain was coming down in great ropes, the horizon bruised and thunderous.

We walked along the beach towards Strallaig, then took the path towards the hill that Finn had said offered views of the whole island. The rain was so heavy that the hill seemed to be disintegrating into a muddy river, and several times we had to lower on all fours to stop from sliding back down. I was soaking wet, blinded by rain, but I kept going until I reached the top. I knew it was ridiculous – I had no binoculars, no way of seeing Saffy from that height, even if she'd stood in the village square – but perhaps, I thought, perhaps *she* might see *me*. Perhaps, if she spotted me on the hill from wherever she might be on the island, the sight of her small, broken mother searching desperately for her would persuade her to come home.

But it didn't.

Back at the bothy, I sat at the kitchen table, shaking with cold and shock, my mind shattered into a million pieces. Finn had taken Cassie home to rest, and I had felt inde-scribably bereft as I watched his car pull away. It hit me in that moment how isolated I was, how alone. How sinister the sea, creeping towards the causeway and finally swal-lowing it.

Isla made me a cup of hot tea and Mirrin set about doing the dishes and gathering laundry.

'The whole island is searching for her,' Isla said gently. 'Everyone's out with their dogs and torches. We'll find her.'

When the phone rang again, I pounced on it. It was Bram.

'As you know, we've spoken with a fair few people on the island. But there's one man we're classing as a person of interest just now.'

'Patrick,' I said.

He cleared his throat. 'No. Not Patrick. I believe you know a man by the name of Finn McAllen?'

IV

I don't really remember much about that day. I was in shock. Finn was a person of interest in the disappearance of my daughter. Rowan had said that she saw him with Saffy the night before she went missing. Another witness stated that they'd seen Finn's car parked near the woods that night. They'd searched Finn's car and found three Polaroids of Saffy in sexual poses.

I tried to retrace Finn's movements over the last week, the times I had seen him and the times he had gone home or gone to work on the rewilding project. Saffy had left the bothy sometime between Thursday evening and Friday morning, which was when Luna had taken her food and discovered she was no longer in the hut in the woods. Brodie had seen her at around four on Thursday afternoon, then spent the evening with Rowan. He returned home at nine-thirty, where he stayed all night until the following morning. His parents confirmed this. Finn was at home on Thursday night with Cassie. I had seen him that afternoon, when I picked up the girls from school. Saffy wasn't there, but then none of the friends she'd made were – they were all still in the woods, finishing up a poetry project. I assumed she'd be home later.

Finn had dropped me, Luna and Clover back home at the bothy.

'Aren't you coming in?' I'd said to him when he left the engine running. 'I've made lasagne. No eggs.'

He smiled. 'I promised Cassie I'd spend some time with her tonight. Didn't I, Cass?'

She pouted and looked from Luna and Clover to her dad. 'But Daa-aad! Luna and Clover said we'd do a pony party tonight. Didn't we?'

All three girls nodded in dejection.

'Aw, come on, Cass,' he said. 'You've got to make time for your old man.'

And she'd relented. But even at the time, I'd noticed that Finn had seemed pointedly unwilling to come inside. A part of me had taken it as a sign that he was distancing himself from me.

I couldn't believe that he'd taken Saffy. But doubt crept in, and I felt horrified at what he might have done to her. Who could I trust?

I retraced my steps, thought carefully about every detail, every word spoken. On Friday evening I'd taken Luna and Clover for a nature hunt around the small island of the Longing. We'd gathered up some shells and flowers, then stood on the outcrop and waved to Basil, who was still hanging around the bay. We'd stood and tried to find the major constellations until the cold forced us indoors. I'd heard the door open and close, and I could have sworn that I heard Saffy go upstairs and climb into bed.

I hated myself for not checking. Two minutes. That's all

it would have taken for me to discover that she wasn't at home.

I don't think I could bring myself to fully imagine why Finn might have taken Saffy. My mind lurched to those moments I could recall her being with us. How had he looked at her? How had he spoken to her? Jokes he'd told, moments where I might not have seen him touching her.

I woke up the next morning, shocked to have dozed off. I was in the living room, still fully clothed and curled up in the armchair Finn claimed was his grandfather's.

'Mum?'

I looked up to find Luna standing there in her day clothes. Her dark hair was dishevelled from sleep and she'd dragged her duvet with her and wore it wrapped around her like a cape.

'Where's Clover?' she said sleepily, looking around the room.

'It's early,' I said, pulling myself to my feet. 'She'll still be asleep.'

Luna looked back at her room. 'She's not in bed.'

I studied her face for a half-second before racing into their bedroom and searching the room. She was right – Clover wasn't there. Nor was she in the bathroom, the kitchen, or hiding in a cupboard.

'Clover, *please*!' I shouted. 'This isn't funny. Where are you? Please come out!'

I opened the front door and lurched outside, where angry white waves were smashing across the causeway. I searched the Longing, taking the rickety staircase two steps at a time until I reached the lantern room.

Empty.

I ran back down and searched the island, clambering

down the cliff face to see if perhaps she'd gone looking for seals on her own and slipped. There was no sign of her. No trace.

Nothing.

Finally, I lifted the phone and called the police.

'My daughter,' I managed to gasp. 'My youngest daughter Clover isn't here. She's gone.'

LUNA, 2021

I

'This is fucking insane,' Cassie says, opening two bottles of non-alcoholic beer in the kitchen. 'I was literally talking about you the other day. And now you're here, sitting on my sofa. I can't get over it.'

They are in Cassie's croft on the west of the island. It used to belong to her father, Finn, and Luna vaguely remembers playing in the kitchen. Cassie has redecorated since – it's charming, with a white living room, large open fire, and dramatic views of green fields rolling down to blue sea. Clover is already asleep on the sofa, worn out from the tumult in the car. Luna's still shaken after the confrontation with Brodie. The minute she stepped inside Cassie's home she felt tearful, a release of everything that had happened before.

Cassie hands Luna a bottle and sinks down in the armchair opposite. 'How long has it been?' she says, dragging a hand through her short blonde hair. 'You were all here in the autumn of 1998. So . . . twenty-two years?'

'You were talking about me?' Luna asks.

Cassie nods. 'There was this headline in the newspaper about a girl called Sapphire. It made me think of the three of you. I told the guy I work with about the summer I met you. You were only here for a couple of months but I never had a best friend like you, before or since.'

Cassie's words are like a warm blanket across Luna's shoulders. 'Was the headline about Saffy?' she asks.

'Oh, no – about a different girl. She just had the same name. They found her here last September.'

Luna frowns. 'Found her here?'

'I'm taking it Saffy has never been found?' Cassie asks sadly.

Luna shakes her head.

'God. I'm so sorry.'

Cassie passes her phone to Luna. There's a news article dated 22 September 2020.

Teenage girl found on Lòn Haven still unclaimed.

'Apparently she was found on the bay,' Cassie says, sitting next to Luna. 'Nobody had seen her before. Nobody reported her missing. She wasn't from the island at all. No family or friends here.'

Luna's eyes fall on the name amidst the text of the article.

She's 15 years old, and says her name is Sapphire. She does not have a local accent and claims to be from northern England. Anyone with information should call the following number.

'What happened to her?' Luna asks.

'I don't know. It couldn't be Saffy though, could it?'

Luna checks the date of the article again before handing the phone back. 'I suppose not.'

Cassie has been living in Edinburgh for the last five years with her wife, Lucia, and is temporarily based in Lòn Haven for two months to work on a restoration project for Historic Scotland. Prior to Edinburgh, she was living in Auckland, New Zealand. A Kiwi twang slides into her voice every now and then.

'What about you?' Cassie says, nodding at Luna's bump. 'When are you due?'

Luna rubs her belly, feeling a little spine pressing against her palm. 'New Year's Eve.'

'Husband? Wife?'

Luna shakes her head. 'Neither. I've been with Ethan for a long time. The plan *was* that we'd get married, but . . .' She tails off, biting her lip.

'Did you split?'

'No. Not yet, anyway. He proposed and I rejected him. It came as a shock to both of us.'

Cassie takes that in. 'Do you think it was to do with everything that's happened? Losing your whole family at the age of ten . . . that's a mindfuck if ever there was one.'

Luna gives a small laugh. 'Don't I know it.'

'Do you think Ethan knows that's why you rejected him?'

'I'm not honestly sure. He took it quite badly . . .'

Cassie gives a small smile and tilts her jaw. 'Wounded pride, perhaps?'

'A lot of that. And I suppose he has his own issues.'

'Don't we all?'

Luna bites her lip. 'I think he's worried that it's *him* I was rejecting. Not marriage.'

Cassie leans forward. 'But . . . have you told him you weren't rejecting *him*?'

'Not in so many words.' Luna rubs her stomach and lays her head back on the sofa. 'Maybe I should.' She smiles at Cassie. 'Thanks.'

Cassie shrugs. 'Every relationship comes with baggage. I fucked up my last relationship so badly that it's made me an expert on communication.' She smiles. 'Lucia and I see a counsellor every year. We don't have any serious problems, but I'm a prevention-instead-of-a-cure sort of person, now.'

'What about your dad?' Luna asks. 'Is he still on Lòn Haven?'

Cassie takes a swig from her bottle and wipes her lips on the back of her arm. 'Fuck no. He moved us both to New Zealand not long after you left. When Rowan accused him of taking Saffy, I think it broke something in him. I don't think he could ever face coming back.'

Luna tries to remember this. It's a small detail buried inside other memories. 'Rowan . . . she was Isla's daughter. Wasn't she?'

Cassie nods. 'And the daughter of the Chief Inspector. Dodgy.' A muscle ripples in her jaw. 'The accusation was false, of course. And there was only a slap on the wrist for little Rowan for slipping Polaroids of Saffy into my dad's car.'

'Polaroids?'

'Nudes that Saffy took of herself. You never heard about this?'

'No. Who took the nudes?'

'Saffy did.'

Luna stares, processing this.

'Dad never said anything more about that time,' Cassie says. 'God knows I tried to get him to open up but I think it was too painful for him. Some of his closest friends stopped speaking to him after it. Mud sticks, doesn't it?'

'It does.' The mention of Isla's name has flipped Luna's stomach. She doesn't want to ask, but she has to know.

'What about Isla?' she asks. 'And Rowan. Are they still on the island?'

Cassie shakes her head. 'Rowan's in Bali, apparently. Lives on some weird commune. I think it's a cult, actually, by the sound of it. Isla's in prison. She got handed twenty years a couple of years ago.'

Luna's eyes widen. 'She's in prison?'

Cassie nods and grins, relishing the opportunity to share this with Luna. 'It was a huge scandal, as you can imagine. Bram – you remember him? Had a heart attack on the job. They brought in a new Chief Inspector, young guy, not so tolerant of bullshit folklore and what have you. About a month later, someone writes anonymously to the police that Isla killed a child in the forest. They dug up human remains and Isla confessed to the whole thing.'

Luna shivers. She presses the bottle to her cheeks, her mood spiralling. She barely knows what to do with this information. Did Isla murder Saffy? Her mind races.

'You never found Clover?' Cassie asks, sadly. 'Or your mum?'

Luna opens her mouth to answer, but holds back. She doesn't know where to start.

'I think it's beautiful that you named your daughter after Clover,' Cassie says. 'The likeness is incredible.'

'She's not my daughter,' Luna says quietly.

Cassie frowns. 'Who is she, then?'

Luna opens her mouth to lie, but despite herself, it all comes out – the phone call, the trip to the hospital in Inverness, fully expecting to be reunited with a twenty-nine-year-old woman.

Cassie looks stunned. She stands and paces, thinking it through. 'That's crazy,' she says. 'And they let you take her?'

Luna explains about her worries that social services will yet come looking for her. She tells Cassie about her theory that Clover has some kind of age regression disease that has stopped her from growing, about the things that Clover has said that *only* Clover could have known: the Longing, Saffy, their mother painting the mural.

She tells Cassie about the glass in the food they ordered at the hotel. About Brodie chasing her.

Cassie cups her hands to her mouth. 'Fuck, Luna. This happened *tonight*?'

Luna nods. 'Right before I saw you in the car park.'

'Why didn't you tell me? I've a crowbar in the boot of my car. I'd have gone after the bastard if you said . . .' She recovers. 'Tell me you at least called the police?'

'I don't trust *anyone* on this island,' Luna says firmly. 'Except you.'

'I've heard about Brodie,' Cassie says after a long silence. 'He's been married a couple of times, had a long stint with drugs, fell on hard times.' She drinks the last of her beer.

'Why would he say I'm meant to be dead, Cassie?' Luna asks. 'What happened after I left?'

Cassie blinks, thinking back. 'It's all a bit of a blur . . . Dad was so out of sorts after the accusation . . . and then Liv went missing and he spent a while looking for her. He took you to the police station, do you remember that?'

Luna shakes her head. 'No, I didn't know that.'

Cassie bites her lip. 'He wouldn't leave until social services were ferried out from Inverness. I remember him phoning them, even when we were in Auckland, to check up on you.' She looks up. 'He said you were in foster care. What was that like?'

'I'm still in touch with one of my foster mothers. Other than that, it was shit from start to finish.'

Cassie nods again, smiles. 'You seem to have it together, though.'

Luna considers briefly telling Cassie about her wayward youth, her years as a shoplifter, desperate to be caught for something, for someone to tell her why she'd been abandoned by her mother.

'You remember the folktale about wildlings?' she says after a long pause.

'Remember?' Cassie says. 'Of course I bloody remember. It was drilled into us before we could talk.'

Luna cocks her head. 'You still believe it?'

Cassie gives a small laugh. 'Are you joking?'

'If I told you that Clover has a burn on her hip, a set of numbers – what would you think?'

Cassie stares. 'I'd say that was very bloody unfortunate and you should make sure she sees a doctor . . .'

'And the fact that she's still a seven-year-old?'

A pause. 'Luna. She *cannot* be Clover.'

'I think she's a wildling.' She feels something change in her as she says it. Saying it aloud is different than thinking it– she feels both relieved and sick to her stomach. How can she believe this?

Cassie's face softens into pity. 'You know it's just a fairy tale. You of all people know . . .'

'I'm not saying I know how it all works,' Luna says, covering her face with her hands. 'I'm just trying to connect the facts. But you know the stories. You can tell a wildling by the mark . . .'

Cassie sits back in her seat, her eyes wide. She clasps her hands and visibly considers her next words. 'OK, so I remember that after Saffy and Clover went missing,' she says, 'there was a rumour about you. People said *you* were a wildling.'

Luna feels her heart race. She tries to remember, but her mind is a whirlwind of images and sounds, cloudy with a thousand emotions. 'A wildling.'

'Now do you see what a ridiculous idea that is?'

'Well, it's obvious that I wasn't.'

'"Obvious" is a relative term.'

'Do you think that has anything to do with Brodie saying I was meant to be dead?' Luna says, and Cassie stares ahead, searching her own memories.

'I don't know,' she says. 'I really don't know.'

II

'Are you all right, Clover?' Luna asks as they lie in the twin beds.

Clover nods, but she looks sad. 'That man was scary.'

She means Brodie. 'He won't hurt you. I promise.'

'I thought we'd see Mummy here.'

'I'm sorry.'

'And the Longing,' Clover adds. 'I don't understand. Why is it like that?'

'That's why we're here,' Luna says. 'To find answers.'

'Thank you,' Clover says, but she still seems sad.

Luna presses a hand to her belly, feeling the baby kick. She squeezes her eyes shut and breathes deep. She knows what has to be done. But it's so, so hard.

'I was thinking we could take a drive,' she says in a thin voice.

'When?'

'Tomorrow. First thing. I thought . . . we could explore the woods.'

'Will Mummy be there?'

'I don't know.'

Clover yawns, deeply. 'OK.'

She turns over, stretching out a hand, brushing against Luna's finger. And there it is again, the beginning of the headache that grows and grows until it feels her head might explode.

She squeezes her eyes tight shut, pressing the balls of her palms against them as though to stop them from exploding out of her head. She wants to cry out, but even amidst the agony of it she knows she mustn't alarm Clover, or Cassie. She gets up and feels her way to the kitchen, hoping to find some kind of painkiller that will numb the pain. The cold on the ground floor of the house is instantly soothing, and so she makes her way to the front door, pulling it open and letting the chill of the night air wash over her.

She looks out over the ocean in the distance, the headache gradually lifting, images swirling in her mind.

She remembers finding an odd shape on the bay by the Longing, a large black hump that looked like the sand had dropped to reveal a stone bank. When she'd gotten closer, she spotted the white marks, the slits indicating gills, and gasped. It was the basking shark, Basil. He had beached, his gills opening and closing slowly as he struggled for breath. He was so large his own body weight was crushing him, and he looked like he was melting into the sand.

Mr McPherson, the fisherman, had appeared with two buckets of water. He poured them over the shark.

'If we do this until the tide comes in, we might save him,' he'd said.

Luna had taken one of the buckets and ran to the tide, scooping it up and tossing it over the shark. It was a phenomenal and strange sight. That enormous shark, long as a bus and helpless as a kitten.

She remembers scooping the water and dumping it over the shark until her arms ached. Finally, Mr McPherson had said, 'That's enough, lass. Say your farewell.' They'd stood in silence for a moment, looking down at the huge body of the shark, his grey skin so rough that Luna had friction burns from where she'd accidentally rubbed her arms against him whilst pouring water over him. He was more rock than fish, all thirty feet of him lying stretched out on the sand. She'd asked Mr McPherson if they could lasso him somehow and get a boat to tug him back out to sea.

'The rope would only hurt him,' he said. 'Yon beast weighs about five ton. We're best letting nature take its course. He shoulda left these waters weeks ago with the rest a the sharks. Maybe he knew his time was up and he wanted to die here.'

Luna was devastated. After the disappearances of her sisters it seemed a cruelty to watch such a gentle giant die right in front of her.

Mr McPherson had urged her to keep away from Basil's body. Once he was dead, toxins would come off his skin that might make people very sick. The coastguard would remove him safely, once he started to decompose.

Luna looks up. Her headache is gone, the cold air a balm for the heat of it. Or perhaps it's the distance she's put between her and Clover.

She's at the bottom of the field in front of Cassie's croft, where the waves can be heard crashing against the rocks below. It's the sky that has her attention. It's so vast, shimmering with stars. She looks up at them and wonders if it's true that we're all made of stardust. The baby kicks again, and she smiles. Her memories are coming back thick and fast. This is what she's always wanted, she thinks. Every birthday, she'd blow out her candles with a wish to remember tucked closely behind the wish for her sisters to return. And now that she's here, in Lòn Haven, it's happening. The unspooling of the past.

But there's one more thing she came here to do.

She turns, and heads quietly into Cassie's kitchen, where she finds the knife block. She selects the one with a long, slim blade, perfect for slitting a throat. She'll slip it inside her bag for tomorrow's trip to the woods.

Behind her, Cassie hides in the shadows. She sees Luna's face in the thin light of the moon at the window, studying the knife, and catches her breath.

III

The snows lifted from Lòn Haven and the sun shone down, and while the people recovered and reeled from the visitation of a wildling to the island, and the near-extinction of our community, Amy revisited her mother's runes and book of spells.

She woke me one night, sopping wet and shivering with cold.

'I worked it out,' she said. 'I think I know how to fix it.'

I helped her out of her wet clothes and lit the fire while she wrapped herself in a blanket.

'I went inside Witches Hide,' she said, shivering. This time, however, instead of climbing back up the tunnel at the entrance, she said she went out the other end that led to the sea. She had expected to step into low tide, but when she went through, she plunged into deep water, the depths almost claiming her.

When she emerged, she swam to shore and sat shivering on the bay. There was a girl with long black hair collecting seaweed, who wrapped her arisaid across her shoulders for warmth. The girl said her name was Marion Darroch. Her father was Christopher Darroch.

The only Christopher Darroch I knew was a child of two years old. A little chubby creature who walked everywhere behind his mother, holding on to her skirts.

'Ask me how long I've been gone,' she said.

I looked out the window. 'You've been gone this night.'

She smiled and shook her head, and there it was again, just for a moment – the wild glint in her eye. 'I've been gone over two months.'

She had hit her head, I thought, or been driven mad by fear. People would cross the street when they saw her, after what had happened to Angus' son Blair. The curse that she'd uttered five years before was dredged up as a likely cause for the wildling.

I rubbed her hair with a towel, and she gasped in pain, pulling at something on her shoulder.

'What is it?' I said.

Slowly, I moved the blanket from the spot that was evidently causing her pain, squinting until I saw the cause – a burn which had caused the skin to rise up in a livid red circle.

'How did this happen?' I asked.

I saw something inside the wound and looked closer – someone had used a sharp blade to carve four small numbers into her skin, all in a row.

1

7

0

7

I knew what it meant, and what it would mean if anyone else were to see.

And I knew how I was meant to act, now that I had seen the mark.

I was to kill her.

I was to burn Amy alive.

LIV, 1998

I

'Isla!' I yelled, hammering on the door of her house.

'You've found them?' she said, mistaking my distress for joy.

I was hysterical. She told me to come inside and I stumbled forward, sinking to the floor. Luna was with me and I wanted to be composed for her sake, but as soon as I saw Isla it felt as though everything I had been holding in spilled out in a tremendous rush.

'Rowan,' Isla called. 'Can you take Luna here and show her what you've been baking?'

I saw Rowan appear. She took Luna by the hand and led her away. Patiently, Isla sat on the floor with me and laid a hand on my arm. 'Easy now,' she said. 'Whatever has happened?'

I told her about the night before. About waking up and finding that sometime during the night a child had come into the house. And no, it wasn't Clover, and it wasn't Saffy – it was a child that looked exactly like Luna.

She sat in complete silence as I told her, my words

rambling and half-crazed. I was at the end of my rope, the end of my wits. And I was perfectly ready to accept that perhaps I was mad, and this was all a dream.

'She was filthy and there were some cuts and bruises,' I said, 'but she is Luna. Her exact double.'

'And she has a mark on her?'

I nodded. 'On the back of her knee. Four numbers. I checked.'

Isla gripped me by the upper arms and stared hard into my face. 'Listen to me and listen well. The child with the mark is *not* your daughter.' She turned and nodded at the kitchen, where I could see Luna helping Rowan lay out cookie dough on a baking tray. 'This is the one without the mark?'

'Yes.'

'*That* is Luna,' she said. 'The other one isn't.'

I nodded but I was barely taking in what she was saying. My mind was racing. Isla told me to come into the living room and sit down. 'Now,' she said, pulling up a chair close to me. 'Walk me through what happened. Step by step.'

'I put Luna to bed last night.'

'What time?'

'I don't know . . . about eight o'clock.'

'And then what happened?'

'I couldn't sleep,' I said, pressing the balls of my palms into my eyes. 'Since . . . I've hardly slept a night since Saffy went missing. And Clover. But I was so tired, I kept drifting off and then waking up.' I squeezed my eyes shut, the horror of it bringing me to silence. Waking was like being plunged into lava. Being torn from the bliss of sleep into the knowledge that not one but two of my daughters were missing.

'I heard a noise at the door. It woke me up. It was still dark. I thought, maybe it was Saffy, or Clover. I shouted their names and ran to the door. Before I opened it, Luna appeared behind me and asked if it was Clover. The noise had woken her up, too.'

'And then what happened?'

'I opened the door. There was a girl standing on the porch. I saw it was Luna, only she was wet and covered in dirt. Like she'd had a fall. She was shivering with cold and begging me for help.'

'And did you?'

'My first instinct was to help her, but then I turned and saw Luna standing in her bedroom. She stepped out and saw the other girl.'

A cold finger of ice ran down my spine. There were two of them. Two Lunas. One crying and begging for help, the other pulling at me, begging me to explain who the other girl was and why she looked like her. In a handful of seconds both girls were crying, their voices identical in pitch, on either side of me, both of them calling 'Mummy' in stereo.

Both of them were asking 'Who is she?' over and over, pointing at the other one. After all that had happened I felt like I was going out of my mind.

II

I felt like I was falling down a never-ending hole of confusion. The other Luna had begged me to tell her what was happening, and she pointed at Luna and asked who she was and why she was here, and then the two of them were crying and shrieking, their voices echoing and braiding, until I shouted, 'Enough!'

I slumped against the wall in the hallway and drew my knees up to my chest, shaking all over. The voices changed – now the girls were working out how to help me.

'You go get her some water,' one of them said. 'I'll get her a cloth.'

'Here you go, Mummy.'

I opened my eyes to see a glass of water held in front of me, and behind it, two versions of my daughter. Standing side by side like twins, reflections of each other, Tweedle Dee and Tweedle Dum. I must have laughed, because they shared a look and said, almost in chorus, 'Are you all right, Mummy?'

My strength had left me. I couldn't speak. I felt pinned

to the floor, the weight of all that had happened collapsing on me like mountains. Saffy's disappearance. Clover's.

And now this.

I heard the girls beginning to talk to each other.

'Are you really called Luna?'

'Yes. Are *you*?'

'Of course I am.'

'This is really weird.'

'I know. Can you tell what I'm thinking?'

'You're thinking about dinosaurs.'

'Actually I was thinking about trees.'

'Cheese? Are you hungry?'

'A little.'

'Do you like cheese?'

'Only in sandwiches.'

'Me too.'

'What's your favourite colour?'

'Blue.'

'Mine too! What about your favourite animal?'

'A narwhal. It's a whale with a . . .'

'I *know* what a narwhal is. It's my favourite animal, too.'

And so it went on. Luna went upstairs to fetch some dry clothes for the other girl and I sipped at my water, finally gaining enough strength to crawl out of the hallway and through to the living room. The girls followed, still chatting. My mind had dredged up the conversation I'd had with Isla and the others about wildlings. She'd said they looked identical to the children they wanted to kill, that the likeness was so incredible that parents were duped, and often grew so confused that they thrust out the wrong child, or both. *The only way to tell them apart is by a small mark that the wildling often bears. A mark that the human child doesn't have.*

I looked up and saw the girls begin to sit down on the floor opposite each other, Luna passing her double a clean T-shirt and leggings to change into. I was standing behind her, and as the muddied girl straightened a leg to pull the leggings on, I saw the red mark behind her knee. Isla's words rang in my ears. I leaned forward, telling her to hold on a moment. I needed to check something.

I looked closer, and there it was – four digits etched into tender flesh, flaming red.

1
9
9
8

'What's wrong?' the girl said. 'Did something bite me?'

I couldn't speak for shock.

'Maybe you scratched it,' Luna said, inspecting the burn. 'I'll get a plaster.'

Ice-cold fear seized me as Luna applied the plaster to the mark. This was something completely removed from anything I'd ever encountered before, something not of this world, and either I had plunged into insanity or I was encountering an actual wildling. And I recalled the warning Isla and the ladies gave me about the little boy who came into my house that night.

Their aim is to wipe out bloodlines.

Luna had brought out one of her toy dinosaurs, much to the imposter's delight. They played on the floor for a while, exchanging facts about sauropods and theropods, and my heart was racing. What would I do? Who on earth could I turn to, and how would I explain it? Would I call the police? What if they took away the wrong Luna?

'Did you sleep in my bed last night?' the imposter asked Luna.

'You mean *my* bed,' Luna corrected. 'Is your mummy called Olivia, too?'

'Well, yes, but mostly she gets called Liv.'

The imposter gave a long, deep yawn into the crook of her arm. 'Sorry,' she said to Luna. 'I got lost last night. I'm so sleepy.'

'Do you want to have a nap?' Luna said. 'My bed's really comfy.'

'You mean *my* bed, silly,' the imposter said. She went to say something else but it was stifled by a yawn. 'Maybe just a little nap. Oh! I just remembered where I put it!'

'Put what?' Luna asked.

The imposter jumped up and pulled one of the armchairs forward, then reached down and held something in the air. 'I found it! Look, Mummy!'

'You found T-Rex!' Luna shouted.

'I was playing with him here yesterday,' the imposter said. Then, 'Do you mind if I take him for a little nap?'

Luna nodded, and I watched, hollowed out with horror, as the imposter went into Luna's bedroom and climbed into bed, the T-Rex clutched to her chest.

Luna came back into the living room and sat next to me. 'Who is that girl, Mummy?'

'I don't know,' I said. 'Have you ever seen her before?'

Luna shook her head. 'She looks just like me. She talks like me, too.'

'And that's when I came here,' I now told Isla. 'I took Luna, put her in the car, and drove her here.'

Isla nodded.

'Where's the other one? The other girl?'

'I left her at the bothy,' I said weakly. 'I didn't know what to do . . .'

Isla looked frustrated. 'You need to go back. It might already have left . . .'

I nodded, reluctantly. I felt like I wanted to be sick.

'You know it's a wildling.'

I squeezed my eyes shut and clasped my hands to my head. I didn't want to agree with her. I wanted to curl into a ball and disappear.

Isla leaned forward and took my hands.

'If you don't act now, you'll never see *any* of your daughters again. Luna included.'

Her voice and eyes were hard.

'What do you mean?'

'You think it's a coincidence that Saffy and Clover are missing, and now this?' She rose from her chair and pulled a long, thin knife off the chimney breast, weighing it in her hands. 'You have to act. If you do what I tell you, you'll be safe.'

I squeezed my eyes shut. 'OK.'

'You'll need rope. And something to light a fire. And you'll need this.' She handed me the knife.

'I can't,' I whispered, looking down at the blade.

'Mummy?' Luna called from the other room. 'Rowan says she can make me hot chocolate. Am I allowed?'

I must have visibly weakened at the sound of Luna's voice – identical to the other Luna's voice – because just then Isla took my hand. 'It's best that you do it. Correct?'

It felt as though the room was underwater. Nothing felt real anymore. I managed to nod.

'I'll come with you,' Isla said with a smile. 'Now, you don't have a moment to waste.'

III

I went back to the bothy, as Isla instructed. To my relief, the other Luna – the one with the mark – was inside, puzzled and upset at my leaving her behind.

'I'm taking you out now,' I told her, offering a thin smile. 'We're going to spend some time together. Jump in the car.'

She wiped her eyes and threw me a cross look before getting into the car. I told Luna to get out of the car.

'Stay in the bothy,' I told her firmly. There was no way I could take her with us. 'Do not answer the door under any circumstances. OK? It doesn't matter who calls. Do *not* open the door.'

She nodded. Her eyes drifted to the other girl in the car.

'Where are you taking her?'

'I'm taking her back to her parents,' I said, lowering my eyes. 'She's obviously got lost. They'll be worried . . .'

'Is she a wildling?' Luna asked fearfully.

I tried not to meet her gaze.

'She is, isn't she?' Luna said, her eyes wide. 'You don't

have to take her away, Mummy. Saffy told me what to do if I saw someone who looked like me . . .'

I told her if she stayed inside she could have as many Pop Tarts as she wanted. She pleaded with me not to take the girl away. She wanted to take her hands, that's what Saffy had told her, but out of the window I spotted Isla's car parking up in front of mine, and I knew I needed to go.

Inside the car, the wildling sat calmly in the passenger seat. 'Where are we going, Mummy?' she asked, and my stomach clenched.

'We're just going for a drive,' I said in that same light-ness of tone that I'd have used if I were speaking to Luna. Isla pulled off and I started my engine, following behind. I could see Mirrin was with her.

Isla drove us out to the large forest on the other side of the island. The wildling kept talking, her voice just like Luna's. I could feel my mind beginning to tear itself apart, the divide between reality and a nightmare beginning to collapse.

'Are we going hiking?' the wildling asked.

'Just a little walk.' I had to force myself to say it.

Isla parked under some trees. She handed me a back-pack and we walked into the forest, Isla's steps quick and swift as she led the way. In the distance I could make out others, and I figured that Isla must have alerted the 'wild-ling committee.' The wildling was a terrible threat, and they'd come to make sure it was taken care of.

My stomach dropping, I took the wildling's hand. It felt exactly like Luna's.

'This is it,' Mirrin told me quietly, nodding at a clearing. I saw a group of trees that looked like they'd been burned. The burning trees, I remembered.

The people from the committee drew closer. I saw some of them were wearing balaclavas, and others were carrying rowan branches. Rowan, I thought. For protection.

Isla flashed Luna a smile, then turned to me. 'You brought everything?'

I swallowed back a sob. 'I think so.'

She took a step closer and placed a hand on my arm. 'I know this is hard. But you must do this. If you ever want to see your girls again, you *must* do this.'

'How do you know?' I said, looking down at Luna. Her tummy was rumbling and she was beginning to whine. Luna always hated walking long distances.

She gripped my hand. 'Remember what I said? If you don't act, you'll lose everything. I promise you – Saffy and Clover will be found once you do this.'

I took off my backpack and, with trembling hands, pulled out the contents that Isla had packed.

The wildling's whining was getting louder, more persistent, and Isla saw it was causing me to soften. She sounded so like my daughter. Perhaps she was. Perhaps there was some other explanation for the two Lunas.

But how could there be?

'Mum, I'm *hungry*,' she said, flopping down to the ground. 'Can I *please* have a sandwich?'

Isla answered for me. 'Of course you can,' she told the wildling, throwing her a wide, all-the-teeth smile. 'But first, we have to play a game.'

'A game?'

Isla nodded. 'You need to follow your mother.'

'What game are we playing?' the wildling asked, her face angled up at me, full of innocence.

I tried to smile, like Isla, but it was so hard to pretend.

So difficult, when she looked so like Luna. 'It's kind of like hide and seek,' I said. My voice sound far off, as though it wasn't mine.

'Only we have to tie you to a tree while you count to a hundred,' Isla added.

It was time. The people from the wildling committee were visible and coming closer. I thought they might hurt me if I didn't do it. I thought of Luna, back at the bothy, all alone. What if they hurt her, too?

I could see that the wildling was getting distressed, her face crumpling. She looked so small, so vulnerable. I pressed a hand to my mouth, and instantly Isla was by my side, reassuring me.

'I know how hard this is,' she said. 'Remember, everything you see before you is not what it seems.'

I nodded, but when the wildling turned I had to crouch down to check the burn on the back of her leg to reassure myself that she wasn't Luna.

And there it was. Four numbers, in a vertical row.

The sight of the numbers sent a fresh chill ripping through me. It was there, just as Isla and the ladies said it would be. The mark of a wildling.

'Stand against the tree,' I said, straightening. But the wildling looked at me with such fear on her face that I felt my resolve weaken again. It felt unnatural to treat a child this way, my *own* child, and yet I clung to what Isla had said. She was a wildling. She had to be.

Tentatively, the wildling stood against the tree, her face full of terror. I tried not to look in her eyes as I moved the rope around her, fastening her there.

Isla placed the bundle in my hands. The long, sharp knife from her home, wrapped in a blanket.

The wildling's eyes fell on the blade and she started to cry. 'I love you, Mummy!' she said. 'Please don't hurt me.'

'Do it now, Liv!' Mirrin shouted from somewhere in the trees. 'Now!'

I raised the knife and willed myself to do what needed to be done. My daughters' faces flashed in my mind. Saffy. Clover. Luna. I was wrong when I'd wished I'd never had them. Despite everything, no matter how terrible our lives had been, it was all worth it.

I would die for them.

And I would kill for them.

'Please, Mummy!'

I looked down into the wildling's face, into the terror that was drawn across it. In that instant, something inside me sparked to life, screaming that *this* was my daughter. My instincts were suddenly loud, stronger than Isla's whispers behind me and the wind in the trees and the fears that screamed in my head.

I brought down the knife to cut the ropes, but Luna had somehow wiggled her arm free and raised it, catching the nick of the blade before I could stop it in time. Blood flew through the air, landing on my face. I moved the blade to the ropes, cutting her free.

I shouted at her to run. Luna darted through the trees, quickly moving out of sight. I glanced around. Isla stared at me, her mouth open. She reached forward to grab me, but I lunged away. Behind her I saw villagers starting to head after Luna.

I broke into a run in the opposite direction, drawing them away from her.

IV

I could not kill Amy. I knew that, as much as I knew I was looking at the mark of a wildling on my wife's skin. I could never kill her, not for anything.

I told her to relay to me what had happened after she'd gone through Witches Hide and met Marion Darroch on the shore. She said that Marion had told her that the year was 1707. The proof, she said, lay in the church graveyard, where a fresh tombstone was marked with the year – 1707, just as the mark on her skin stated.

Amy was mesmerized, she said, and terrified, for although she looked for me, she could not find me.

She climbed back into the cave and went through once more, hoping to arrive back in 1667. She went dozens of times, the cave spitting her out at whim to the years before her own birth, before her mother's birth, and far into the future. She said she passed through the cave and it sent her where it wished her to go, branding the year on her skin each time like a burn.

Slowly, she lifted her right sleeve. Just as trees are ringed inside their bark with each passing year, so too did the flesh of her arm report hundreds of fiery red numbers, etched painfully into her skin. All marking the years to which she had travelled.

'Time's stigmata,' she said, fingering a particularly livid wound.

She told me she spent two months in 1921, hiding in an abandoned croft on the south of Lòn Haven and living off crops and stolen milk from a nearby farm. She knew she had to work out the spell to enable her to return to her original time. And once she did, she went through.

'So . . . do you know everything that is to come?' I said, feeling sick at the thought of it. What would that kind of knowledge do to a person?

'The boy they killed,' she said. 'Angus' son. He wasn't a wildling. He had travelled through the cave from the future.' She turned her face to the fire, her jaw set. 'I'm going to tell the Privy Council that the mark isn't what they think. That it's not the mark of the fae.'

I told her, as gently as I could, that they'd never, ever believe her. They would believe she was bewitched, or in league with the Devil. They would kill her for possessing the mark.

It had to remain a secret.

'Why don't we go through the cave together?' I told her. 'You've worked out the spell that sends you back to the time you came from, have you not?'

She nodded. 'There is a problem with that idea,' she said. There was a possibility of encountering yourself in the past, or in the future. In such a case, there would be two of you. Two Amys, or two Patricks.

I could not comprehend this.

'If this happens, you must be careful not to hold hands with your other self. If you do, the two of you will become one.'

She was both in awe and fearful of the magic, of interrupting the course of events. We were taught, as children, not to dabble with the course of nature. This was the same; she had seen her sister in the past, but did not approach her for fear of changing the order of time. And while she ached to prevent her sister's death, she knew that there were consequences to using such magic.

We planned one day to go through the cave together. We just had to decide on the year.

But the Privy Council had other ideas. Despite her efforts to conceal the marks on her skin, Isobel Boyman, one of Amy's good friends, spotted them while they were walking. She told the elders, and a charge was given to apprehend her immediately.

Not just Amy.

They also came for me.

'Amy and Patrick Roberts,' a voice called from the front door. I looked through the slats of the wood and saw a crowd of ten men, maybe more, all of them armed.

'Come out now or be forced out by fire!'

SAPPHIRE, 1998

I

'I've done it,' Brodie says as soon as he climbed up the rocks. 'I told Rowan it was over.'

She studies his face, scared to believe what he is saying. 'You told her.'

He nods. 'Aye. I told her.' He kisses her again, his tongue quick and searching. She pushed him back.

'And what did she say?'

'She wanted to know . . . if . . .'

'If what?'

'If I was in love with you.'

'What did you say?'

He looks away. 'I said, yes. I'm in love with you.'

His tone isn't convincing. 'And was that it? She was OK with it?'

'Aye. She was fine.' He grinned, slipping his hand under her shirt. 'Now, about that payment you promised.'

II

The next day is Samhain. Saffy doesn't go to school. She feels like a coward, but the thought of seeing Rowan's sullen face, stained with tears, no doubt hissing to everyone in earshot how Saffy stole her boyfriend, doesn't exactly appeal. And at least she'd not have to endure any more poetry.

And she needs to process what had happened with her and Brodie, the so-called loss of her virginity. She didn't feel like she'd lost anything. It had felt like a violence to her body, and that was really what she needed to process – why an act of love should feel so much like violence. He hadn't even kissed her, hardly even touched her. Just pushed her knickers to one side and shoved himself in, and she'd whimpered for him to stop but he kept going, panting like a dog for thirty seconds until it was over, and she felt blood wetting her legs.

Only then did the fear set in that she might get pregnant.

'Did you use a condom?' she whispered as he buttoned himself up.

He shook his head. 'Pull-out method. Just as safe.'

She had no idea what the pull-out method was. She'd ask Machara, once she went back to school.

She spends the day in the hut in the woods, smoking and listening to music. She doesn't need food or water. She doesn't feel hungry at all, isn't even cold despite the shade of the trees and the damp clinging to the walls of the hut. She's stopped bleeding but inside she feels bruised and uncomfortable. She tries to quell her misgivings about sex by recalling Brodie telling her that he loved her. The weak look on his face when he'd climaxed, and the way he'd laid his forehead against hers, as though they were the sole survivors of a cataclysmic event, bonded by the agony and ecstasy of sex. Perhaps the ecstasy part will happen for her, one day. For now, she hopes she didn't have to do it again for a long time.

She didn't hear the first couple of knocks on the door of the hut. She was absorbed in her book, the grimoire. She's learned about wildlings, and she wants to tell the whole community of Lòn Haven that they were wrong. Or at least share the book with them. Maybe it was fictional, but it was very convincing.

Another knock. *Luna*, she thinks. *Or maybe Liv.* She removes her earphones and stands up, yanks the door open, and makes to pull her little sister into a hug.

But it isn't Luna. And it isn't Liv.

'Hi,' Rowan says. Saffy's stomach drops. She looks over the figure in her doorway, dressed in a long black cape over a purple velvet dress. She doesn't look upset or angry. She looks calm, even friendly. As though she's popped by for a chin-wag over a bottle of vodka.

'Hi,' Saffy says warily. 'How did you know where I was?'

'I need to talk to you.'

Saffy hesitates. She feels suddenly trapped. Why had she even opened the door? She straightened. 'What's this about?'

'This,' Rowan says lightly, producing a thick wadge of paper and holding it out to her.

Saffy takes it. 'What is this?'

'Have a look and see,' Rowan says. 'They're all over the village.'

Saffy takes one of the sheets of paper and stares down in horror. It is a photocopy of her posing naked in the Longing. One of the Polaroids she had given Brodie.

'How did you get these?' she says, grabbing the rest from Rowan. There are dozens of photocopies. Hundreds. She starts to tear them up frantically. 'Why did you do this?'

'Me?' Rowan says, affronted. 'I didn't do anything. I came to warn you. Brodie made copies.'

Saffy covers her mouth, utterly horrified. '*Brodie*? Why would he make copies?'

Rowan gives a little smile. 'They're everywhere. He said he even sent them to your old school back home.'

Saffy bursts into tears, letting the papers fall from her hands to the ground. She has never felt such crippling shame, and now it comes to rest in her, like a weight on all her organs.

'You poor thing,' Rowan says, stooping to gather up the papers before they blew into the trees. 'Brodie told you he'd broken up with me, isn't that right?'

Saffy nods, tears rolling down her cheeks.

Rowan gives a coy smile as she curls the papers into a thick scroll, removing a hair band from her wrist and sliding it down the tube. 'Well, he didn't. He thinks I don't know about you, but I do.' She glances behind her. 'You want to go for a walk?'

III

Saffy isn't sure what Rowan was up to, whether she had really come to warn her or if she is just wanting to gloat. She offers Saffy weed. Hell yes, she wants weed. And she wants to scream into the air and punch Brodie's stupid face and erase everything that's happened.

They head towards the moonlight that streamed through the trees, and when they reach the road, she can see lights from the village in the distance, a low thrum of music.

'They're celebrating Samhain,' Rowan says. 'It's the biggest event of the year on the island.'

'I thought you'd be celebrating,' Saffy says.

Rowan smiles. 'I am. But obviously I needed to tell you about this.' She holds up the scroll, and Saffy takes it, holding her spliff to one end until it catches alight. She stands for a moment, holding the sheaf of photocopies alight like a torch. She feels daring as it blazes, letting it move down close to her hand before dropping it to the ground and stamping it out.

'I hate him,' Saffy says, punctuating the words with a fresh stamp on the photocopies.

Rowan takes a long drag of her joint and exhales in Saffy's direction. 'What you have to understand about Brodie is that he likes to control people.'

'Is that why he made the photocopies?' Saffy asks, looking at the ashes on the ground. She could burn twelve more sheafs and it wouldn't stop the pictures spreading. He has the Polaroids. She was stupid to have done that.

'I think it comes from a deep-seated fear of not being good enough,' Rowan says wisely. 'The control impulse. Like he has to force people to do things that they'd probably do anyway if he was just kind to them.' She gives a little shrug of her shoulders and a smile, as though this was acceptable.

'Why did you spend three years with him, then?' Saffy says.

'Because I love him,' Rowan says, blowing a ring of smoke.

Saffy wants to say something to that but her thoughts have become soggy, a big sopping mess of anger and confusion. She hadn't felt ready to have sex with him, but at the time she'd felt like she was just being stupid. He'd coaxed and made a little joke about payment, and her confusion over her own feelings had blindsided her into acquiescing. She wanted to be wanted, and at the same time she *didn't* want to sleep with him. At least, not so early. Not in a way that felt like she was paying him.

But she did it anyway, because it felt like too hard a thing to explain.

They make their way slowly to the Longing, the conversation spinning off into music, TV shows, and they have a long conversation about how Quentin Tarantino glorifies violence against women in his films but manages to get away with it because of his talent ('You have to admit *Pulp Fiction* is crazy-brilliant,' Saffy offers), and also because Hollywood was basically the patriarchy. Saffy still wasn't clear on the purpose of this chat. Maybe Rowan just wants to get to know her. She's been Brodie's girlfriend for a long, long time. Maybe she was just trying to clear the air so that there was no bad feeling between them.

'So, are you really a witch?' Saffy asks. 'Like, can you cast spells and stuff?'

'Can *you*?'

'Well, no, but I never said I was a . . .'

'I call myself a witch primarily as a form of protest,' Rowan says. 'In defiance of centuries of genocide in Europe against women. To say I'm a witch is to recognize my ancestors who were tortured to death.'

'Oh,' Saffy says, surprised. 'So . . . it's a performance, then?'

Rowan turns to her and frowns. 'Just as much as your grunge-girl, Courtney-Love-wannabe look is a performance.'

Courtney Love wannabe? Saffy pulls at her blonde hair. Grunge? She feels a stab of disappointment in Rowan. She'd almost figured her for the real thing, an actual witch, capable of conjuring darkness.

They are at the Longing now, the tall, menacing shape of it looming over them. Rowan tugs the door open and gestures at Saffy to follow her inside.

'My mum painted this,' she tells Rowan, flicking on a work lamp to reveal the half-finished mural in all its multicoloured glory. They stand for a moment in dreamy, drug-infused silence. 'I suppose you'll recognize the runes, being a witch and all.'

Rowan looks up at the mural. 'Oh, yes. It's the sign for love.'

Saffy can't help but smile to herself. Rowan hasn't got a clue what the mural meant, and for a moment she relishes standing in the Longing.

Now that they've stopped walking, she feels woozy, and her cheeks are aflame. She presses a hand to her chest and feels the skeleton key there.

'Look what I have,' she tells Rowan.

Rowan's eyes widen when she sees the key. 'For the cave?' she whispers, and Saffy sways, her eyes taking in the grooves of the key. Her mind turns to the history of witches, a cinematic scene of naked, shorn-headed women being flung into a pit. How apt that they chose a phallic building in which to torture women and call them witches. The patriarchy, Alpha and Omega, eternal without end.

'Let's open it.'

They slide down the long narrow neck of the entrance, both of them collapsing with a loud 'ow' on to the wet floor at the bottom.

Saffy wrenches herself up into a sitting position, though it takes a staggering amount of effort, like a triathlon—were there triathlons that involved sitting up? She hurt her knee on the way down, but the drug has made the pain fabulously distant. Her head is crazy heavy. She wonders if she might be wearing a crown made of some kind of metal that weighs a ton.

'Am I queen now?' she asks Rowan, completely serious.

Rowan stands and dusts her dress down. 'I don't think so.'

The cave spreads out in front of them like the mouth of an enormous beast. Jagged remnants of limestone skewer upwards from the floor like fangs and the uneven, craggy floor glimmered with rock pools. Somewhere moonlight is seeping in, and it is astonishing that such a massive space exists beneath the Longing. It would be terrific for candle-light orchestras, Saffy thinks, though the damp would probably affect the instruments. The air is cool and clammy, the kind of dampness that got into your bones. It is exciting, really, being in such a weird place with such a weird girl.

She turns to Rowan in a dizzy haze. 'So this is Witches Hide. They killed witches here.'

Rowan laughs. 'You mean, they killed *women* here, silly. I know this is Witches Hide. I've lived here all my life?' She produces a lighter from some hidden pocket in her dress and flicks it.

'So you've been in here before?'

Rowan looks away. 'They've always had it locked. But I've seen photographs. Most of the islanders are terrified of this place.' She rights herself, flicking her long black hair over one shoulder. 'But I'm not.'

They walk a little farther into the cave, into the part where it seems to swell and deepen, the walls green and damp with algae and shadows swirling on the ground. Rowan walks ahead, holding her lighter to the walls until she finds what she seemed to be looking for. Markings on the walls. She shivers and raised a hand reverently, as though not daring to touch the marks.

'This is incredible,' she whispers.

'So,' Saffy said, in what she deems a valiant attempt to bring herself around, 'you're OK with me and Brodie, then.'

'I never said I was OK with it,' Rowan says. She said it so easily that it took a long minute for the words to spiral in the air and sift their meaning to Saffy's brain.

'Then how come you're here?'

Rowan is suddenly sitting next to her with her legs crossed, looking around the cave. She is probably admiring the beautiful ceiling too, Saffy thinks, with its symbols of black magic that had started to glow bloodred, as though a rich sunset was bleeding its light all along the cave floor and up into the engravings.

'I have a proposal for you,' Rowan says.

'A proposal?' Saffy rolls onto her belly. She feels happy and snug. 'Do you want to marry me?'

'No, silly,' Rowan says. 'I want to cut you.'

Saffy isn't sure how it happens, but one moment she is on her belly kicking her legs, and the next she is sitting upright staring at a sharp knife that Rowan is holding in front of her.

'What are you doing?' Saffy says, the knowledge that she is in danger pitching her into semi-soberness.

'It's the law of return,' Rowan says, as if Saffy is stupid. 'You took what wasn't yours. So now you have to pay.'

'No,' Saffy says, rising awkwardly to her feet. Is she dreaming this? Is Rowan really suggesting that she *cut* her? She tries to will herself sober, but her head is spinning and the ground beneath her feels light as clouds. 'I didn't take anything,' she says.

'Yes, you did,' Rowan says, with surprising clarity. 'Three times is what he said. And so you owe me. Three cuts.'

Saffy laughs, but a glance at Rowan's face tells her she is deadly serious. 'I'm not letting you fucking touch me,' she says, backing away. She looks left and right, realizing with panic that she can't remember how to get out of the cave. Which way is it? The cave seems like an endless loop, with no indication of whether she needs to go up or down, left or right.

'You said you came to warn me,' Saffy says, her heart racing. She reaches to the side and feels the wet, rough contours of the cave wall, a gasp of wind on her skin telling her she is near an exit.

'I did,' Rowan says. 'I didn't lie. But I had promised myself to him, and you took him.'

And with that, she lunges forward, blade landing in Saffy's shoulder. Saffy screams, the pain both distant and so gut-wrenchingly real it knocks her to the ground. But when she looks down, her hands are red with blood, and suddenly she is on her feet, running to the night sky ahead. The sea is howling, calling her name. She can hear Rowan calling after her, telling her not to go that way, doesn't she know where it leads? Come back, she is shouting, come back!

But Saffy gropes her way to the sudden glimpse of daylight ahead, pulling herself to the sea, falling endlessly into the cold, black depths.

LUNA, 2021

I

'What time is it?' Clover asks.

'Almost seven.'

'Is seven early or late?' Clover says through a yawn. 'It's dark so I think it's late.'

'Actually, the sun's coming up, so it's early.'

Clover leans her head back and closes her eyes. Luna watches her in the rear-view mirror. She is wide awake, her mind sharp and her thoughts clear.

She has to do this.

The road is marked with new signs leading to the forest car park. Luna parks up, relieved that there are no other cars nearby. There's a gate leading to a public footpath through the forest. She has no idea if this is where the burning trees are, but she's prepared to walk as long as it takes. She's packed some sandwiches and a flask of tea. And the knife.

The day is cold but dry, and the sunrise is glorious, streaking the sky vivid orange. They follow a path marked with a yellow post, past fir trees that soar into the clouds.

She could almost marvel at the beauty of it – muscular oaks fluffy with moss, the multicolour branches of a eucalyptus.

Clover has woken up a little. She marches along, arms swinging, giving Luna a running commentary about the parts of the woods she supposedly remembers. It moves Luna, that desire to remember. She can relate.

The path rises uphill, then joins another path that forks. 'Which way?' Clover asks.

'I'm not sure,' Luna says. She looks around, paying particular attention to the thick oaks that have evidently been in the forest for hundreds of years. Can she remember them?

'This way,' she tells Clover, taking her steps slowly, consciously breathing in the smell of the forest, listening to the sounds of the ocean in the distance, the birds calling in the trees. Slowly, images gather in her mind, and she tunes out Clover's chatter with the noises that nudge at her memory.

She remembers being in Witches Hide the night she went to find Saffy. She remembers the etchings in the walls, and now she remembers spying a hole at the end of the chamber. Saffy was nowhere to be found, and now she had two choices – turn back and scale the tunnel at the entrance, or go out the other end where the ocean was visible. The water wouldn't be that deep, she thought. Probably only up to her knees, and then she could wade to shore.

After a few minutes of deliberating she stepped down into the water, yelping when she felt the cold.

But it wasn't knee-deep at all. She plunged down, gulping down mouthfuls of salty seawater, before shooting back up to the surface and gasping for air.

She'd expected then that she'd drown. The shore was suddenly so far away, and the rocks were sharp at her legs and no one was around to help. Arching her head back, Luna spotted a house light in the distance. It was a marker of the beach. So she wheeled her arms and kicked her legs in the water, and not long after she felt sand beneath her feet and fell forward into a mound of seaweed, hacking and coughing.

She sat upright on the beach and huddled her legs to her chest. She was near the spot where she'd spent much of the afternoon with Mr McPherson, pouring buckets of seawater over Basil the basking shark. Mr McPherson had told her to keep away from the body, that toxins would make her sick. But the huge shape was nowhere to be seen. She stood and scanned the bay all the way to the cliffs. The moon was bright, and she could see the bay clearly, but there was no sign of Basil's body. And he was so huge she couldn't imagine missing him.

She turned to the waves to see if the tide had carried him away. There, cutting through the surface just thirty feet away, was a dorsal fin. It was Basil! She jumped and shouted. She'd saved him! He was alive!

She couldn't wait to go home and tell her mum. Maybe Clover and Saffy would be there, too, and she'd tell them, and they'd all laugh and be happy again. But in her excitement she took a wrong turn and found herself in the woods, tripping over branches. The forest seemed endless, no sign at all of the bay through the trees. She was scared out of her wits, jumping at every hoot of an owl and call of the wind.

Something caught her ankle and she fell forward, right over the edge of a ravine. It felt like she'd never stop falling.

Tumbling head over foot through mud and brambles and nettles, until at last she landed flat on her back at the bottom. She'd lain there, wondering if she'd broken her neck, staring up at the sky. Navy blue and streaked with stars. She could taste mud and something else, something like metal. She wiped her nose on the back of her hand and saw a liquid shining there. Blood.

After what felt like hours she managed to roll over and pull herself on to all fours. A small tree stuck out of the hill on the other side of the ravine, and she pulled on to it, hoisting herself up.

She has no idea what time she got home, but it was light. Her mother answered. Luna burst into tears as soon as she saw her, but the relief was soon swept away by something else – confusion. Standing behind her mother was another girl. The girl was wearing Luna's nightdress. She also looked exactly like Luna. She had the same hair, same mouth, same *everything*.

'What's your name?' she asked the girl, curious.

'Luna,' the girl said. 'I'm Luna.'

II

Cassie gets into her car and reverses quickly down on to the road. She woke to find Luna and the girl gone, and a horrible knot in her gut is telling her that it's going to end badly. Luna thinks the girl is a wildling. Those nutcases from the island have wormed their fucking stupid ideologies into Luna and now her vulnerabilities are rising to it. She's seen it so many times – intelligent people, capable of reasoning and critical thinking, giving into these stories the moment they experience grief, or some kind of emotional upheaval. Coming back to Lòn Haven must have taken balls, but now Luna's alone, and dealing with her childhood all over again. Cassie needs to warn her.

She messaged her dad late last night back home in Auckland, where he was enjoying an early morning surf at Takapuna Beach. Finn is recently divorced, has taken up veganism and surfing as part of his 'new me' regime. He works in forestry. At fifty-seven years old, he's the healthiest he's ever been.

She asked about what happened after the Stay girls went missing back in 1998.

He told her the rumour that had spread across Lòn Haven: folk said there had been two Lunas, one a wildling, one the 'real' Luna. He's pretty sure it was nonsense. Luna was found. He was the one who had taken her to the police station – he'd been worried that Isla might take her to the burning trees – and insisted they call social services until her mother was found. He had helped the search teams look for Liv for two months solid, swept every part of the island. But to no avail.

She told him about Clover. About how Luna said she has a mark on her, that she suspects she's a wildling.

'What do you think, Dad?' she asked. 'Why would she be a kid instead of a grown up?'

'I have no idea,' Finn said. 'But you need to get them both off the island. Now.'

III

'Why are these trees all black?' Clover says, screwing up her face.

They're at the burning trees, and Luna is shaking. She has to do this.

'Can you stand against this tree?' she asks Clover.

'Why?'

'Please?'

Clover looks at her darkly before stepping towards the tree.

'This is weird,' she says.

Luna positions herself in front of Clover, taking everything in: the small form of her amidst the trees, the wet, black branches above like spikes, the leaves at her feet. The faint smell of fire lingering in the burnt wood, stoked by the wind. She steps forward, lifting her hand in the air, and Clover flinches.

'What are you doing?' she whimpers.

IV

'Come out, you dogs! We know you're in there!'

Through the slats in the door I could make out about fifteen of them. Angus and his men – Stevens, a bear in human form, as wide as he was tall, holding a length of rope and a scabbard, Fotheringham with a pail of oil, and Argyle clutching a dirk. There would be no trial. They wanted blood, and they'd take it.

I boarded the door as best I could, then pressed a knife into her hand and my coat across her shoulders. 'Run,' I told her. 'Do not look back.'

'I'll go to the cave,' she said, her eyes wild. 'Promise me you'll follow.'

I didn't get a chance to answer. The door was beaten down and in a moment Stevens was lifting his scabbard and bringing the butt of it down hard on my head.

When I came to, we were in the broch surrounded by the men. Amy had not made it to Witches Hide, though we were in the broch. Amy was crying and shaking with fear, and I wanted to comfort her.

'No, you don't,' Stevens said, his sword at my throat. He uncurled his filthy fingers to show me a handful of stones before plunging them into my mouth, breaking my teeth. They dragged Amy to a milking stool and began to hack off her hair, tossing her long black locks to the ground. They were so rough, hacking so close to the scalp that blood began to ooze out. I yelled at them, and with a terrific lunge Stevens' plunged his knife deep into my chest. I fell to the ground, unable to breathe.

They had lit a fire, the hiss and crackle of it in the courtyard indicating that it was already a good size. When I came to again I saw Angus Reid at the back of the barn, watching darkly. He wanted to be sure the punishment was done before the Council found out.

'Patrick,' Amy wailed, and I looked up to see her being dragged off, naked as a babe, to the stake.

'You needn't worry,' Stevens replied gruffly. 'He'll be joining you soon enough.'

I heard her cries as they tied her to the stake, the terrible shrieks that fell quickly to whimpers. I felt like I had stepped outside my body. Everything was happening so fast, and the smell of the fire had wrenched me back to the day I'd witnessed my mother being murdered.

A voice in my head shouted that Amy would not suffer the same fate, not if I acted. Amy would find a way. She had brought fish back from the dead. She had cursed the cave to thrust living people into the distant corners of time itself. She wouldn't die. I just had to get to Witches Hide, like we'd planned.

We would escape. And so would the child that was growing in her belly.

The men were murmuring about whether the stake would

topple if they added another body to it. I stayed put on the ground, feigning collapse, as they decided whether to take Amy off before tying me to the stake. Soon a decision was reached, and they began removing her, leaving me unattended.

And so, I ran for the cave, my heart clanging wildly, my feet torn up by the stones on the ground. The men gave chase, but I outran them and headed to Witches Hide, dropping down the tunnel to the narrow chambers. Soon I could see daylight, a shaft of light bouncing off the wet black rock. I was bleeding badly from the wound Stevens had inflicted, dark blood covering my hands. I was woozy from it, but the knowledge that I had to get through that cave if I was ever to see Amy again powered me on. I moved quickly towards that light, so relieved by the sight of it that I didn't feel the edges of the cave slicing up my legs.

I passed the rock hewn with numbers, then pressed my palms on the outer wall of the cave and hauled myself out, falling head first into black sea.

LIV, 1998

I

I raced through the forest, branches tearing up my face and arms. I could hear Isla and the others behind me, calling and gaining speed. I had to keep focused on my path, weaving through the trees towards the sound of the waves. I'd get Luna, and we'd get in my car and drive before the others could reach us.

If they hadn't already taken her.

I was drenched in sweat and gasping for breath by the time the Longing came into view. I darted across the road, my heart in my throat. Was Luna there? I reached the door to the bothy, put my hand on the door handle, and from the corner of my eye I spotted someone stepping towards me, their arms raised in the air, holding something heavy. Before I could glance at them they brought it crashing down on my head. The pain was sickening, knocking me clean to the ground.

And everything went black.

II

Colours flickered at the edges of my vision. Someone or something shuffled close to me, and in the distance, there was roaring.

I was lying on my belly, raised up from the floor.

Gradually, I recognized where I was – in the Longing, lying face down on the wallpaper table I'd used to spread the mural out before painting it on the walls.

My head throbbed. I could smell vomit on my T-shirt from where I'd been sick. My vision was fuzzy, but gradually it cleared enough to bring the floor of the Longing into focus. A set of feet moved towards the door, locking it.

Patrick.

'It turns out that I have made a bit of an error,' he said. 'Language is everything. Did you know that? It really is.' He shook his head. His eyes were wide and his hair askew. Terror ripped through me. He had beaten me over the head and dragged me here. He looked and sounded like he'd lost his mind.

'All these years, I'd misinterpreted a single word,' he

said, 'and this misinterpretation has caused needless misery. As you might have gathered, I've been trying to find Amy. I can see you're not Amy at all. No marks on your skin.'

I opened my mouth to tell him to let me go, but just then he moved something tight across my mouth and fastened it behind my head. I shouted into the strap but it came out as a muffled whimper.

'So, it's back to Plan A. You've helpfully painted the runes I need for that on the walls of the Longing. We'll also need a bit of fire, and one more crucial thing, which you're also going to help me with.' He leaned close to my face. 'Living bones.'

The bone triangle in the lantern room flashed in my mind.

'Now, I know what you're thinking,' he continued, pulling down the waistband of my trousers.

He's going to rape me.

'"Why hasn't Patrick tried bones before now?" To that, I'll say that I have. I've removed the bones from countless creatures, painstakingly putting them in the right place on a full moon and so on. And guess what? Nothing. No Amy.' He started to laugh. 'And do you know what? Just the other night I was looking into my translations of old Icelandic. The word I'd interpreted as "living" actually means "human". Can you believe that?'

I felt a quick sting in my buttock. A flash of a needle told me he'd injected me with something.

He ran a blade up the back of my T-shirt, tearing it off. The cold air settled across my arms.

'This has to go, too,' he said, slicing the strap of my bra. I could feel my toes and legs, the blood in my hair from where he'd struck me, but not my back. He'd anaesthetized me.

380

He's going to kill me.

'The lower ribs,' he said, tapping the blade against my skin. 'You don't actually need them. But I do.'

And then he plunged the knife into my skin.

Crushing weight. Darkness, and a fire inside, close to my kidney. Pressure, and a wetness between my legs.

Something began to scrape and whine against bone.

Pulling.

He wrenched so hard that my whole body lifted off the table.

I could see liquid pooling on the ground beneath me, and for a half-second I thought it was grape juice.

Blood. It's my blood.

I must have blacked out, because when I came to, a threaded needle appeared in front of me, pinched between a finger and thumb.

'I'm stitching you up now,' he said. 'I'd prefer that we stick to the *living* part, just in case. OK?'

And then the tug of the thread, binding my skin together. I was slipping under, the fringes of my consciousness starting to flicker and darken.

Smelling salts ripped me back. Patrick's face appeared at the fringe of my vision. 'Stay with me, sweet Amy looka-like.' He smiled and stroked my cheek with a bloodied hand.

'We're not done yet.'

III

It was night when I came to. My wound had stopped bleeding, and to this day I have no idea why I didn't die – Stevens had stuck his knife close to my heart, and the blade had twisted when I pulled away. I felt weak and light-headed, forgetful for a moment of all that had gone before. Above me the stars told their stories as they had done for centuries before. The sea nudged at me to get up, and slowly the memory of what had happened before crystallized in my mind. Amy. The flame. The cave.

I pulled myself upright. It was dark, but the moonlight fell on the broch, white, restless waves dancing all around it. I was freezing cold and the desire to curl up and sleep was insistent, but somehow I managed to half-crawl, half-stagger my way to the broch.

It was empty. No sign of Amy or Angus and his men, but also no sign of the stakes. No smell of flame on the air, no scorch marks on the stone.

I used the last of my strength to make for the woods, where I made a small shelter to protect against the rain and a fire to ward off the cold, and wolves. Then, I took a stone, set it in the flame to cook it, and when it was hot enough I used two sticks to pick it up and hold it to the wound in my chest, suturing it.

There was a fresh wound on my arm, the skin raw as though I'd been burned, and a small row of digits confirmed the year:

1

7

4

2

The next day I explored my surroundings, frantic, terrified. The island looked almost the same, wild and windcombed, the sea beating thick clods of creamy foam up the beach. A man and a child were standing there, watching me. I wanted to ask them where Amy was, but there was no use – it was almost a century since she had been born.

I went through Witches Hide again. But when I fell out the other side, I did not arrive in 1662. I arrived in 1801. I went back again, and again, and each time I emerged coughing and spluttering on the shore and branded with fresh digits.

I had to change my approach. Amy had discovered the secret to the cave's magic. I had seen her write down the runes in her book of spells, had learned a small amount of Icelandic. I would have to take time to remember, to get it right. Otherwise I risked losing her forever.

When I emerged for the last time, the broch seemed to have sprouted into a white tower. A lighthouse, I later learned, designed to guide ships. I was branded with a year I'd never imagined. 1994. Three hundred and thirty-two years after Amy's birth.

I built a shack on the small piece of rock that seemed to have been spewed from the larynx of Lòn Haven by the bay, forming a smaller island where some old dwellings had been left to ruin. I covered one of them with branches, then leaves, fashioning a roof. I stole clothing, visited the village. Much had changed, and it daunted me. I spent those first weeks in a perpetual state of dizziness, like a small child. I turned nocturnal, sleeping during the day and exploring the new world at night. It seemed easier, somehow, to sniff out the corners of this new version of the island like a fox when no one was around. I had to relearn much of what I knew.

I remembered my father's box of treasure that I had mocked as a boy, buried in the hill. I did not dare trust that I would find it, but I did, and even then I did not trust that the objects therein might earn me more than a week's food: my great-grandmother's rings and a bag of old coins. But an antiques dealer found them extremely valuable, and overnight I went from owning just the shirt on my back to becoming the wealthiest man on the island.

I bought a house, and the Longing. I bought land. And I bought a boat. Somehow travelling the ocean soothed me. It felt as though I was getting somewhere, that I was travelling back to her. I ventured to Iceland, where her ancestors had hailed from, and where her mother's knowledge of spells had originated.

I wrote, in the back of this book, all that I remembered. Amy's runes came back to me, little by little, in dreams, and sometimes at unexpected moments.

I had vowed to her: I would never rest until we were together.

And I would do anything, absolutely anything, to make it so.

IV

'There we are,' Patrick said.

I was falling in and out of consciousness, but the lightness of his tone – chatty, convivial – dragged me back into the present. He was speaking to me as though we were on a coffee date, or as though he'd just mended a hole in my T-shirt instead of slicing up my back. I felt spit filling up my mouth, trapped by the strap he'd tied across it. Images of my father filleting a fish flashed in my mind; the jab of the knife, the spine ripped out, then the heart. The metallic smell of blood reached my nostrils. *My* blood.

My lower back was still cold, numb, but the thought of what he had just done to me, in this filthy, disgusting place, rife with insects and bat droppings . . .

My vision started to blacken again, the world around me collapsing to an atom.

Luna will find me here. She'll be completely alone.

Or Patrick will do to her what he's just done to me.

I came to as he started to head up the staircase. On the floor beneath me I could make out a pair of discarded vinyl gloves smeared with blood. Something clicked in his hands as he moved up the stairs.

My ribs.

He had my fucking ribs.

As soon as I heard him reach the lantern room, I lifted my head as high as I could and looked around. Patrick had a phone. Where was it? I had to call someone. Finn. The police.

But just then, a new smell reached me, the dense, earthy scent of an open flame, teasing out my primal instincts, a new alarm bell shrieking in my head. He was shouting in the lantern room, and the taste of smoke on my tongue was unmistakable.

The spell only works with the runes, bones, and fire.

I saw the hole in the floor, the one that had been covered by the grille. The wood had been shifted to one side, the grille removed. Slowly, painfully, I raised myself on to my knees. My lower back was still numb, my left arm, too, and despite how close I was to fainting, the rest of me had feeling. Adrenaline powered through me.

Luna was still in the bothy. I had to get to her.

But as I moved, I slipped down the hole in the floor, falling painfully to the ground below.

I heard a terrible crunch as my ankle snapped. A sharp pain shot through the bones of my foot, hot and gut-wrenching. Tears came quickly to my eyes, and I clamped a hand to my mouth to stifle a scream.

I straightened and glanced around. The hole that I'd fallen down widened outwards into a huge cave, with streams of light at the far end indicating the exit.

And I wasn't alone.

The little boy I'd spotted, the little boy with straggly

pale hair, was standing behind a long pillar of rock. I crawled towards him.

'Are you a ghost?' I managed to whisper. Maybe I was dead. Maybe this was the afterlife.

He gestured for me to follow. Somehow I raised myself to my feet, staggering after the boy.

'Olivia?' I heard above me.

My stomach lurched. It was Patrick.

He'd spotted that I'd escaped, and it wouldn't take long for him to work out where I was. Smoke billowed down the hole after me. The Longing was ablaze.

I moved as fast as I could after the boy through the cave, towards a rocky chamber that narrowed until my shoulders rubbed against the side.

A thin strip of daylight fell into a pool of water ahead. It marked the end of the cave, nothing but sky and ocean. The boy was a few steps ahead of me. He turned and looked back at me before closing his eyes and crossing himself. Then he jumped.

I stood on the lip of the cave and looked down at the water below. It didn't look terribly deep, maybe three feet deep. And there was no splash. No ripples to indicate where the boy had fallen. And yet I'd seen him jump. Perhaps Finn was right; maybe he was a ghost.

I took a breath and stepped forward, the shock of the cold knocking the air from my lungs.

It took a long time for me to surface. It felt like the water was holding me, looking me over, deciding whether or not to give me back to the earth. And then it let go, and I surfaced.

I broke the surface and gasped. I remember the current pulling my legs, dragging me into the bay. I felt cold sand brush against my cheek, my body shaking from shock. I remember thinking that Patrick must have done to Saffy and Clover what he'd done to me. I wanted to die, then.

Heavy boots crunched across the sand towards me. Patrick, I thought. Come to finish me off. I opened an eye to look up at him.

'You bastard,' I whispered.

But the man staring down at me wasn't Patrick.

'Liv?' he said, astonished.

LUNA, 2021

I

'Luna! Stop!'

Luna hears a shout. She turns to see a figure moving up the hill through the trees, her arms waving above her head. Cassie. She runs up to Clover and pulls her away from the tree.

'What are you doing?' Cassie shouts, holding Clover behind her. She looks over Luna. No sign of a knife or a rope.

Luna stares, her memories swamping about her. She feels as though she's underwater.

'I . . . I wanted to remember,' she stammers. 'I remembered my mother tying me to a tree, and lifting the knife . . .'

'But doing the same to Clover won't change things,' Cassie pleads.

'I wasn't,' Luna says, turning to look at Clover, who has sat, cross-legged, at the base of the tree, twirling a sycamore seed. 'I was . . . retracing my steps. I needed to fill in the gaps. And I thought . . . if I came to the forest, the place I feared most . . . it would happen.'

'And has it?' Cassie asks cautiously.

'I think I understand what happened,' Luna says, a catch in her voice. 'I think I know why Clover is seven years old.'

II

They sit in Cassie's car, the doors locked, Clover watching a movie on Cassie's phone with headphones.

'You're saying the shark somehow made it back to sea?' Cassie says, replaying Luna's story of the basking shark in her mind. 'You're saying he came alive again?

Luna shakes her head. 'I saw him die. I think what happened was that when I went through the cave, I went back a day. A day *in time*.'

Cassie presses a hand to her forehead. 'But . . . if that's the case, then *all* the so-called 'wildlings' were just kids who went through the cave . . .'

'. . . and travelled to another time,' Luna says. 'And that's probably what happened to Saffy and my mother. They've gone to another time.' Her voice catches. 'And I'll never find them.'

'What about that girl they found?' Cassie says. 'The one called Sapphire they found here last year. She *could* be Saffy. Couldn't she?'

Luna nods. It's possible, but she's terrified of investing

too much in it. She's still processing the truth about Clover, about her own childhood. And the girl who was found is no longer here. The police won't divulge the information easily. It's not like she can tell the truth.

Hey, officer. The girl you found might have time-travelled from 1998. Can I have her address in case she's my sister?

Luna thinks of Isla, her hardened stare. She remembers running from the people in the woods, from her mother, holding the knife. She remembers the fear and confusion that felt like a living creature, a monster with its teeth bared, snarling after her.

And she remembers finding a grove of trees and stopping there, exhausted, sinking down behind a large trunk to catch her breath. But she wasn't alone. In front of her was a girl. The other Luna, still wearing her nightie. She was afraid. Why was she here? Was she something to do with the reason her mother had tried to kill her?

The other Luna looked worried for her.

'It's all right,' she said. 'They've gone the other way.' She held out her hand.

'We have to take hands, remember? That's how it works.'

At that, she'd remembered what Saffy had told her, the night she asked about the book of spells. *If you see yourself in human form, you have to take hands. One of you is from the future, and one of you is from the past. If you take hands, you become one again – in the present.*

She reached out and closed her eyes, clasping hands with the other Luna.

When she opened them, she was alone. The other Luna was gone.

No, not gone, she thinks. Inside her memories. Her memories, she thinks, have combined both versions of her. One and the same.

III

The ferries are back on. Ethan is waiting for her at Cromarty. Cassie says her goodbyes at the port.

'I don't think I can let you go,' Cassie says. 'You've only just got here.'

'Promise you and Lucia will visit us in Coventry,' Luna says.

Cassie nods. 'I'll do my best to find out where Saffy is. I'll ask around.'

'No, don't do that,' Luna says, remembering the night she encountered Brodie. 'I don't want to put you in danger. Promise you won't.'

Cassie cups a hand to her face. 'As long as you promise me, dear friend, that you will tell Ethan the truth.'

'That I wasn't rejecting him,' Luna says.

'Exactly.'

She smiles. 'I promise.'

Cassie waves her off as Luna gets into the car and pulls away, ready to drive on to the ferry. Foot passengers are queuing to board, the engines roaring.

As the car in front moves forward, Luna spies a figure among the foot passengers moving beside her. There's a girl there, a teenager, tall and skinny. Her blonde hair is piled up in a messy topknot and spiked with a pen. She's wearing nine-hole Doc Marten boots and a lumberjack shirt underneath a denim coat. She has a familiar walk.

Before she knows what she's doing, Luna's stepping out of the car and shouting, 'Saffy! *Saffy!*'

The girl turns. She removes her sunglasses and squints at Luna. Then she breaks into a run towards her.

IV

I have done a lot of wrong things in my time, and I'm sorry for most of them.

But doing what I needed to do in order to find Amy? No, I'm not sorry for that.

And as I said, I was a skilled butcher. I had learned anatomy, both animal and human. The woman I had mistaken for Amy would live.

Her bones completed the spell, and for that, I wish her a long and happy life.

After I took her ribs I placed tall branches all around the sides of the Longing and set them alight; as the flames climbed to the windows I rushed through to the end of Witches Hide, diving deep into the water and coming to shore.

I tore off my clothes from 1998 and began to race towards the forest. I recognized Lòn Haven as it had been, that raw, wild landscape dotted with white crofts, the forests thick and lush again.

But a scream from the bay stopped me in my tracks.

I turned back and saw smoke rising from the bay. The broch squatted there, bleak and ominous as it had once been. I ran towards the broch and was astonished by what I found: Stevens and his men tying Amy to the stakes, her head bloodied and shorn, just as I had left her.

Amy was already dead, I thought, her body limp against the stakes. My knees buckled and I sank to the ground, the horror that I had arrived too late to save her thudding in my bones.

'Bring her down,' a voice called out. It was Father Ross, newly installed at the kirk after the death of Father Skuddie. 'She has not stood trial.'

I lifted my head from the cold rock and watched as the men laid Amy's body on the stone. A moment later she coughed, and relief flooded through me. She was yet alive. I inched forward towards her. Stevens spied me and raised a baton to knock me down, but Father Ross prevented him.

'Douse the flames,' Father Ross said, and though the men grumbled they did as he asked.

'This woman bears the markings of a wildling,' Angus said, lifting the blanket that I'd placed upon her to reveal the livid numbers there. 'You know the mandate as well as I do, Father. No trial is needed to deal with a wildling.'

'Wildlings take the form of children,' Father Ross replied, looking over the marks. 'These markings look like they were self-inflicted. I have seen such, on the limbs of those who are in mourning.' He looked at me for confirmation, and I nodded. I had taken the bones of an innocent woman to get here and I would lie to a priest. Anything to be with Amy.

'I think you are mistaken, Angus,' Father Ross said. 'This woman is not a wildling, and you are to return her to her home. May God forgive your soul.'

Angus was visibly angry, but he did as Father Ross instructed. Buckets of water were thrown over the stakes to put out the flames, and the man who would be our executioner took Amy and me back on his horses to our croft, where Mrs Wilson, a healer, attended to our wounds.

The violence meted by Stevens and his men caused Amy to lose the child she was carrying. 'I'm sorry, wee lamb,' Mrs Wilson said as she attended to her. 'There may be a chance of another.'

We mourned our loss. But I told her where I had travelled, and for how long.

We learned from that day.

We swore we would not meddle with history. We lived in dangerous times, but we had glimpsed danger in every time, past and future. We could face the danger, so long as we were together.

At first, we decided to block the entrance to the tunnel. It seemed a simple and effective way to spare more children's lives, and so I commissioned a blacksmith to make a grate – or a gate, I told him – that we would put across it. However, we quickly found that the presence of the grate only served to heighten curiosity with older children devising stories about the origin of the grate, and then methods to get around it. We put wood over it to conceal it. But it wasn't enough.

We lived quietly. We planted, and reaped, and watched bitterly as wildlings were found and killed, knowing them to be the children of the very people who killed them. What could we say that would stop them?

I made a stone to commemorate our mothers and Amy's sister, and the nine others who had been killed. Father Ross spotted me at work, and invited me to place the stone within the kirk.

'I'd rather not,' I told him. 'There'll be an outcry.'

'An outcry?' he said. 'They've paid for their sins, and it is up to God to judge them now. Their memory is no stain, but a warning.'

I could not agree with him about the warning part, but I consented. Slowly, the presence of the stone stirred up more than I could have imagined – some of the older members of the community stopped after the church service on the Sabbath to lay wildflowers by the stone. Sometimes I would hear them mutter remembrances about Finwell, or my mother.

I cannot say whether the stone acted as a warning or not. But while witches continued to be burned all around us, there was never another witch trial on Lòn Haven, though the legacy of wildlings persisted.

One day, I hoped that, too, would cease.

SAPPHIRE, 2021

I

'Lunch money?'

'Got it,' Saffy tells her foster mother. She throws her a tight smile before heading out the front door and walking briskly to school.

It's been six months since she came out of Witches Hide. Six months since she was found on the bay, bleeding, and in shock. Six months since she sat in the police station and had been told that the year was 2020. She didn't believe them. They'd asked for her next of kin. She gave them her mother's name and date of birth. They couldn't find her. She gave them her uncle's name and address. He'd died ten years ago. She couldn't take it in. What was going on? If it wasn't for the wound in her shoulder – a two-inch stab wound that missed her subscapular artery by millimeters – she'd have thought she was being pranked. Payback for how horrible she'd been to her mum and sisters. But the strangeness of her surroundings didn't lessen, the odd way people dressed and the cars and the mobile phones. Like a form of magic. And when a social worker came, it started to sink in. She *was* in 2020.

And she was entirely alone.

She's been staying with a foster family, the McKennas, in St Andrews. They have a beautiful home, a four-bedroomed chapel conversion with ocean views that they'd hoped to fill with their own children but never could. Michael works as a lawyer and Jenn's a full-time foster carer. They're quite taken with Saffy, and she with them. She has an iPhone 8 and a laptop and an Instagram account. She has friends at the local school. She's on antidepressants and sees a counsellor. No one has been able to trace her family. No one and nothing has been able to fill the gaping hole in her heart.

So today, she's running away. She's left a note for Michael and Jenn with a bouquet of wildflowers she picked yesterday tied with some gardening yarn. She doesn't want to hurt them, they're lovely people, so she's taken time to think carefully about what to say. She hopes they're not upset.

She's going back to Lòn Haven to find out for herself what happened. She's already worked it out. When she went through Witches Hide, she moved forward in time. The stuff she'd read in the grimoire was all true. The witches from Lòn Haven put some kind of spell on the cave in revenge for the way they'd been treated, and rightly so. But now, she's in 2021. She's spent time learning how to use the internet. Four weeks ago she found a Facebook page with her face on it. *Find Saffy Stay!*

There was a name on the 'admin' section of page. Luna Stay. Luna had set it up. Luna was a grown woman, now. Saffy marvelled at the thought of this – of course she was. It was 2020 – Luna was thirty-two! And she was looking for her.

Saffy was astonished. At the click of a button, she had

found her sister! She could go home, at long last. But Luna hadn't responded to any of Saffy's messages. Maybe she'd done it wrong.

She refused to be discouraged. The Facebook page proved that Luna had been looking for her, that she was out there. Perhaps, she thinks, if she retraces her steps, she'll find her family.

In a public toilet, she changes out of her school uniform into jeans and a shirt, then checks the cash she's been squirrelling away in her purse. The McKennas give her a weekly allowance on a credit card, but she's been drawing it out. It's taken such patience to do this instead of just bolting, but a credit card can be traced. She knows the route she has to take – a bus, then a train, then a ferry. And then she'll be on Lòn Haven.

As she boards the bus, she checks the route on her phone, running a thumb over the image of the island. Her heart aches to find her family. How ironic, she thinks, that the whole time she was on Lòn Haven she fantasized about running away, about leaving her mother and sisters, and now all she can think about is going back.

About throwing her arms around her mum and apologizing for being such a diva. About telling her sisters that she loves them and she'll never, ever shout at them again.

LIV, 2021

I

A limpet is a creature without eyes, limbs, without so much as a brain, and yet it creates for itself a spot on the rock that is its home. It leaves its mark on that spot, wearing away the rock until its shell forms a perfect seal. The home scar.

Maybe time is like that. Maybe we always move exactly to where and when we belong, even without realizing it. It certainly feels like that for me. As though everything in my whole life has led me to where I am now.

Finn found me that day on the beach. Finn, who had left Lòn Haven for New Zealand many years before, who hadn't so much as visited in twenty years, after being accused of having an affair with Saffy. Even when Rowan confessed to slipping the Polaroids through a gap in his car window, the rumours spread. He'd stayed in Auckland for twenty years, then decided on a whim to fly back to Lòn Haven to spend Christmas 2021 with Cassie. And that morning, he'd felt a pull to walk along the bay next to the Longing.

He saw a strange creature drag herself up the beach. He

saw that she was injured, a horrific wound in her back, rough stitches holding together a hole the size of a fist. And when he bent down, he recognized me.

I used to tell myself that I regretted the choices I'd made in my life. But every choice, including the wrong ones, made me who I was. And the same applied to you, Luna, and you, Saffy, and you, Clover – both the good and bad experiences strengthened you, shaped you. We are not just made of blood and bone – we are made of stories. Some of us have our stories told for us, others write their own – you wrote yours.

Finn took me to hospital, where they pumped me full of antibiotics and wheeled me into surgery. When they told me what year it was, I thought I was hallucinating.

2021.

I didn't believe them until they showed me a newspaper with the date printed.

And the world had changed beyond recognition.

I drifted between consciousness and a black hole in which I was falling endlessly. When I woke, I tried to piece together the truth. The police came. They told me they'd found a burn on my shoulder, with a number painfully scored into it. I said that Patrick must have done it. He'd removed three of my ribs – what was a few small numbers carved into my skin? But they said Patrick Roberts was dead. He had been dead for years.

I remembered the numbers I'd found scratched on your leg, Luna. I'd thought they meant that you were a wildling. But I now had the same mark, numbers on my shoulder. The cave had done it.

The mark signified the year you'd been thrust into by whatever magic lingered in that cave.

Twenty-three years. I had been gone for twenty-three years.

I can't tell you the grief that accompanied this realization. Finn told me you were all alive. The relief brought by this news spiralled quickly into sorrow. Who had raised you all these years? What had happened to you in the time I'd been absent? What must you all have thought?

I thought of the little boy I'd discovered in the cave. And all the children who'd gone missing on Lòn Haven. The wildlings. Most likely, they'd simply gone into the cave to explore. Then they'd fallen out the other side to another time. A day in the past, a century in the future.

The wildlings that people had murdered were their own children. They just didn't understand how. The stories that had been passed down year upon year had given the people of Lòn Haven a way to make sense of what they saw: whenever a child disappeared, the stories of wildlings and witches provided a way of making connections between past and present.

But I've learned to be wary of easy connections. The best way to tell a false narrative, I think, is to consider how neatly cause and effect have been fastened together.

While I was in hospital, they told me the cancer had spread to my liver and stomach. All they can do is extend my time. Is it weird that I found this ironic? I said yes to chemo, of course. I've been allowed to have it at Cassie's home.

So you see, I kept my promise. I saw someone.

Finn tells me that Cassie had managed to track you down. He tells me, Luna, that you've just had your son, Charlie, and that Saffy and Clover are both with you. I can't tell you how happy I was when he broke this news to me. He says you're heading to Lòn Haven, even as I write. I know the ferries have had to be cancelled on account of the winter weather; I've been thinking of that night the four of us had to sleep in my old Renault 5, the wind shaking the roof and the rain beating against the glass. I hated it at the time, and now I'd give anything to go back and spend one more second with you all.

Forgiveness is a kind of time travel, only better, because it sutures the wounds of the past with the wisdom of the present in the same moment as it promises a better future. I've travelled forward in time. I don't know how. I'm only glad that I lived.

But I'm not sure if I'll make it, Luna. I'm not sure I'll be able to hang on long enough to see you one last time. I'm going to try. But if not, if I slip away before I get the chance to hold you again, I wanted to write down the story of what really happened on Lòn Haven.

As you'll see, cause and effect in this tale do not fit easily together. The pieces are odd and mis-shaped because truth is messy and porous.

I want you to know that I never abandoned you. I want you to know that I'm sorry for being deceived, even enough to take you into the woods. I think that everything I've done in my life has been pulling me back to you.

Right now, I'm sitting in Cassie's living room watching cars move along the road at the bottom of the field, and every time I see someone my heart leaps. Snow has whitened the hills; already night has drawn a black curtain over the horizon. I'm wondering if you've chosen not to come. If you've decided that the years between us are too many, the trauma too great to put aside.

I'll understand that, Luna. It will never make me stop loving you.

But now, I see a woman walking up the garden path. There's a baby strapped to her chest, and by her side is a little girl with red hair that dances in the wind. I feel a flash of recognition.

'Easy, Liv,' Finn says as I get up from my seat. 'You need to rest.'

But I pull myself up, and he puts an arm around my waist to help me.

'It's them,' I tell him, breathless. 'It's my daughters.'

LUNA, NOW

'We're here, Charlie,' Luna tells her son, unclipping his seat belt and holding his hand as he jumps out.

'I'll take the flowers, Mummy,' Charlie says.

She's pregnant again, and on medication for the migraines that returned with a vengeance at the start of her second trimester. Luna only learned what they were when Ethan happened to mention them to one of his Pilates clients. She'd felt stupid, thinking that somehow Clover had been causing them. But then, she'd never had a migraine before she was pregnant, so how was she to know?

They walk through the graveyard, taking the familiar route past the huge oak tree with a twisted trunk and holes that Charlie can sometimes spy squirrels darting into. Their home is thirty minutes from here, a rustic, five-bedroomed villa on the outskirts of Stratford-upon-Avon, with oak-beamed ceilings and views of the Malvern Hills. They moved a couple of years ago, just after she and Ethan spent a month in New Zealand instead of splashing out on a wedding. The flat was never going to be spacious enough for them all. Luckily, when Ethan set up his own Pilates studio, it took off, and they could finally buy a house.

Their downstairs neighbour, Margaret, took the move personally and refused to say goodbye.

Luna lays the rowan wreath on Liv's grave, then stands for a moment in silence, as she does every year. She remembers the night she received the call from Cassie.

'Are you sitting down?' she'd said. 'You need to sit down for this. Trust me.'

And then, the long drive north with Clover, Ethan, Saffy, and Charlie, to see her mother. She had been turned inside out with anxiety the whole way there. When she'd walked into Cassie's home, she saw a woman in the chair by the fire. She was young, and she looked ill, her hair gone and her face puffed up from the chemo. But Luna knew who she was.

She'd promised herself not to cry. But when she saw Liv, it had spilled out of her, and the room spun and she was transported back to being a child again. 'Mum!' she shouted, a word and a tone that had not left her lips for many years. She wrapped her arms around her mother's waist, and Saffy and Clover had fallen against her legs. And they wept.

Liv died three months later. It was longer than the doctors had predicted she'd live, and her last days were spent in Luna's home. Before she passed, she and Finn had a small ceremony, and he adopted Clover and Saffy as his own. Luna knew she'd be looking after her sisters in England, that Finn would stay in Scotland, or perhaps he'd go back to New Zealand. But he would also FaceTime them every week. And every Christmas, they'd travel to Cassie's home in Edinburgh, and celebrate Hogmanay with first footing, a Scottish tradition designed to bring good luck for the new year, and whiskey.

Luna was tested for BRCA gene mutations to detect her

chances of developing cancer. She tested low risk, but planned to be screened regularly, just in case. And to have both Clover and Saffy tested once they turned twenty-one.

Clover is eleven now. She's in Year 7 and obsessed with clothes, science, and Minecraft. Sometimes she calls Luna 'Mum', and Luna doesn't correct her. She can see the resemblance herself, even when she looks in the mirror. And sometimes, when she looks at Charlie, she can see a flash of her dad, Sean. Especially around the eyes. Life continues outrageously, she thinks, in whatever form it can. An unstoppable circularity, the past always in the present.

Eilidh contacted Luna soon after they arrived back in Coventry. By then, Clover was overjoyed to be reunited with Saffy, which made her relocation to Coventry and embracing of life without her mother a lot more bearable. Eilidh called right as Clover was laughing her head off in the background, and although she's been placed on file for a check-up with local social services, there hasn't yet been a call.

Saffy is nineteen. She's studying history at Glasgow University and shares a flat with her boyfriend, Florin, and an assortment of house plants. For her birthday, Luna bought Saffy a Leica digital camera that sends images via Bluetooth straight to Saffy's laptop. Saffy still can't get over the magic of it. Everything, all the technology she can get her hands on, is a kind of magic. She's amazed nobody else feels this way, but then nobody else has bounced from 1998 into the 2020s like she has. She podcasts under a pseudonym, *Ph0t0copied Grrl*, about the witches that were killed in Scotland, with particular emphasis on the ones from Lòn Haven. She gets messages sometimes from people researching the period and has gathered more information

411

about the women. It humanizes them, she thinks, to know their names, and details about their lives.

By accident, she came across Brodie's Facebook profile. She laughed a little too hard when she saw how he turned out. And then she blocked him.

Luna's thought about the cave every day since she was found, and wondered how it had happened. She's researched wormholes and the conversion of mass into energy. She's researched resonance frequency – all human bodies have their own frequency – and whether something within the ancient rock of the cave, formed three million years ago, transferred the resonance of her body into a different temporal frequency. A physics professor in Cambridge told her he'd found microbes that he believed were from another planet trapped inside caves in Japan. Yet another emailed a long screed about dark matter particles found in rock samples collected from the Arctic, about quantum radiation creating wormholes deep within the earth. Another explained time as Russian dolls, the past and present stacked within the present like eggs inside eggs – when she went through the cave, she'd simply cracked one and slipped inside the other.

None of this explains how she got the numbers on her leg, etched as delicately as though writ by a human hand.

She still doesn't believe in magic. It's a technology, she's decided. Just one that she doesn't understand yet.

Saffy and Luna have decided to destroy the cave to stop anyone from the past coming through. Luna has been on the look-out for a specialist contractor. Someone to do the job right, without drawing attention. It'll have to be done quickly, at night, and with discretion. No trucks rolling up, no drilling. The explosion will have to coincide with a noise elsewhere on the island. A fireworks display, perhaps, organized by Cassie. A distraction.

Her phone bleeps. It's a message from the contractor.

Yes. I can do this.

The price is eye-watering, but she doesn't hesitate.

The past belongs in the past.

'Should I put the flowers in the vase now?' Charlie asks as she weeds the grave and cleans the headstone.

She points at the ones that have died. 'Take those out first,' she tells him, watching as he stretches his little hands to the old, droop-headed roses with the browning petals, replacing them with the new.

AUTHOR'S NOTE

I came across the story of Scotland's witches by accident. I moved to Glasgow in late 2019, just before we went into national lockdown. I'd been working at the University of Glasgow for four and half years, and in all that time, I'd not yet heard that the Scottish witch trials were the worst in Europe, nor that around four thousand people – mostly poor women – were tortured and killed on false charges of witchcraft. I'd not yet learned that their conviction meant that their memory was forever tarnished, that their loved ones were left without a body to bury, and without a gravestone to pay their respects – in fact, they were left without a single way to remember their loved one with fondness. I can only imagine how profoundly traumatic and complicated their grief must have been.

When we finally relocated to Glasgow – mostly to spare me the 163-mile commute from our home in Whitley Bay, next to St Mary's lighthouse – I learned, completely by chance, that we lived twenty minutes from a small plaque marking where eleven people were executed for witchcraft. Two of them were young boys, roughly the same age as my son, and in fact they had lived close to our new home. I had heard about the witch trials in Salem, USA, and in

England, but knew very little about the ones in Scotland. Gradually, my research revealed this dark stain on Scotland's history, and I found myself astonished again and again by both the magnitude of this history and its persistent invisibility. For example, close to my home, I was able to find the megalithic Kempock Stone, known as 'Lang Stane' or Granny Kempock. Sat opposite Sainsbury's at the top of a short path, the stone forms part of a story concerning a woman named Mary Lamont, who was accused of dancing around the stone and plotting with the Devil to throw the stone into the sea to sink ships. She was sent to the gallows on the grounds of a church nearby. It will take you to scour the depths of the internet to find this information. Although the stone is marked by iron signages and a plaque, there is no mention of Mary, not even on the Kempock Stone's Wikipedia entry. I drove to the church where she was burned and found no mention of her execution there either.

There are now some excellent projects dedicated to uncovering the stories of Scotland's witch hunts. The University of Edinburgh has an online database which led me to discover the witches named in this book. (http://witches.shca.ed.ac.uk) I was moved to find names of women there who were killed on the same day, and who were likely related to each other – mothers, daughters and sisters, executed together. Although historical information is scant, the good research resources out there pointed me to numerous cases whereby an accusation made against a single person led to additional accusations, as the person accused was often tortured – even when it was outlawed – which, reading between the lines, caused them both to 'confess' to cavorting with the Devil and naming others who had done the same.

I came across cases of accused individuals buying their way out of execution, suggesting that it was the most vulnerable and voiceless in society that were led to the gallows. Women were not even allowed to be witnesses at their own trials. In his book, *Daemonologie* (1582), King James VI suggests repeatedly that women, as the 'weaker vessel', were more likely to be deceived by the Devil. It is hard to read the witch fervour that flooded Europe for centuries as anything less than misogyny. 'Witch' continues to be a gendered term, aimed entirely at females.

I stayed on the Isle of Bute several times to write the book, and discovered that a Bute woman named Amy Hyndman had been convicted of witchcraft in March 1662. Although Lòn Haven is a fictional island, I based it partly on Bute. Amy is mentioned in the Highland Papers, a now-digitized historical record that reports on numerous witch trials. Amy is mentioned once; she was named by another woman who had been accused. As with almost all of the witch trials, Amy is voiceless and vulnerable, and I wanted to imagine her story as it may have been.

As I wrote I came across other efforts dedicated to telling the story of Scotland's witches. One of them is the Witches of Scotland project (www.witchesofscotland.com), a campaign for justice initiated by Claire Mitchell QC and by Zoë Venditozzi, who are engaged in attempting to secure a legal pardon, apology and national monument for the people who were accused and convicted under the Witchcraft Act. Quite rightly, they point out that, while there are statues around Scotland commemorating many individuals, mostly men and – bizarrely – a bear, there isn't a single statue dedicated to those who were accused and killed on false charges of witchcraft. At Edinburgh castle, a plaque at the

'Witches Well' marks the spot where some three hundred people were executed – but not a single name, and certainly no monument.

Although the stories of Scotland's witches are from a distant past, they feel remarkably part of a story of the moment: the #MeToo movement, the depiction of then-presidential candidate Hillary Clinton as a witch on social media in 2016, the arrests of women at the vigil held for a woman was who murdered by a man while walking home from a friend's house. For me, Amy's story from the 1600s echoes in the 2000s. It is my sincere hope we can change the narrative in the future.

QUESTIONS FOR YOUR READING GROUP

1. How do you think the setting influences the story? How does the island's isolated location affect its inhabitants?

2. What did you make of the wildlings? How does this novel explore superstition and folklore?

3. In what ways does the novel explore the history of witch-craft and witch hunts? What parallels did you find between the historical narrative and the modern narratives?

4. What do you make of Patrick? Do you understand why he acts as he does in 1998?

5. *The Lighthouse Witches* follows multiple protagonists – Luna, Liv, Saffy, Patrick. Who did you find yourself most drawn to?

6. Liv's relationship with her daughters is key to the novel, and Luna spends much of the novel pregnant. How does the book explore parenthood and parent-child relationships?

7. The novel explores the relationship between the three sisters, Saffy, Liv and Luna. How are they different, and how are they similar? How do their different ages and life stages affect their different experiences on Lòn Haven?

8. 'There were two of them. Two Lunas.' How does *The Lighthouse Witches* look at identity?

9. How do you think Luna, as an adult, has been affected by the events of her childhood? How does this novel explore memory?

ACKNOWLEDGEMENTS

To Alice Lutyens, Sophie Burks, Kimberley Young, Danielle Perez, Loren Jaggers, Jessica Plummer, Candice Coote, Deborah Schneider, Luke Speed, Felicity Denham, Sarah Bance, Sophie Macaksill, and Andrew Davis, my sincere and indebted thanks for everything you've done to help create this book with me. I am eternally grateful to work with such brilliant, talented, and patient individuals.

Thanks to Emma Heatherington and her partner Jim McKee for advising on mural painting, and to Helen Stew for advice on social services – all errors are mine.

Thanks to Fez Inkwright, for her book *Folk Magic and Healing: An Unusual History of Everyday Plants* (Liminal 11, 2019), and Alice Tarbuck, for her book *A Spell in the Wild: A Year and Six Centuries of Magic* (Two Roads, 2020) – both proved useful while researching this book. All errors are my own.

To Kris Haddow for pointing me in the direction of *Witchcraft and Superstitious Record in the South-Western District of Scotland* by J. Maxwell Wood.

To my colleagues at the University of Glasgow: Elizabeth Reeder, Zoe Strachan, Sophie Collins, and Colin Herd,

Louise Welsh, and especially Jen Hadfield, for teaching me about the home scar.

I came to Zöe Venditozzi and Claire Mitchell QC's wonderful project *Witches of Scotland* (www.witchesofscotland.com) much too late, but nonetheless I'm indebted to their excellent podcasts for refining my thinking while completing my edits.

Thank you to all the book bloggers, booksellers, librarians, and readers who champion my books. You are absolute rock stars.

My love and thanks to my children, Melody, Phoenix, Summer, and Willow. To our dog Ralph for being the perfect writing partner. And to Jared Jess-Cooke, least of all for helping me research how to remove ribs from someone (despite it grossing him out) without suspecting me of being a homicidal maniac (right??). I love you.

Read on for an extract from
C.J. Cooke's new novel

THE
GHOST
WOODS

Then

Mabel

Dundee, Scotland, May 1959

I have a ghost in my knee. There's a small pocket just behind the kneecap and she's hiding in there, all tucked up in the soft mattress of cartilage. She's very small and terrified, so I'm sitting with that leg slightly straightened so I don't disturb her. I've not said a word about this to anyone. They'd think I'm mad.

'Mabel? Are you listening?'

Ma's eyes are wide, as if she's trying to wake herself up, but her hands tell a different story. She's holding on to the strap of her handbag, knuckles white, as though we're on a fairground ride.

'Did you hear what Dr McCann just said?'

I nod, but I didn't hear, not really. I'm always doing this – sliding off into a daydream. I look over the file on the desk beside us. I can see my name. Mabel Anne Haggith. Date of birth 12 March 1942, ninety-eight pounds, five foot two. Dr McCann peers down his spectacles, his fat red fingers laced together like a sea creature. The air in the room pulses with the sense that I've done something wrong.

'When was the date of your last menstrual period, Miss Haggith?' he asks.

'I'm not sure.' Embarrassment hits me like a slap. Nobody has ever asked me that before. It's a private thing.

'Do try and recall,' he says wearily. Ma nudges me as though I'm being rude.

'My . . . my monthlies have always been irregular,' I stammer.

'I only need to know about one menses, Miss Haggith.' Mr McCann sighs. 'The last one.'

'Just before Christmas,' I say, remembering how the ground seemed to tilt that morning in the bakery when I was putting in the first batch of mince pies. A strong twist in my groin, and I knew what was happening. Unlike now.

Dr McCann scribbles something down before flipping through the calendar on his desk. More scribbling, and muttering. The ghost in my knee gives a cough.

'Five months,' Dr McCann announces suddenly. 'Which suggests a due date around the end of September.' He licks his finger and thumb and plucks a leaflet from a pile on his desk. 'Here,' he says, passing it to Ma. 'I expect you'll wish to make enquiries as soon as you can.'

Ma takes the leaflet with a sob. The ghost is restless, unable to sleep now. I rub my kneecap furiously until Ma pulls my hand away, irritated.

'Who was it?' she snaps, her eyes flashing. 'Was it that awful boy, Jack?'

'Jack?' I say, frowning. 'I don't understand. What's wrong with me? Am I dying?'

'Dying?' Dr McCann starts to laugh. 'Come on, Mabel. You're seventeen. You're not a child.'

'. . . would have thought you'd keep your legs crossed,'

Ma hisses, angry tears wobbling in her eyes. 'And that dirty, disgusting boy. I knew it would come to this. I *knew* it.'

It's only when I see the title of the leaflet that it dawns on me, a slow realization like creeping fingers along my neck. *St Luke's mother and baby home.* The front of the leaflet bears a picture of a woman sitting in bed, a man and woman beside her. They're all smiling, and she's handing a baby to them. A subheading reads, *Adoption is the best option for unwed mothers.*

They think I'm expecting a baby. That's what this is.

'I'm not having a baby,' I protest loudly, and I almost go to tell them about the ghosts that sometimes sleep in my lungs or hide in my gums, and that maybe there's a ghost in my womb and they've mistaken it for a baby. But instead, I say, 'I'm a virgin,' which causes Dr McCann to splutter into a laugh. But it's true – I *am* a virgin. I've never had sex, not even the type you do with your hands.

Dr McCann looks at Ma, whose face is tight, lips pursed. A fact I heard once drifts into my mind – the average person tells one or two lies a day, but is lied to up to *two hundred* times a day. I know I've told the truth. So is Dr McCann lying?

My stepdad Richard is waiting for us in the car when we go outside. 'Everything OK?' he asks Ma, and she presses her face into his chest as though we've just fled a war.

He narrows his eyes and looks from her to me. 'What did you do?' he says.

I keep my knee straight for the ghost, but she's moved. I can feel her in my tummy now, dancing.

'It's that Jack,' Ma whispers, stricken. 'He's got Mabel in trouble.'

Jack's my friend from two doors down. We've been seeing

each other, but we've never gone further than kissing. 'It's not Jack!' I say, afraid that she's going to pin blame on him when he's innocent.

'Mother of God,' she hisses, crossing herself. 'There's a squadron of potential fathers.'

Richard stares at me, his face darkening. My heart flutters in my chest. I don't know what I've done wrong.

We pull off for home. Our house is a four-storey terrace on Rotten Row. There are nine bedrooms, seven of which are usually occupied by strangers. We've lived there my whole life, but it's only been a guest house since Da died ten years ago. It's how Ma met Richard. He came to stay six years ago and never left.

We stop outside Mr McGregor's butcher's shop. Richard winds down the window and the smell wafting from the shop door is like an open crypt. I scramble for the door handle, certain I'm about to be sick.

Adoption is the best option for unwed mothers.

'You can go for the mince, Mabel,' Ma says, handing me some coins. 'A quarter pound and not half an ounce more, do you hear? On you go.'

I press the lapel of my coat to my nose and walk into the butcher's. An inch of sawdust carpets the floor, plucked chickens are strung up by their necks, and a row of dead pigs hang upside down along the back wall.

Mr McGregor's son Rory is working today. He's a little older than me, and he's deaf. When Rory's working, they use a notepad and a pencil for the customers to write down what they want. Sometimes Rory writes back little messages, like 'nice day for a BBQ!' or 'you're looking well today, Mrs Haggith!'

What was I to order again? A dead chicken? When I

reach the top of the queue, Rory has been replaced by an older man I've never seen before. He must work for Mr McGregor because he's wearing a bloodstained striped apron and he's wiping his hands on a towel and staring at me. He has a tattoo on the side of his face. A spider's web.

'What'll it be?' he says. 'Got a great deal on pork sausages today. A pound for ten pence.'

I'm still too deep in my body to speak to him. I pick up the notepad and pencil.

Chicken, was it?

I take a fresh page on the notepad and write, but the words don't make sense. They say:

There's a man in the car with a knife to my ma's neck. He'll kill her if you don't give me everything in the till.

I hand the note to the man with the spider's web tattoo. He looks up at me with a look of wild confusion, and suddenly I'm relieved because he's every bit as green about the gills as I feel after what happened in Dr McCann's office. Why did I write that? One of the ghosts must have written it. I can feel one of them lengthening along the bone of my index finger, fidgeting.

The shop is empty. The man glances again at Richard's car parked outside, and whatever he sees must convince him because he makes a quick dash for the till and starts stuffing handfuls of money into a plastic bag. He hands it to me with a grim nod, the bag full of coins and notes swinging in the foul stench of the dead things. I find my arm lifting, my fingers unfolding from my palm, the bag jangling in my hand, my feet turning and cutting a fresh path through the sawdust. And then I'm outside, and I get into the car and hold on to the bag of money. I'm not sure what's going on.

'Pass me the mince,' Ma says, snapping her fingers at me. 'And the receipt. He better not have overcharged you. Always adding on a few more ounces than I asked for, that McGregor.'

I hand her the bag. She opens it and stares down at the cash. There's a moment of complete silence, when all the ghosts inside me are still and Ma's too bewildered to say anything at all. But it doesn't last. She turns sharply and stares at me in alarm.

'Mabel?' she says.

Now

Pearl

Scottish Borders, Scotland, September 1965

1

This place is in the middle of goddam bloody nowhere. It's getting dark, and I swear my bladder is going to explode if I don't pee in the next two minutes.

'Do you think we could pull over?' I ask Mr Peterson. He's the Church of England's Moral Welfare Officer.

'Oh no, is it that time?' he says, tearing his eyes from the road to glance at me with horror. 'Do we need to find you a hospital?'

'What? No!' I say. 'I'm not in labour. I just need to empty my bladder.'

The car wobbles slightly as Mr Peterson decides what to do with this information. He flicks the indicator – a pointless act, given that we're the only car for miles – and slams the brakes on, pulling to the side of the road in a cloud of gravel dust.

I burst out of the car and scramble through the bushes at the roadside, arranging my heavily pregnant body before squatting down with relief. It's only when I'm finished that I realize I'm ankle-deep in a bog, and my attempts to yank my feet free of the sucking mud flicks up enough of it to ruin the expensive dress my mother bought for me to impress the Whitlocks. Fat chance they'll be anything but disgusted now.

'Oh dear. Did you have a fall?' Mr Peterson asks when I return to the car. I had to reach into the bog to retrieve one of my shoes, so am now sleeved and socked in black slime. He produces a handkerchief from his breast pocket, and I use it to scrub off the worst of it, but the smell makes me gag.

'Let's go, shall we?' I say.

'Right.' He clears his throat and turns the radio on before heading back to the road. The Beatles' 'I Want To Hold Your Hand' comes on, and he moves a hand from the wheel to change the station.

'Oh, can you not?' I say. 'I love the Beatles.'

He's miffed, but leaves the radio as it is.

'I went to see them, you know,' I tell him. 'Last April. When they came to Edinburgh.'

'Did they?' he says, and I laugh. As if anyone on the planet didn't know this.

'I signed the original petition to get them to come to Scotland.'

'You must be quite the fan,' he says.

I tell him how Lucy, Sebastian, and I camped out for two nights on Bread Street to get tickets. It was freezing cold, a long row of sleeping bags huddled together on the pavements, but I never laughed so much in my life. And then, the night of the concert, the sight of the four of them on the small stage of the ABC Cinema, all in grey suits. When they played 'I Want To Hold Your Hand', you could barely hear them for the hysteria. Everyone around us immediately burst into tears, even Sebastian. It feels like a hundred years ago that we did that.

'I'm more of a Glen Miller man myself,' Mr Peterson says, and he gives into the urge to flip the station to the eight o'clock BBC News.

I wonder how often he makes this trip, driving knocked-up girls to mother and baby homes – although the place we're headed to *isn't* a mother and baby home, per se. It's a residential home. Lichen Hall, a sprawling sixteenth-century manor house owned by the Whitlock family, who lovingly take in girls like me on occasion to spare them the indignity of entering an institution. I'm grateful for this, really I am. But I'm so anxious I've broken out in hives. Lichen Hall is situated on the Scottish Borders, half an hour from the little fishing village of St Abbs – or, like I said, in the middle of goddam nowhere. What am I going to do all day? I should have asked if they have a record player, or, at the very least, a television. I'm used to being busy, up at five to start my shift at the hospital, then straight out to dinner or a nightclub with friends.

'I don't suppose you know if this place has a television?' I ask Mr Peterson.

'I'm afraid I don't.'

'They'll have a phone, won't they? I'll be able to ring my family?'

'You didn't find that out before you agreed to stay?'

Truth be told, I was too ashamed to do anything other than resign myself to whatever fate my parents planned out for me. Pregnant and unmarried at twenty-two. I'm such a disappointment.

'It's not too late to apply for a place at an institutional

mother and baby home,' he says, hearing the fear in my silence. 'They've changed, you know. Not as Dickensian as they used to be.'

I don't believe this for a moment. I visited a mother and baby home last month. It was one of the smaller ones, in a terraced house on Corstorphine Road, run by the Salvation Army. The atmosphere inside chilled me. The matron was charming, but the walls were cold and bare, and from the pale, fearful expressions of the girls there I suspected she ruled the place with an iron fist.

'Mum says she knows the owners of Lichen Hall,' I tell him. 'She says they're my kind of people. Mr Whitlock's retired. He was a scientist. A pioneering microbiologist, if I'm correct.'

'A microbiologist? And they own a mansion?'

'He held professorships at Edinburgh University and Yale. Mrs Whitlock's father bought Lichen Hall, back in the day. I'm sure they'll have a telephone.' I say this more for myself than for Mr Peterson. 'And anyway, how would it look if I cancelled so late in the day?'

He arches an eyebrow. 'Your mother is a friend of the Whitlocks?'

'Well, friends *of* friends.' I try to read his look. 'Why? And don't even think about telling me the place is haunted. My brother's already tried that one.'

Charlie kindly cooked up an elaborate tale last night and decided to regale me with it while I was packing. Something about a fairy queen who took issue with the original owners after they killed a fairy baby. According to my brother, she haunts the place and curses everyone who steps inside it. Such a bastard, is Charlie. He knew full well how anxious I was about coming.

We take a right turn and park outside tall black gates, two gold 'W's pronged at the top. This must be it, though it's quite a concealed entrance for what I imagine to be a large estate, just a wee nook on the bend of the road clutched by trees.

Mr Peterson turns off the car engine and pulls a folded piece of paper from his jacket pocket. 'Instructions for the key,' he says. I watch as he steps out and roots around for a while in the dim light, bending over a bush and then heading back to the gates with what I assume to be the discovered key. He opens the gates and returns to the car to drive us through.

'I think you were about to tell me Lichen Hall is cursed,' I say. 'Or that the Whitlocks are murderers.'

'I'm not at liberty to say . . .'

'Oh, for God's sake, spit it out,' I laugh. 'You can't build me up like that and then clam up.'

'It's just a rumour,' he says, braking too hard at a bend and throwing us both forward in our seats.

'*What's* just a rumour?'

He scratches the bald spot on the crown of his head. 'Well, it was a while ago now. '57 or '58, I can't remember when . . . An awful car accident just past Berwick. Smoke for miles. Neither of the Whitlocks was involved, but their son was.'

'My God,' I say. 'Their son?'

'Their only son, only *child*. Rumour goes that once word of the crash reached the Whitlocks, they went straight to the morgue and insisted the body be given over to them.'

I wait for him to tell me he's joking, but he doesn't. 'That's . . . unusual.'

'Well, that's not the worst of it. About a week later, their son – his name escapes me – was spotted in the village, right as rain, apparently. No sign of injury.'

I digest that for a moment, then shake it off. Lichen Hall is one of the largest properties in the Scottish Borders. It sounds like they've been the victims of vicious gossip.

'That's all I know,' Mr Peterson says, very serious.

'I'll bear it in mind.'

I won't let him talk me out of this. I'm not going anywhere near an institution, thank you.

The drive to Lichen Hall is a single lane tarmacked road with a wall on one side and tall trees on the other, and I crane my head to spot the house at the end of it. Oh God, there it is, lit up by the car's headlights. Four pointy turrets and dark stone walls laced with red ivy. It looks like Dracula's holiday home.

We drive to the main entrance, marked by pillars, broad stone steps, and a forbidding front door. Mr Peterson suddenly looks nervous.

'I'll leave your bags by the steps,' he says, cutting the engine. He jumps out of the car, and I follow, watching him as he hefts the bags out of the boot and dumps them on the ground.

'Can you at least help me carry them inside?' I ask, annoyed at how carelessly he drops my belongings on to the wet cobblestones. He's already heading back to the front of the car, and I assume he's getting some paperwork, some last detail before handing me over to my hosts.

But then the engine sounds, and with a squeal of tyres he's driving off, the back end of the car fishtailing as he disappears down the driveway.

The Ghost Woods is out autumn 2022